Praise for Isabel Ashdown

'Ashdown skilfully incorporates big moral questions into a thoroughly compelling thriller' - *Mail on Sunday*

'So atmospheric' – *Crime Monthly*

'Had me gripped throughout, with a heroine worth rooting for' – Ian Rankin, author

'Beautifully crafted and satisfying' – Mari Hannah, author

'Satisfying on every level' – Elly Griffiths, author

'Tense, edgy and nerve-wracking. I loved it!' – Helen Fields, author

'With atmosphere and surprises aplenty, this will keep you gripped' - *Heat*

'A dark, unrelenting psychological thrill ride' – *Publishers Weekly*

'Addictive' - *Fabulous*

'A heart in your mouth read' – *Red*

'Ingenious' - *Sunday Times*

'It's action all the way and a compulsive read' – *The Sun*

'This tautly written thriller will make you question everything' – *Stylist*

'A gripping, twisty thriller' – *My Weekly*

'Gripping, clever and beautifully written, Ashdown's star is about to soar' – Phoebe Morgan, author

'Beautifully-written, and ultimately very moving ... I loved it' – Steve Mosby, author

'Twisty, gripping, and utterly unpredictable' – Will Dean, author

'A tense and claustrophobic read' – Lesley Thomson, author

'A craftily plotted, intricate read. Highly recommended' – Mick Herron, author

'Kept me up three nights in a row' – Holly Seddon, author

'A stylish, confident thriller . . . hard to put down' – Kate Rhodes, author

'Had me gripped from start to finish' – Louise Candlish, author

'A great story . . . and a thoroughly satisfying ending' – Katerina Diamond, author

'Draws you in, right from the first page' – Sam Carrington, author

Homecoming

For news, previews and book prizes, join Isabel's newsletter at
www.isabelashdown.com

You can also find Isabel on:
🐦 @IsabelAshdown
📷 @isabelashdown_writer
📘 IsabelAshdownBooks

Also by Isabel Ashdown

Glasshopper
Hurry Up and Wait
Summer of '76
Flight
Little Sister
Beautiful Liars
Lake Child
33 Women

Homecoming

ISABEL ASHDOWN

ORION

First published in Great Britain in 2022 by Orion Fiction
an imprint of The Orion Publishing Group Ltd
Carmelite House, 50 Victoria Embankment
London EC4Y 0DZ

An Hachette UK Company

1 3 5 7 9 10 8 6 4 2

A CIP catalogue record for this book is
available from the British Library.

ISBN (Mass Market Paperback) 978 1 3987 0389 6
ISBN (eBook) 978 1 3987 0390 2
ISBN (Audio) 978 1 3987 0391 9

Typeset by Born Group
Printed and bound in Great Britain by Clays Ltd, Elcograf S.p.A.

MIX
Paper from
responsible sources
FSC® C104740

www.orionbooks.co.uk

For my children, with love, always

'Liberation does not come from outside.'

Gloria Steinem

PROLOGUE

Present day

No one in The Starlings, least of all Katrin Gold, could ever have imagined things would end this way: that their safely gated sea-view community would be the scene of such a shocking crime.

Since the start of the year, everyone had been looking forward to the private estate's first anniversary party, and after months of neighbourly plotting and planning the day had arrived, along with a lively five-piece jazz band and a vintage ice-cream van. Even the sun had turned up, unseasonably hot for the end of May, and the laughter flowed as easily as the champagne as the generations bonded over a barbecue on the lawns, and young parents did their best to ignore their sugar-fuelled offspring, who tore about the gardens, unchecked. Bordering the circular green, the red-brick horseshoe of the Victorian mansion block loomed large, its central clocktower gazing proudly across the lawns towards the majestic modern home of Bill and Katrin Gold, whose vision had transformed the abandoned site into this idyll they now called The Starlings. All around, giant daisies and alliums bloomed, their heads nodding brightly in the light sea breeze, and many were heard complimenting the work of old Thomas who had, until recently, tended those flowerbeds with such devotion. When the local press arrived to photograph the event at midday, there must have been a hundred happy neighbours arranged beside the ornamental koi pond as the band played on. Under the eye of the imposing clocktower, handsome young families stood shoulder-to-shoulder with respected elders, while cross-legged teenagers sat in the front row, straight teeth dazzling as they thrust their peace signs towards the endless blue sky. Frida, of course, was one of them. The photograph should make that week's edition of the *Highcap Press*, the young journalist informed Katrin as he hurried off to his next assignment, not knowing then that another, far more prominent story about The Starlings would instead take its place.

As afternoon slid into evening and a kaftan-clad Ginny wafted around the fairy-lit courtyard, topping up the drinks of the dozen or so tipsy adults remaining, everyone agreed: the day had been an unparalleled success, a day of nothing but good feeling and happy memories made. Most of those still up were the couples with children old enough to put themselves to bed, and, now that the band had packed up and the sun was going down, they'd all moved to the courtyard at the rear of the residential block, where their laughter and chat wouldn't disturb those who'd already turned in. Belinda Parsons was there with her daughter Poppy, as were Graham and Dylan from No.21, Michael and Joy Bassett and of course the Gold family, with the exception of Frida, who was now minding the little ones back at Starling House. Anne Ashbourne had retired a little while earlier, with her mother who was visiting from the care home for the weekend – but otherwise, all the founding residents were there to reflect on their first year at The Starlings. *Aren't we lucky*, Hugo remarked as he set down his tumbler and pulled his willowy wife to his lap, *to live in a place like this*? His heavy-eyed older brother tilted his glass in agreement and knocked back his tipple in a single gulp. Amélie, already rake-thin only weeks after giving birth to her little boy, rested her head against Hugo's like a sleepy cat. *C'est vrai*, she replied. *We ARE lucky, mon cher.* Not even the recent gossip surrounding the family had been able to mar the occasion, and certainly, to anyone looking on, the day itself, honeysuckle-scented on a warm sea breeze, could only be described as perfect.

Perfect, that was, until now.

Now, it is just a few minutes after nine, and everything has changed.

In the distance, emergency sirens peal into the night air, their cries growing closer, as a darkening starling cloud swirls and blooms in the crimson sky above the clocktower at the heart of the community. Years from now, residents will talk of that red sky, of the unseasonal spectacle of starlings dancing in May and the ominous feeling that crept over each of them, the remaining friends and neighbours enjoying Ginny's nightcap, when they first noticed that one of their number was missing. Of course, it will be impossible to know later whether that feeling of dread truly existed before the incident, or was falsely inserted into those recollections in the grim moments that followed Frida Pascal's night-splitting scream.

I knew something was wrong, an ashen-faced husband will tell the investigating officer, standing on a path ablaze with spinning yellow lights, while squad car doors slam, and uniformed officers secure the area. *She'd been gone for almost an hour; I should have looked for her sooner.* A week or two from now, neighbours he once considered friends will question his depth of feeling, his potential culpability – his possible *motive* – and he will wonder, in his sleepless nights, what the correct response should have been. But, right now, those same neighbours look on, shock-faced around the green, edging as close to the nightmare

3

as the hastily erected police tape will allow. Others who had already retired to put young ones or themselves to bed are gazing from their overlooking windows or emerging from cosily backlit doorways to investigate, and for a short while no one has a clue what the drama is really all about.

Because things like this just don't happen at The Starlings.

PART ONE

One Year Earlier

1. Katrin

Taking a moment to gather herself in the shade of the clock-tower, Katrin looked out across the bunting-festooned courtyard, security gates flung wide, and felt a wave of nervous anticipation at the task ahead.

This was it, the moment she'd been working towards – the official opening of her most ambitious and certainly most personal project to date. The Starlings. After five tireless years of negotiation, planning and reconstruction, this forty-one-home gated community was now rising from the ashes of Highcap's long-forgotten Victorian hospital. Reborn, The Starlings presented a perfect union of heritage restoration and comfortable contemporary living – and with its unequalled views of sea and hilltop, situated on the edge of a vibrant market town, it really was a location to inspire and aspire to. It would be, she would reiterate to prospective buyers today, *Dorset's safest community*. That was what her marketing materials and the polished plaque on the brick entrance pillar promised, a guarantee she intended to make good on once the community was up and running.

All she needed to do now was find her residents, which, with a fair wind, she would do today, she told herself, in spite of her racing pulse and nagging self-doubt. Yes. Today, Katrin would find her buyers, secure her family's future, and together they would live there happily ever after. That was the goal. That was the vision. That was the dream. That had always been Katrin's dream.

Overhead, a lone seagull cut through the cloudless blue sky as the wall-mounted speakers either end of the north wall crackled into life, and 'Sunny' played out via the sound system rigged up in the lodge cottage adjoining the front gate. A few seconds later, old Thomas appeared from behind the rose-flanked door, theatrically cupping one hand over his ear, until she gave him the thumbs-up and he shuffled back inside again, like a weathervane man with no matching wife. Facing Thomas's house, just inside the entrance gates, a small white gazebo was set up, where Belinda Parsons and her daughter Poppy were busy laying out nibbles and prosecco glasses in readiness for the first guests.

To the obvious dismay of her daughter, Belinda's hands shot up into the air in response to the music. 'Any sign of Amélie?' she called over.

'No sign of her yet!' Katrin replied with a shrug. Bloody Amélie; she should never have asked her to help – she'd only done it as a favour to Hugo, who had a theory that his wife's problems would all miraculously vanish if she had a bit less time on her hands. Katrin wasn't so sure. Some people could never be relied on; some people were too wrapped up in themselves. 'She'll turn up!' she added with a casual wave, and Belinda returned a sympathetic smile. There weren't that many people who actually liked her sister-in-law, Katrin realised, and she wondered briefly what it was that Hugo had seen in her when they'd met – apart from the obvious.

Alongside the main path, Anne Ashbourne, dowdy in flat brown loafers and a calf-length floral number, was securing large cardboard arrows to direct visitors to the clocktower entrance, where there was a brief photographic history of the sanatorium, pinned up on the sealed wooden door to distract from the fact that it wasn't yet safe to enter. Even from here, Katrin could see the anxiety pouring off the woman as she fiddled with the signage ties, repeatedly pushing her wire-rimmed glasses up her little pink nose only to have them slide right down again. Poor old Anne; she was like a bad advertisement for life over forty, a milestone Katrin was rapidly approaching herself. *God, shoot me if I ever give up the fight like that*, Katrin thought, immediately hating herself for being so mean. Anne might not be particularly sophisticated, but she was a good person, an incredibly bright woman, and as a published historian she brought a positive spin to the Starlings development. And boy, did they need a positive spin if potential buyers were to look beyond the dark past of the site to imagine a shiny new future for themselves within these walls. First impressions were going to be everything, and that was why the whole family were *meant* to be present at the 2pm meet-and-greet. The Gold family: Katrin and Bill, family-first stars of the show, she pretty and persuasive, he twenty years her senior but still disarmingly handsome, their twin boys a credit to their good parenting; and Hugo, Katrin's business partner and brother-in-law, a darker, more boyish version of his older sibling, with his wife Amélie at his side, captivating them all with her ex-model looks and exaggerated French accent, her lovely teenage daughter Frida in tow.

That was the plan, but the others were nowhere to be seen. Katrin checked her phone again and pinged off another text to Bill. *Where are you?!*

On the far side of the square, Frida, back from boarding school early, was pulling the twins around in their bright red Radio wagon, causing them to squeal as she rounded the ornamental pond on two tyres, looking set to tip them into the lavender before righting the cart at the last minute. Ted was sitting up front crying out for more, like a tiny blond gladiator, while behind him his opposite, Max, had one chubby hand clamped over his mouth, feigning terror. The four-year-olds were completely lost to their pretty big cousin, and it suddenly struck Katrin just how much the girl had grown up since she'd last headed off to school in the New Year, dressed in her private girls' school uniform and still looking every bit the teenager she was. Now, Katrin observed, with her fawn-like legs – too, too long in that short, short skirt – with her nipped-in waist and platform trainers, her black curls worn loose, the fifteen-year-old could pass for several years older, and an ancient fear tugged at Katrin's guts, threatening her with unwanted images from her own distant past.

'Frida!' She beckoned across the courtyard.

With the boys still in tow, Katrin's niece broke into a jog, limbs moving with a kind of graceful gawkiness, one arm pulling the boys, the other swinging free. She was now, Katrin noted, a good inch taller than her. Frida set the wagon down and draped her arms around her aunt's shoulders in an unexpected embrace.

'Are you OK, Auntie Kat?' she asked, stepping back, studying Katrin's face. 'No need to be nervous – I'm not saying you are or anything, but – anyway, you'll kill it. You look like a celeb.'

Katrin threw her head back and laughed, reaching out to pat Frida's cheek. 'You're still a big idiot, I see.'

'Hey!' Frida planted her hands on her hips, looking her aunt's outfit over. 'I'm serious. You could be a dragon, you know? Like on *Dragons' Den* – on the TV. Verr-rry stylish. Dressed to impress.'

It was true: Katrin had put much thought into her launch outfit, a smartly fitted power dress in midnight blue, bought just last week on a rare shopping trip to the city, away from Bill and the kids for an entire day. While there, she'd had her dark blonde locks expensively highlighted, her nails French manicured, and her face scrubbed, buffed, micro-cleansed to within an inch of its thirty-nine-year-old life. Bill had taught her many years earlier that you must dress for the job you want, not the one you have, and here she was now, happy, affluent, and dressing for the job she'd wanted *and* got. Despite everything that had been against her from the start, Katrin had survived, and she was now at the helm of Gold Property, a vibrant family-run business already up for several heritage awards – and, if today was a success, on the brink of turning a fine profit. Katrin had every reason to feel confident. *Yes.*

'Thanks, sweetheart,' she said, taking up Frida's hand to kiss her on the knuckles, a distraction from the heavy thumping deep inside her chest. 'Now do me a favour and find out where your mum has got to. She's meant to be here for the meet-and-greet, and people are going to start arriving in half an hour.'

At the pond, the twins had now clambered on to the low perimeter wall to chase one another in dizzying circles. Ted halted suddenly and stumbled, before hitting the cobbles with a dull thud. 'Maaaaaa-aax!' he screamed furiously, tugging at his brother's trouser leg until he successfully brought him down too. Katrin stared at the tangle of them, inwardly cursing her conveniently absent husband as she checked her watch and wondered how she ever got a thing done without the blessed help of their weekday nursery. Too bad it was the weekend.

'Shall I take the boys with me?' Frida asked, already gathering them up. 'I don't mind, honest – I haven't seen them for months. It'll be nice.'

'Oh, Frida, you're a lifesaver!' Katrin exhaled gratefully, already striding away. 'Remember, tell Amélie to get over here asap. We kick off at 2pm sharp! And if you see Bill, give him a kick in my direction, will you? He and Hugo went into town this morning, and they should've been back by now.'

Frida rolled her eyes and made a drinking gesture with one hand, before charging off with the boys either side of her, all three of them arms outstretched like bomber planes about to do battle.

At the entrance, a couple of early arrivals were already dawdling by the gates.

'Jesus, Bill, where the *hell* are you?' Katrin muttered to herself, before shining a broad bright smile on her first potential buyers. 'Hello! Lovely to see you! I'm Katrin Gold – are you here for the Open Day?' She approached them as though welcoming old friends, and their uncertain faces lit up in response. 'We'll be ready to invite you in properly in about twenty minutes,' she told the couple. 'But in the meantime, I'll leave you with Belinda, who'll talk you through the brochure and offer you some refreshments.'

Beyond the gates, Hugo's open-top Audi sped into view. Bill was in the back seat, one stylishly crumpled linen-clad arm draped over the side, his silver waves tousled, looking every bit as though he'd been on some great adventure. In the passenger seat beside Hugo was a woman Katrin had never seen before, platinum blonde beneath a Liberty silk headscarf, Audrey Hepburn shades covering a well-preserved face of indeterminate age. She could be anything from late fifties to early sixties, Katrin thought. It was so hard to tell these days, especially when you had money, as this woman clearly did.

'Katrin!' Bill beamed as the car idled a moment on the path. 'We've scooped up another punter for you! Ginny, meet Katrin

– she's the one you need to impress if you want to get your name down for a place.'

As Hugo held the door for her, the woman stepped out of the car and removed her scarf with a little tug at her chin. 'Darling, aren't you just beautiful?'

2. Ginny

That morning, Ginny hadn't intended to stick around in Highcap town centre any longer than it took to sign the legal papers, but somehow, with the sun shining overhead and the positive lift that came from the finality of one door closing, she had allowed nostalgia to lure her on to the high street.

It was a Saturday, and the pavements were packed with market traders and buskers, with young families browsing stalls, and locals chatting outside coffee shops. Gaggles of beachy-haired teenagers weaved through the crowds on skateboards, dodging toddlers and walking sticks and dogs. So many dogs! The air smelled of freshly ground coffee and cinnamon buns, of lavender soap and freshly cut mint, of car fumes and sun lotion, and – there – the distant whiff of the harbour blowing in from the shore. It was a scent so familiar to Ginny, she was immediately transported back to that earlier time, both to the good of it and the bad, intertwined as they had become with the passing of years.

Momentarily overwhelmed, she had paused in the shade of an estate agent's awning, facing out on to the square, where a colourful folk band played, and onlookers chatted in good-humoured clusters. Across the square, two men, one silver-haired, one dark, both strikingly handsome, appeared from the doorway of the Knotsman's Arms and strode across the busy thoroughfare in Ginny's direction. Brothers, she guessed by their close resemblance and gait, though clearly several years apart. As they passed through the entrance to the estate agent's, Ginny found herself turning to browse the properties displayed in its window, checking off those she recognised against those she did not. Several new housing estates had popped up, beige-bricked monstrosities with names like Sunshine Way and Twiner's Fields. Some of the run-down council houses were now being marketed as 'investment' opportunities, and several of the town's rope mills had been converted into studio flats and maisonettes. On the top row were the million-plus properties, including the now derelict White Rise out near Golden Cap, which had just gone at auction for two point five million.

'Excuse me, I hope you don't mind me asking, but are you in the property-buying market?' It was the older brother, now leaning out on the door frame and grinning rakishly. 'Because if you are, we've got a series of premium homes just going on the market today. The location is out of this world, and, well, you look like exactly the kind of resident we're hoping to attract.'

It was flattery that got Ginny inside the estate agent's office, but it was morbid curiosity that had her agree to a viewing.

As the car sped along that familiar road towards The Starlings, Ginny felt something inside of her give way, for just a second or two, as the familiar shape of the Victorian building rose up on the horizon.

'There she is!' the younger of the brothers said, gesturing towards the old hospital. 'What a beauty, eh?'

'Just wait till you get inside,' the silver-haired one added from the back seat. 'My brother and I have already moved our own families in, so we're hoping to "hand-pick" our neighbours, for want of a better phrase. I hope you know I wasn't being insincere when I said you're the kind of resident we're hoping to attract.'

Ginny laughed then, and turned to raise an eyebrow at him, not once betraying the fact that this wouldn't be her first visit to the site of the Highcap Sanatorium. 'And what kind of resident is that, darling?'

3. Frida

At No.1 The Starlings, Frida was in the living room with her twin cousins Max and Ted, scrolling through the kids' channels until she landed on their favourite and hers, *SpongeBob SquarePants*.

The two boys were seated like bookends on the cream leather sofa, a plastic tub of popcorn between them, their faces zoned-out. Frida had finally worn them out, playing chase on the green for the past half-hour, and she was now in need of a change of clothes after a well-fought tussle had made grass-stains on her favourite skirt. Beyond the front window, Anne Ashbourne was hurrying with a clipboard along the sunny east path, but, other than her, the close was empty. Strange to think that within the hour The Starlings would be buzzing with new people, people who might even end up being their neighbours. Maybe some of them would be Frida's age.

Checking her phone, she could see that both Meg and Rose had read her last message to them, sent two hours earlier. Read, but not responded. She certainly could do with a new friend, she thought with a sinking sense of desolation. Someone to confide in, someone to help her work out how to deal with the mess she was making of her life right now. Maybe this would be one of those *Sliding Doors* moments people talked about, when things would change for the better in a single instant, with just one look or a word from stranger.

She should get changed, she decided, look her best, just in case. Giving her goggle-eyed cousins a parting glance, Frida headed out to the front hall, where the familiar sound of the Dyson starting up on the first floor told her they weren't alone in the house.

'Hi, Cathy,' she called out, spotting the cleaner on the landing as she ascended the stairs. 'You seen Mum anywhere? Auntie Kat's been looking for her.'

'I think she's in the shower, love,' Cathy replied, dragging the vacuum hose aside to let Frida pass. 'She just told me she'd rather I did the downstairs first.' She smiled kindly, and Frida wondered for a moment just how much Cathy knew about her mum and her problems.

'The twins are in the front room,' Frida explained, for want of something to say. 'Just so you know. I've got them for an hour, while Katrin meets the people coming for house viewings. Hey, you might get a bit more work out of it, if any of them want a cleaner too . . .' She trailed off, feeling inexplicably awkward about the exchange.

Cathy nodded mildly, unoffended, and started down the stairs. 'You're home early from school this term, love. My two don't finish till June or July.'

'Exam revision,' Frida lied, and she darted along the landing before she had to explain any further.

In the en-suite, Frida found her mother standing in front of the mirrored wall, in just her underwear, pulling back the skin of her temples and checking herself out, this way and that. She wondered how long it would take before Amélie registered her appearance in the reflection behind her, and she felt the old rage boiling up with every second that passed. She stared at her mum's thin frame and huffed loudly.

'*Chérie*,' Amélie said at last, still holding her face tight, eyes on herself. 'What d'you think? Is it time?'

'Time for what?' Frida replied, knowing full well she was talking about Botox or fillers or some other rubbish. She sighed, recalling a time long ago when her mother could almost have been described as fun, back in the years before Hugo, when they were still living in London. Yes, she had been crazy, unpredictable and more often than not disappointing – but, while Frida's father had been absent her entire life, Amélie had always been there. Sometimes, when she really, really tried, Frida could conjure up the fragrant memory of her mother's kiss, and the tuck of the duvet snug around her feet, to keep her feeling safe whenever she was left alone. *Bonne nuit, mon petit lapin.*

Downstairs, the vacuum cleaner thrummed through the house.

'Cathy said you wanted her to start downstairs today,' Frida said, challenge in her voice. 'Have you only just got out of bed?'

Amélie curled her lip, finally meeting Frida's gaze in the glass of the mirror. 'Ha! The cleaner? She came bursting into my bedroom, uninvited, throwing back the curtains, stinking the place out!'

'Jeez, what the hell is that supposed to mean?'

'Bleach! She always smells of bleach, *chérie!*'

Frida shook her head. 'So, she woke you up at – what, one-thirty in the afternoon? Oh, yeah, really inconsiderate of her. And smelling of bleach too, after scrubbing your toilet clean. Poor bloody Amélie. Must be so hard being you.'

In the mirror, her mother shot her one last withering look, before stalking across the room to snatch up her brush and tame her thick dark hair into submission.

Frida took a breath, working hard on bringing her anger to heel. 'Anyway, Mum, I only came here to tell you Auntie Kat is down at the front gates, wondering where you are.'

'*Pourquoi?*'

'*Parce que*,' Frida replied, adopting her mother's language in a well-practised show of sarcasm, 'you're meant to be helping her with the meet-and-greet. It's Open Day, remember? She's pretty much on her own down there. Hugo and Bill have gone walkabout too. Do you know where they are?'

Amélie sniffed, feigning upset. 'How should I know? Nobody tells me anything.'

'Oh, don't be so pathetic, Mum. If you didn't spend half your life in bed, you'd know just as much as the rest of us.'

'Why don't *you* go and help Katrin if you're so bothered, *chérie.*'

Frida picked up her mother's Chanel fragrance and sprayed it over her own neck and wrists, carelessly, as she glanced about the room, having already spotted the faintest smear of white powder left behind on the black polished windowsill. Setting the glass bottle down, Frida delved into her mother's cosmetic bag and, with no searching at all, located a small paper wrap.

'So, you're using again?' she said, holding it up between them as Amélie at last granted her her full attention.

For a few seconds neither said a word, and then Cathy walked in with her cleaning bucket, and stopped dead in the doorway. Discreetly, Frida dropped the wrap back where she'd found it.

'Can't you knock?' Amélie screamed, her French accent dialling up to the max. 'Have you no manners?! Ah! Go!'

Cathy's face drained white. 'I'm sorry, Mrs Gold – I thought I heard you downstairs – I thought—'

But Amélie wasn't listening. Frida watched on in horror as her mother threw out a dismissive arm and Cathy retreated down the hall to the furthest bedroom, to start up the vacuum cleaner again.

'Mum, *what the fuck*?' Frida hissed.

Amélie snatched up her silk robe, muttering under her breath. 'These immigrants, you know, Frida? No manners!'

'Mum! Have you even spoken to her? Her name's Cathy and she's Dorset born and bred. She's from the town! She's not an immigrant. And anyway, *you're* an immigrant – my dad was an immigrant, for God's sake – or so you tell me—'

But Amélie wasn't listening. 'That is not the same thing and you know it. I have a British passport and I'm married to an Englishman. And you, you have a British passport too. We have money, *non*? This—' she said, gesturing around the sparkling bathroom '—this is *not* the home of an immigrant.'

Frida stared at her mother angrily tying the belt of her robe, and tried to recall the last time Amélie had spoken to her with any warmth. 'Mum . . .' she ventured, consciously softening her tone, realising she might not get another opportunity to catch her mother on her own again for a while. 'Maybe we should talk about what happened at school, you know – the thing – why they sent me home early?'

Amélie made no response, except to turn back to face herself in the mirror.

'You haven't even mentioned my suspension letter.' Frida's heart was pounding now; it was the first time she'd brought up the subject since she'd arrived home, and the waiting – the waiting for Amélie to mention it was killing her. 'I want to tell you what really happened.'

Avoiding her daughter's gaze, Amélie scraped her hair into a bun, tight concentration on her face, before pushing a half-finished mug of coffee into Frida's hands. 'I read the letter. I know what happened, *chérie*,' she said, flashing her dark eyes.

'What you did, it was embarrassing to you, *non*? And him? So. You learned a lesson and you won't do the same again. It is over.' She reached for her make-up bag, and turned back to her own reflection.

This wasn't how the chat was meant to go; how was Frida meant to put her side across? Why did no one want to hear what she had to say?

When Frida stepped out on to the landing, Cathy did so too. At that exact moment, from behind the closed door of the en-suite came the familiar sound of Amélie vomiting into the toilet bowl. Frida thought of the way Katrin looked at her boys, the way her feelings spilled out of her whenever they were around, and she knew that was all she had ever longed for, some of that overflowing, absolute love. As her eyes locked with Cathy's, she set her face to conceal her shame, and headed for the stairs.

'Do that room last?' she called back to the cleaner, casting up a small smile of apology, all the while praying Cathy wouldn't think they were the same. *I'm* not *the same*, Frida longed to cry out. *Please don't hate me for being my mother's daughter.*

4. Katrin

'I can smell beer on your breath,' Katrin scolded her brother-in-law, when he returned from parking his car.

Hugo answered her with an affectionate peck on the cheek. 'You know these officials, Kat – they need a bit of oiling. Anyway, it wasn't our idea; Bill asked them if they wanted a bite to eat and they insisted on the pub.'

Katrin pursed her lips. 'I believe you.' They were standing in the shade of the north wall, as Belinda and Poppy went through the preliminaries at the welcome tent, and Bill circulated, wooing prospective buyers with his you're-in-safe-hands charm. Katrin ran her pen down her checklist again with a little huff.

'Relax, Kat,' Hugo whispered, nudging her shoulder with his. 'Today will be perfect.'

She gave him a withering look.

'Come on, go easy on yourself, will you? You work harder than the rest of us put together – why not try to enjoy the day a little, eh?'

She laughed, thankful for her brother-in-law's pep-talk. 'Sometimes I think if I let myself enjoy it,' she sighed, attaching her pen to the top of her clipboard with an efficient snap, 'if I take my foot off the pedal for even a second – then all of this – everything I've worked for – will disappear in a flash. *Poof!*' She made a little exploding motion with her fingers.

'Nonsense. Enjoy! You earned it!' He kissed her cheek again, and she marvelled at his ever-positive approach to life. How different it must be to be one of the Gold brothers; to never fear loss, having never known a time when they had nothing.

'So, how did you get on with the planners?' Katrin asked, steering the conversation away from herself. 'How long till we can get started on the White Rise project?'

Hugo ran a hand through his dark waves of hair, a mannerism so familiar to her that if it weren't for the fact of their differing hair colour and Hugo's slightly warmer eyes, Katrin could imagine she was standing beside her own husband years earlier.

'We've got a few more planning hurdles. But the good news is, the building isn't protected and with any luck we'll be granted the go-ahead by the autumn. At any rate, it'll be an easier project than this one by far.'

Katrin checked the time on her phone. 'OK, let's make a start, shall we? Looks like we've got around forty or fifty bods to me – not bad, and hopefully we'll get more as the afternoon goes on.'

At the front gate, Katrin kissed her husband and stepped on to a makeshift podium to greet the crowd, giving away nothing of the sleeplessness she'd suffered last night. Still no sign of Amélie, she noted, quickly pushing the irritation away to shift into full-charm mode.

'Good afternoon, everyone!'

The crowd, already responding to the loosening-up effects of the free prosecco, gave an appreciative murmur.

'I'm Katrin Gold, and these are my business partners: Bill, my husband – and Hugo, my brother-in-law. Together, we launched

Gold Property five years ago, when we became the owners of this long-abandoned historic site. Now, hopefully you each have a brochure, in which you'll see there are forty-one properties in the community, with a staggering quarter of them already having been sold by the time we cut the ribbon last month. We hope that you'll recognise it as a testament to our personal investment that we partners have all recently made The Starlings home to our own families. In fact, you could say we've developed this place with our own family values in mind: those of comfort, convenience and care. Now, I'm sure you're all desperate to see the place for yourselves – but, before I release you, just a word to say that we anticipate the properties going very quickly, so please, if you have a solid interest, I do recommend you grab Bill here to get your name down before you leave today. And Belinda and Poppy – fellow residents, by the way – will be right here in the tent if you need a top-up or directions to the loos.'

'*Perfect*,' Bill whispered approvingly, taking her hand and stealing another kiss as she stepped down. 'Break a leg,' he added, before heading over to the drinks tent to field questions and hand out more property particulars.

Still smiling after her husband, Katrin divided the visitors into two groups, with Hugo leading one set via the west side, while she headed off down the east path with her group following in murmuring pairs. The woman Bill and Hugo had brought from town gestured towards the rest room, signalling that she would catch them up on the way round, and Katrin's group continued their tour.

'This,' she began as they passed the gatekeeper's cottage with its green-painted bargeboards and leaded windows, 'is the original lodge house. It dates to the early 1800s, I believe, and is today the home of Thomas, our grounds manager, whom we'll be meeting any minute now. He's got quite the history here.

Thomas is a keen sea swimmer,' she added, waving towards the bright red swimming towel drying on the line to the side of the building, and suppressing her annoyance that he'd failed to take it down for the viewings.

The group continued along the path at the rear of the East Wing gardens, until they reached the Japanese greenhouse, lush with growth, its windows propped open to release the fragrance of early tomatoes and herbs. Katrin rapped on the frame and pushed open the glass door. Thomas appeared in the doorway, dressed for the occasion in a pale linen shirt and khaki shorts, taut brown legs rooted firmly in well-worn walking boots. He nodded gravely, hands behind his back, his white hair neatly combed. She would never say it out loud, of course, but Thomas always looked to Katrin like the oldest Boy Scout in town.

'And this is the famous groundsman himself. Rumour has it that Thomas has never missed a day's work in his life!'

The old man's expression brightened, and the crowd stirred warmly.

'Now, Thomas here has very long associations with The Starlings. Thomas, perhaps you could tell us more?' Katrin stepped back to give him the floor.

'Of course. Back in the early 1900s,' Thomas informed the group in a clearly rehearsed voice, 'the place wasn't known as The Starlings. Then, it was still the original Highcap Workhouse, originally funded by local philanthropist William Jarman back in 1846.'

A few murmurs of surprise told Katrin the group's interest was piqued.

'By all accounts, conditions were terrible – only the poorest and most desperate would voluntarily admit themselves, and my grandmother was one of them. She'd been widowed in the months before – her husband lost to a farming accident – and, with six children and another on the way, she had no choice but to come here for help. My mother was that unborn child, and she drew her first breath here.'

The group were clearly enthralled by Thomas's story, and Katrin made a mental note to thank him properly later.

'Did they get out in the end, your mum's family?' a middle-aged woman asked. She was cradling a small black and tan dachshund as though it were a baby.

Thomas nodded. 'They did. My grandmother got back on her feet when she met a fellow widower in the congregation of the Highcap Anglican Church. They were married within the month.'

'A happy ending!' Katrin said, and Thomas allowed himself a small acquiescence of pride. 'By the 1930s the workhouse had closed down, hadn't it?' she prompted him.

'That's right, which was when the building was repurposed as a sanatorium,' Thomas expanded. 'But it wasn't the end of my family ties with the place, because my mother – a married woman by then – got a job just along the cliff at White Rise, as housekeeper to the next generation of the Jarman family, where she would go on to serve them for over five decades.'

'White Rise,' Katrin interrupted, 'which is, coincidentally, the next renovation project on our list!'

Thomas continued with a stoic nod. 'By this point, the founder's great-great-grandson, Stanley, was an eminent doctor working at the sanatorium, following in his father's footsteps in his pursuit to do good with his wealth. The family was always very kind to my mother, and a few years on, when I was fifteen, I was apprenticed here as a gardener. And I've been here ever since, looking after the place.'

'Why's it called The Starlings?' a young man asked.

Thomas gestured towards the clocktower, visible above the roofs of the East Wing, its presence sentry-like, overseeing the entire estate. 'They've roosted here for decades,' Thomas replied, his face suddenly grown childlike. 'On cold, clear nights their flight display is quite the sight!'

'How could we call it anything else?' Katrin said, laying a hand on Thomas's shoulder. 'Even during the past decade, when the buildings stood empty, Thomas was given special permission to stay on in the gatehouse, which is why the outside spaces have remained so well-tended. Of course, the moment we became the new owners, we could see Thomas was really part of the fixtures and fittings, so we were delighted – and very lucky – to keep him on as grounds manager.'

With that, Thomas gave a small bow, and returned to his greenhouse. The group moved on, and Katrin felt great relief at having covered the subject of The Starlings' grim past with no great dramas.

The older woman, Ginny, caught up with the group as they paused on the east path.

'Of course, it was a mother and baby home in the seventies and early eighties, wasn't it?' This again from the sausage dog lady. 'My old neighbour used to work here in the laundry back then and she said it was a tragic place. Don't think the conditions were that much better than that workhouse – the girls were forced to give up their newborns, you know? That's if they were lucky enough not to die in childbirth.' She pulled a sour face, casting about the group for affirmation. 'Plenty of them did.'

'Oh, God, that's horrible,' said a pregnant young woman at the back, to a murmur of assent.

Katrin smiled warmly at the dog lady, pegged her as a catastrophist, and agreed. 'Well, like so many old buildings, this one certainly has seen its share of human experience.'

Watchfully, she hesitated, delaying the moment when her group would see the development in its full glory. They were standing at the sea-facing end of the East Wing, where views of the ocean broke through the high perimeter hedges, and where, a couple of steps from here to the west, Katrin's own architect-built home would come impressively into view.

'OK,' she said, just slightly raising her voice to ensure all attention was back on her. She laid one flat palm to her chest. 'Time for full disclosure. There is a reason I was so keen to take on this huge project; a reason why I was determined to make something good of a building that for so many, had represented great sadness and loss. Because The Starlings actually has very personal significance to me . . .'

Now, she gestured for them to walk on, and the group found themselves at the very heart of The Starlings – at the open end of a majestic horseshoe of red-brick mansion buildings, set out around the grand oval green of the communal lawns. An audible gasp passed through the assembled visitors, and, as though on cue, beautiful young Frida went gambolling across the green, laughing, limbs flying, in pursuit of Katrin's own perfect twin boys, Teddy and Max.

'Oh, Justin, it's divine,' Katrin heard one voice whisper.

'Good grief, it's lovely,' uttered another, and then their voices fell away as they surveyed the awe-inducing grounds and imagined how it might feel to live here. To call it their home.

For a few long moments, nobody spoke.

Katrin felt a gentle hand on her arm. 'Darling, you said this place had personal meaning for you?' said the woman called Ginny, in a voice like a mug of warm cocoa. And at this the spell was broken and the rest of the group, eyes shining with new longing, turned to hear her answer.

'That's right,' Katrin replied, gazing up as a small cloud passed behind the watchful eye of the grand central clocktower. 'It's personal, because I *was* one of those newborns given up here, in 1981. I was born right here in The Starlings, and now – I've come home.'

Dorset Life Property Pages, special feature
Monday 24 May

Local Orphan Renovates Victorian Hospital

For the past decade, the long-abandoned Highcap Sanatorium on the coastal Dorchester road has stood empty, a decaying local reminder of the wrongs of the past. First erected by philanthropist William Edward Jarman in 1846, the building was initially the town workhouse, a.last-resort destination for the desperate poor of the parish. But, following the abolition of the British workhouse system, the site was used first as the county insane asylum, and in later years as the infamous Highcap House Mother and Baby Home until its closure in 1981. For two further decades it operated as a residential psychiatric unit, before finally closing its doors in 2001, to stand empty but for the roosting starlings which quickly took over the building's central clocktower.

But that is all about to change, as the gates to the site open once more this week to reveal The Starlings, a prestigious development of 2-, 3- and 4-bedroom houses and apartments, in an ambitious renovation project led by developer Katrin Gold. Gold, herself an orphan, moved to the area six years ago when a prolonged search into her own history led her to the town of Highcap. 'It was a sad time,' Gold told us in a recent interview. 'While I was overjoyed to confirm that Highcap was indeed my birthplace, that joy was short-lived when it became clear that the records had been destroyed in a fire in 1981, soon after I was born.'

But that was not to be the end of the journey for Katrin, who, on discovering that the old site was up for sale, persuaded her husband Bill that they should buy it. 'It was a crazy plan, I know! I guess I just wasn't ready to let go of the place, and I suppose you could say I went with my heart over my head on this occasion,' Katrin says. 'I might not have found my birth mother, but I did get the opportunity to build something wonderful from what remained of the past. I'm incredibly proud of what we've achieved.'

For full details of properties available, contact Bill, Katrin or Hugo Gold at Gold Property Ltd.

5. Ginny

By the end of July, Ginny had packed up her old life in Kensington and moved the chattels of the past three decades into her new home at No.40 The Starlings.

It was reckless, she was certain most would say, to have made such a decision at her stage of life: uprooting so impulsively, to move to a place where she had no friends whatsoever. But the truth was, these days there *was* no one to talk her out of it – no husband or sibling or best friend or close confidante – and, with fate conspiring in the way it had with that unplanned viewing in May, and her cash-buyer status elevating her to the top of Katrin's offers list, she'd simply acted on gut instinct.

She wanted a new life, and she'd said yes.

Her feeling of warmth towards Katrin was immediate, and that, for self-confessed snob Ginny, was rare. There was something about the younger woman she was instantly drawn to; something of herself reflected back, perhaps? Katrin had an attractive refinement, yes – though Ginny suspected that quality had been more than a little nurtured by her dashing older husband over the years – but also the hint of a hidden darkness, of some long-ago damage overcome.

'Ginny, can I top you up, gorgeous?' This from Hugo, already refilling her champagne flute and snatching a cutesy kiss on her cheek.

'I don't know why you bother asking, darling,' she replied, enjoying the safe flirtation with Katrin's charming brother-in-law, who had now moved on to fill the next glass. He really was a sweetheart, and she couldn't for the life of her think what he saw in that dreadful French woman. Were all men, even the best ones, really that easily hooked by a pretty face? Even at her age, Ginny didn't have the answers – in some ways the world was as much a mystery to her now, she realised, as it was when she was a naïve young girl.

The views from here – from the balcony edge of Bill and Katrin's modern roof terrace garden – were majestic, and, as she accepted a salmon tart from the tray of a passing hired help, Ginny felt the warm glow of pleasure that came from easy entry into the inner circle of the beautiful people. Today was Katrin's fortieth birthday, and, despite the neighbours still being relative strangers, Bill had pulled together a select group of a dozen or so, to share in their celebrations.

The stocky little woman beside Ginny addressed her with a mildly anxious smile. 'Lovely nibbles, aren't they? Outside caterers – Tino's in town, I think,' she said, wiping her fingers on a napkin before offering them to Ginny. 'I'm Anne Ashbourne – No.32.'

Ginny extended a gracefully downturned hand. 'Ah, yes,' she said, taking in the dowdy school-matron attire, the slightly haphazard up-do. Frankly, she was the only person present who didn't look as though they belonged here. 'The historian?'

Anne pushed her little round spectacles up her nose with a self-conscious bob of her middle finger. 'That's right,' she said, with a pleased flush. 'Isn't Katrin's home just gorgeous? Mind you, I wouldn't expect anything else from Katrin – she's just so, so . . .' Her eyes shone as she tried to conjure up the right words.

'Glorious?' Ginny suggested, and Anne nodded emphatically. '*Glorious*,' she echoed, casting her eyes about in starstruck wonder. 'Well, they all are, aren't they? Katrin is just stunning, and so, so, *accomplished* to have achieved all this! And have you ever met a man more handsome than Bill Gold? Apart from his brother, of course . . .' She laughed self-consciously and flapped a loose *don't-mind-me* hand in the air between them.

Ginny smiled sympathetically at poor smitten Anne. 'And do you have family living here with you, Anne? It's just me at No.40.'

'We-ell,' Anne replied, flushing deeper still in the presence of Hugo as he topped up her glass, 'I'm actually going through a divorce at the moment, and there are no children—'

'You're young, free and single!' Ginny declared to Anne's great delight. 'Best way to be, darling!'

Anne's gaze trailed after Hugo for a moment, as, graceful as a dancer, he slipped a hand around the tiny waist of his glamorous wife. 'Hardly young,' she murmured. 'I was forty-two last year – I think that was what gave me the push to leave Raymond. I just thought, I'm now firmly *in* my forties and what am I doing with my life? What will I become if I stay?' She gulped from her wine glass, hazy-eyed.

It was evident to Ginny that Anne was not a seasoned drinker. 'And what will you become now that you have left?'

Anne's face lit up. 'A writer!' she said. 'I'm researching the history of The Starlings – all the way from its foundations as the union workhouse in 1846, right through to the present day.'

She waited for a response, but Ginny's attention was now on the small figure of an elderly man shortcutting along the edge of Katrin's garden below, a red towel draped over one shoulder. There was something about him, something—

'Anne, tell me, who is that man making his way down to the beach?'

Anne squinted behind her glasses and pressed against the balcony for a better look. 'Thomas? Oh, he's a bit later than usual. He's the grounds manager – haven't you met him yet? He lives in the lodge house at the front gates, but you'll usually find him in the greenhouse or around the grounds.'

Now Ginny thought about it, she had seen him around, many times. But never at this distance, she realised, the vantage point of which allowed her to see him for who he really was. For the younger man he used to be. *Thomas King.*

'Katrin and Bill let him cut through their garden to get to the beach,' Anne continued, clearly a person unable to leave a silence unfilled. 'Swims every day, all year round, you know? I don't know where he gets the energy.'

'And does Thomas have a surname?'

'Yes, it's King. Actually, he's been really useful in terms of research for my book, because he's been here for years, ever since he was apprenticed as a gardener.'

How was it possible that he was still here, after all these years? Heart thumping, Ginny tried to bring her shock to heel. 'So, your book?' she murmured, for want of something distracting to say.

'Oh, yes! I'm particularly interested in the 1960 to 1981 phase, when it was the Mother and Baby Home, because—'

But now Ginny had spotted Katrin across the room, radiant in teal, and she'd had enough of this woman, this historian, this Anne, and she turned her attention back with an apologetic smile.

'Oh, I'm sorry, Anne, darling – this sounds completely fascinating, but I promised I'd give Katrin a hand with the caterers. Do you think we can continue this later?'

At dinner, Katrin and Bill took the rattan carver chairs at either end of the large veranda table, while guests were arranged girl-boy, except for Belinda Parsons and her daughter Poppy, who made an unnecessary fuss about wanting to be placed beside one another. At Katrin's end of the table, Ginny was seated with Michael Bassett to one side of her and one of the boys from the North Wing to the other. (Graham, or Dylan? She could barely tell them apart, interchangeably dressed as they were in, she supposed, vintage-inspired cardigans and horn-rimmed spectacles.) Across from her, the lovely Hugo was sandwiched between earnest Anne Ashbourne and Michael's wife, Joy, a well-groomed and rather-too-pleased-with-herself 'professional' homemaker, who was already draining the life from her neighbours with tales of her remarkable eight-year-old.

'His coach says he's got the best under-elevens front crawl he's seen this year. I can barely doggy-paddle, so I don't know where he gets it from!' she hooted to the horn-rim on her right, who responded with a patient smile and a glug of his wine.

Katrin reached past Michael for the water jug and gave Ginny a wicked wide-eyed blink in response to Joy's bragging. Only this morning they had bumped into each other on the green, and in confiding tones Katrin had recounted her reaction to finding Bill's 'surprise' fortieth birthday guest list on the kitchen worktop. 'Poor old Bill – I tore a strip off him, and he was only trying to do something nice. But I wouldn't have invited half the people we've got coming. I mean, take Joy. She's such a *bore*,' she'd gasped at Ginny, glancing conspiratorially in the direction of the Bassett family home. 'And her children are so bloody accomplished. Last week she asked me what clubs the twins attend, and I had to lie, just so she wouldn't judge me.

Because, believe me, she *would* judge me. I couldn't think quickly enough and said they were top of their class in tai kwondo. Ginny, they're four, for pity's sake,' she'd said with a shake of her head. 'I don't even really know what tai kwondo is!' Ginny had thought this marvellous, and she'd howled with laughter.

At the slow creep of dusk, tiny white fairy-lights lit up all around the balustrades, and, with the last of the sun just about disappearing beyond the sea's horizon, Katrin's veranda felt like the finest place on earth to be. This time last year, Ginny reminded herself, she'd been in London, rattling around in her lonely great maisonette in Kensington, with nothing to look forward to and no one to share it with. *And look at me now*, she thought. *Just look at me*. That it took a man's death to release her should have come as no surprise to Ginny, and yet she still felt the wonder of it, day after day in this place. *The Starlings*. Despite everything, it seemed somehow so right that she should be back here now, after so many decades of averting her gaze in fear and shame.

'So, Michael, done any good loss-adjusting lately?' Bill called down the centre of the table, leaning back to allow one of the waiting staff to set down his starter, while an unsteady Amélie rose from the seat beside him and headed inside.

Next to Ginny, Michael puffed up his feathers. 'I'm a forensic accountant, actually, Bill, old chum. I investigate big business fraud.'

Bill laughed, the baiting chortle of well-concealed insecurity. 'Lawks. Sounds like the FBI. I guess I'd better keep on your good side, Agent Bassett, in case you start crawling all over *my* business.'

'No fear of that, Bill – your little property biz is far too small-fry for me, I'm afraid. I'm more your international corporation kind of investigator.' He tipped his glass Bill's way. 'For my sins.'

'Ignore him, Bill!' Joy piped up, and good-humoured laughter erupted around the table, as in return Katrin waved a breadstick at Bill and told *him* to stop winding everyone up. As the last of the starters arrived, conversation resumed in little pockets around the table.

'You know I'm only pulling his leg,' Michael murmured to Katrin in a confidential tone. 'Because the truth is, I'm dying to know how on earth he managed to get his hands on this place? It must've cost a fortune for the land alone, let alone the renovation costs.'

Katrin smiled enigmatically. 'I guess, with the age difference between me and Bill, everyone assumes that he's the pioneer, don't they? That it was bought with his money.' Her gaze landed briefly on her brother-in-law. 'Or at least, Gold family money.'

Hugo snorted. 'Some chance. You ever met my old man? Tight as a gnat's—'

'But it's not,' Katrin cut him off. 'Hugo and Bill are joint partners with me, but I actually bankrolled the whole project.'

Of course. Ginny hadn't been able to put her finger on it thus far, but there was an interesting dynamic between Katrin and Bill Gold. It was something to do with the balance of power, Ginny now recognised, quite clearly. Financially, it would seem, Katrin quietly held the upper hand, while allowing her husband to let the world believe he was running the show. Clever girl, Ginny thought; if it works, it works.

'Wow,' Anne Ashbourne breathed out. It was the first word she'd uttered in a while, and her cheeks were now shiny with intoxication. 'You're such an inspiration, Katrin.'

'You received an inheritance?' Michael asked, desperate to get to the bottom of this puzzling conundrum.

Katrin shook her head with a hard laugh.

'A lottery win, then?' he pressed on, and it was only then, once the game of 'guess the windfall' seemed to have taken hold, that Katrin began to withdraw, her eyes casting down to the asparagus tips on the china plate before her.

'Oh, come on,' Michael goaded loudly, provoking a glare from Joy a few seats down. 'Tell us, you terrible tease!'

Amélie passed their end of the table on her return, weaving slightly, releasing a bitter 'Ha!' over Katrin's shoulder, before returning to her seat and drunkenly toppling a glass of wine over Bill's plate. 'You telling them all your money story, Kat-er-ina?' she sing-songed down the table, her expression savage. Bill's face darkened and he whispered into his sister-in-law's ear, before pouring her a glass of water and making her drink from it. A resigned-looking Hugo went to get up, but his brother gave a subtle 'no-need' signal, and the poor man was off the hook.

Meanwhile, Katrin had left her own seat and was now crossing the expansive living area towards the sound system, where she skipped the current track to a Billie Holiday number before returning to the group. As she pulled out her chair, Ginny noticed the firm set of her jawline, and the brightly confident tone in her voice. 'Do you give up?' she asked, bringing her palms together with amusement. 'Well, it was none of the above! It was actually a compensation payout.'

'Some payout!' Michael gave a whistle. 'I thought you had to lose a limb or something to get that kind of cash. How much?'

'Oh, Michael!' his wife chastised from a few seats down. 'I don't know what it is you're saying down there, but please stop it!'

'What?' he chuckled in response, and Ginny concluded that he was a social buffoon of the first order.

'Michael, I really don't think it's the done thing . . .' Ginny added, to Hugo's gentle agreement.

At last Michael raised surrendering hands. 'Sorry, God, yes – rude of me. *God*. Blame the wine! Or my profession! So used to talking about money like it's nothing. Good job the wife's distracted with the gay film producer, or she'd be giving me a right bollocking.'

Hugo gave a rueful little shake of his head. '*Jeez*.'

Next to Ginny, Graham leaned in and cleared his throat. 'Actually, I'm the film producer. My husband's the conveyancer. And, you know, I don't *only* make gay films—'

'Oh, I didn't mean—' Michael stuttered, as Graham's stern expression slowly morphed into a mocking smile.

Ginny screeched with laughter and slid her seat back a fraction to improve Graham's view of a now puce-faced Michael.

Katrin laughed too and placed her hand over Michael's to give a reassuring squeeze. 'I think that's enough money talk for tonight,' she said, and she left the foolish man none the wiser as to the real source of her wealth.

Along the table, Joy Bassett jumped in, to shut her husband down, Ginny suspected.

'Katrin, I've been meaning to ask you about the clocktower. Are you still planning a games room over there? Maggie and Taff keep asking when it'll be ready – you know, they're real little pros when it comes to table tennis!'

Katrin sighed meaningfully. 'It's going slowly, Joy – but you can tell the kids it's still going ahead. The roof is full of asbestos, which needs professionally removing, but we can't do a thing until the bird people have worked out what to do with the starlings. Thomas says we need to apply for a special licence to get them relocated, but even then, we can't do anything until nesting season is over.'

'The plans show it's got a concealed basement,' Bill added from the far end of the table. 'I hate to think what secrets are buried down there.'

'Oh, stop it, Bill,' Katrin laughed. 'You and your grisly imagination!'

'And how's your next project going?' Belinda asked, leaning in to join the conversation. 'White Rise? It's an amazing looking building – Joy, it's that lovely old place just along the coast here. The one with the boarded-up windows.'

'Again, it's going slowly!' Katrin replied. 'It's in a terrible state of disrepair, but still, beautiful. It's not listed, so we're confident permission to redevelop will go through easily enough – but we're at the mercy of the verrrry slow Dorset planning department.'

'You absolutely have to chase them,' Joy said, knowledgeably. 'Every day, if you really want to get things done.'

'Yes, we've had quite a lot of dealings with them, renovating this place,' Katrin replied, catching Ginny's eye. 'But it's a good tip, Joy, thanks.'

'We had to do that with our new windows in Bridport, didn't we, Michael?' Joy pressed on. 'In the end I was on the phone to them *every* single day.'

Michael gave a sage nod.

'And you need to be firm. Don't take any nonsense.'

'I expect you're right,' Katrin said, catching Ginny's eye again, with a mischievous glint.

'Wise words, Joy,' Ginny replied, returning a knowing smile, but then for a second or two she felt entirely outside of her own body, and very far away. She saw herself up on top of Golden Cap as a young child, hand in hand with her mother, looking out across the sprawling patchwork of field and farm, her gaze roaming over White Rise and Highcap and the world beyond. What was the feeling? Freedom? No, not quite that. *Possibility*.

'Ginny, are you alright?' Katrin asked quietly.

As her focus returned to the room, Ginny took in Katrin's concern and quickly offered up her brightest smile. 'Never better, darling!' she said, lifting her wine glass. 'Though I think I could do with a little top-up!'

Hugo, attentive as ever, reached for a fresh bottle and began cutting the foil.

After dessert, the neighbours moved inside to take coffees on the trio of comfy sofas arranged around a vast Persian rug, facing out to sea. On the dark horizon, the small lights of a container ship winked like stars.

'This place really is beautiful,' Belinda Parsons said. 'Isn't it, Poppy?'

Her daughter bobbed her head in reply. 'So beautiful. I love modern architecture.'

'It's completely different from our old place, isn't it, Kat?' said Bill. 'We spent the past twenty years in a Victorian terrace in Battersea – gorgeous place: high ceilings, lovely little roof terrace, just a stone's throw from the park.'

'Why did you move?' Graham asked.

'Well, we'd struggled to have children for a good ten years,' Katrin replied candidly, 'and when my money came through, we just decided it was time for a change. We thought we'd be spending a big chunk on IVF – but then, in one fell swoop, I became pregnant naturally and we found The Starlings.'

'We were lucky to get permission to build something so modern on the existing site.' Bill cast a tender look at his wife. 'And we do love it, don't we, Kat?'

Ginny reflected what a truly beautiful couple they were: a perfect match, age difference be damned.

'You've got the best of both worlds, really, *Bill*, haven't you? A state-of-the-art modern *château*, and a view of the *océan*.' This was Amélie, Hugo's wife, and her slurred delivery was more than a little challenging. She was sitting on the central sofa, between the two brothers, and she laid a hand on her brother-in-law's thigh with a little squeeze. 'Not to mention a perfect view of the rest of us *petites bestioles*. You know, Katrin and Bill have a telescope in the top room—' she waved a casual hand towards the ceiling, with a slow blink of her cat eyes '—in the glass penthouse? The *master bedroom*.' She said this last with louche intonation, scanning the room for some reaction.

For a moment nobody spoke, and it seemed to Ginny that every person in the room was wondering what kind of game Amélie was playing. She really was the most dreadful woman.

'Oh, don't listen to her!' Bill brushed her hand from his leg with a dismissive flick. 'It's for looking out to sea, you smutty woman – not at our neighbours!'

Hugo rubbed the heel of his hand across his brow and smiled good-humouredly.

'Still, you must have a good view of the whole estate from up there,' said Dylan (Ginny had worked them out now – Dylan's voice was the decidedly more estuary of the two). 'With or without a telescope.'

Everyone laughed; the music played on; out on the veranda the hired help discreetly cleared the detritus of their evening meal.

It occurred to Ginny that Belinda's daughter seemed uncommonly quiet for a teenager, though not exactly unconfident. 'How old are you, Poppy?' she asked.

'Fifteen,' Belinda answered on her behalf.

'Nearly sixteen,' the girl corrected, stiffening in the way that the young so often did, when unexpectedly placed under the spotlight. *Narely* sixteen. You'd never guess she was a local. These privately educated girls ended up so very universal in their demeanour and accent that they could pass themselves off as hailing from wherever they liked. Ginny herself claimed to be from the Cotswolds originally, and not a soul had ever challenged her on the fact.

'Oh, similar age to your daughter, Amélie,' Ginny remarked.

Amélie gave a bored little jerk of her chin.

'Frida,' Ginny recalled. 'She's around tonight, somewhere, isn't she, Katrin? Do you know her, Poppy?'

'She's in the same year as me at St Saviour's.' A fleeting smirk crossed the girl's face. 'But of course Frida hasn't been boarding this term—'

'Actually she's babysitting the twins for us tonight,' Katrin said warmly, rather quickly cutting off Poppy's words, as Amélie indicated towards her empty glass and Hugo did the honours. 'I expect she's in the snug now, watching a film or something. Feel free to join her, Poppy. You don't have to stick around us oldies out of politeness.'

Poppy glanced up at her mother with unconcealed dread. 'No, I'm fine, thank you very much.' Her eyes darted from Amélie to Katrin and back to Belinda. 'I mean, I quite like being around the oldies.'

As laughter filled the room once more, Belinda stepped in to save her daughter's blushes. 'Anne! I'm dying to hear more about your writing project. Katrin says you're researching the mother-and-baby years here at The Starlings.'

Anne, whose face was quite aglow by this point, sat forward in her seat and helped herself to a second brandy. 'I've got a long way to go,' she said, 'but already, oh, my God, the *things* I'm discovering. I knew it was bad from the little my mother has told me, but her memory's not so good now and—'

'Your mother?' Ginny interrupted. 'What does she know about the place?'

'I must've told you, Ginny?' Katrin said. 'Anne's a Highcap orphan too. Turns out we were born within a couple of years

44

of each other. Though, unlike me, she's been lucky enough to trace her birth mother.'

Ginny anchored her fingers to the pearls around her neck, and rearranged her limbs, which now felt oddly heavy. 'But what led you to her, Anne? I'd heard all the Highcap records had been destroyed?'

Anne was scrolling through her phone, to show them all a photograph of her mother, a woman who looked a fair deal older than her fifty-nine years. 'You're right. The records went up in a fire that pretty much wiped out the chapel and the far end of the West Wing. When I discovered that, it seemed like a dead end to me. But then, two or three years ago I sent a DNA sample off to one of those genealogy companies, just in the hope that I could discover a bit about where I came from. You know, my ancestral profile. Turns out, I'm sixty-nine per cent English, five per cent Scandinavian and twenty-six per cent Irish. Not all that interesting. But!' She raised a finger in the air, emboldened, her eyebrows shooting up. 'The bit I wasn't expecting was that within a couple of months a family match came up with a fourth cousin, and quickly after that another.'

'And you didn't know these people?' Michael asked.

'Not at all! I was adopted at birth, and there'd been no paperwork to tell me who my mother was, let alone a father.'

'So how . . .?' Ginny murmured, her words trailing off as her mind flooded with the endless scenarios now possible.

'Well, I didn't do anything at first. I mean, fourth cousin is miles off being a close relative. But then, some weeks later, this happened.' Anne took her phone back, and brought up a screenshot of her Ancestry.com profile, which displayed a list of possible DNA matches. She returned her phone to Belinda, who passed it along to Ginny. At the top of the list was a match with the username *Dottie2017*, and next to it the words *Close*

Family. 'Turns out *Dottie2017* was my maternal half-sister – and she was able to tell me my mother was still alive. After literally years of searching, I'd found her, with nothing more than a bit of spit in a bottle. Easy as that.'

'It's like something out of a film,' Joy Bassett said, her jaw hanging slack. 'Graham, maybe you could make a movie about it?'

'It really is quite incredible,' Graham agreed. 'And she's in your life now?'

'Yes!' Anne laughed, before her expression clouded. 'Soon after we met, she had a diagnosis of early-onset dementia, but until a year or so ago it was slow-moving, which means she's been able to tell me a lot about what happened to her, and how I came about. The most criminal part of the story is that, when I was born, she was actually told I had died.'

'No!' A collective gasp travelled around the table.

Anne nodded. 'Apparently, if any of the girls showed signs that they'd kick up a fuss when it came to giving up their babies, the staff would tell them they'd died during labour – my mum was one of those. And then she had to stay on for three months of unpaid service, cleaning and looking after other babies, to "pay back" the charity the institute showed her – all the while believing her own child was dead. Anyway, last year we moved her into a nursing home in Studland, so she could be nearer to me. Even after this short time, we're so close, it's like we've *always* been mother and daughter.'

Ginny knew it would look strange to not engage in this conversation, and she swallowed her anxiety down to speak. 'So, Katrin, you say you've had no success tracing your own birth mother?'

Katrin glanced over at her husband with regret. 'We tried for years to find her, didn't we, Bill? With no records this end it was almost impossible, although through my foster papers we were able to work out that I was born here during the mother-and-baby-home years. But then the trail runs cold. I have a log number for my birth mother, but sadly, no name. It was a system Highcap used to protect anonymity in closed adoptions.'

'Hey, you should do a DNA test, like Anne!' Poppy piped up, suddenly animated.

Amélie yawned loudly and closed her eyes, dropping her head against Bill's shoulder.

'Oh, I don't know,' Katrin replied, denying her rude sister-in-law the benefit of her attention.

'I'm not sure rummaging around in the past always bears positive fruit,' Ginny said mechanically, a sense of vertigo threatening her as the conversation continued to hurtle down this troubling path. 'It often causes more harm than good.'

Joy nodded earnestly. '*Yes*. Do you worry about hurting the feelings of your adoptive parents?'

'No, I—' Katrin began, frowning deeply, her discomfort with the subject clear. 'I was brought up in care – a mixture of children's homes and foster families – so there are no adoptive parents to worry about.'

'Oh, in that case,' Poppy declared, 'you really should do it.'

The ensuing murmurs of sympathy and surprise appeared to make Katrin more uncomfortable still, and she shifted in her seat, bringing her feet up on to the sofa beside her and waving the topic away. 'I don't know – I suppose I feel like I've expended far too much energy on it already. The endless disappointment can be pretty exhausting. I'm not really that bothered any more.'

'Nonsense! That's a fabulous idea, Poppy!' Bill exclaimed, linking his hands behind his head. 'Where do you get it done, Anne?'

'I'll jot the website down for you,' she replied. 'You order the kit online, and after you've sent it back it just takes a couple of months to get your results. It's really easy.'

'Well, that's settled!' Bill said, looking very pleased with himself, and a small, hopeful smile appeared at the edge of Katrin's mouth. Ginny could only look on, feeling helpless. 'I'll order them tomorrow, my love, an extra little birthday present for you. We'll see if we can get you a new mother to go along with that diamond eternity ring I just coughed up for.'

'Ooh, do show!' Belinda cried out, as Amélie rolled her eyes and headed to the bathroom for perhaps the sixth time that evening.

The women crowded around Katrin's outstretched hand, and, for now, talk of DNA and missing mothers was forgotten.

Forgotten, that was, by all but Ginny.

As she lay in the darkness of her own bed later that night, *she* could think of nothing else. Nothing but that and the spectre of Thomas King. Maybe this whole 'new life' plan of hers was a terrible idea, after all?

6. Frida

In fact, Frida had not been in the snug when her name came up at Katrin's birthday party that night. She'd been right outside the door.

With the twins soundly asleep, Frida had finally managed to gather up enough courage to join the rest of them on the sofas for a while, on Katrin's promise of a bowl of the Eton mess she'd helped the caterers unload earlier that evening. Really, she was looking forward to a bit of time spent in the warm glow of Auntie Kat's company, and, though she hadn't been keen to be in the same room as her mother for even a minute more than necessary, it was Katrin's birthday, and she'd do anything for her favourite aunt. Her only aunt.

Standing in the shadows on the threshold to the sea room, feeling like an overgrown kid in her stripy beach shorts and daisy-print vest, Frida had been paralysed by the sound of Poppy Parsons' confident vowels, and mortified all over again. Reminded all over again that her secret was not really a secret at all. Not at St Saviour's where the gossip about Frida Pascal was a source of endless interest. Tonight, they hadn't actually been discussing the details of Frida's recent suspension, but that wasn't the point; Poppy had alluded to it, and Frida had heard the mockery in her voice.

She had shrunk back along the hall and returned to the quiet comfort of the Gold family snug, where she curled into the corner of the sofa and scrolled through her phone to locate the only photo of Barney and her together that she had kept, password-protected to prevent anyone else from discovering it. No one would understand, he'd told her, as he insisted she delete their entire text history, along with her cherished WhatsApp messages and pics. Others would just judge them, he'd said; like a modern-day Romeo and Juliet, but from two different schools. Those losers could never understand what they have. *And they'll break us up if they find out.* That was all it had taken to guarantee her silence, she realised now, as she studied the photograph for concrete signs of his devotion. Because he did love her, didn't he? Otherwise, what else was this all about – this risk, this heartache, this pain?

I miss you, she typed into a new message window. Her thumb hovered over the screen a few moments, before, with a jolt of her heart, she pressed send.

Seconds later, she received a reply. *Me too.*

She hadn't expected him to respond so quickly; so positively. Her pulse raced. *How was the sixth form party?* she asked.

A series of emojis volleyed back: cocktail glass – dancing – crazy face – puking face.

Standard, Frida replied, pulling her legs up beneath her and settling into their old rhythm and ease.

We shouldn't be doing this, he messaged.

I know, she responded. *But I don't care.*

Several seconds passed, a minute perhaps. Frida stared at the screen in one hand as she bit down on a hangnail on the other, second-guessing herself, mad at herself. She'd been too pushy. Too familiar. Too in his face. They were meant to be avoiding each other. They were meant to be 'respecting boundaries'. Giving each other 'a wide berth', as Mrs Bateman had put it.

At last, his reply came. *Send me a pic. September's too long to wait.*

Frida stared at his words. It wasn't over. As far as he was concerned, they still had something, didn't they?

What kind? She pinged back, along with a pink-cheeked smiley face.

You know what kind.

'Hello, gorgeous.'

Frida gasped at the low growl from the doorway, clutching her phone to her chest, before throwing a cushion at her stepdad with a little shriek. 'God! Hugo! Don't do that! I nearly had a heart attack.'

Hugo placed his tumbler on the mantelpiece and sunk to the sofa beside her, lightly slapping her thigh with the back of his hand. 'You're jumpy as a jack-in-a-box at the moment, sweetheart. Are you sure you're OK?' He cast a meaningful look at her under those ever-shifting dark brows. 'You know you can talk to me, right? You know I'm still here for you, no matter what.'

No matter what. Adjusting her position, Frida leaned into him, allowed him to slide his arm over her shoulder, to hold her steady for a while. *Please God, don't let Mum come in now*, she prayed silently. Neither of them needed that. 'I'm fine,' she murmured, afraid that if she opened up, it would all come spilling out.

'Nothing you want to talk about?'

In truth, there were so many things she wanted to talk about, but she didn't know how to say those things in a way that he would understand. She couldn't articulate the terror she felt

51

when her head hit the pillow in the darkness of night, when her fear and regret and shame and uncertainty came creeping in, and her loneliness threatened to swallow her up once and for all.

'I mean it, lollipop, you can tell me anything,' he said, squeezing her shoulder lightly.

Lollipop. He'd called her that the first time they'd met in a noisy café in Bermondsey all those years ago, and he'd won her over then, in the easy way he'd made her mum smile, from morning till night. But that was then.

'I love you,' Frida said now, but her words seemed pathetic, so completely lacking in the depth with which she meant them. She thought about all the things her stepdad knew about her, and all the things he didn't. Would he hate her, if he knew the truth? She visualised the growing stash of unopened cosmetics and sweets beneath her bed at No.1, about her daily resolve to give up her shoplifting habit and dispose of the evidence before her luck ran out. She thought about Amélie, wasted and wasting away, bent over the windowsill in her underwear, vanishing white stuff up her nostrils, oblivious to her daughter. And she thought about the exhilarating feeling when she caught Barney watching her across the refectory, so intensely, and how it wasn't creepy when he did it, unlike the other boys, who'd stare and blush and stammer like the little perverts they all were. 'I'm sorry about all the trouble I've caused between you and Mum,' she murmured.

'Enough of that,' he said, shifting to face her, his tone serious. 'We all get to fuck up once in a while, Frida. You're fifteen, right? Now's as good a time as any. Your schoolfriends will all have forgotten about this by the time you go back in September, and you'll just start again like new.' He paused, waiting for her to cheer up, but all she could manage was a petulant huff. 'Look, I know your mother's still being offhand with you,' he continued.

'But she loves you, and she'll get over it soon enough. I reckon she'll even be talking to you again in, what, a year or two—?'

Despite herself, Frida found she was smiling and nodding and wishing Hugo didn't have to go back to the party without her.

'I see Poppy Parsons was invited tonight,' she said, withdrawing her hand as she sensed him preparing to leave.

Hugo pushed up with the effort of a man several drinks in and crossed the room to retrieve his crystal tumbler. 'Snooty little madam, isn't she?' he replied.

With a smile, Frida fell back against the plum velvet sofa, waving him goodbye with a waggle of her foot.

Maybe Hugo was right: maybe her schoolfriends *would* forgive and forget everything that had happened this year. But how could he be so wrong about her mother? Amélie wasn't just offhand; she was virtually absent as far as her daughter was concerned. Frida thought about the warm embrace Katrin had pulled her into earlier that evening, after opening her gift of perfume and chocolates, the warmth of her joy so welcome in contrast to the coolness of her own mother.

Not for the first time, Frida wished Katrin were her mother, not Amélie. But more than anything she wished that she could turn back the clock a few weeks; that she could unsay what she'd said about Barney that day, and set everything back to just how it was before.

7. Katrin

'We're so lucky.'

This was the first sleepy thought that rose in Katrin's mind as she woke the following morning, just very slightly hungover after her birthday celebrations the night before. Indeed, it was the first sentence she uttered as her husband appeared in the doorway of their en-suite only moments later, filling the room with the warm scent of sandalwood. He was, as Ginny put it, devastatingly handsome, not to mention year-round tanned from so many weekends spent out on the water with Hugo, and there was no denying that middle age suited him well. Katrin knew they were fortunate to have what they had; they still loved each other, and they still looked good together, and they still regularly – as a hazy recollection reminded her they had last night – made love with the fervour of real desire.

'Luck?' Bill replied, with just a hint of arrogance. 'Luck has nothing to do with it, my love.'

But Katrin knew Bill and his brother had benefited from more of a leg-up than most, although if you were to probe either of them on the subject they were likely to play their advantages down, reluctant as they were to admit that their success was borne of anything but hard graft and God-given talent. It was a quality Katrin had often noticed in the comfortable classes, who so often appeared to Katrin as secretive about their privilege as she was about her absence of it. The truth was, the Gold brothers' stable childhood couldn't have been more different from Katrin's, and their self-possessed grasp on the world signified just that.

'Yes, lucky, you total ingrate,' she smiled, drawing her pillow to her cheek as she curled over to watch him dress. 'We're the luckiest people I know.'

Sunlight streamed in through the shimmering drapes of their master bedroom, and through the open windows the cries of seabirds travelled on a sultry summer breeze. She thought about the age gap that his family and friends had questioned, about how their marriage had thrived to conjure up not one but two beautiful children in one fell swoop, to complete their lives in this dream home – this dream life. How on earth had she ended up here?

Cocooned in the soft comfort of freshly laundered Egyptian cotton, Katrin closed her eyes as her handsome husband leaned in to kiss her on the lips, and she told herself, yes. She had every reason to feel lucky.

Breakfast was a leisurely affair, thanks to the thoughtfulness of young Frida, who, on waking in the snug to the sound of her cousins squabbling, had spirited them downstairs for a bowl of cereal before whisking them across the square to spend the morning with her at No.1.

'I wish Amélie was a bit nicer to her,' Katrin remarked as Bill poured her a second cup of coffee.

'What do you mean?' he replied, frowning.

'You know what I mean. *Frida*. Amélie barely speaks to the girl. She's her mother, but she behaves more like a wicked stepmother. She's so – so – *disdainful*.' She clicked a sweetener into her coffee, watching it fizz on the surface. 'And that business at school this term, whatever it was – well she's just sticking her head in the sand about it, making out to everyone that Frida was home early on revision leave. But you heard Poppy last night; there's obviously more to it than any of them are letting on.'

'Yes, what *is* that all about?' Bill asked, taking the seat across from her, absently flipping the pages of the Sunday papers. 'I did wonder. Boy trouble?'

'To be honest, I'm not really sure. All I know is that Frida was suspended for the remainder of term, and Hugo said it wasn't drink or drugs.'

'Huh, that's something.'

'But if it is a boy, it would have to be something pretty big to get suspended – which worries me, because she's only fifteen, Bill.'

'Nearly sixteen,' he corrected, spooning honey on to his toast. 'Anyway, it's an all-girls' school, isn't it?'

'Yes, but that never stopped anyone, did it? They're right next door to the mixed sixth form college. Frida once told me they share the same canteen, which means she'll be rubbing shoulders with lads as old as eighteen.'

Bill sighed. 'Teenage girls – no one wants to admit it, but they're all at it, really, aren't they?' He looked up in response to Katrin's silence and was met with a blank stare. 'Oh, God, me and my stupid mouth. I didn't mean – oh, you know what I mean, Katkin. Sorry-sorry-sorry.' He flashed an easy smile at her and she wondered how it felt to always be forgiven.

'Actually, I don't think they are *all at it*,' she said in a clipped tone, 'and those who are have often been led down a path they had no idea existed. Look at Frida: she's turning into a young woman before our eyes. I mean, she's beautiful, isn't she?'

'No doubt about that. She's a cracker. Good genes – any child of Amélie's was going to do alright on the looks front, eh?'

'Yes, but what I'm trying to say is, men and boys will be looking at her and seeing one thing, when the reality is, she's still just a kid. She's too young to be getting involved with anyone.'

'She'll make mistakes; we all do, Kat, and we survive them, one way or another.'

'Well, actually, not everyone does survive their mistakes, Bill,' she snapped. Suddenly riled, Katrin pushed her plate away, croissant uneaten, inwardly cringing at the smugness of her earlier waking thoughts. Her life was not perfect by any stretch, but must she constantly pretend to herself that it was? She thought of that word, 'luck', and of Bill's firm belief that you made your own, that it was all there for the making; for the taking. But in Katrin's experience good luck *was* a real thing, a phenomenon that could, sometimes, just fall into your lap like a gift – like beauty or inheritance or good weather on your wedding day. But so too could bad luck throw itself into a person's path when they least expected it. Otherwise, how could you explain childhood cancer, or aircraft disasters, or miscarriages or lightning strikes or simply meeting the wrong person in the wrong place at the wrong time? All at once Katrin felt a rush of fear and responsibility for Frida, and she hated Bill for his blasé attitude and male privilege.

'For Christ's sake, Bill, she's your niece,' she said with a heavy exhale. 'Don't you have any protective instinct towards her at all?'

'Well, she's not really my niece, is she?' He pulled *that* face. 'I mean, strictly speaking. In the same way that she's not really Hugo's daughter.'

'We've known her since she was *nine*, Bill. She sees *you* as a real uncle – and I see myself as her aunt. It doesn't matter that we're not related biologically.' Sometimes it seemed to Katrin that, passionate as she was about the importance of family, Bill was just as happy to not bother at all. Take his parents over in Tenerife. Most people would do all they could to stay connected to distant parents, but not Bill; he hadn't even taken her to visit yet. But family was *everything* to Katrin. 'What if we had a fifteen-year-old daughter – what if it was her?'

'Well, that would be different, of course.'

'*Of course*. But in the meantime, you wouldn't lose any sleep if Frida got into some bother with a boy at school? If, say, some older lad talked her into having sex before she was ready – or worse.'

'Worse?' He looked genuinely confused.

'I'm talking about abuse, Bill – assault, rape. Don't you watch the news? This stuff happens to girls every single day, and it's not just confined to deprived inner-city schools, you know. The private ones are just as bad. And if the girls in our lives can't count on us adults to look out for them, then who will? *God*. After what happened to me, I would have thought you'd be more—'

'Oh, give me some credit, Kat. What happened to you was different. Completely different. That was – that was, I don't know, a broken system. Shit social workers, a rough neighbourhood. Bad luck, even.'

And there it was. 'I thought people made their own luck? Must've brought it on myself in that case.'

'I don't mean that, and you know it! Stop putting words in my mouth. What I mean is, you didn't have a family to look after you, so it's no wonder you went off the – anyway, why are we even arguing about this? This is meant to be your birthday weekend. We're supposed to be having fun!' He made his way round to her side of the table, to drop a kiss on the top of her head. 'Look, if you're that bothered, I can ask Hugo if Frida's alright. Would that make you happy?'

Katrin picked up her mug and plate and crossed the large kitchen to place them by the sink. 'No, don't worry about it. Hugo wouldn't have a clue. God, if her mother weren't such a car crash I'd go over and check with her. I'll have a chat with Frida myself when the moment's right.'

Feeling bad about her outburst, she looked round to give Bill a conciliatory smile, only to find he had his back turned, his full attention now on a text message he was typing into his phone. 'That's great, darling,' he replied, without looking up. 'You do that.'

Something in his pose signalled threat to Katrin. The familiar turn of his shoulder, the barely perceptible smile that twitched at the side of his mouth.

'Who are you messaging?' she asked in as casual a tone as she could muster.

She watched him slide his phone into his breast pocket before energetically raking fingers through his hair. 'Oh, no one,' he said with a bland roll of his eyes. 'Just a boring work thing.' Avoiding her gaze, he made a show of taking in the weather beyond the patio windows. 'You know, sweetheart, I think I might go for a run. Shame not to on a day like today.'

Katrin's stomach sank with the awful sense that they'd been here before. Because they had, hadn't they? Several times over.

8. Ginny

She'd started having the dream again, the one in which she is trying to hold on to a newborn baby, pulling it close as its cries vibrate through her ribs like a heartbeat. Desperately she wrestles to keep it, turning from her attacker, only to feel frantic fingers slipping beneath hers, loosening the crocheted blanket and snatching the infant away. There is blood in the air, and ammonia, and the smell of sweat and fear, and in her arms: nothing. The baby is gone.

Every night the same, Ginny would wake from the dream, hair damp, pulse racing at the vivid clarity of it, and the sense of it never having gone away. *The cause of it is obvious*, she thought: *it's this place. It's The Starlings. And it's the troubling spectre of old Thomas King.*

While Katrin's party had started on such a celebratory footing, as the evening progressed, several topics had unnerved Ginny, and she'd spent that night tossing and turning in bed, revisiting the past, and wondering what kind of madness had compelled her to return. Maybe she *was* mad, she considered, mentally weak, 'like her mother', as her father so often would say. Because what sane person lived through something so awful as Ginny did and then return to the scene – not just out of fleeting curiosity, but to stay, to move their whole life there, permanently? Perhaps she was punishing herself, still driven by guilt for the best part of her life? In the early hours, awake, her mind kept fixating on that frump Anne Ashbourne, who was not only raking up the dirt of the past in the self-serving hope of publication, but now also encouraging others to have their DNA tested. It was immoral, surely? Because it was all well and good celebrating those stories like Anne's which had happy endings, but what about the mothers who didn't want to be found? Those who had gone on to build new lives, with new families who were blissfully ignorant of their loved one's tragic past. What of them? Anne was playing God, and Ginny was certain her actions would only lead to pain for dear Katrin and countless others. And then there was all that talk of secrets buried in the basement of the clocktower. So morbid; so upsetting.

So alarming.

After weeks of private agonising, Ginny decided it was time to take control of herself – and the situation – or else leave for good.

Katrin answered on the third ring. 'Hi, Ginny,' she replied, breezily. 'What're you up to?'

'Oh, not a great deal – actually, I'm at a bit of a loose end. I was meant to be meeting an old pal in town for lunch today, but they've just stood me up. It's a devil, because I'd managed to book us into Cornelia's, and you know how hard it is to get a table there on a Saturday lunchtime. I don't suppose you'd like— '

'To join you? Ginny, I would love to! My niece, Frida, has been badgering me to earn a bit more babysitting money, so I'm sure she'll come and sit with Max and Ted.'

'And Bill?' Ginny asked, having already seen him leaving with his brother an hour earlier.

'Oh, the boys are out on the boat today – I won't see them until the late hours, at least!'

Ginny gazed from her screened front room window towards the Golds' impressive architect-built home, where she could just make out the faint outline of Katrin against the sunny glass walls of the upper floor. 'The penthouse' as her horrible sister-in-law had described it. 'Oh, that's wonderful. I have a proposal for you, too – something I think might help you out.'

'Intriguing!' Katrin replied. 'I'll be all ears.'

'That's sorted, then! The table's booked for one-fifteen, so shall we meet at say, half-twelve – outside mine?'

When she hung up, Ginny stood quite still, her lying heart hammering behind her ribcage, while she watched Katrin from her safe distance, as she too remained at the window, phone in hand, eyes on the clocktower at the heart of The Starlings.

'Today,' Ginny reassured herself. 'Today is another day.'

At Cornelia's, Ginny managed to charm the management into shifting the seats around a little, so that they could have an outdoor table beneath the Bedouin tents which had recently been installed to accommodate more diners.

The heat of the early August sun glowed orange through the canopy, while overhead plantation fans cooled the air to a perfect bare-shouldered temperature. Already the place was filled with chatter and the low-level melodies of Frank Sinatra piped from speakers hidden within the glossy leaves of potted palms. Without consulting Katrin, Ginny waved over the most attractive young waiter, and ordered a bottle of 'very cold Bollinger, with an ice bucket, *s'il vous plaît*'. She could feel Katrin watching her, wide-eyed at her no-special-occasion extravagance, and she flashed her a wicked smile and said, 'If you can't splurge at my age, darling, then when can you?'

Katrin rewarded her with a laugh that betrayed her less refined beginnings, and when the champagne arrived the two women toasted 'to new friends', and Ginny felt entirely confident about the proposal she had planned for Katrin.

'Oh, no, there's Belinda,' Katrin murmured, nodding discreetly towards the inner restaurant. 'I hope she doesn't see me.'

Ginny slid along in her banquette seat to better obscure Katrin. 'You're hiding from her?' She smiled wickedly, breaking off a corner of olive bread and popping it in her mouth. She rarely ate bread, for her figure, but for some reason she was ravenous today. Nerves, perhaps. Or daytime drinking; she was certainly out of the habit.

'Not exactly hiding,' Katrin replied. 'She texted me a few days ago, asking if I fancied a day out shopping this weekend, and I said I couldn't get a babysitter, which wasn't exactly true – and now, here I am, with you. Drinking champers.' She winced guiltily.

Ginny snatched a furtive glance over her shoulder. 'And there was I thinking you two were so close. She was your right-hand woman at the open day back in May, wasn't she? What's the story?'

Katrin drained her champagne flute, and Ginny indicated to the waiter that they needed topping up. 'No real story,' Katrin said. 'It's just – you know what it's like, when you're thrown together with people through circumstance rather than choice? For a while you think you have lots of things in common, but ultimately those things don't last.'

'Lordy, you could be describing most marriages, darling!'

'Well, it's a bit like that with Belinda. She's really nice, so I feel like a cow just saying it. I mean, I don't think she has a bad bone in her body, actually.'

'How dull,' Ginny said, one eyebrow lifting.

Katrin grimaced guiltily, dropping her voice. 'She went through a divorce last year, and I think she's turned into a bit of a born-again singleton. Always saying how great it is to be on her own and how she's "embracing the grey" and doesn't "have to dance to anyone else's tune". These days, I can't help feeling she's judging the rest of us married folk with pity.' Katrin paused for breath. 'Perhaps our friendship's just run its course.'

'I believe one only makes really *true* friendships a handful of times in our short lives. So many of the people we end up spending time with aren't real soulmates, don't you agree, darling? It's such a waste. Still, at least you've got Anne,' she added with a mischievous wink. '*She* thinks you're the bee's knees!'

'Oh, don't be mean,' Katrin replied, before giving into laughter again. 'Anne's lovely. But I'd be lying if I said she wasn't getting on my nerves a bit lately too. She's forever finding excuses to pop by with historical questions I've no hope of answering, and then asking me where I bought this outfit or that. The constant compliments make me feel a bit awkward.'

Ginny pursed her lips, trying to keep a straight face. 'Shame she doesn't follow up on any of your retail recommendations. She could certainly do with a style overhaul.'

'*Stop*,' Katrin gasped, raising a halting palm. 'You're bringing out the worst in me, Ginny LeFevre. And I'm enjoying it far more than I ought to!'

The waiter arrived to take their orders, and Ginny spotted 'the boys', as she liked to call them – as she liked to call most men younger than her – at a table in the furthest corner. She attracted their attention with a wave of her red napkin, before blowing them a kiss. Dylan laughed, and Graham removed his spectacles before recognising her and sending one back.

'Oh, you are a breath of fresh air, Ginny,' Katrin said. 'How do you make life look so effortless?'

'At the risk of sounding like your old friend Belinda, being single doesn't hurt. Although, between you and me, I'm far from ready to "embrace the grey"! That and no money worries, and—' she lifted her glass '—a little of what you fancy, every now and then. Anyway, I hear you sold the final property last week? That's got to be worth celebrating – and champagne certainly puts a lovely glow on things.'

'You're not wrong about that,' Katrin agreed. 'Thanks for ordering the fizz, Ginny – it's just what I needed. I tell you what, sometimes I can see the benefits of single life, alright. Bill really wound me up last week, and I don't know what it is, but I can't seem to shake off my bad mood with him. It's not like me, but honestly, I was glad to see the back of him this morning.'

Ginny sensed Katrin wasn't the kind to open up like this, and she held back from probing too hard. 'Maybe it's the weather, darling? Too much heat makes *me* horribly grouchy.'

'Sometimes I think Bill and Hugo haven't got a clue how the real world works,' Katrin continued, seemingly warming to her subject. 'They're like a couple of spoiled overgrown boys, with their yachts and cars and well-turned-out wives.' She laughed. 'And not just because they're posh – you're posh, but you don't behave like them.'

Now it was Ginny's turn to laugh. 'And how do they behave?'

'As if nothing's off limits. Oh, that's not fair – Hugo's not like that at all; he's lovely, in fact. It's Bill. He just behaves as if he *knows* he can have anything he wants, so long as he smiles nicely and raises his voice loudly enough.'

'Oh, I'm not so very different, darling.' Ginny winked, and she raised her heavily bangled arm and beckoned the lovely waiter over once more. 'You'd better put another one of these on ice,' she instructed him, with a smile that she knew knocked years off her. 'We lunching ladies have decided to make an afternoon of it.'

'God, I don't know if I could manage another bottle, Ginny,' Katrin said, halting the blushing waiter in his tracks. 'I mean, I've got the kids to get back to—'

'Nonsense! Bill's away, and Frida's perfectly capable of looking after the twins – you said so yourself. She'll be happy for the extra hours. Look, I know I'm being completely selfish, darling – but I haven't enjoyed myself so much in a long time, and I don't want it to end!'

Katrin looked momentarily caught off guard. She turned to the waiting waiter. 'What would you do?' she asked him.

After a beat, he gave a decisive nod. 'I agree with your mother,' he replied, and the two women fell about laughing and sent the poor boy away to sort out that second bottle of fizz.

'Now, darling,' Ginny said as their starters arrived, 'I wanted to talk to you about this blasted clocktower business you've got hanging over you. How would you feel if I offered to take over the job of chasing up the bird removal certificate? The sooner we get the starlings relocated, the sooner we can get the builders in to fit out the games room.'

Katrin's face shifted through the various expressions of confusion, surprise and delight. 'I don't know—' she began, but Ginny was quick to cut her off.

'Here's the thing: I've got all this time on my hands now I'm retired, and meanwhile you're run off your feet with work and home. I'd love a project to get my teeth into, and of course, it's win-win for me if it frees you up for the occasional lunch date like this with old Ginny!'

'Ginny, I don't know what to say,' Katrin replied. 'Except for, yes please! You know we've got this new project about to start over at Golden Cap, so I'm going to be working all hours on that come the autumn. I know I should be pushing the clocktower delays through a bit harder, but I never seem to have the time.' She stopped speaking and gazed at Ginny in apparent wonder. 'God, you really are heaven-sent, aren't you? Ginny, it would be a huge burden off my shoulders. I can't thank you enough.'

'Nonsense, darling. You'll be doing me a favour.'

In her more rational moments, Ginny was quite sure there was no truth to the silly dinner-party chat of secrets buried in the clocktower basement. But at the time it had felt worryingly similar to the rumours she recalled from her own day, of small bodies discarded without a care, hidden, forgotten. Ginny reached across the table and topped up Katrin's glass. With any luck, her friend would soon be so distracted with her new project that the clocktower would be the least of her priorities, soon forgotten.

Yes, these things were best not left to chance.

9. Frida

At 5pm the pizza arrived, and Max and Ted fell on it like tiger cubs, telling Frida in hushed tones that Mummy didn't normally let them eat on the carpet in front of the telly.

'Good job I'm not Mummy,' she replied, sitting cross-legged on the sheepskin rug between them, making them laugh as she drew out a long string of mozzarella between her mouth and her outstretched hand.

She'd been at Katrin's since midday, and when the text had come through asking her to stay on later she had been pleased, both at the extra money she'd be earning and at having an excuse to stay longer away from home. She'd barely done anything or seen anyone outside of The Starlings since she'd arrived back from school under her cloud in May, but, now that the holidays had officially started, she had hoped she might at least see Rose and Meg, who would be back home for the summer break. Except, they were ghosting her, still ignoring her calls, and with creeping dread Frida was coming to the conclusion that she was going to come out of this thing at school far worse off than Barney was.

For the first few years of her life – her mother's modelling years – Frida had never really had a best friend to speak of, as she and Amélie had moved around so much. But when she was nine they'd moved in with Hugo, and together relocated to his old family town of Dorchester, 'for a better life in the country', less than an hour's drive from the boarding school that would soon become her home. On her first day at St Saviour's in Year Seven, Frida had met Rose Pitt and Meg Fitzarnold, recognising immediately, by some kind of mutual instinct, that these two would be her friends for life. Placed in the same house, D'Urberville, at registration, the trio – all of them boarders with family nearby, all of them only children – had stuck together solidly, sharing dorm rooms and day trips, and secrets and 'firsts'. They'd even got their periods within a few months of each other, Frida's arriving on an overnight stay at Meg's house, where an unfazed Amanda Fitzarnold handed her a stack of sanitary towels and a change of underwear, and congratulated her with the words, *Welcome to the club, doll.*

Now, after four years as close as sisters, Meg and Rose seemed no more than strangers. Had it all meant nothing? But this morning, after several weeks of radio silence, Frida had woken up with renewed optimism and, hoping Rose and Meg would be more receptive, she had pinged off a new message, as casual and nothing-to-see-here as she could make it.

Fancy meeting up in Dorchester this week? Milkshakes at Binky's?

After twenty minutes of obsessive screen refreshing, Frida had been able to establish with complete certainty that both friends had not only received her message but also read it within seconds. But no answer had returned, and her mood quickly shifted from optimism to paranoia. That had been nine hours ago. Now, she snapped shut her empty pizza box, slid her mobile from her back pocket and began scrolling again.

'You got a boyfriend?' Max asked her, leaning in and manoeuvring her hand so he could see the screen. He and Ted were still wading through their shared extra-large stuffed crust margherita.

'No, why d'you ask?' she replied, wiping his greasy fingerprints off her screen.

He smirked, chubby cheeks still chomping away at a bulging mouthful.

'Ted thinks you're pretty,' Max said, making the most of his brother's inability to protest.

Max's eyes scowled a warning at his twin, and Frida pouted her lips and batted her lashes for effect, and said in a terrible American accent, 'Why thank you, young man. *Ah* am flattered.'

The boys fell about, careless of the red pizza stains they were grinding into Katrin's lovely rug, and Frida left them to it, happy as they were watching *Finding Nemo* for the millionth time this week.

In the kitchen, she slid on to a bar stool and scrolled through Instagram, checking out the accounts of her various schoolmates. Meg's account was, as ever, full of lovely-looking meals, photos snatched at the serving hatch of her parents' Michelin-starred restaurant and hinted at as her own creations. May-Louise was in Trinidad eating roti and visiting waterfalls with her local cousins. Ivy Trott was in California at a sports camp for élite young swimmers, tweeting every day in a different swimsuit and describing herself as an 'influencer'. And Rose – for some reason, she couldn't locate Rose's account. She tried again, changing the search terms, and sifting through their mutual friends' comments, until finally she came to the one horrible conclusion that made sense.

She messaged Meg again: *Has Rose BLOCKED me?*

This time Meg replied immediately. *Think so. Tbh I'd meant to too, but just hadn't got round to it.*

They were together. Frida knew it at once. Meg was never so bold, so bitchy, without the back-up of Rose at her side. Heart racing, she fired a message back, desperate to get answers before she was ejected from Meg's timeline too. *WHY?*

Meg: *You know why.*

Frida: *Because of him?*

Meg: *OMG, Frida. Can you even hear yourself? There was no 'him'!*

Frida's mind was racing. What did Meg mean, *there was no him*? Meg and Rose were the two people she'd confided in when things started to get serious between her and Barney, and they knew *exactly* what had happened, exactly how they felt about each other. Sure, Frida had had to deny everything to the teachers when the shit hit the fan, but just because she'd had to change her story, well, it doesn't mean it *didn't* happen, does it?

Frida: *I don't understand.*

Meg: *Listen, Frida, no one believes you. You made us two look like mugs, with all your lie.*

Frida: *What?!!!*

Meg: *Mrs Bateman told us to look at the evidence, and she's right – you got suspended for making it up WHICH YOU ADMITTED and he didn't, did he? I can't believe you accused him of THAT. It's pretty disgusting tbh.*

Frida: *I didn't accuse him of anything! The first time Mrs Bateman had me in her office, I just told the truth. And then before I knew it everyone else started using the R word – but it wasn't like that. That's why I said I'd lied in the first place – to stop everyone saying those things!*

If it weren't for the fact that Barney had sworn her to secrecy, she'd tell them everything now – she'd send Meg and Rose that pic of them together, if proof was what they wanted.

There was a pause, in which Frida could only imagine Rose and Meg conferring. A new message pinged through.

Meg: *It's pretty shady the way you just left school and didn't come back last term. Looks totally guilty*

Frida: *But I was suspended!*

Another pause.

Meg: *Whatever. Anyway, you do know you can wreck people's lives with toxic lies like that, Frida? That's what my folks said.*

Oh, God, her parents knew about this too? Frida's thumbs hovered over the screen, but her mind was so clouded, she couldn't think what to say next. She stared and stared at the word 'toxic', and for a moment she thought, perhaps they're right, perhaps that's why my own mother can't stand to be in the same room as me. Because I'm toxic.

Meg: *Me n Rose have been talking and basically we can't be friends with a liar. We don't want to get tarred by association. I told Rose I'd block you too so – bye.*

Tarred by association? What kind of talk was that? Were those Mrs Bateman's words? Seconds later, Frida's Follow list decreased by one, and she was officially friendless. Outside, beyond the glass doors of the dining room, the afternoon sun had grown hazy in the sky. She stared into the light, her gaze following the soaring gulls that drifted in and out from the shore, dipping from view before circling high again.

Without warning, she was sobbing. These long-pent-up tears weren't just about the loss of her two closest friends; they'd been stored up for weeks now, ever since that meeting with the Head and Mrs Bateman, which Amélie had failed to turn up to. Ever since the letter home, hopeful of 'lessons learned' as it detailed her lies and set out conditions of a possible return to school in the autumn. The shame of it all, the betrayal, the hurt, the not being believed – all of it spilled over now, in a noisy, howling, snot-nosed heap on Auntie Kat's state-of-the-art breakfast bar.

'Good lord, what's all this?'

Frida looked up to see Uncle Bill standing in the back-door entrance, a life jacket hanging from one hand, two bottles of wine dangling from the fingers of the other. His silver hair was wind-tousled and surfy, and his teeth shone brightly against his beachy tanned skin. Frida made a grab for the kitchen paper and hid her face as she rubbed it dry, cursing herself for being such an idiot.

'Sorry,' she mumbled, dropping down off her stool to deposit the crumpled paper towel in the bin. Her nose was so blocked from all the bawling that her voice came out congested, like someone pretending to have a cold when they've phoned in sick. 'It's nothing,' she said.

Bill dumped the life jacket on the floor and plonked the bottles on the worktop. 'Doesn't sound like nothing to me, sweetheart. I could hear your wailing from a street away.' He gave a teasing smile as he said this, and she knew it was meant to make her laugh, but somehow his kindness just got her crying all over again.

Uncle Bill swooped her up, pulling her solidly into his arms, and it struck Frida how very like Hugo's his embrace felt, and that was at the same time comforting and strange to her. A few seconds passed, before Bill released her. He pushed back her hair and cupped her face, running two big thumbs across her cheeks to swipe away the tears. Reaching up, he brought down two glasses, holding one up like a question. 'I'm going to have a glass of wine, Frida. You look like you could do with one yourself?'

While Uncle Bill removed the foil from the neck of the bottle, Frida gave a nod and pressed Send on that photograph Barney had been begging her for all week. If she had Barney, she wouldn't need Meg or Rose or anyone else, for that matter. A reply returned straight away, pinging brightly into the large echoey room.

Barney: *Now I can die happy* ❤

She smiled at the message and responded with a volley of kisses. The rest of them could all just go to hell.

10. Katrin

It was gone seven by the time Katrin stumbled in that evening, and the first thing she heard from the floor above was the sound of Bill and another woman, howling with laughter.

Dumping her bag, she located the twins in the downstairs lounge, lying on their bellies, constructing a new dinosaur town, with several empty crisp packets discarded on the floor nearby. She stooped to kiss them a quick hello and kicked off her shoes to hurry up the broad wooden staircase on bare feet, her stomach tightening with every step she took closer to the sounds of laughter, her mind leaping into all sorts of disturbing places.

The door to the snug was ajar. Inside, on the sofa, were Bill and Frida. From her vantage point, she could see that they were both focused on the widescreen TV on the far wall, sitting side by side, so that their shoulders were almost touching, despite the generous proportions of the seat. On the coffee table in front of them was an almost empty bottle of red wine, two glasses and a feasted-on platter of bread and cheese.

'Watching anything good?' she asked, startling them both, causing them to spring apart as they turned.

Was that guilt she saw in Bill's face? In Frida's?

'Auntie Kat!' Frida cried out, making a grab for the remote control to pause their show. 'It's *The Office*. The American version, which is waaay better, in my humble opinion.'

Bill gave an approving nod. 'She's right. Haven't laughed so much in ages.'

Katrin's heart continued to pound away, stuck as she was in this heightened state of emotion, still reeling from thoughts of the scene she had imagined walking in on. She stared at Bill – at Frida – and had to stop herself from saying, *You're right, Bill, we haven't laughed much lately, have we? What with me walking around on eggshells, second-guessing who you're texting, when you think I don't hear the click of your phone from the room next door. Or when I sit alone late at night while the boys are in bed, torturing myself as I wonder who you're really meeting up with when you say you have an 'overnighter' in the city that can't be helped.*

Katrin despised this jealous version of herself. She despised the woman her husband was turning her into, collusive in her unwillingness to challenge him, instead watching on dumbly, while he infected their beautiful life with his lies.

'Auntie Kat? Is everything OK? You look really weird.' Frida was on her feet.

Katrin stared at the girl, and she wondered: did Bill have any real moral limits? So far, his conquests had been, well, adult, at least. But here was Frida, a child in a woman's body, almost, and – well, not very much younger than Katrin had been, when a thirty-something Bill had made his first move on her. Did Katrin need to worry?

'Yes, you do look a bit peaky, my love,' Bill agreed, dropping an elbow over the back of the sofa and reaching out a hand she would not take. 'Anyway, where've you been?'

She rested a steadying hand on the doorframe, feeling herself return, as though the essence of her had been, for a moment or two, somewhere else altogether. What had she been thinking? Bill might wander from time to time, but he would never step over *that* line.

'Sorry, I'm tired, that's all,' she replied. 'I was with Ginny – she treated me to lunch at Cordelia's. It was lovely.' Katrin looked at Frida, in her skimpy shorts and T-shirt, and she was gripped by the strongest need to embrace her; to protect her. 'Come here,' she said, and with heartbreaking gratitude Frida stepped into her arms. 'Let's get you home, before your mum starts wondering where you've got to.'

Dashing the short distance through the drizzle to No.1, Katrin and her niece were met by the unexpected presence of a woman knocking at Frida's front door. The grey-suited woman was a stranger: early thirties, petite-framed, hair pulled back into a neat chignon and a face absent of make-up. Katrin was certain she was there under some authority or other, intuitively recognising the confident, businesslike stance of her posture.

'Hello?' Katrin called over as they approached, suspicion in her tone. 'Can we help you?'

The woman turned and extended a hand. 'DS Ali Samson. Mrs Gold? Do you mind if I come in?'

The police?

DS Samson glanced at Frida, smiling. 'I'm guessing you must be Frida?'

With an air of caution, Frida unlocked the front door and Katrin and the detective followed behind. In the entrance hall, there were shoes racked and coats neatly hung, a tidy stack of letters on the sideboard and a large arrangement of fresh flowers filling the space with scent, and yet still the place felt somehow vacant.

There was something so temporary about the way Amélie and Hugo lived. Was that his influence or hers? Frida had once told Katrin that before Hugo, she and her mum had never lived for more than a year in any one place, and Katrin wondered now if their big, spotless, soulless home was merely a reflection of that restlessness – an extension of Amélie's lack of commitment.

Katrin gave the DS a flat smile and gestured her through. What was this all about?

'Erm, Hugo must be at the gym,' Frida said timidly, leading the way into the kitchen, where she stood awkwardly for a second or two. Inexplicably, she reached into the fridge for a carton of juice and drank from it, head thrown back, her eyes closed against the soft sea light beyond the patio windows.

Tuning into the sounds of the house, Katrin concluded that Amélie was out too, but before she was able to explain her relationship to the family the detective jumped in, gesturing for them to take a seat at the breakfast bar. *God*, Katrin, thought, feeling suddenly as though she were in trouble herself and hoping the officer couldn't tell she'd been drinking all afternoon.

'Mrs Gold, Frida, I'll get straight to the point. We've been investigating reports of shoplifting at one of the shops in town, and Frida, your image has come up several times on the CCTV footage filmed this week.' She paused for a moment, taking in Frida's trapped expression.

'How—?' Katrin asked, instinctively reaching for Frida's hand.

'One of the shop girls recognised you, Frida. And just now, I showed your image to the gardener, and he pointed me in the right direction.'

Without warning, Frida began to cry, as her words came tumbling out in a rush. 'I'm sorry – *I'm sorry*. I don't even need the stuff! I don't even use it! I'll give it back? Can I give it back?'

'Are the things here? The items you stole?' The detective was speaking in a low, kindly voice, and Katrin wondered what a senior detective was doing following up on so trivial a crime.

Frida jumped up from her seat. 'It's all upstairs, under my bed.'

DS Samson jerked her chin, giving her permission to run up and fetch it. The moment the girl was out of sight, she spoke. 'Has Frida ever been in trouble before, Mrs Gold?'

Katrin shook her head emphatically. 'Never. She's been through a lot lately, detective. Trouble at school,' she said, and then in case she was giving the wrong impression, added, 'She's been the victim of bullying – and this, well, I'm pretty sure she's just acting out.'

DS Ali Samson sighed, in such a way as to suggest she'd dealt with this kind of situation a million times before. She lowered her voice. 'In that case, I'm going to give Frida a warning – frighten her off doing anything like this again, OK? The retailers don't usually want to prosecute if it's just a one-off. You're lucky – half the station is off sick with some stomach bug, and normally one of my uniformed colleagues would be here. I suspect some of them would be pushing for a charge.'

Frida reappeared in the doorway, cradling an armful of cheap drugstore make-up and chocolate bars. She leant in and dumped the items on the counter, before stepping away again, eyes downcast.

'OK, Frida. Now, I understand this is uncharacteristic for you, and, given your clean track record and the fact you didn't try to deny the crime, I'm going to let you off with a verbal caution, *just this once*. Do you understand? But if anything like this comes to our attention again – well, we'll have no choice but to take you down to the station, and, from there, to court.'

Frida's skin had drained to grey. She nodded earnestly, and the detective stood and led them back through to the front door.

'Frida, you've got your mum here to thank for putting in a good word for you,' she said, shaking the teenager's hand firmly, 'so you be sure to keep in her good books, eh?'

With that, DS Samson was gone. For a few long, silent moments, Katrin and Frida stood in the airy entrance hall, staring at the back of the door.

'I paid for your birthday present,' Frida said quietly. 'I just want you to know – that wasn't stolen. I paid for it myself.'

'That's good to know,' Katrin replied gently, turning to look at her. 'Listen, I've done my share of stupid things too, Frida. You might not believe this, but I've stolen before, and I've lied and cheated just to get myself out of trouble – and it's rarely ever worth it.'

Frida gaped back at her. '*You?*'

'Yes, me! I spent my childhood in care, Frida, and I can tell you "dog eat dog" is the expression that comes to mind. Listen, all I'm trying to say is that there are better ways of working out your pain or upset or whatever it is you're feeling right now, yeah? I'm always here for you, sweetheart – just promise me you won't do anything like this again? You really don't need a criminal record to add to your list of things to worry about.'

Sheepishly, Frida nodded, and the pair moved closer to the front window where they could peer at the retreating police vehicle outside. 'So, *I've got my mum to thank*?' Frida repeated the detective's words with a smile in her voice.

Katrin continued to watch through the window. 'I didn't like to correct an officer of the law,' she replied, deadpan, before the pair of them descended into a suppressed bout of tears and laughter, and Frida clung gratefully to her aunt like a drowning girl to a raft.

'So, where is your mum?' Katrin asked, when Frida finally let go to return to the kitchen to wipe her face dry.

'Dunno. In bed, probably.' She placed her palms flat on the breakfast bar between them.

Katrin glanced at the microwave clock. 'At half-seven in the evening?'

'Pretty standard,' Frida mumbled, blowing her nose into a sheet of kitchen roll.

'Frida,' Katrin ventured, 'is your mum OK? Could she be depressed, do you think?' It was an inappropriate question, she knew, but she was still drunk, and it had come out of her mouth without thought.

Before she had a chance to take it back, to her shock Frida made a scoffing sound and then mimed the act of snorting drugs from the marble countertop, before casually swiping imaginary powder from her nostrils with the knuckle of her forefinger. It was such an adult gesture, so blithely delivered, that Katrin was at once pierced with profound fear for this girl, her niece. 'I actually thought that woman, that DS Ali, was here for her,' Frida said, 'about her drugs or something.'

'And is everything alright with *you*?' Katrin asked, concealing her shock, careful to keep her voice low. 'You had some bother at school, I know. But do we need to worry about you? Is there anything we – *I* – can do to help?' She should have had this conversation earlier – she should have made it a priority, instead of pushing it from her mind and hoping it would work itself out.

Across the counter, Frida blinked, her amber eyes appearing huge. She said nothing, and Katrin recognised the signs of numb denial. It was almost like looking into her own reflection twenty-five years earlier.

Oh, God. What was it? What wasn't she saying?

'Frida,' she whispered. 'You don't have to tell me anything you don't want to. But just tell me, is your mum looking after you? And Hugo? Have you got someone to talk to when things get tough?'

Frida's eyes appeared to grow larger and shinier, until a single huge tear dropped on to the worktop. 'She hates me,' she murmured, swiping at her cheek, unblinking. '*Amélie*. She hates me. When I got suspended, you know she didn't even come to the meeting at school – I mean, she said she would, then at the last minute she just didn't turn up. No message, no nothing.'

'Where was she?'

'London. On a last-minute casting call for a modelling job. Which she didn't get, by the way, probably 'cause they took one look at her and realised she's a junkie.'

'*Frida*, don't say that,' Katrin cautioned. 'She's your mum.'

'Try telling her that!' Frida straightened up, her volume rising. 'She put me in care when I was a baby, did you know that?' she hissed, glancing guiltily towards the kitchen door.

Katrin could do no more than nod for her to continue.

'In Paris. Apparently she just walked down to the local adoption agency and left me there. By the time she'd changed her mind, I was already with foster parents who wanted to adopt me. But *she* wanted me back, so I had to stay in care while she had blood tests and stuff to prove she was my mum and convince them she could look after me. And now that's her story – that she "fought" for me, like some fucking hero!'

Katrin had known nothing of this. Nothing at all. But then, what did she really know about Amélie? She knew she had begun travelling the world in her teens at the start of her modelling career, that she'd seen early success in a profession that Amélie claimed 'threw you on the fire' at thirty. But other women continued modelling after thirty, didn't they? Did Amélie's career end not due to age, but to drug abuse, as Frida claimed? Katrin thought of Hugo's past – the 'family secret', as Bill called it with some sibling glee – of Hugo's own previous struggles with cocaine, his never-mentioned-for-the-sake-of-the-family stays in The Priory.

'What about Hugo, Frida? He's not—'

Frida shook her head. 'And he'd go mad if he knew Mum was – he's totally anti-drugs, you know? They made a pact when they met in therapy.'

And then it all fell into place. Hugo and Amélie hadn't met at a meditation retreat, as the Gold family narrative went. The timing of Amélie's first appearance as Hugo's fiancée only weeks after he'd re-emerged from rehab suddenly all made sense: they'd met at The Priory. Bill would have known this, because he and Hugo told each other everything, and yet Katrin, despite being in their lives now for over twenty years, hadn't.

This discovery of an entirely different version of Gold family history felt like a fresh blow. Bill had been keeping her outside of the whole picture ever since they first met, and, with sickening clarity, she realised he was never going to change.

She glanced around the big, vacant kitchen. 'Frida,' she said, 'you'll be back at school the week after next, won't you? How would you like to stay with us for a few days – make the most of your last bit of summer hols? We could take a few day trips together, if you like.'

Frida's bleak countenance evaporated. 'Really, Auntie Kat? *Really?*'

'Go and pack a bag, and I'll square it with your mum. And don't worry; I won't mention the police visit.'

On the upper landing, Frida gestured towards the double doors of Amélie and Hugo's bedroom. 'I'll see you downstairs in a minute,' she whispered, disappearing into her own room.

Katrin knocked on Amélie's door. From within, she heard a barely audible 'Huh?' and she turned the handle and let herself in.

Inside, the room was dark and stuffy, as though it had been sealed for days, despite the August heat. Amélie was no more than a long, thin mound beneath the white sheets of her large four-poster, illuminated only by a narrow strip of evening light breaking through the drawn curtains. Katrin crossed the room and gently pulled back the drapes. Amélie, in response, drew the duvet up over her face.

'Amélie?' Katrin said. 'Are you awake?'

'Go,' her sister-in-law mumbled, her French accent unmistakable in even that one small syllable.

'I'm sorry, Amélie, but I need to talk to you. Are you unwell?'

Easing her head from the covers, Amélie regarded Katrin with one suspicious eye. 'What are you doin' in my bedroom, Kat-er-ina?'

She did this, Amélie; it was her thing, purposely mispronouncing names, as though it afforded her power.

'I'm here because Frida is downstairs alone and I thought you should know. Hugo's at the gym, and, well, you're up here in bed.'

'What do you want me to do about it?' Amélie pouted, stretching lazily and rubbing a palm over one mascara-streaked eye.

Thanks to the second bottle of champagne she'd polished off with Ginny, Katrin's usually well-managed filter was off. 'Well, d'you know what, Amélie, I expect you to haul yourself out of bed and get downstairs to cook some supper for your fifteen-year-old daughter. Have you any idea what she's been through this summer? Now, I don't know what that trouble at school was all about, but I do know that her friends appear to have stonewalled her, that her stepdad comes and goes as he pleases, and that her mother seems to have decided that her work as a parent is done.'

Amélie's face remained impassive, and she raked her eyes slowly up and down Katrin's body, in the way that men did when they wanted you to be scared.

'Jesus, she's right – you really don't give a shit, do you?' Katrin said, with a small, hard laugh.

'Frida *said* that?' Amélie replied, her mood shifting quickly from nonchalance to anger.

Katrin bit down on her lip; she'd said too much.

Amélie propped herself up on her elbows, and it saddened Katrin to witness the sharp, unyielding lines of her sister-in-law's shoulders, the knotty quality of her overworked yoga arms. 'You tell her to come up here to see her *maman, oui?*'

Katrin exhaled, a long slow breath. 'No, Amélie, I won't do that. Because Frida's coming to stay with me for a few days. I can't bear to see her on her own like this. I'd like your blessing, please.'

After the aggression of the exchange, she expected Amélie to object. But instead Amélie flopped back against her pillows and turned away. 'Fine,' she said, her voice thick with resentment. 'Take her.'

As Katrin stepped out on to the landing, Amélie called her back. 'Katrin?'

'Yes?'

Her hesitation hung heavy with significance in the musty air. 'Your life isn't perfect, you know?' Her tone was altered; disturbingly mild. 'Your husband – you'll never be able to trust him. He's not like Hugo; he's not faithful. Your Bill is like a handsome dog, *non*? Pissing wherever it is he likes the smell.'

A familiar chill settled in the pit of Katrin's stomach. Softly, she pulled shut the bedroom door.

11. Ginny

Despite only having been at The Starlings for six short weeks, Ginny really was starting to feel as though she'd been part of the community for years.

Very quickly, she'd got to know her nearest neighbours – Marcie, a fiercely outspoken eighty-seven-year-old Polish Holocaust survivor with an equally fierce sense of humour – and, the next door down, Andrea and Jim, a lovely young couple who ran a deli in town, and who frequently knocked on Ginny's door with treats left over at the end of the day. Andrea was expecting her first child in January. Recently Ginny had started to do a little pruning and weeding around the flowerbeds to the front of their three houses, giving them pause to chat now and then, and she enjoyed her neighbours' companionship, without any danger of over-familiarity. In fact, except for old Thomas King, whom Ginny had been studiously avoiding ever since she'd heard he'd taken a particular interest in her, just about everyone at The Starlings was a delight.

But it was Katrin with whom Ginny connected most strongly, and, as their friendship flourished, so did Ginny's outlook. She'd missed out on so much in her life – her father had seen to that after her mother's death, with his punishing approach to child-rearing – and, with no other family to speak of, she had always wondered whether she was even capable of maintaining a relationship of the maternal kind. But here was Katrin, this plucky young career woman, beckoning her into the private sphere of her family as though they'd been in each other's lives since the year dot. And of course there was Bill too, who it seemed couldn't welcome her warmly enough, and those gorgeous boys of theirs, who after just one afternoon of Ginny babysitting had now taken to flinging themselves into her embrace at every chance meeting. They were adorable, and she didn't mind admitting to herself that she was completely in love with them all.

Over the past week, Katrin's young niece had been staying at Starling House too, and with Bill away on business again, and Katrin juggling admin duties during the day, Ginny had spent several evenings with them, helping out with the twins and cooking supper. Despite her reservations about the teenager – she was, after all, the daughter of that dreadful woman poor Hugo had saddled himself with – Ginny was warming to Frida, who she knew had encountered some problems at boarding school before the holidays. It wasn't natural to coop girls together like that, like livestock; it was no wonder they all turned on each other every once in a while.

On Frida's last night before her return to St Saviour's she and Ginny put away the dinner plates as Katrin read to Max and Ted upstairs.

'Are you looking forward to going back to school, darling?' Ginny asked the girl gently.

Frida was cradling a large frying pan, running the tea towel slowly around its circumference, as she gave the question some thought. 'Partly yes, partly no,' she replied. 'I had a bit of grief last term, so, you know . . .'

'Am I right in thinking you've had a bit of boy trouble?' Ginny asked. St Saviour's always used to be a girls-only school.'

'Oh, it still is,' Frida replied, 'But there's a mixed sixth form college next door now.'

Ginny nodded, and waited, and Frida shook her head. 'It's complicated. Anyway, I told my best friends all about it and instead of keeping it a secret, like I asked, they blabbed to just about everyone in the school. Long story short, the Head heard about it, and I got called to her office "to explain".'

'I would imagine the school doesn't take kindly to their girls mixing with the older boys?'

'Ha, you could say that. They even talked about him getting charged, 'cause of my age, and in the end, I said I'd made it all up, just to make the whole thing stop. So then I got suspended for lying, and he just got told to stay out of my way.' She looked down at her hands. 'And now my friends all think I'm a liar too.'

'What's this young man's name?' Ginny asked.

'Barney.'

'And he let you do that, did he, darling, this Barney? He let you take the fall?'

After a pause, Frida merely shrugged, and Ginny wondered if she'd just hit on the real hurt in all this. It was the oldest story in the book: she liked him more than he liked her. She switched off the dishwasher and wiped down its door. 'I think these friends of yours all sound rather dreadful,' she said. 'Blindsiding you like that. And Barney – well, I don't think he sounds much better!'

Frida didn't reply, and Ginny felt sorry for her harsh dismissal.

'You must miss them, though,' she added.

'Yeah. But also, I *hate* them. So, I guess I'm gonna have to make some new friends, and that might be scary, but also it might be cool.' She gave a decisive little nod, shook out the tea towel and returned it to the hook on the wall.

'That's the attitude!' Ginny replied, pulling off her rubber gloves with a snap. She hoped the poor girl felt as bold when she got back to school tomorrow. That those nasty little madams cut her a bit of slack. And as for that lad, Barney—

Katrin appeared in the doorway, muttering curses under her breath.

'What is it?' Ginny asked.

'I've messed up,' Katrin replied. 'I've offered to drive Frida and Poppy Parsons back to school tomorrow morning. Belinda's working and Amélie – well, Amélie's away.'

'At the "spa",' Frida said, making quote marks with her fingers.

Of course Ginny knew where Amélie really was; everyone in the close did. She'd left under cover of darkness three days ago according to Katrin, headed off to a famous London rehab centre, for a 'rest'.

'And?' Ginny prompted.

'And I'd completely forgotten that my car's going in for its service. The garage just texted me to say they'll be picking it up in the next hour.' She stared at her phone, her brow furrowed in concentration. 'I'd normally use Bill's car as a back-up, but with him away too . . .'

Frida's shoulders dropped.

'I can drive us!' Ginny suggested at once. 'Don't object – I can see you want to object, Katrin, but, really, you've got to get better at accepting help when it's offered. No, I insist – I rarely get a chance to take the Caddy out, and you need a lift.'

'What's a Caddy?' Frida asked.

'It's the Cadillac, darling,' Ginny replied proudly. 'A 1960 Pompeian red Deville convertible, and an absolute dream to drive. Imagine turning up to school in that!'

The teenager's face lit up.

'It'll be fun,' Ginny added brightly, still sensing Katrin's hesitation at accepting her, or indeed anyone's, help. 'A girls' morning out! I haven't been to Bournemouth in years, and I completely, utterly and totally insist.'

Katrin threw her hands up in defeat, before wrapping them around Ginny in so strong an embrace, she felt quite knocked for six. 'You're a godsend, Ginny LeFevre,' Katrin said. 'Isn't she, Frida?'

Ginny laughed. 'I'm nothing of the kind!'

The next morning, after Ginny and Katrin had dropped the twins at nursery, they pulled up outside No.1, where Frida and Poppy, conspicuously standoffish with each other, loaded their bags into the trunk while Katrin popped back to Starling House to fetch her bag. It was a squeeze to get everything into the Deville, but they managed, and before 8am they were ready to set off, with Frida and Poppy sitting like stiff little dolls in the back, separated by a large Fortnum & Mason hamper Ginny claimed she was dropping off with a friend in Bournemouth.

'Shall we have the top down, darlings?' she asked from the driver's seat, knotting her headscarf under her chin and sliding on her huge dark shades.

Without waiting for an answer, Ginny flicked a switch, and slowly the soft-top eased back to reveal a china-blue sky stippled with thin white clouds. She could see Katrin making her way back from Starling House, evidently trying and failing to shake off her superfan Anne Ashbourne, who was matching her step for step. Ginny helped her friend out with an aggressive rev of her engine and turned up the Connie Francis on her gleaming music deck, determined to get the girls in the back to crack a smile.

'*Who's sorry now?*' she sang, pitch-perfect, '*Who's sorrrry now?*' At last she was rewarded with a little laugh from Frida, and, on checking the rear-view mirror, a reluctant smile from Poppy.

As Belinda Parsons toot-tooted a farewell to her daughter from her retreating car, Katrin slid into the passenger seat of Ginny's, and the four of them cruised steadily over the speed bumps that ran all around the central green of The Starlings, on to the path that encircled the mansion buildings within their high walls. Briefly, sunlight bounced off the all-seeing eye of the clocktower, a reminder to Ginny of her promise to chase up the planning department. She had let Katrin believe she was waiting for a call back from the bird relocation expert, but she couldn't keep that little white lie running forever. A few more weeks wouldn't hurt, she thought, and besides, Katrin was so busy right now with Bill away on business, Ginny doubted it was top of her priority list. At the entrance gates, she picked up speed past the ivy-clad gatehouse, relieved to have avoided Thomas along the way, and they accelerated out on to the open road for the sixty-minute drive to St Saviour's School for Girls.

'Are you sure you're alright in the back, sweetheart?' Katrin asked, but Frida quickly waved the question away. 'She's not a brilliant traveller in the back seat,' Katrin whispered to Ginny in explanation, and it occurred to Ginny just how lucky the girl was to have Katrin take so much interest in her, when her mother did not.

It was another clear day, the roads quiet post-summer holidays, and before long Ginny had the girls Bluetoothing their favourite tracks to her stereo and talking animatedly between themselves in the back.

'You're quite cool for an old person,' Poppy remarked with certainty. 'I mean, most people over forty don't even *know* what Bluetooth is.'

Ginny hooted with laughter and flashed a red-lipsticked smile at the spoiled little madam in the rear-view mirror.

'*And* you drive a kick-ass car,' Frida said.

'So, you approve?' Ginny asked, snatching a glance at Katrin in the seat beside her, shades down, eyes closed, a gentle smile just perceptible at the edges of her mouth.

To Ginny's great pleasure Frida raised a firm thumbs-up, before dropping back into conversation with Poppy, as though their earlier animosity had never existed at all.

'She's going to be alright, you know,' Ginny murmured to Katrin, suppressing a shudder of recognition as they approached the wrought iron entrance gates to St Saviour's. 'She's going to be absolutely fine.'

12. Frida

Frida watched the Cadillac drive off, with Katrin and Ginny waving all the way down the long drive and out through the school gates into the world beyond.

Maybe this term would be the fresh start she'd hoped for after all. The journey here with Poppy had been just fine, fun even, thanks to Ginny, and, with the sun shining overhead and the distance the summer holidays had put between last term's embarrassments and the here and now, Frida felt almost positive.

'How come she gave you that hamper?' Poppy asked, nudging the large wicker basket with her toe. 'Didn't know you and the old biddy were that close.' It was as though the new and improved Poppy of the car ride here had vanished, as soon as she'd landed on St Saviour's soil.

'She's not an old biddy,' Frida replied blandly, wondering about the hamper herself. As they'd unloaded their bags on to the school steps a few minutes earlier, Ginny had presented Frida with the unexpected gift, stuffed full of treats, and told her to give this term 'a jolly good go'. In her final embrace, she'd said quietly, 'I know how cruel girls can be, Frida. If they're stupid enough not to see the good in you, sod them all – rise above them, darling.'

Why was Ginny being so kind to her? she wanted to know. Her own mother hadn't given her anything to take back to school – she hadn't even stayed around long enough to see her off. 'Don't think she's got any kids of her own,' she murmured, only now realising that Poppy was already halfway across the gravel drive, her focus fixed on another group of girls laughing in a huddle on the lawns.

Frida gathered up her things, stacked them on to one of the wheely trollies lined up outside the entrance and, stomach fluttering with nerves, headed directly for her room on the second floor. The sounds of girls' shrieks and laughter echoed all around: bouncing along the corridors, drifting up through open windows from the lawns below, passing muffled through closed doors. The walkways had that all too familiar scent that came from an old place being shut up for a few weeks, overlayered with the disturbance of footfall, the fragrance of freshly cut grass, and the mixed eau-de-toilette waft of a hundred and fifty teenage girls. On her landing, she paused at the floor-to-ceiling window to look across the lawns towards the sixth form college next door, where the older kids could be seen coming and going through their front entrance. Only a couple of hours before lunchtime, Frida thought; maybe she'd see Barney in the refectory then. Last week, he'd said not to text him again until they'd settled back into school – just to be on the safe side – and it was taking every ounce of her resolve to stick to it. If it weren't for the promise of seeing him again, she would never have returned to school for this final year; if it weren't for him, she would have dropped out without a thought.

Footsteps on the stairs propelled her to get going along the narrow corridor to her own dorm room, which she could see from this distance was already open. Which could only mean that either Rose or Meg had arrived first and were in there before her, setting the tone. *Shit.* She'd hoped to be the first to arrive, to re-establish herself quietly, so that she might feel a little less like a visitor in a strange place after so many months away. She breathed deeply, mentally preparing for the reunion. *It'll be fine,* she told herself – *I'll just walk in and dump my bags on my bed, and say hi, and unpack, as if nothing ever happened. They might be a bit off with me, but they'll come round. All these years of friendship can't mean nothing, can they? We'll make it up,* she thought, *and soon everything will be back to normal, just like Hugo said.*

But the moment Frida reached the open doorway she could see *nothing* was normal. Her three-bedroom dorm was now, in fact, a two-bed, and she saw that her own name had been removed from the plaque outside the door.

Rose was sitting cross-legged on her own bed, in a new Suicide Squad T-shirt, with a restyled choppy blonde haircut that made her look several years older than the last time Frida had seen her. She squinted cautiously at Frida, who was helplessly planted to the wooden threshold, neither in nor out, and seemingly incapable of speech.

'Oh, so you came back?' Rose said, prompting Meg to appear from the concealed corner of the room. '*Bold.* Didn't think we'd see you again.'

Frida shook her head, struck dumb.

'I'd be too embarrassed, if it was me,' Meg said, plonking down on the mattress beside Rose, leaning into her so that the pair became one through Frida's stinging vision. 'I'd be *morti-fied.*' Meg blinked her cool eyes, slowly unscrewing a lip-gloss wand and running it over the contours of her mouth, round and over, over and round. 'But then, I'm not you,' she said, with a smack of her lips. 'So . . .' She got up, apparently bored, and wandered back to her corner of the room, out of sight behind the open door.

'Where's my bed?' Frida gestured limply towards the space where a large wooden desk now stood.

Rose flopped back against her pillows with a huff and spoke to the ceiling. 'End of the corridor. Room 24. They've given you one on your own. Mrs Bateman thought it would be for the best.' Now she turned and fixed her gaze on Frida's. *'Under the circumstances.'*

The door slammed shut, and the howling laughter of Frida's ex-best friends pealed out on the other side. Frida was left staring at the paint-crackled door of the room she'd called home for the past four school years, and wondering whether she could really do this – whether she had the strength to get through even a day, let alone a year of this.

Down in the refectory, she sat at the end of a table for ten, alone. She was hungry, but she couldn't eat. All she could do was sit and wait, sit and watch. There was no rush, because moving-in day was for exactly that: settling in at a leisurely pace, catching up with old friends, picking up timetables, preparing for the official start of term the next day.

She glanced around the increasingly busy canteen, her nerves on edge at the growing clamour of voices and footfall, as she took in the way the older girls and boys interacted with one another after the abstinence of the summer holidays. She watched the playful movements of these other girls, and Frida thought not one of them had experienced the adult intensity of feelings that she had, the obsession of longing and belonging in the arms of someone they loved. She felt those girls' judging eyes on her, of course – she wasn't an idiot – and she comforted herself with the thought that they were themselves pitiable, every one of them. The way they were around those boys reminded her, to her disgust, of her mother. Like Amélie, they were no more than needy children, playing childish games.

At the front of the queue, she spotted Poppy Parsons, attempting to pay for a tray of food, while frantically searching her bag for a purse Frida knew she'd never find. She ran her thumb over the missing item secreted in her jacket pocket and felt glad she'd been astute enough not to trust Poppy's phoney friendship on the journey here. *Stuck-up little madam*, she thought, echoing Hugo's verdict. *Stuck-up little bitch*. If Meg and Rose were here, she'd tell them what she'd done, and they'd probably laugh together at the sight of the unflappable Poppy panicking in the dinner queue in front of the whole school. Frida's feelings of rejection at the hands of her school-mates converged around memories from four nights ago, when Frida had watched her mother from her bedroom window as she disappeared into the waiting taxi below and sped off into the night. She hadn't spoken to Frida all that day, not even to explain where she was going, or to say goodbye. After she had gone, Hugo had come in to check on Frida, had lain beside her and held her in his arms as she silently wept, but even he was still caught up in the lie of making excuses for bloody Amélie. Maybe those falsehoods had worked when Frida was little, but not now, not since she'd grown a brain and opinions of her own. *What kind of mother just runs off in the middle of the night like that?* she'd wanted to scream at him? The truth had crashed in on Frida, like a terrible epiphany, that she meant nothing to her mother. Nothing at all.

Her eyes followed the strip of sunlight that flooded in from the skylight overhead, cutting the refectory in half, a slash of light that landed on him. *On Barney*. There he was in all his glory, larking about in the sixth formers' queue, and she saw him see her, *really* see her, as their eyes locked. *I love you*, she projected at him, silently, fervently. And she felt him say it back, she really did, and she knew she could weather this storm with him in her life. If she had Barney, she'd no longer be entirely alone. So what if they must keep it a secret for now? This time, she wouldn't do a thing to jeopardise their relationship; this time, she would keep her head down, work hard in her studies, tell no one her secrets, and disappear off the radar. No one was going to miss her at The Starlings, and not a single person would notice her disappearing into herself here at school. Here, she would make herself so invisible as to be nothing; here, she could be content being nothing and nobody – for everyone, that was, except Barney. For him, she intended to be everything, and this time nobody else need know.

Frida shrank back at the sight of Meg and Rose entering the refectory, and, by the time she glanced up again, Barney and his group had disappeared behind the mass of bodies now filling the clamouring room.

On the table, her mobile buzzed, startling her with a new message.

You look hot, it read.

Even before she had a chance to respond or look up and locate him, her phone vibrated again, and heat rose to her cheeks like flames.

Rumour has it you've got a room of your own.

13. Katrin

As Ginny drove away, neither woman spoke for a few minutes, both seemingly caught up in their own thoughts since dropping the girls at St Saviour's.

Would Frida be alright? Katrin wondered. She had no siblings to lean on, no other family nearby, and she had more to cope with than the average teenager at her twenty-grand-a-year boarding school, that much was clear. Amélie's drug habit had put her in rehab once again, and, while Hugo was a kind man, he had no idea when it came to parenting a teenage girl.

Katrin closed her eyelids a moment, inhaling a long, steadying breath as the warm breeze washed over her skin. Amélie's last words had continued to replay through her mind for days now, and, rather than ebbing with time, the private anxiety provoked by that conversation seemed to be intensifying. *You'll never be able to trust him. Like a handsome dog.* But what did Amélie know? She might be married to Bill's brother, but that didn't make her an authority on the rest of the Gold family.

Katrin's mind flitted back to that Sunday morning in their kitchen in July. Her birthday weekend. After his beach run that day, he'd avoided her attempt to greet him with a kiss at the door, instead sprinting straight up to the shower in shoes that looked suspiciously absent of sand. Was it really possible he was lying to her again, even after the threats she'd made the last time? The twins had been just a year old then, and she'd discovered his affair when she'd returned to work after her maternity break and spotted a damningly suggestive email from a woman he'd met at a conveyancing firm in Axminster. For a while, she had felt broken by the betrayal – the third that she knew about since they'd married ten years earlier – but when Bill had sworn that nobody else knew, that it was all over between him and this other woman, Katrin had made the decision to stick it out. To work it out. It would be hard to rebuild the trust they'd once shared, but they – she – had too much invested in this beautiful life of theirs to throw in the towel so easily. And so, drawing on some inner determination she didn't know she had, she'd issued him with his final warning and, as far as she knew, he'd never strayed since.

Opening her eyes, Katrin took in the rolling English landscape all around them, and, inexplicably, found she was thinking of Hugo. She'd long felt that she and her brother-in-law had developed some unspoken sympathy with one another, borne out of being hitched to these two demanding peacocks as they both were. But it went further back than the arrival of Amélie, didn't it? They had always been close. Once, at the end of a boozy night, long before the twins were even conceived, Hugo had told her she was the strongest woman he knew, and at the time she'd thought it was perhaps the nicest thing anyone had ever said to her. How would his opinion of her alter, she wondered now, if he found out she was prepared to put up with Bill's so-called 'lapses', not just once, but several times over? Katrin knew what *she* would think. She would think herself pathetic. Weak. Afraid.

A fraud. A worse thought slid through her mind: maybe Hugo and Amélie had always known about Bill's transgressions. Maybe they talked about it, about her – them – in private? Perhaps they'd been laughing at her all these years, or, worse still, pitying her?

'Is this the right way?' she asked, suddenly aware that Ginny had turned down an unmade country lane, instead of dropping on to the main road.

'Just a quick detour,' Ginny said, speaking for the first time since they'd left the school, carefully manoeuvring the vehicle over the rutted earth of the hoof-turned track. She pulled up outside a dilapidated block of stables and got out.

'What are we doing here?' Katrin asked, joining her to walk the perimeter of the now derelict building, stopping to survey the area. All around were the decaying signs of the building's past, half hidden in the overgrowth of bramble and nettle. Here a discarded tooth-bit and a sodden chamois; there, a cracked leather saddle and a collapsed canvas bag of sprouting horse feed. It appeared that the place had run to ground a good few years earlier.

'I used to ride here,' Ginny explained. 'When I was at St Saviour's'

Katrin took a moment to absorb the information. 'You were at the girls' school? I swear you've never mentioned that before, Ginny.' She turned to her friend, whose eyes were still concealed behind those large sunglasses, and briefly she reflected just how little she knew of this woman's past. There was something veiled about Ginny, an armoured quality that Katrin could certainly relate to. 'I thought you grew up in the Cotswolds?'

Ginny wafted the question away. 'Oh, I was here, there and everywhere, darling, but yes, like our lovely Frida, I boarded at St Saviour's. Some of it was good, some of it bad – I never really thought to bring it up, to be honest. It's a long time ago now.'

She turned on her heel and strode with purpose towards the farthest brick building, an ancient stone construction with small unglazed windows, open to the elements. Katrin followed as, cautiously, Ginny stepped inside the broken doorway.

'Do you have a light on your phone, darling?' she asked, holding out a hand, as if this were the most ordinary of detours.

Katrin swiped on to torch mode and stepped in behind Ginny, who now eased the wooden door shut, plunging them into damp-stone darkness. Katrin gasped, lifting her phone to illuminate the small space.

'May I?' Ginny took the phone and aimed the beam at the back of the ancient door. With slow deliberation, she scanned the scarred wood by torchlight, passing over countless carvings of initials and love hearts and doodles and obscenities, until her focus rested on what might have been the oldest and deepest engraving of them all.

Victor + V Forever

Katrin watched on as, deferentially, Ginny ran her fingers over the letters before snatching her hand away and exiting the hut. Katrin had never seen Ginny even close to flustered before, but the energy that radiated off her now was darkly electric. They returned to the car in silence.

Standing together at the driver side, Katrin frowned at her friend, bemused. 'Are you OK?'

Ginny smiled weakly and still hiding her true emotions behind sunglasses, she thrust her car keys into Katrin's palm. 'You said you'd never driven a Caddy before. Fancy taking the wheel?'

As they drove away from the deserted stables, Ginny sat quietly in the passenger seat, while Katrin tried to make sense of what had just happened. She thought about Ginny's sudden eagerness to drive them to St Saviour's today, and her habit of glossing over the past whenever Katrin and Anne talked of The Starlings and its tragic history.

'Victor and *Virginia*?' Katrin asked after a while, clarity dawning on her. 'The V stands for Virginia? Did you carve that on the back of that door, Gin?'

For a few long seconds, there was silence.

In her lap, Ginny folded and unfolded her hands, smoothing out the creases in her herringbone slacks. 'He was my first love,' she explained, simply, in a voice much smaller and quieter than the one Katrin recognised. 'Victor. The stable boy, as cliché would have it. He was my first love – my only love, I suppose and I . . .' For several moments she fell into silence again, while they passed alongside rolling country fields and out towards the open road. 'I just wanted to make sure I hadn't imagined the whole thing.'

14. Ginny

That same evening, after they had collected the twins from nursery, Ginny offered to cook supper for Katrin, so that she could catch up on some paperwork and emails after her day away from the office.

With Bill still in Somerset on business, and Hugo concentrating on their next big acquisition, Katrin was having to deal with more of the day-to-day running of the business – and despite outward appearances Ginny could see it was taking its toll. She'd looked tired today, she reflected as she stood chopping vegetables at Katrin's kitchen counter, and preoccupied with more, she suspected, than just young Frida.

At six, Ginny popped her head inside the study door, and held up two crystal glasses, tinkling with ice. 'A Ginny-and-tonic for the worker?'

Katrin snapped shut the lid of her laptop and pushed her chair away from the desk. 'Ginny, sit down with me a minute, will you?'

Masking her surprise, Ginny arranged herself on the office sofa beneath the window, where Katrin joined her. Beyond the doorway the boys could be heard sliding about in their socks on the polished floor downstairs, screaming with glee every time one of them went over.

'Is everything OK with you?' Katrin asked, concern softening her voice. 'It's just, you seemed really rattled earlier. At the stables. I've never seen you so, so – shaken, I suppose.'

Ginny took a measured sip from her drink. She should have known Katrin wouldn't be able to leave this alone. Even as Ginny had walked about the place, she had been aware of herself giving in to a moment of weakness, a lapse of longing to make some sense of the past. As was always the risk, surrender to her emotions had opened her up to scrutiny. Why were this generation so obsessed with talking about emotions? What was wrong with simply getting on with it, and looking ahead?

'You know, I had a strange upbringing, Katrin,' she said. She paused long enough to place her glass down on the table beside her. 'I was only eleven when my mother died, and of course, my father didn't hesitate in sending me away to school. I'd come home in the holidays, but his new wife treated me little better than a domestic servant. Ours was a rambling great place, miles from town, and really, I couldn't bear to be there after Mummy had gone. I used to spend the whole time dreaming of escape back to school; exactly the opposite of what all the other girls were dreaming of! At least at St Saviour's I knew the routine. There, I was the *same* as everyone else, in many ways. Anyway, despite my school pals, I suppose I was a lonely child. And for a long time I went looking for affection in all the wrong places.'

'Oh, Ginny.'

She put her hand over Katrin's. 'Please. Don't feel sorry for me, darling, I couldn't bear it.'

Katrin shook her head, and nodded sadly, and listened intently, and Ginny suspected her young friend knew just as much as she did about loneliness and uncertainty, the absence of belonging.

'When I was sixteen, I struck up a friendship with Victor, who worked at the stables where I rode. The stables where we stopped today. He was seventeen, shy, and quite the most handsome boy I'd met in my entire life. Believe it or not, I was a shy little thing too, back then, so we gravitated towards each other, I suppose.'

'Was it love at first sight?' Katrin asked.

'You know, I really think it was,' Ginny replied, recalling with sharp clarity Victor's dark, intelligent eyes, the angular lines of him. 'It didn't take long before we were both smitten. Victor came from a much poorer background than me, so nothing could ever have come of it, but for those few hours we had together each week I could dream of a different future. I think I still believed in the fairytale ending back then, silly girl that I was – a little part of me really thought we might actually find a way to live happily ever after together, surviving on nothing more than fresh air and love!'

'It's a reasonable dream, when you're sixteen,' Katrin said. 'I think I dreamed of much the same thing myself at that age. Hearts usually win over heads when you're young.'

Ginny reached for her glass. 'Of course, my father wouldn't have stood for it. So, Victor was my secret.' Despite her calm exterior, she felt as though she was standing at a cliff edge, about to leap, about to let the whole sorry story of her life spill out of her as she hit the rocks below. In some way, it was a relief just to be speaking these few true words out loud, to share them with another human being. 'But, poor or otherwise, I've never met another man who matched him since.'

'You know,' Katrin ventured in a pause, 'I've noticed you seem to know more about this place than you originally let on. About The Starlings.'

Ginny felt herself withdraw her hand from Katrin's, to the safety of her own lap. She felt herself falling, inside; some part of her was about to break away, and she wasn't sure she could stop it from happening.

'Gin, since we got back this afternoon I've been reading some of Anne's notes about the mother-and-baby years here, and it got me wondering—'

But Katrin's question was cut short by the vibrating ring of her mobile phone on the sofa between them. Ginny exhaled a silent juddering breath, the pressure behind her ribs releasing.

'Speak of the devil,' Katrin murmured. 'It's Anne. I promised I'd get back to her about something this morning.'

'Take it,' Ginny urged her, pushing the phone closer. '*Really.*'

Reluctantly, Katrin accepted the call on speakerphone. 'Anne, hi! Sorry, you must be chasing me about the email?'

There was a long pause down the line, and Katrin inclined her head, waiting for her friend's reply. 'Anne?'

Ginny's hammering pulse began to slow, released as she was, at least for now, from Katrin's scrutiny, from her own weakened defences. She reached for her glass and shifted back into the corner of the sofa, increasing the space between her and Katrin; between herself and the mistake she had almost made in opening up.

'Hi, Katrin,' Anne's voice lifted suddenly into the room. 'The email . . .?' she replied, sounding confused.

'You know, I'm a bit tied up right now, Anne. I'll take a look at it later, if that's OK.'

'That's fine,' Anne replied distractedly, and Katrin made a smiling frown at Ginny.

'Is everything OK?' Katrin asked.

Anne sighed. 'Listen, Katrin – I really don't want to be the one to do this, and honestly, I agonised over making this call.

107

But you're my friend, and I thought, I'd want to know if it was me. I'd want to know about it before everyone else – before the gossipmongers got hold of it.'

At these words, the colour drained from Katrin's face; she looked like a woman cornered. Suddenly, the room seemed too brightly lit by the lowering summer sun, the glow of it illuminating Katrin's horror too cruelly. Ginny knew that whatever this was about, she should take Anne off speakerphone now – or leave the room for Katrin to deal with it privately – but she seemed paralysed. She felt like a bystander about to watch a juggernaut plough into Katrin's beautiful family.

'Katrin?' Anne pressed on. 'I was meeting an old friend at the Wessex Hotel this afternoon. She works there, on reception . . .' Another pause. 'And I know you said Bill was away in Somerset this week, but . . .' Clearly Anne was having trouble getting her words out. 'Katrin? Are you still there?'

Ginny nudged her gently.

'Yes, Anne – I'm here,' she replied, slack-faced.

'OK, I'm just going to come out and say it. OK? I saw him. *Bill.* I was in the lobby and we – my friend and I – were just about to leave, and he walked in, straight past us, and into the lift. He's not in Somerset, Katrin. He's been staying right here at the Wessex Hotel under the name Mr Smith, would you believe? God, I'm so sorry to say this,' Anne stuttered, 'but, but . . .'

Katrin slammed her palm down on her own thigh, her face contorted. 'For fuck's sake, Anne! Will you just spit it out?'

A long pause. 'He wasn't alone, Katrin. My friend Stella doesn't know Bill, but when I pointed him out, she said he's been staying in the honeymoon suite, with a woman. *Mrs Smith.*' Anne waited for Katrin's reply, but none came. 'God, I feel awful. I'm sorry. Do you hate me for telling you? I'm really, really sorry, Katrin.'

'Did he see you?' Katrin's voice was now strangely calm.

'No. He looked in a hurry to get through reception. Probably worried someone might recognise him.'

'And the woman he's with? Did your friend describe her?'

The next pause seemed to go on forever. 'Er, not really, but . . .'

Ginny had had enough. 'Anne, it's Ginny here. Will you please just put this woman out of her misery and finish your bloody sentence?'

'She said she was attractive – and quite a bit younger than him, and—'

Good God, Ginny thought, could she have been more insensitive? Beside her, Katrin dropped her face into her hands. Ginny snatched up the phone and brought it to her ear as though it weren't still on speaker. 'Thank you, Anne,' she said firmly. She felt bad for yelling at her now; it wasn't her fault. It wasn't her fault these bloody men couldn't keep it in their trousers for even five minutes away from their wives. The truth was, she felt grateful to Anne for interrupting them this evening. Her phone call had stopped Ginny from giving away more of herself than she was ready to, and for that she was thankful. 'You did the right thing,' she said, more gently now. 'I'll stay with Katrin tonight, so you've no need to worry about her. But, Anne?'

At the other end of the line, Anne's voice sounded tiny. 'Yes?'

'We'd really appreciate it if you could keep this to yourself?'

15. Katrin

She'd survived worse than Bill's affairs before; far worse.

Over the years, Katrin had developed a hardwired ability to separate emotions from events, to reshape hurt in such a way that the event itself receded in importance and any negative emotion transmuted into a drive of another kind. It didn't mean she forgot the wrongs she'd suffered in the past – she just didn't let them screw up her future. As far as Bill's affairs were concerned – most of them work-related – the small acts of vengeance Katrin had been able to wreak on his lovers had gone some way to soothing her humiliation, in lieu of a public showdown. A laxative-laced coffee served with a smile; an anonymous tip-off to a clueless husband; unwanted pizzas delivered at two in the morning; and her particular favourite, an overripe herring dropped into a handbag, stinking juice and all. It was trashy, she knew, but, boy, did it soften the raw edges of her private degradation. She'd often wondered if her handsome husband ever realised that she was the perpetrator of these various menaces, because if he did he had never let on, but then Bill always was one to take the easy option in life.

For Katrin, the next few days slid by in a numb blur, as she tried to focus on the needs of her children and the business of gathering building tenders for the renovation work up at White Rise. Never in her adult life had she felt so exposed, so raw – not just at the revelation of Bill's latest affair, but in the knowledge that, this time, others were aware of it too. Ever since that dreadful call on Monday night, Anne had been bombarding her with concerned texts asking forgiveness for telling her, offering Katrin 'a shoulder to lean on', as though she were some kind of victim. But Katrin was no victim, she kept telling herself, although she was certain that was the way others would view her, once news got out. Because it surely would get out. The imperfections of her life and marriage had been exposed, and in the aftershock of the phone call Katrin had asked a confused Ginny to leave, ignoring her subsequent calls for want of time to think. But her new friend was stronger-willed than her, and Katrin had found herself agreeing to Ginny coming over on the eve of Bill's return, to make supper and chat and 'put the world straight'.

The evening was mild, so, with Max and Ted asleep upstairs, and several strong cocktails inside them, the two women reclined on patio loungers in the dusk, as Katrin confided the details of her less-than-perfect relationship for the first time in her ten-year marriage, and the unshockable Ginny listened on. And, once she'd finally started to open up, Katrin found the words tumbled out of her, as she tried to make sense of the thoughts she'd only ever wrestled with in private.

'Darling, do you love him?' Ginny asked, once Katrin paused to take breath. Despite matching her drink for drink, the older woman managed to appear completely sober.

'I've given him so many chances in the past,' Katrin said, eyes on her friend as she reached out to pierce an olive with a deft cocktail stick. She thought of the last woman Bill had been involved with, a temp Katrin herself had recruited briefly to get them through a busy patch. She'd been pretty, in an obvious way, and even as Katrin had poured salt into the petrol tank of the girl's Fiat 500 she had concluded that she only had herself to blame, for putting temptation so squarely in Bill's way. 'And you know what upsets me more than anything, Ginny?' she continued, taking another slug of her third Tequila Sunrise of the evening. 'He's made a victim of me. And, God knows, I swore I'd never be anyone's victim again.'

'*Again*, darling?'

Katrin rested her glass on the patio beside her. *Slow down, Katrin*, she cautioned herself, sensing her control, her reserve, slipping. She didn't know what it was about Ginny, but, when she was with her, a piece of her armour peeled away, and she felt herself edging towards territory she would otherwise avoid at all costs.

'Oh, you know what I mean. I feel stupid, that's all.' The truth was, she despised herself for her own complicity in the sordid lie of their lives – in the perfect lives of Bill and Katrin Gold. This was not how things were supposed to turn out.

Casually, Ginny reached out for Katrin's hand, bridging the gap between their loungers. 'Look,' she said, raising their clasped knot of fingers. 'They're practically the same size.'

Katrin blinked slowly at the comfortable tangle of their digits. They came from different worlds, she and Ginny, and they were more than two decades apart in age, and yet, when they were together, they barely stopped for breath, so flowing was their conversation, so easy their laughter. It was a cliché, but Katrin really did feel as though they'd known each other forever. Since she had ejected Ginny so swiftly on Monday night, they hadn't returned to her story of Victor the stable boy and whatever secret trauma was wrapped up in that part of Ginny's history, but somehow Katrin knew the time had passed, for now. Right now, she had enough of her own problems to wade through.

'Yes,' she replied, releasing Ginny's hand and reaching for her glass, only to find it empty. She was, she suddenly realised, hopelessly drunk. 'In answer to your original question: I do still love him.'

'Of course you do, darling,' Ginny replied.

'Pathetic idiot that I am,' Katrin added. 'You know, before Anne's call, I'd got it in my head that we'd start trying for another child now that we've got The Starlings off the ground. I had it all planned out: I was going to cook him a romantic homecoming meal, oysters and steak and champagne and . . .' She trailed off with a self-disgusted little scoff. 'Because I always wanted a big family, and I know Bill would love a girl, and I'm *forty*, so we need to get on with it if we're going to—' She broke off, aware she was only going to repeat everything she'd already said.

'Can you forgive him?' Ginny asked, swinging her legs off the lounger to face Katrin.

Groggily, Katrin sat up to mirror her. She felt exhausted. 'I've forgiven him God knows how many times before. Because I figured, there's always hope, isn't there? But this time feels different, Ginny – I had every hope pinned on The Starlings being the start of a fresh chapter for us, a new place, away from London and the reminders of past mistakes. But now he's gone and tainted even this. I'm not sure I can get over it.'

Against the six-foot hedge of Katrin's huge garden, a white-haired man could be seen making his way down to the shore, bare-chested and deeply tanned in his khaki shorts and walking boots, a red towel over one shoulder.

'Good grief,' Ginny gasped, 'he scared the life out of me.'

'Oh, it's just Thomas. You know, the groundskeeper?'

'Yes, I realise that,' Ginny replied, suddenly alert as a guard hound. 'But why?'

'He swims every night, and we let him use our shortcut to the beach. Saves him walking all the way round.'

'And you don't mind? I wouldn't want him lurking about in my garden.'

Katrin laughed, surprised by Ginny's mistrust. 'Who, Thomas? I know he's a bit awkward, but he's harmless enough. Anyway, he checks our perimeters while he's at it – it's quite reassuring, actually.'

The temperature had dropped a little now, and Ginny collected up their glasses and the two women headed inside.

'Right. Here's what you're going to do,' Ginny announced, once Katrin had checked on the boys and she'd put a sobering pot of pasta on to boil. 'Bill's home tomorrow, right? You're going to cook him that homecoming meal you'd planned, and you're going to pretend none of this ever happened.'

'But—'

'Look,' Ginny cut her off, 'your marriage may or may not survive this. But if you want another child, this could be your last chance. Think of yourself, darling. Woo him, have that baby, and, with a fair wind, have the best bloody life you possibly can.'

'But what about the affair?' Katrin protested. 'I can't just pretend none of this happened.'

'That's exactly what you're going to do. For now, you're going to make yourself the centre of Bill's universe. If you don't, this life of yours will implode, and you're not ready for that. Nor am I, to be frank! I've grown very fond of you all – you, Bill and the twins – and if I'm honest I'm not ready to lose you just yet.'

Katrin shook her head at Ginny's brutal honesty and fantasised about cutting Bill's brake wires. Because wasn't the truth of it that life would actually be easier without him? She was financially secure, she did most of the heavy lifting when it came to the business – she had her boys, and, well, now she had Ginny too, didn't she? *Snip-snip.* Katrin gave a bitter little scoff at the idea.

'And it's not only you it affects, is it?' Ginny continued when Katrin didn't answer. 'What about Frida? And Hugo? I see how much you adore him, darling – *everyone* loves Hugo. But you know, he'd have to choose his brother over you, if pushed. You'd lose him too.'

'So, you're saying I should "stand by my man"?' Katrin asked bitterly. 'Just roll over and accept it?'

'Not at all!' Ginny replied. 'It's called not cutting off your nose to spite your face. If you want to leave Bill, darling, that's fine! But before you do, you make sure you've got your affairs in order. Get legal advice so you know where you stand. Ringfence your finances. Have that third baby you've always wanted – and *then* make your mind up. But don't make a hasty martyr of yourself out of pride or fear of weakness. It's harder to stay, Katrin, believe me. You do this on your terms, you hear?'

'But, what if—'

'If he does it again, you'll be in a position to act quickly.'

'But right now – how can I look him in the eye when I know this is going on behind my back? How can I watch him with the twins, as though everything is normal? How can I bear to let him touch me?'

'I could have a little word with him,' Ginny says, thoughtfully. 'Gently. Let him know he's been spotted – advise him to give her up, before all his friends and neighbours find out.'

'And Anne?'

'I've already spoken to Anne.'

Of course you have, Katrin sighed to herself.

'You're safe there, darling. I think the thrill of being in on the secret is enough to secure her silence.'

In the garden, a fox stalked over the dim lawn where Thomas had walked just half an hour earlier. It halted, gazing into the illuminated kitchen, staring directly at the two women through steady eyes, before vanishing into the darkness of the hedge. Katrin thought of Frida, desperate for the love and attention of a mother, friendless in her boarding school bedroom. She thought of herself, back when she was that age, perched on a single bed in a halfway house dorm room, afraid, with no one to call family and nowhere to call home. She had family and a home now, not only in Bill and the twins, but in Hugo, in Frida, in this place, The Starlings – and, now, in Ginny. And Ginny was right, of course – she had too much to lose.

Katrin nodded decisively. 'Sod him,' she said as Ginny served up pasta and poured them both a glass of sparkling water. 'I'm not going anywhere.'

Thank God for Ginny, and her no-nonsense approach to life. Katrin had been left reeling after this latest blow – ready to pack the whole damn marriage in – but, with Ginny's support, before long she began to regain at least some sense of control over her feelings.

To her shame, she had covertly linked Bill's Find My Phone function to hers in the days after Anne's call, only to find, in the weeks that followed, that her husband really was wherever he claimed to be. The only explanation, she decided, was that the 'affair' had been in fact no more than a fling, over as quickly as it had started. That didn't make it all right, but it certainly made the fact feel less catastrophic.

Determined to maintain her renewed positivity, Katrin persuaded Bill that they ought to get away for a few days to a spa retreat in north Cornwall, while Ginny looked after the twins at home. For four peaceful autumn days they stepped off the treadmill of their working life, to walk the coastal paths over-looking the wild Cornish sea, stopping for impromptu lunches in cosy firelit pubs before heading back to the hotel to fall into bed for wine-soaked siestas and afternoon lovemaking. Sometimes, when he looked at her in the way he did during those intimate moments, as though she were the most important woman on earth, she could almost imagine Bill's affairs had never occurred at all.

On their final day, Katrin surprised him with a 'couples after-noon' in the hotel's spa sanctuary, where side by side, they were massaged and steamed until pink, before being released into the ambient waters of a private aromatherapy whirlpool, complete with champagne on ice.

'I'm glad you talked me into this,' Bill said with a contented sigh, topping up their glasses before sliding his arm around Katrin's waist, completely clueless that his wife had timed their minibreak around her ovulation cycle. 'I think it's done me – us – the world of good to get away from it all, don't you? All work and no play makes Bill a dull boy.'

Katrin kissed his cheek, remembering the first time he'd ever said that to her, back when they'd met in Fulham, after she'd been placed at Arnold's estate agents on the high street as part of the youth employment scheme for careleavers. She still remembered the thrill of the pre-work shopping trip with her social worker, Cara, picking out a smart bootleg trouser suit and new shoes in the Dorothy Perkins sale – clothes that Bill would quickly upgrade on another shopping trip, in Knightsbridge, only a matter of weeks after first meeting her. His ambitious nature, both for himself and others, had been one of his most attractive qualities; that and his film-star good looks. Even now, after two kids, several rocky patches and a stretch mark or two, Katrin could look back on those days and recall how it felt to fall in love so helplessly. Because that was how it had been: instantly, she had worshipped him. Of course she had. She was a seventeen-year-old care system reject; he a successful thirty-seven-year-old man who promised her the world. In her head the story didn't sound so bad, but increasingly Katrin found herself playing down the age difference and omitting the fact that she'd fallen straight out of a foster home and into the arms of a grown man. How much had their age difference influenced her choices? If the relationship had been less skewed from the start, would she have stayed so long?

'We work too hard,' she agreed now, breathing in the soothing aroma of lavender and eucalyptus. 'We always said we'd ease up a bit once The Starlings was off the ground, but even now that we've sold all the units, we seem to be working harder than ever. What with the office and the twins and this new White Rise project – we hardly see each other these days.'

Bill pulled her closer, kissing her damp hair. 'I'm sorry about that, sweetheart. You know what it's like: the more you have, the more you seem to need. I'll be happy to take my foot off the pedal once we've cleared those bloody nightclub debts. Shouldn't take more than a couple of years, I reckon.'

Those 'bloody nightclub debts' were Bill's, and Bill's alone, an investment gone bad when he'd taken his eye off the ball – around the time of his first affair, as it happened, when Katrin had been expecting the twins. As quickly as she was making money from her successful renovation projects, Bill had been skimming the profits to repay his debts, and she'd be lying if she said his poor business decisions hadn't been a disappointment to her. They were comfortable, yes, but not quite as well off as they might have been otherwise. Bill would be sixty on his next birthday, ten years older than the age by which he had always intended to retire. She glanced at him sideways, taking in the sun-striped creases at the corners of his eyes, the slight loosening of skin around his once taut jaw, and wondered what he would think if he knew she'd been crawling all over their financial affairs with divorce in mind. Because in the aftermath of Anne's revelation Katrin had followed Ginny's advice and carried out a full and discreet financial audit on their businesses, moving certain funds around and safeguarding others, to ensure she had ample control in case she ever needed to exercise it. So far, Bill had failed to notice the adjustments, further evidence if any were needed that he'd been taking a rather more relaxed approach towards the business of late.

'Shame that project in Somerset didn't come off.' The words were out before she could stop them.

'Oh, you win some, you lose some. We just couldn't agree on a deal. On reflection, it wouldn't have been great – too much travel for starters.'

He lied so effortlessly.

'Yes, but I know how you love a challenge,' she said, running her index finger in slow circles over the soft hairs on his thigh. That was really the core of the problem, wasn't it? she thought to herself. Bill's love of the challenge.

He hesitated momentarily. 'Well, yes, but – you know how these things go,' he replied finally. 'Anyway, we've got enough on our plate with White Rise, haven't we?'

'We sure have. You know, it's in far more need of renovation than you boys had really considered when you placed your bid.'

According to the solicitor, the previous owner had spent his final years in just two rooms on the ground floor, with the rest of it – six bedrooms, three storeys, a huge scullery – piling high with old newspapers and books and rotting rubbish. Katrin shuddered at the thought; she recalled watching a documentary with Ginny about hoarders, and the chaos of the way these people

119

lived profoundly troubled her sense of order. Every one of them had mental health issues; every one of them trauma in their past. At the time, Ginny had said they'd be better off setting a torch to those places than attempting to sort them out, and, having seen the disgusting state of White Rise when they took it on, Katrin could kind of see what Ginny meant.

'Yes, but I think we'll turn a very good profit on it,' Bill continued. 'Hugo says the architect's plans should be approved in a week or two, so you'll be able to get down to County Hall and start talking with the chaps in Planning. Talking of which, what's going on with that clocktower of ours? I had McGowan's on the phone last week, asking if we were ready for them to start work on the games room. I had to tell them no, it's still full of bloody asbestos and starlings!'

Katrin took a small sip of champagne; all weekend she'd been drinking just enough for him not to suspect her baby plans. Ultimately, whether they stayed together or separated, Katrin was determined she would have the third child she'd always hoped for. If Bill was allowed secrets, she figured, dispassionately, so was she.

'I'll have to ask Ginny how she's getting on with that bird relocation certificate – last time I asked she was waiting for the council to call back. It seems to be taking forever – I hope they're not just fobbing her off.'

'I'll pop into the council office when I'm in town next week, if you like? Give it a little nudge along.'

Katrin smiled at the easy way in which work pulled them together. Really, this was when they were at their best: when they had something other than the kids to talk about, when they were wheeling and dealing and getting stuff done. She liked the old sleeves-rolled-up, hard-grafting Bill far more than the louche, wine-swilling playboy that she seemed to glimpse more often these days. He spent more time entertaining clients over swanky lunches than manning the boring office, all the while with one eye on the weather forecast, anticipating his next trip out on the boat.

'We'll be planning our retirement before too long, I promise,' he said as though reading her mind.

'Maybe *you* will,' she said, laughing, 'but not me! I've only just turned forty – although I could certainly do with a bit more help. I know I've got Cathy to clean and Thomas helping with the garden, but there are still not enough hours in the day. And when Max and Ted start at school next year I'll have even less time than the nursery gives me now, unless I put them into after-school clubs, which I'd rather not. Where's the point in having kids if you're going to just farm them out?'

'Oh, it doesn't hurt them,' Bill replied with a gentle nudge. 'In fact, it probably does kids no end of good, a bit of time away from their doting mothers.'

'Try telling Frida that,' Katrin replied, careful to keep the bitterness out of her voice. 'You know, Amélie hasn't spoken to her once since she went back to St Saviour's in September.'

Bill gave a little grunt of acknowledgement. 'Anyway, it's nice that you've got Ginny as a friend now,' he said, deftly steering away from talk of Hugo's selfish wife. 'She's a godsend, isn't she?'

'She really is,' Katrin replied.

'You know, she's a very attractive woman for her age. Very well preserved.'

Katrin pulled her chin in. 'Ha! "For her age"! She's not far off you, my love. But you know Ginny: "a woman never divulges her age".'

'Has she ever been married?' he wondered aloud. 'We've talked at length, but you know, I don't think she's ever mentioned a partner – or much else about her past, for that matter.'

'No, never married,' Katrin said, remembering with sadness Ginny's story of Victor the stable boy.

'Hmm, surprising. Siblings?'

'None. Her mother died young and her dad remarried, and she got sent away to school – to St Saviour's would you believe, where Frida is? Probably why she's so independent. You know, she worked as a window-dresser at Liberty's in the eighties – and she has no end of amazing stories about famous people she's met, or places she's been. Apparently, she used to go to the Cannes Film Festival every year, "before it got tacky"!' Katrin laughed. 'But I've noticed that whenever anyone probes too deeply, she has this stock phrase: *the past is the past*. She's fobbed me off with it countless times. *Oh, darling, do drop it! The past is the past!*'

Bill threw his head back and laughed too. 'Oh, yes, you've got her down pat! So, she's the mysterious type, is she? I'll have to see if I can charm a little more from her next time we all have dinner together.'

'Good luck with that,' Katrin replied, sleepily kissing him on the neck.

Bill curled himself around her, sliding his fingers beneath the elastic of her bikini briefs. 'How about we head back up to the room to "sleep" off this champagne, my sweet?'

Extracting herself from his arms, Katrin stepped gracefully out of the little pool to slip on her bathrobe, fastening the belt with seductive leisure. 'I'll see you up there,' she said, and she left her deceitful husband in the swirling water, looking every bit as proud as a handsome old dog.

16. Ginny

On the first day of December, Ginny found herself sitting with Katrin at the best table in the Aqua Shard restaurant, overlooking a rain-splashed London lit up for the festive season.

It had been Bill's idea, a thank-you to Ginny for all the support she'd given Katrin with the boys since moving to The Starlings, along with a beautiful pair of diamond studs he'd picked out for her with Katrin's help. Of course, she'd protested at his generosity, complaining that she loved looking after Max and Ted, that it was a favour to her that they let her do so, when they'd only got to know her these past six months.

'You're practically family now, Ginny,' Bill had disagreed, sweeping her up in a gregarious hug. 'And anyway, you girls deserve a day out together. I've booked the table already, so you can't say no – and that's that!'

The waiter, Adriano, an effusive young man who bestowed compliments liberally, brought them each a peach Bellini while they perused the menu. 'Sisters?' he joked as he set the drinks down.

'He'll get a tip,' Ginny whispered to Katrin when he walked

away. 'One never gets too long in the tooth for a bit of old-fashioned flattery, no matter how insincere.'

Katrin laughed and raised her glass. 'To you,' she said. 'My lovely friend.'

Ginny lifted her own glass in reply. 'To *us*. This is such a treat, darling,' she said, sitting back in her chair and taking in the sweeping cityscape, mottled with cloud shadow as a splinter of midday sun attempted to break through. 'I adore The Starlings, but I'll admit there are times when I miss the bright lights of London! Don't you, Kat?'

Katrin gazed out over the view, daylight reflected in her shining eyes. 'I think my London was a little different from yours,' she replied, thoughtfully. 'I wouldn't go back *there* for a million pounds.'

Ginny put her hand out, and Katrin took it without hesitation. What had this poor child been through? Ginny thought. How could the system have discarded her so easily? She had no way of knowing the hardships Katrin had endured, but she knew enough to suspect that her past was a dark spectre over the light of her present life.

'I'm just thankful that whatever powers exist in the universe brought us together, darling,' she said softly. 'You know I've never been happier than I have these past months, and that's down to you. And Bill. I know he's not perfect, but then, who is? He's warm and generous and giving. And together – you, Bill, Maxie and Teddy – together you really are perfect. You do know that, don't you?'

Briefly, Katrin's gaze met hers, and Ginny saw the raw emotion right there on the surface, a fragility rarely displayed, laid bare. Katrin pushed her seat back from the table and excused herself as a single fat tear dropped to the tablecloth, soaking into the starched white linen. Was it Bill? Ginny wondered. Was the stupid boy up to his old tricks again? She hoped not. She herself had already warned him off soon after Anne's revelation. *You'll lose her*, was all she'd needed to say as he'd walked her to her front door late one night after babysitting. *Not to mention the respect of your family and friends.* He'd kissed her on both cheeks and nodded meaningfully, and to his credit had since then treated her as warmly as ever before the conversation.

When Katrin returned through the double doors on the far side of the restaurant, Ginny spotted the change in her immediately. They'd been in close proximity all morning, and she'd not noticed, but at this distance it was suddenly, remarkably clear. Some people called it 'the glow': a kind of serene radiance subtly illuminating the skin, a secret held close. Dressed in a flowing two-piece, Katrin showed no other tell-tale sign as she made her way across the busy room and into her seat, but one look into those lucid eyes told Ginny everything she needed to know.

'Sorry,' Katrin apologised, smiling, embarrassed. 'I'm a bit over-emotional at the moment—'

'You're pregnant,' Ginny replied, pulling her friend into a fervent embrace. 'Oh, darling, darling, darling! I couldn't be happier. Really, I couldn't!'

Laughing, Katrin extracted herself, handing Ginny a napkin to blot her tear-streaked face. 'You mustn't breathe a word, though, Gin – I haven't even told Bill! I only took the test this morning before we left, and God, my mind has been racing ever since. Promise me?'

Ginny made a zipping motion across her sealed lips, and sat back, hands clasped beneath her chin, feeling proud as a mother. 'You've made my day,' she sighed. 'My *year*. Will she call me Auntie Gin, like the boys do?'

'You're assuming it's a girl,' Katrin laughed. The smile on her face was so pure and unguarded, it seemed years dropped away from her, affording Ginny a glimpse of the young girl she might have once been. 'Of course she will,' Katrin added. 'In fact – and obviously, I haven't spoken to Bill, but I know he'll agree wholeheartedly – I was wondering if you'd do us the honour of being godmother? Not in the religious sense, but in the being-a-fabulous-role-model sense. Whether it's a boy or a girl, I can't think of anyone who would do a better job.'

This was all Ginny had ever dreamt of: family and belonging. Who would have thought she'd find it at Highcap House – at The Starlings? It was as though the whole circle of her life up to this point suddenly had meaning.

'Adriano!' she waved, catching the waiter as he passed with an empty tray. 'Two glasses of your finest champagne please – we're celebrating!'

It was gone six by the time their train pulled in at Dorchester, where Ginny agreed to hand her car keys over to Katrin, who'd earlier insisted she couldn't drink her champagne in light of her recent news.

As they drove the half-hour trip back to The Starlings, Ginny sat in the passenger seat and a peaceful mood settled over them after their long day in London. The moon was high over the water as the hills parted on the horizon and the ocean came into view. This really was one of the most beautiful places on earth, Ginny reflected. She glanced at Katrin at the wheel, her features set in a serious, contemplative attitude, and she wondered, not for the first time, what thoughts passed behind those eyes of hers. Here and there, roadside houses were lit up with fairy-lights, and, as they approached the outskirts of Highcap, Christmas trees twinkled outside pubs and farm shops, a promise of a happy season ahead.

At The Starlings, they idled a moment as the security gates drew back for them, pausing again on the other side as Ginny fiddled with her remote control, eventually locating the 'close' button. All around the courtyard, little white lights flashed and twinkled ahead of the official switching-on ceremony that coming weekend, when the community would come together to drink mulled wine and decorate the eighteen-foot tree that had been specially shipped in. Already Ginny was looking forward to the occasion, even more so since the happy news of today.

Directly to their left was the front window and door of Thomas's lodge cottage, and as they paused to check the gates were shut behind them she couldn't resist the urge to take a quick look at the place, lit up as it was inside, with none of the curtains drawn.

Just as Katrin began to pull away, Thomas's door flew open and a woman's screeching voice tore out across the quiet courtyard entrance.

'What the hell—?' Katrin said, employing the brakes and craning her neck to look back at the commotion. She pulled on the handbrake and stepped out of the car. 'Thomas?' she called over. 'Anne?'

From Ginny's position in the passenger seat, she could see that two women were now out on the path – one of them, by the look of it, Anne Ashbourne – while a ghost-faced Thomas swiftly retreated behind his door.

'Yes! You!' the older woman was screaming, while Anne tried to wrestle her into an overcoat and steer her away. But the woman shook herself free, sending Anne's papers flying across the path. As Anne scrabbled about retrieving her notes, the other woman folded down into herself, while a violent sobbing escaped her. She reminded Ginny of old news footage of Greenham Common protesters, women balling themselves up to make the job of the police more difficult. And it was working, because poor old Anne was having a hell of a time getting a grip on the woman, who was now lashing out blindly between frightened sobs.

Ginny didn't know what to do. She couldn't get out and risk coming face to face with Thomas, but at the same time she felt she ought to be supporting Katrin in some way. She watched in the side mirror as Katrin laid a hand on Anne's shoulder and talked softly. Anne's face appeared almost featureless in the lamplight, her mouth a little pink 'oo' as she spoke to Katrin, shaking her head every now and then, her hands gesturing helplessly towards the lodge cottage.

Katrin banged on Thomas's door, calling out his name, just as the woman broke from her pose and rushed towards Katrin, arms flailing. In a heartbeat, Ginny was out of the car and marching towards the pair, inserting herself between them and taking a blow across her forehead in the process.

'Mother!' Anne screamed at the sight of Ginny's injury, a superficial nail scratch which instantly drew blood to the surface. Before either really had a chance to register what had just happened, Anne hooked her arm through her mother's and dragged her away, apologising profusely.

Heart hammering, Ginny turned to check on Katrin, when the door to Thomas's cottage flew open, bathing the two women in the full glow of his entrance light.

'Thomas,' Katrin started. 'I've just been speaking to Anne, and she said her mother attacked you. She's mortified, of course—' But Katrin broke off when she realised that Thomas wasn't looking at her at all. Instead, he had his eyes fixed firmly on Ginny, who, in the glare of his attention found she couldn't get her feet moving fast enough to back away into the shadows.

'Thomas?' Katrin repeated, looking from him to Ginny and back again.

Thomas blinked, his lips slightly parted, a deep crease scored between his white brows. 'It *is* you,' he said, almost imperceptibly.

Katrin turned to Ginny for an explanation, and she rearranged her expression into one of mild bemusement.

'Of course it's me! I'm at No.40, remember? I've been living here for the past six months, Mr King!' These past few months Ginny had successfully managed to avoid him, using her back door to exit whenever he was gardening at the front, and timing her daily stroll around the grounds to coincide with his evening sea swim. But she'd known it was only a matter of time before they collided, and that time, it seemed, had arrived.

Thomas took a step back inside, doubt now creeping into his features.

'Katrin, why don't we leave Mr King to get on with his evening?' she said, regaining her sense of control, having successfully shut Thomas down. 'Perhaps you can follow this up tomorrow, in the clear light of day? I expect Thomas here has things to do.'

'Is that alright with you, Thomas?' Katrin asked, clearly relieved that the altercation was, for now, at an end.

Thomas nodded. 'Night, Katrin,' he said, snatching a last cautious glimpse of Ginny before his door clunked shut.

'What was that all about?' Ginny asked, back in the car.

'Poor Thomas,' Katrin replied, starting the engine. 'Anne was there to interview him – for her book – and she'd thought her mother might like to meet him, as they'd likely have been here at the same time, back in the late seventies. I'm not sure they got very far before the mother got upset.' She shook her head. 'Dementia – it's a terrible illness.'

Ginny remained silent for the next few minutes, as they cruised slowly over the speed bumps and into her car port at the back of No.40. 'Aren't you worried about him?' she finally said. 'Thomas?'

'Do you think I should be?' Katrin replied, switching off the engine and returning a puzzled look.

Ginny raised an eyebrow. 'You saw him just now – he didn't even know who I was!'

'I thought he seemed to think he knew you . . .'

'Yes, he was confusing me with someone else, wasn't he? He certainly seemed muddled.' Ginny took the keys from Katrin, locked the car and walked around to link arms with her. 'He must get terribly lonely, all by himself in that little house. I'm sure I could smell booze on his breath. You don't think he's a drinker, do you?'

Late that night, Ginny stole out through the frosty back path of her east side garden, sticking to the shadows of the perimeter fence, until she reached the gatehouse, now in darkness.

On soft feet, she made her way to the rear courtyard, navigating the dark path with ease, and stood on the tread-worn back step, breathing deeply, willing her pulse to slow down. With a firm hand, she knocked, *one-two-three*, and waited until a light flickered on behind the netted windowpane, and a bolt slid free on the other side of the door.

'Virginia.' Thomas stood inside his kitchen, dressed in a chequered bathrobe, an old cast-iron press gripped in his fist.

'What are you going to do, Thomas King,' she said, eyeing the iron with disdain, 'bash my brains in?'

With dignified poise, Thomas placed the iron on the floor at his feet. 'Why are you here?'

'Well, I think we need to talk, don't we? Straighten a few things out.'

'I meant, why *here*? Why come back to Highcap? You swore you'd never come back unless this place was razed to the ground, Jarman and all.'

Ginny barked a hard little laugh. 'God, so your memory's intact, then. Forty years is a long time.'

A flicker of sadness flashed across his features.

Ginny took a step closer, her voice low and menacing. 'You think I'd have bought a place here, at The Starlings, if I'd thought for even a second that I'd run into you? I thought – I hoped – you'd have moved on, or, better still, died long ago.' Seeing the shock in his face, she withdrew, despising herself for letting her composure slip. 'I saw you, not long after I moved in, from Katrin's balcony, and I knew it was you, the way you moved like an apology, as though you were somewhere you oughtn't to be.'

Looking into Thomas's tired eyes, she saw in him the younger man he once had been, the memory of him clear as day: he in his overalls, at the window of the maternity wing, she on the other side, trapped and full of rage.

'You were walking down to the beach, through her garden,' she continued, 'and seeing you there – well, it was like a punch in the gut. I swear, I almost called back the delivery van there and then. '

'So, why didn't you?' he asked.

Ginny glanced back towards the mansion blocks, and thought of Katrin and the boys, sleeping peacefully in their seafront home, oblivious. 'I don't know,' she murmured.

'If Katrin knew—' Thomas started.

'If Katrin knew what, Thomas King?' she hissed. 'There's nothing to know. The past is the past.'

'But—' he began, losing his momentum as he met her fierce gaze. 'She deserves to know the truth.'

'*Whose* truth?' Ginny spat. 'Your truth? The governor's truth? Mine? The truth of a thousand other women who passed through those doors?' She waved an arm in the direction of the old maternity wing.

For a few moments, they stood in silent standoff, the distant drag and pull of the moonlit ocean the only audible sound.

Ginny took a step forward and placed her hand on the door-frame. 'Let me in, Thomas,' she said, doing her best to inject a grain of warmth into her voice. 'Let's just sit down and have a cup of tea, and we can talk about this in a respectable manner. It won't do either of us any good if we're spotted out here in the middle of the night.'

Thomas stepped back and let Ginny inside. She glanced around the old kitchen, unchanged after all these years, the 1950s cabinets lining the walls, the quarry tiles imbuing the place with an unwelcoming chill of frugal self-denial. Unplugging the kettle and filling it at the sink, Ginny could feel his eyes on her, alert as cornered prey.

With great effort, she turned kind eyes on him and softened her tone. 'Look, let's start again, shall we?'

Thomas blinked at her from across the room.

'I shouldn't have said those things. I don't wish you were dead, Thomas, I'm just in a bit of a state.' She waited for a response, until he nodded meekly. 'I really am sorry.'

Behind her the kettle reached boiling point and clicked off loudly, breathing steam into the chilly kitchen. 'Milk, one sugar?' she asked with a gentle smile.

Finally, Thomas's guard lowered and he gave a little bob of his head before taking a seat at the table.

'So, what was going on with that woman earlier?' Ginny asked as she reached into the cupboard to find mugs, still kept where they always had been. 'Anne's mother?'

'She was confused,' Thomas replied, cautiously. 'She thought I was someone else.'

The obvious next question might have been *Who?*, but a more pressing imperative preoccupied Ginny's mind, one of absolute clarity. Thomas King had to go.

17. Katrin

For as long as Katrin had known Bill, it had been a Gold tradition to meet for a festive lunch the weekend before Christmas, as a way of getting the far-flung members of their immediate family together once a year.

This year she dreaded the celebration more than ever, her sense of charade heightened since her private struggles of the past couple of months. Despite her efforts to shrink the pain of Bill's betrayal over the weeks since Anne's revelation, the knowledge of it was always there beneath the surface, like an unexploded bomb. If it weren't for the twins and the baby, and the diversion of this new renovation project up at White Rise, Katrin's resolve to make her marriage work might have broken once and for all.

On the morning of the lunch, Hugo suggested Katrin and Amélie drive ahead in her car, while he and Bill chauffeur their parents, who had flown in from Tenerife two days earlier, and were already complaining that they hadn't seen enough of their boys. Ginny had agreed to stop by beforehand to fetch Max and Ted, after their grandparents – who were at great pains to remind everyone they were paying for the meal – had suggested the boys might be an unwanted distraction over lunch, when the adults 'ought to be able to converse unmolested'. '*Unmolested!*' Katrin had gaped at Bill in the privacy of their bedroom as they'd dressed that morning. 'Your parents are mental.' Bill hadn't disagreed. Fully appraised and knowing that today the couple were planning to share their baby news, Ginny had arrived, embraced Katrin and whispered, 'Break a leg!' before corralling the boys out of the front door with promises of baking.

For the first few minutes of their drive to the Highcap Hotel Amélie didn't speak, while Katrin consciously resolved not to be the one to break the silence. Frankly, she was fed up with the way everyone made allowances for her sister-in-law's rudeness, and she was sick of the way she treated Frida like an inconvenience. Only this week, Hugo had asked if Bill and Katrin could have Frida over Christmas, as he and Amélie had booked a romantic getaway in Paris, to iron out a few differences they'd been having lately. Naturally Katrin had said yes, wholeheartedly ready to take in her niece, but, deep down, she'd wanted to explode at the wrongness of it all. She fantasised about breaking into Amélie's house while she was out, to hide her passport, the selfish cow, but she wouldn't do that to Hugo, much as she was tempted. Of course, Katrin was aware her hormones were in some ways to blame for her heightened intolerance, but you didn't need to be pregnant to come to the conclusion that Amélie was a pretty selfish human being all round. Let her make the first move, Katrin thought now, stubbornly fastening her jaw as they drove out along the Charmouth road; let her feel just a little of the discomfort she inflicts on others.

As they paused at a junction, to Katrin's surprise, Amélie broke the hiatus.

'It is hard work, having the parents in your house, *non*?'

Katrin glanced at her in the passenger seat, dressed in black rollneck and slacks, her crimson belt and slip-on shoes the only pop of colour. She was slumped low in a posture of boredom, her bony arms crossed loosely at her ribs, her long legs slung one over the other, face hidden behind enormous shades. With lips painted out in a matte shade of nude, she could have stepped straight out of a fashion magazine, Katrin thought, already aware of the baby pounds stealthily obscuring the lines of her own cheekbones.

'It's exhausting,' she replied. Without warning, Katrin's pent-up irritation at the old couple came tumbling out, unleashed. 'They're obsessed with food – all they can think about is the next round of eating. They're not in the least bit interested in their grandsons and yet they talk constantly about their friends in Tenerife, who we've never even met! They just sit around waiting for food, Henrietta talking non-stop and George agreeing with everything she says. I certainly couldn't manage more than a few days with them.'

Amélie laughed, a rare authentic sound, a momentary accord between the two women. 'I'm glad they prefer to stay with you – with Bill. They hate me, don't they?'

Katrin considered lying, as she would do under normal circumstances, to save a person's feelings, but she knew such platitudes would be pointless with Amélie. 'Yeah,' she said. 'I think they do.'

'*Pah*. I'm used to it. They've barely spoken to me since our wedding. Five years!'

'Don't take it personally, Amélie. They're not much more friendly towards me.'

'Hmm. But at least they don't *hate* you. They made their minds up before they even met me, *peut-être*.'

'What makes you think that?' Katrin asked, lowering the sun visor as they dropped on to the coastal road, where the mirror-bright sea spread out before them.

'Hugo says they would prefer if he'd married a nice English girl. No baggage, you know.'

'Baggage? *Oh*. Frida.' It made sense; George and Henrietta found it hard enough to show affection to the grandchildren they were related to, let alone an incomer.

'A single mother,' Amélie continued, carefully enunciating the words. '*Disgusting*. And, worse, Frida's not even the right colour.' She laughed again, more bitterly this time. 'Ah, if only I'd been a quiet little virgin, with no child, no history at all – maybe then they'd like me.'

'They can be, let's say, a bit old-fashioned in their views,' Katrin offered.

'Ha! Old-fashioned! They're racists, Katrin, you know? Big fat racists!'

Half-laughing, Katrin started to defend them, if only out of loyalty to Hugo and Bill. 'Oh, come on, they're not that bad—'

'*Non?* You don't believe me? The last visit, the mother, you know, she asked Frida: "Are there any other *coloured* girls at your school?"'

'No! What did Frida say?'

'Frida? She held out her hands and looked at them, shocked, and said, "Oh, my God, am I not white, *Maman*? I can't believe I had to find out like this!" Hugo's mother – ha! She looked like she swallowed an egg!'

Katrin's laughter filled the air. 'Go, Frida!' she said as she pulled into the hotel's gravel driveway and parked the car facing out towards the ocean.

For a few seconds, Amélie sat quite still, her gaze fixed on the horizon, and Katrin allowed herself to wonder if perhaps there was more to her sister-in-law than she gave her credit for. If it was possible the two of them might, one day, be friends.

'*Oui*,' Amélie sighed. 'It was a proud moment. I was a proud *maman*.'

'Did you tell her that?' Katrin asked, gently.

After a beat, Amélie shot her an unvarnished glance, and exited the passenger seat, graceful as a cat. 'Don't try to tell me how to be a parent, Kat-er-ina,' she said, facing her across the roof of the car. 'I am Frida's mother, not you.'

The spell was broken; Amélie and Katrin were never going to be friends.

Inside the hotel restaurant, they were shown to the large window table overlooking the sea – the same table at which Bill and Katrin had dined on their wedding day, and the seat they always requested when returning for anniversary dinners.

The Art Deco ballroom was bedecked for Christmas, with mistletoe arrangements adorning every window, and a vast, tastefully decorated tree dominating the far corner, beside the white Steinway piano. The room was already a hubbub of conversation and cheer, as the pianist played a leisurely rendition of 'I'm Dreaming of a White Christmas' and the waiting staff moved about the room, graciously attending to their patrons' needs. Ginny would love it here, Katrin thought, and she made a note to bring her before the festive season was over.

Already a slave to her bladder in these early weeks of pregnancy, Katrin excused herself to the ladies', glad to absent herself from Amélie for a minute or two. As she dried her hands, she silently berated herself for imagining that things could ever be friendly between her and her sister-in-law. Just because she was married to Hugo, that didn't mean Katrin had to like her – or even *try* to like her, for that matter. God, she was such an idiot! As she faced herself in the mirror, she recalled that last stinging confrontation when Amélie had compared Bill to a pissing dog, leaving his scent wherever he liked the smell. '*Fuck you, Amélie,*' Katrin murmured to herself in the mirror, and she topped up her lip gloss before returning to the restaurant.

On her return, Bill, Hugo and their parents were seated at the table, and Katrin joined them, subtly suggesting a switch-around that placed her on one side of the circular table between Hugo and Bill, and Amélie opposite, sandwiched between George and Henrietta. She kissed Bill on the cheek as he held out her chair, giving a friendly little wave to his parents as she sat.

'So, here we are!' Hugo said, perhaps sensing the tension on his wife's side of the table. 'How lovely that we're all together.'

Henrietta smiled at her youngest son, a tight, pinched acquiescence of sorts. 'Nice of you to spare us your precious time. I know you're all run off your feet.'

Bill smirked, reduced to a teenager. 'Mum ticked me off on the way here, for texting in the car. I wouldn't mind, but I wasn't even the one driving!'

Everyone laughed; the ice was broken.

'So, who were you texting?' Katrin asked Bill, her voice low enough for only him to hear. She loathed herself for asking.

'Ginny,' he replied discreetly. 'She says she found a couple of empty vodka bottles in the greenhouse when she was returning some gardening tools last night. She thinks Thomas might have a drinking problem.'

'Really?' Katrin scowled. 'Thomas?'

'Well, Ginny seemed to think she's smelt it on his breath a few times too. Anyway, we'll talk about it later. Can't have our groundsman pissed on the job.'

138

'Your girl's not here,' George announced, breaking Katrin's thoughts of Thomas, as he helped himself to bread with arthritic fingers, scattering crumbs across the white cloth.

'*Frida*,' Henrietta reminded him.

'Frida!' he repeated, as though he'd remembered the name himself.

'She's at boarding school, Dad,' Hugo replied.

'Shouldn't she be home by now?' Katrin asked, although of course she knew the reason why Frida was still away. When Amélie and Hugo had been meant to fetch her on Friday, they had instead been in the middle of one of their famously explosive rows, and, in the hours that followed, they'd simply forgotten. Katrin had received Frida's SOS call early that evening after they'd failed to turn up, and, while she'd offered to drop everything and drive out to fetch her, Frida wouldn't hear of it. There were some revision clubs running for a couple more weeks, she'd said, and she'd rather stay on there than be at home listening to those two at each other's throats.

Amélie glanced at Katrin under dark lashes. 'She has exams coming. She wanted to stay on a little longer with her friends, to revise.'

'Good girl,' George said around a mouthful of bread. 'Needs all the advantages she can get!'

Katrin knew he meant this in the general sense, in the 'kids need all the help they can get these days' sense, but still, she caught Amélie's eye again and widened hers, a provocation.

'What do you mean?' Amélie asked, taking the bait and turning sharply towards George. 'Because she has brown skin?'

George's pink cheeks flushed deeper still. 'Good grief, woman! I meant nothing of the kind!' He looked to his son, who was already shaking his head uncomfortably. 'Hugo?'

Hugo's palm was tensely pressed to the tablecloth beside Katrin's, and she gently brushed the side of his hand with the tip of her small finger, in a way that was visible for all see. To Bill and the in-laws, it would appear to be a gesture of sisterly caution; to Amélie, Katrin knew, it would feel like a challenge.

'Amélie, that's not what George meant,' Katrin said, tolerantly. 'Come on, he's just making conversation. Let's have a nice lunch, huh?'

She rose and reached in for the breadbasket, allowing one hand to linger on Hugo's shoulder, and fixing her eyes on Amélie as she did so. Without a thought, Hugo's nearest hand went to the back of her chair as she retook her seat, a natural, warm instinct. She and Hugo were so at ease with each other, he didn't even seem to notice the moment, sitting back and chatting as he was to his brother on her other side. But Amélie noticed, and Katrin felt a surge of energy as she recognised her own dominance in this setting.

The waiter appeared with a bottle of champagne, and, once he'd filled their glasses and left them to look at the menu, Katrin stood up. She touched Bill's hand gently, before clinking the side of her glass with a spoon.

'Bill and I have an announcement,' she said.

Amélie reached for her glass, and drank from it ahead of the toast, obscuring her sour face.

'Someone else is going to have to drink this for me,' Katrin said, lifting her own glass with a broad smile. 'Because – we're expecting again!'

Beside her, Hugo cried out and broke into noisy applause, attracting smiling attention from the neighbouring diners.

'Marvellous!' George said, thrusting his own glass into the air, obviously delighted that the conversation had shifted on to more pleasant topics.

Henrietta's features softened, her attention now on her firstborn. 'Well done, darling. That really is marvellous news.'

Hugo pushed his chair back and swallowed Katrin up in an embrace that seemed to go on forever. 'Oh, Kat, that really is wonderful, wonderful news!' He released her, stepping out to do the same with his brother.

'We're only six weeks in, so keep it to yourselves for now,' Bill replied with unrestrained pride. 'But yes, Kat and I couldn't be happier.'

Katrin glanced at Amélie across the table.

'You'll be next, Hugo,' she said, turning to her brother-in-law as the clamour died down. In response, Amélie sat quite still, her gaze firmly on Hugo, across the table. This was a low blow; Katrin knew they'd tried and failed to get pregnant for a number of years. 'You and Amélie will make beautiful babies, when the time comes.'

A self-conscious silence travelled about the table.

'Actually,' Hugo said, dropping his eyes, 'we're not sure we'll be able to, Kat. We had some more tests done recently, and we haven't got a very good chance with my . . .' He glanced towards his parents, chastened, childlike.

Katrin felt a rush of remorse, at having used her advantage in so crass a way. What the hell was wrong with her? There was something about this pregnancy that made her feel reckless in new ways – was reckless the word? No, careless was more like it. She cared less about the consequences of her actions, and this feeling, this cavalier, full-steam-ahead Katrin was not who she was meant to be. That Katrin scared the hell out of her. Silence descended, obliterating their good news, and she was overcome with self-loathing. In her drive to put Amélie in her place, to position herself as the golden daughter-in-law, Katrin had dragged poor Hugo over the coals, and that was unforgivable.

'Oh, God, I'm so sorry, Hugo—' she started, tears springing to her eyes, but her sentence trailed off at the sound of Amélie dinging a spoon against her own glass across the table.

When all attention was on her, Amélie raised her champagne flute and drained it, placing it sedately on the tablecloth before her. 'Actually, we have some news of our own,' she said.

Hugo frowned. 'We do?'

'We do, *chéri*. We will be mothers together, Kat-er-ina,' she replied with a slow, sure smile.

'We're having a baby?' Hugo gasped.

'Bravo!' George piped up.

Amélie nodded at her husband, her green eyes never leaving his face. 'It's a miracle.'

'How many weeks gone are you?' Katrin asked, in an attempt to sound pleased.

Now Amélie looked not at her, but significantly at Bill in the seat beside Katrin. 'Three and a half months,' she replied without a hint of joy at the news.

Three and a half months.

Henrietta seemed not to know quite how to react to the unexpected announcement, and so she simply clapped her hands and said, 'Well done, boys. You clever things!'

Still laughing at this joyous revelation and displaying no sign of being even slightly annoyed that Amélie had chosen to break it to him in this public way, Hugo nudged his brother roguishly. 'Cousins!' he said. '*Cousins!*'

'Cousins,' Bill murmured in the seat beside Katrin. Why wasn't he jumping up to congratulate Hugo in the way his brother had for him? 'Good on you, Hugo, mate,' he added, his tone unaccountably subdued. 'I'm really pleased for you.'

Katrin watched, rigid with shock, as her husband made his way round the table to Amélie, whom he embraced like the good brother-in-law he was. Over his shoulder, Amélie's gaze finally met Katrin's, and Katrin was at once reminded of that week in early September when Bill had been spotted with his lover in the Wessex Hotel – the same week, she now recalled, with the hindsight of a fool, that her sister-in-law had been away 'on retreat'. As the family around them continued to chink glasses and laugh, Amélie gave Katrin the tiniest of nods.

Beyond Amélie and the mistletoe-swagged window, the sea swelled, and the waves broke against the shore, the same as ever before. But, for Katrin, *everything* had changed, forever. She thought of Anne Ashbourne, and the way her face had grown vivid as she'd described a sense of profound recognition when she'd finally met her mother for the first time; a sense of belonging. Katrin's eyes passed over the strangers assembled at the Gold family festive table, and she felt as though a light had just come on inside her mind. *These people aren't my family*, she recognised, with absolute certainty. *I am nothing to them.*

'Did I mention,' she heard herself say as Hugo ordered another bottle of champagne and Bill returned to his seat, 'I'm going to send my DNA off to one of those testing companies – see if I can find any close family matches.'

As the rest of the group murmured the standard noises of interest and encouragement, Katrin turned to her husband beside her and held his attention just a few halting seconds too long; long enough to see his expression turn to unease.

'Family's everything, isn't it, Bill?' she said.

With a slow blink, Bill broke out his most dazzling deceitful smile and kissed her on the lips. 'Of course it is, my love. *Of course it is.*'

It was time for Katrin to start making plans for a future without him.

18. Ginny

Ginny poured two sparkling elderflowers into champagne flutes and insisted on an optimistic toast.

'Happy New Year, Katrin!' she smiled, with a clink of crystal. 'To fresh beginnings.'

'To fresh beginnings,' Katrin echoed sedately.

Poor Katrin. Despite displaying all the physical signs of pregnancy bloom, she was clearly struggling with the sentiment. It was New Year's Day, and, apparently fed up following a day spent with a painfully hungover Bill and two stir-crazy twin boys, Katrin had called Ginny with the suggestion of an evening in together. By now of course, Ginny was fully appraised of *the situation* with the sister-in-law, and Katrin's assertion that she was the woman Anne's friend had seen at the hotel with Bill in September. Worse still was Amélie's pregnancy announcement, and the unbearable implication that Bill might be the father.

Ginny was, of course, furious with Bill, the stupid man, not only for the pain he was causing to Katrin, but for the fracture he had shot through the heart of his beautiful family. What kind of fool did his business right on his own doorstep – and on his brother's, at that? But she couldn't express those opinions; Katrin simply wasn't ready to hear them yet. For now, all Ginny could do was be there for her friend and support her in whichever path she took.

'Any news from the council about the bird licence yet?' Katrin asked as they ate.

Ginny passed over the parmesan with a heavy sigh. 'I'll chase them up again in the morning. Bloody useless, the lot of them!'

'Bill was saying we need to get the starlings evacuated before the end of Jan at latest, otherwise we'll have to wait another whole nesting season before we can get to work on the roof. I've had a number of residents asking me when the games room is going to be ready, Joy Bassett among them. It's the last outstanding phase of the project—'

'Yes, yes, I'll phone them again first thing tomorrow. I promise.' Ginny smoothed out the tablecloth and offered Katrin more salad. 'Any thoughts on Thomas?' she asked, fishing for an update since her recent suggestion that he might be drinking on the job.

'Actually, I had a chat with him last week,' Katrin replied. 'And he didn't take it very well at all. His reaction – well, it was as if I'd accused him of something far worse than having a sneaky drink.'

'Guilty conscience,' Ginny said, raising an eyebrow.

'I don't think so. More a sense that he was mortified to hear I should think so badly of him. I felt stupid when he told me he was teetotal – he said he hasn't touched a drop of alcohol in over fifty years! Anyway, the upshot is, he hadn't a clue how those bottles got into the greenhouse.'

Inwardly, Ginny cringed at her own stupidity. She'd gone to the trouble of pouring away two more half-litres of cheap vodka last week and planting the bottles in the greenhouse after dark, for Katrin or Bill to find. 'I wonder where those empties came from, in that case?'

'God knows. Anyway, Thomas said he'll start locking the greenhouse at night, just as a precaution.'

'Good idea,' Ginny agreed, before adding for the sake of prudence, 'Reassuring to know it wasn't him. I hope he wasn't too upset by the whole thing.'

'Bill bumped into him on the green later that day, and said he seemed flat. I hope he doesn't hold it against us. We'd hate to lose him.' Katrin's serious manner shifted as she put down her fork and gave Ginny a lopsided smile. 'Apparently, he was asking after you again, Gin – said to send you his best regards. I think you might have a bit of an admirer there.'

'Urgh, don't be disgusting, Katrin. As if . . .'

Ginny felt a chill thread through her veins. This was a message, she knew. Their last meeting obviously hadn't been persuasive enough to put him off his insane idea of 'coming clean'. What was wrong with the man? It was clear she was going to have to pay Thomas another visit.

'Oh, Ginny,' Katrin said, her face dropping. 'I'm only pulling your leg! I'm sure his interest is purely neighbourly.'

Waving away the silliness of it all, Ginny began clearing their supper plates and busied herself preparing her hastily defrosted dessert at the kitchen counter across the room. 'How is Frida?' she asked over her shoulder, keen to move them away from the uncomfortable topic of Thomas King.

'She's fine,' Katrin replied. 'I'll be driving her back to school in a few days. I think it's done her good to stay with us over Christmas – given them all a break from each other. Poor girl is all over the place, though. She's got GCSEs this year, and I think she's got some boyfriend back at school who's messing her about – and of course Amélie has no interest in her whatsoever.

Hugo does his best, but it's not the same, is it? A girl needs her mum – and the announcement that she can expect a new brother or sister – right before they buggered off to Paris – hasn't exactly gone down well.'

As Ginny slid a slice of cranberry cheesecake across the table, she caught despair in Katrin's expression.

Katrin smiled awkwardly. 'Of course, it's done us – me and Bill – good too, having Frida staying,' she said, eyeing her friend steadily, making it clear that she was ready to talk; that she just needed a little encouragement to do so.

'How's that?' Ginny asked.

'Well, having another person in the house saves us from having to acknowledge the obvious, doesn't it?' Katrin fed a forkful of dessert into her mouth. 'The obvious being that Bill's been screwing around again – this time, God help us, with his own brother's wife – and that it's about to catch up with him. I mean, the evidence is set to arrive in six months' time, isn't it? That's if Amélie doesn't kill the poor thing with a drug overdose first.'

Ginny was silenced by Katrin's sudden outburst.

'I suppose at least if it comes out looking like Bill,' she continued, 'people will put it down to family resemblance, rather than inter-family shagging.'

Ginny hated seeing Katrin like this, so caten up by the wrongs of others. 'Does Hugo have any doubts about the baby?' she asked. 'Does he even know about the affair?'

Katrin shook her head. 'Not as far as I know. I think he's just happy to accept it as a "miracle", as she's selling it. Ha! Amazing what you can believe, when you don't want to face up to the truth.' She ran her index finger around the rim of the glass. 'Bill and I haven't even talked about it. Pathetic, isn't it?' Her eyes clouded over in deep thought. 'I bumped into Anne the other day – she must be conscious that I've been avoiding her. When

I told her I was pregnant, honestly, Gin, her pity nearly undid me. All she said was, "And are *you* OK?" in that well-meaning way she has, and I wanted to lash out at her, just for knowing the humiliating truth about my sham of a marriage.'

'Oh, darling,' Ginny sighed. 'Everything will be better once the baby arrives.'

Katrin looked weary. 'I think this could be the end of the line for us, Gin. Bill's been behaving as if nothing has happened – his usual upbeat self. But I can't do it any more. Because it's one thing deceiving me, as I'm quite well aware he has done on multiple occasions, but to do that to Hugo – to the boys – to his horrible parents, even! Who does that? Who blows up an *entire* family for the sake of a fling?'

'He isn't the first, darling, and he certainly won't be the last.'

'And don't even get me started on the business. We – *I* – have worked so, so hard to build up Gold Property! So hard! You know, I only took six weeks off after the twins were born? Everyone told me I was crazy to go back to work so soon; everyone except Bill, who was delighted to hand the donkey work back to me. And here I am, pregnant again, and still doing all the donkey work—'

'I know, Kat. I know.'

'If I file for divorce,' Katrin continued, warming to her subject, 'it won't matter that it was my money that launched the business – he'd still retain his share. Gold Property would never survive. I couldn't rely on him to pull his weight without me chivvying him along as I do – and I doubt very much he'd sign his share over to me. You know, I come from nothing, absolutely nothing, Ginny – and Bill, well, he's never known anything but privilege. How dare he?'

Ginny's own sadness swelled like a hard knot in her throat. Never before had she witnessed so much rage in Katrin, and it scared her, just how much it reminded her of her own younger self, the way in which she reared up and hardened off when backed into a corner.

'I'd have to sell Starling House – maybe move into town—'

'You can't do that!' Ginny gasped, fear at what she might herself lose overriding her concern for Katrin's marriage.

'Why not? You don't know Bill. Yes, he's lovely and funny and charming, but he also has that core of steel rich white men possess – you know what I'm talking about – and I think we'd see a very different side to him if he felt exposed in any way.'

She was right, of course. Ginny's own father had been one of those rich white men, and he had been ruthless to the end.

'Because it would all come out, wouldn't it? And if I humiliated him like that – by showing the world the less-than-perfect truth about him – I think he'd hold on to the business just to punish me.'

Katrin took a shuddering breath and slumped back in her chair, drained. Ginny stared at her across the table, her thoughts racing. These men, *these men*! She wanted to scream. We women think we have it all these days, but still *they* have the power to manipulate our lives.

'I could buy him out,' she said, softly.

'What?' Katrin leaned onto the tabletop, arms folded, a hard line between her brows. 'Ginny, what are you talking about?'

'I could buy his share – become a partner with you and Hugo.'

'But the business is worth several million. You haven't got that kind of—'

'I have.'

Katrin blinked wildly. 'You're serious?'

Sudden panic surged in Ginny, and she felt herself teetering again, just as she had that day when they'd visited Victor's stables: wanting desperately to come clean – to own her past, every bit of it – while at the same time persisting with the drive to protect herself, and her lies. She clapped her hands together, bringing the conversation to a close. 'All you need to know, darling, is that I'm deadly serious.' She paused to draw breath. 'But for now, promise me one thing? Don't do anything rash. If you're a smart girl, you will sit tight and play the happy wife, for the next few months at least. If you still want to go through with a divorce, you'll have a far better hand with a new baby in your arms. By all means seek professional advice – but do it discreetly, and bide your time, my darling girl.'

'God, Bill would *kill* me if he knew I'd been discussing our marriage like this,' Katrin sighed. 'But honestly, fucking *Amélie*, of all people.'

'Yes, fucking Amélie wasn't his smartest decision,' Ginny agreed in her cut-glass accent.

Katrin frowned, and then they were both laughing, and crying, and clasping each other's hands across the table like two drunk sisters at a wake. Katrin exhaled a long breath and gazed at her friend. 'How did I ever manage before you came along, Ginny? Honestly, you're the best thing to happen to me in a very long time.'

Ginny allowed herself the pleasure of letting the warmth of Katrin's words sink in, before her inevitable sense of deceit quickly snatched the feeling away. 'You soppy thing,' she said with a tut, stacking the dessert plates one on top of the other and pushing them aside. It really was time to change the subject. New Year; new start.

'Now, darling, I've been thinking,' she said, fingering the pearl choker at her collarbone, one of the few remnants of her mother's life. 'We attract a certain type of woman here at The Starlings, don't we? Interesting, bright women – if you don't count Joy Bassett, of course, who could bore heads off for England!'

Katrin shook her head. 'You're so mean.'

'I've noticed many of our women don't go out to work in the conventional sense, which can, quite frankly, rot the brain. It's important to stay interested in the world, don't you think? Bill and Hugo have their sailing and social clubs – why shouldn't we girls have a bit of fun too? So, I've been thinking: why don't we launch a monthly club at The Starlings – just for us girls?'

'You mean like the Women's Institute?' Katrin ventured, drawing down the corners of her mouth.

'Not *at all*! I'm thinking less rhubarb jam and bowling, more wine-tasting and galleries. I thought we could meet monthly – we could discuss books, organise cultural day trips, invite the occasional speaker? And it would certainly take your mind off all that other nasty business, darling. What do you think?'

'I think it's a brilliant idea. Let's do it!'

'Oh, that's wonderful! Because I've already got a name for us.'

'Naturally,' Katrin said, with a smile.

'The Starling Darlings!'

Katrin bellowed with laughter, and the world felt right again.

How strange, Ginny thought as she kissed Katrin on the cheek and watched her walk the short distance across the frosty path towards her own brightly lit home. How strange that her own emotions had become so entirely intertwined with Katrin's that she could only be truly at peace when her friend was. She supposed the feeling must be something like the experience of a parent, when their child was fully grown.

The moment Katrin was out of sight, Ginny pulled on her coat and slipped out through her back gate on to the dark path beyond. It was time for her to tackle the problem of Thomas King once and for all.

19. Katrin

Frida wasn't due back in Bournemouth until midday, so when she returned from her house at 8.30, bags packed and obviously desperate to get going, Katrin invited her to accompany her on a few errands she needed to run around the estate.

'Thanks again for the lift,' Frida said as she perched on the edge of Katrin's bed, an arm around each of her cousins, who were still fluffy-headed in pyjamas, having woken at the sound of the front door banging shut. 'I didn't want to ask Mum – you know how sick she's been with the baby. She says it ruined the Paris trip. And Hugo offered to drive me, but I'd rather go with you. So long as you really don't mind.'

Katrin brushed her hair in the mirror and smiled back at her niece, swallowing down her antipathy towards the poor girl's mother. Ted waved a sleepy hand at his mum's reflection; she blew him a kiss, sending a second one to Max as he caught on. The nursery school was still on shutdown, and Katrin had arranged not to return to the office until the end of the week, to draw out the last of the winter holiday with her boys. Let Bill and Hugo deal with the New Year admin for a change, she'd told herself, and she was quite enjoying the big peaceful space Bill left, after two weeks of continuous contact over the Christmas break. She too was suffering with morning sickness, but, unlike her sister-in-law, she was doing her best to get on with it, despite not being able to manage anything more than a ginger biscuit before mid-morning and feeling constantly as though she was running on empty.

'Your poor mum,' she said, sweeping a blush of colour across her cheeks, eyes on Frida. 'She's still feeling sick? I have to say, I haven't seen her for weeks.'

'Join the club,' Frida replied sulkily. 'She saw the doctor yesterday and he told her to take bed rest. She hasn't put on as much weight as she should've by this stage, and he reckons that's why she feels sick all the time. Low blood sugar, or something.'

'Frida, she's not dieting, is she? I know how Amélie hates to put on even a pound, but you can't mess about when you're expecting.'

The twins were now in a frenzy of giggling, writhing and rucking up the duvet in their attempts to get away from Frida, who was tickling them both and not letting go. The teenager was shrieking with laughter as the boys fought back ferociously, and Katrin realised her words were lost on the girl. As if Frida had any influence on her mother's choices anyway. Katrin despised herself for caring a jot about Amélie's welfare, but this was a baby they were talking about, a tiny, living human being who would soon make its way into the world to take its first breath, and it just wasn't fair. *We don't get to choose our family*, someone somewhere had once told Katrin, and the wisdom of the words struck her as profoundly today as they ever had.

'Come on, you lot,' she said, ushering them off the bedsheets, now in chaos. 'Let me get dressed.'

Half an hour later, the four of them were in the courtyard, dismantling the Christmas lights and packing them away in plastic storage boxes.

'Shouldn't Thomas be doing this?' Frida called from her position high up on the stepladder.

Katrin was on the ground below, winding the lights around her arm as Frida fed them down to her. 'He should – but to be honest I got fed up waiting for him to return my call, so I thought – *Teddy!* Don't throw stones in – you'll scare the fish! Or worse, kill them!'

Frida laughed, and put her fingers to her mouth to emit an ear-splitting whistle. 'Ted! See if you and Max can collect all the stars up?' She pointed to the gold wicker stars hung around the square. 'Teddy, you put the ones you collect on the bench and Maxie, you put yours next to the pond. We'll see who got the most at the end. Ready! Steady! Go!'

The boys roared in accord and sprinted off to take up the challenge.

'You're so good with them,' Katrin said with a sigh. 'You know, I really do wish you could stay on at ours, Frida. In fact, if it weren't for your GCSEs, I'd insist! Sometimes I could do with another woman in the house.' She smiled up at Frida, and although it was a comment made flippantly, she meant it, and she hoped her niece understood her words to be sincere.

'Don't speak too soon, Auntie Kat, 'cause I might take you up on that,' Frida replied, her face still turned towards the tree. 'Though I think I'd probably drive Uncle Bill mad with my mess.'

Katrin smiled up at Frida and held the ladder steady for her descent, her mind now on Bill. Only last night, as they'd made love, he had murmured into her neck, *It's over, sweetheart, you've got nothing to worry about* – his one and only acknowledgement of this latest lapse of his. But Katrin had understood his real meaning: it was over, until the next time. Her feelings towards him – towards their marriage – continued to confuse her; one moment she felt close to him, the next as though there was some great chasm between them.

'So, what about Thomas?' Frida asked again, breaking into her thoughts as she relieved Katrin of the heavy load of looped cable. 'You haven't seen him about?'

'No, and it's really odd, because when I last spoke to him he told me he was going to start taking the decorations down, because he had plans to work on these raised beds here for the rest of the week. I said he shouldn't work on the bank holiday, but he insisted he wanted to.'

As the twins shot past, fighting to reach the last star, the two women turned in unison towards Thomas's lodge cottage, the windows of which Katrin now realised were in complete darkness.

'Frida, when did you last see him?' she asked, dread rising.

Frida shook her head. 'I don't remember seeing him at all over the past week – but then, it's been the holidays, and we haven't been out all that much, have we?' She glanced back at the cottage with a grimace. 'Oh, God – you don't think he's in there, you know, like – dead, or something?'

Before she even had time to stop and think, Katrin was across the cobbles, hammering her fist at Thomas's front door, and calling his name.

'There's no one in the front room,' Frida called over, pressing her face close to the glass. 'Should we go round the back?'

'No, I'll do it. You go and keep the boys busy, and I'll go round to the kitchen. I'm sure he's fine,' she added, dismissing Frida's anxious scowl. 'He's probably just slept in.'

But when Katrin entered the cottage and walked, breath held, through the small, dim rooms of Thomas's home, she knew he wasn't there. And, judging by the stillness of the place, orderly yet thinly veiled in dust, he hadn't been there for a good few days.

She stood for a moment, taking in the absolute silence; that and something else – sadness, perhaps – something deep in the old walls and the quarry tiles beneath her feet, like the ghosts of past inhabitants. Everything was so very spartan; not a single item could be described as superfluous or without use, with the exception of a small silver-framed photograph on his bedside, of a woman and a boy, whom Katrin presumed to be Thomas and his mother back in the early sixties. Beside the photograph was an empty spectacles case, a half-filled water carafe and a small, age-worn family bible, the kind that was passed down through generations as a record of family history.

Curious, Katrin lifted the solid little book and leafed through the first few yellowed pages, where, sure enough, a list of King family births dated back for several generations, ending with Thomas's name and date, the absence of more recent additions a hint that the King ancestral line would end with him. Katrin considered the irony: here she was, with no past, compelled to create a new future and a new family line – while Thomas King, with all this history, was apparently content to live his life from day to day, without a care for what he might leave behind. Who, Katrin wondered, would inherit this bible when old Thomas was gone?

Absently, she flicked through its pages, wondering where the old man might be, when another photograph fluttered from the book to land on the candlewick bedspread, face down. Feeling an urgent tug of conscience at her snooping, Katrin snatched up the picture and turned it over. It was a group shot, an organised sitting, with a studio caption printed along the bottom border: 'Highcap House Mother and Baby Home, May 1971'. Some ten years before her own birth there. The black and white picture had been taken in front of the doors to the imposing clocktower, revealing enough of the surrounding area to show Katrin that the grounds had barely altered in the fifty-odd years that had passed. As for the subjects, the standing back row and the seated middle were made up of young women and girls in matching grey tabards, 'patients', she presumed, though the picture had been choreographed to obscure their shameful pregnancies. In the front row were seated twenty or more uniformed women – nurses, cooks and orderlies – flanked either side of an austere bespectacled gentleman with pale skin and a heavy black moustache. The only other males stood at either end of the back row: an older man in overalls and cap, and a boy in his teens, his thin legs made skinnier in too-big shorts and heavy boots, and sporting a short-back-and-sides haircut. To his side, he held out a garden fork, presumably positioned by the photographer and incongruously resembling a trident. This boy was, unmistakably, Thomas.

Katrin's eyes passed over the girls' faces, faces which gave nothing away of the torments they might have witnessed – faces that looked not so very dissimilar to those of the young women on the front row, with their clean white collars and brightly polished brogues. The faces, in fact, looked not unlike those of the many girls Katrin herself had rubbed shoulders with during her sixteen years of institutional care.

Without a thought, Katrin slid the photograph inside her jacket pocket and headed back to the kitchen at the rear of the cottage. As she passed through, she paused one final moment, and her eyes caught on a single sheet of paper on the little melamine table, pinned beneath an old pressing iron. There, in careful handwriting, were Thomas's words, written, at a guess, before he'd left the lodge cottage some days ago.

Dear Katrin,
I am so sorry.
Warmest regards, Thomas King

Careful to leave everything else the way she'd found it, Katrin closed the back door behind her and returned to the courtyard, her mind astir with possible explanations as she put through a call to the local police station, to report Thomas missing. While she waited for them to arrive, she typed out a quick text message to inform Bill and Hugo of Thomas's strange absence, before calling Ginny to join her and the kids at the lodge cottage, for moral support. Whether it was a sudden drop in temperature, or simply Katrin's nerves at work, she had grown icy cold, and when Ginny arrived she was grateful for the warm embrace she received.

'You say he left a note?' Ginny asked as she pulled back, rubbing her palms up the lengths of Katrin's arms. She glanced at Frida, who was standing on the cobbles, with the boys either side of her, now subdued by the sudden change in atmosphere. 'Oh, darling, she's shivering!'

'Do you want me to fetch you a warmer coat, Auntie Kat?' Frida asked. 'I can run back with the boys and get you one. I'll get them a snack while we're there.'

Katrin nodded, and pressed her keys into Frida's hand, watching her gratefully as she sped off with Max and Ted, for their sake making a game of what was turning out to be a horrible morning.

'The note?' Ginny nudged.

'I left it where it was – I thought the police wouldn't want anyone moving it, which is silly, I know, because he's clearly gone somewhere of his own accord, but—'

Ginny sidestepped her mid-sentence and pointed her clicker towards the entrance pillars, having spotted the police car approaching on the main road. Katrin turned to watch the iron gates parting, and a squad car passed slowly through, coming to a halt directly outside Thomas's home beside them.

Two officers stepped out, one uniformed and one not, and greeted them with easy smiles.

'DS Ali Samson,' the non-uniformed officer introduced herself. 'And this is my colleague, PC Terry. We've met before, haven't we, Mrs Gold?'

Katrin extended her hand. 'Yes, of course – call me Katrin, please. This is my friend and neighbour, Ginny.'

'And it was you who called the station, Katrin? You say you're the freeholder here?' DS Samson asked, turning over a page in her little notebook. 'I understand you're worried about an employee. A Thomas King?'

'That's right,' Katrin replied, gesturing towards the lodge cottage. 'He's our grounds manager – he lives here, on his own. He's in his late sixties, or maybe early seventies.'

As DS Samson made notes, the PC wandered across to the cottage and peered in through the front windows, much as Frida had done just half an hour earlier.

'Is it normal to send a detective out so soon?' Ginny asked with a frown.

'Not really. But I was at the station when the call came in, twiddling my thumbs,' DS Samson replied brightly. 'And this is an elderly gentleman we're talking about, missing in a cold snap, so we can't be too careful.' She tucked a tendril of shiny black hair behind one ear, from where it had escaped her neatly coiled bun.

Katrin recalled the detective's kindness towards Frida over the shoplifting incident last year, and she sensed they were in good hands. DS Samson was straight-talking and that had to be a good thing. 'Thank you,' Katrin said. 'We really appreciate it.'

'Now, has anyone else been inside the cottage, apart from you?'

'Not to my knowledge. I told Frida to wait outside with the boys while I went in. The back door was unlocked.'

'*Frida*,' she said, writing it down. 'Ah, yes, I remember. Your daughter.'

'My niece, actually,' Katrin replied, taking in the officer's frown and wincing inwardly at her earlier unintentional deception. 'I, um – she spends a lot of time with me. People often assume—'

Almost as though on cue, Frida now jogged back into the courtyard, holding out a large padded jacket for her aunt, with the two boys dawdling behind and chomping down on crumpets, big globs of butter dripping from their fingers on to their freshly laundered sweaters. Katrin looked at her watch, mindful of Frida's need to get back to St Saviour's.

'Hello, Frida,' the officer said with a smile, glancing at Frida's school uniform and quickly reading the situation. 'So, Katrin, tell me when you last saw Mr King?'

'Well, I've been thinking about that since I called the station, and I'm pretty sure I haven't seen him since January the second. I remember it because we'd only been talking about him when we were together the day before, hadn't we, Ginny – which was New Year's Day.'

Ginny nodded her agreement, and the officer wrote the detail down.

'I didn't actually speak to him,' Katrin added, 'but we waved. I think he was on his way down to the beach. My husband and brother-in-law are at the office this morning, and I've already texted them to ask if they can remember the last time they saw him.' She checked her phone again. 'Oh, Bill just replied – neither recalls seeing Thomas at all since Christmas Eve, when they dropped a hamper round to the lodge. To thank him for all his hard work this year,' she added, unnecessarily. She was, she realised, feeling unshakeably responsible.

'And you, Mrs – Ms—'

'LeFevre,' Ginny offered, 'Capital L, capital F. Ms. Yes, I think I saw him that afternoon too. Thomas is a keen sea swimmer, officer. He tends to go before last light – he enjoys walking home with the sunset at his back, he once told me.'

Katrin eyed her friend with surprise. Since when did she know so much about Thomas? Ginny seemed to catch her silent question and blinked archly, returning her attention to the DS. 'So, what time is sunset at the moment?' she mused. 'Four-ish? In which case, I'd estimate I saw Thomas at around three that same afternoon – on his way to the beach.'

The constable was now back at DS Samson's side. 'Did you speak to him?'

'No. We don't know each other all that well, really.'

'And would you say Thomas is a man of habit? That's to say, is this absence out of character for him?'

Katrin nodded firmly. 'Completely out of character. We've been at The Starlings since May, and he's never missed a day's work. He's utterly reliable – and I'm sorry to say, he doesn't seem to have any family or friends to speak of.'

'And nothing's happened lately that might cause him to just up and leave?'

Katrin glanced at Ginny, who looked away. 'I suppose there was an incident a couple of months back,' she offered cautiously. 'We thought he'd been drinking on the job, but – well, it was just a misunderstanding in the end. We cleared it all up at the time, so—' Katrin blinked at the officer. 'But that note I mentioned, the one on his kitchen table, the apology – that seems to suggest something's not right, doesn't it? Maybe he's still upset after all.'

DS Samson pressed her lips together regretfully. 'PC Terry and I will take a look inside now, if you wouldn't mind just waiting here. We won't be long.'

'God, Ginny,' Katrin exhaled as the officers disappeared around the back of the cottage. 'This doesn't look good, does it? You don't think he's done something stupid, do you?'

'He's fine, I'm sure,' Ginny said, slipping an arm through Katrin's and giving it a little squeeze. 'You know, that detective? DS Samson? She's pregnant. Two months gone, I'd hazard a guess.'

'Really? How can you tell?'

Ginny took a second to respond. 'Call it a sixth sense, if you like. There's a particular quality; you can't miss it,' she laughed. 'It's an incandescence of sorts. It's hard to explain. But if that woman isn't pregnant, I'll eat my hat.'

While Ginny and Katrin waited outside the lodge, Frida and the twins ran circles around the frozen pond, and the occasional resident peered out of the overlooking maisonettes, interest piqued at the rare sight of a police car. *God*, this sort of thing never happened in The Starlings. She must circulate an email later, she thought, to reassure everyone that it was just a routine police check, that there was nothing to worry about. But ten minutes later it became apparent that there *was* something to worry about, as the officers returned holding Thomas's note sealed inside a clear evidence bag. As she watched them approach, Katrin's eyes landed on the small patch of grass between the lodge cottage and Thomas's brick store. She had known something wasn't quite right about the scene earlier, when she'd entered the property herself, but now it was suddenly clear.

'DS Samson,' she called over. 'Thomas's towel is missing.'

'His *towel*?'

Katrin pointed to the short length of washing line that hung between the two buildings. 'His swimming towel. Unless he's at the beach, it's pretty much permanently pegged up. It's bright red, so you can't miss it.' She hesitated, horrified by the direction her thoughts were heading. 'He only ever really takes it off the line if it's raining, or if he's at the beach.'

DS Samson gazed across the cobbles to the empty line hanging over Thomas's little patch of grass. 'It's been dry all week, hasn't it?' she said, her brow furrowing. 'We haven't had a drop of rain at all.'

With Max and Ted in Ginny's care, Katrin was relieved to finally get away with Frida mid-morning, leaving DS Samson and the PC to carry out their house-to-house enquiries around The Starlings.

As they passed along the A35, the Dorset patchwork spread out to either side, rolling towards a cool slash of ocean, as breathtakingly beautiful to Katrin today as it had been all those years ago when she'd laid eyes on it for the very first time. Seemingly in tune with Katrin's reflective mood, Frida sat silently in the passenger seat, intermittently checking her mobile phone, and photographing the billowy clouds as they moved across the horizon.

Guilt pricked away at Katrin, as her mind replayed that conversation with Thomas, when she'd wrongly accused him of drinking on the job. Had he spent the whole of Christmas completely alone, with that anxious fear still worming through his mind? We should have invited him to Starling House for a Christmas drink, she thought now; we should have been better neighbours.

'Do you think . . .' Frida finally broke their silence, a good twenty minutes into the journey. 'Do you think Thomas is OK?'

Katrin took a moment to answer. 'I'm sure he's fine, Frida. All we can do right now is hope for the best. The police seem to be taking it seriously.' She glanced at her niece sitting side-on in the seat beside her, one leg curled around the other as she scrolled through photos on her phone. 'So, have you got a picture of your boyfriend you can show me?'

Instinctively Frida pressed the power button, and her screen went blank. She cast Katrin a withering look.

'How are you feeling about going back to school?' Katrin asked.

Frida shrugged. 'I dunno. I'm not sure what I feel to be honest. I'm anxious, for sure, but I'm just going to take it one day at a time.'

'They sound like wise words to me.'

'Well, you're the one who said them,' Frida replied, with a little chuckle, 'that, and "don't let the buggers get you down"!'

Katrin laughed. 'Yeah, that does kind of sound like me. But seriously, every day is a new one. And you've got my number.'

Frida waggled her phone between them. 'I know,' she said. 'Thanks, Auntie Kat.'

When they arrived at St Saviour's, they sat for a few minutes in the parking area, from where they could observe the hive of activity outside the grand front steps, as returning girls hugged their parents, before heading off to lug too-big suitcases on to trollies and shriek with friends they'd missed over the Christmas break.

'See any of your mates?' Katrin asked.

Frida made a 'hmph' sound and crossed her arms over her chest. 'You know, I'm not exaggerating when I say I don't have any friends, Auntie Kat. They have literally all dropped me.'

Katrin shook her head, annoyance getting the better of her. 'Really? Over this boy, for God's sake? When will girls ever learn?'

Frida sighed heavily. 'Did I tell you, I've got a single room now? No one wants to share with me. They think they might catch my unpopularity.' She snorted, making light of the situation.

'You're too young to be so cynical, Frida,' Katrin said, sadly. 'You've just got to get through your exams now, and then you're free! Your true friends are all still out there, waiting to meet you! Have you thought about plans for next year? I guess you'll do A-levels, or something?'

'I'll go to sixth form next door – Bartholomew's,' she said, nodding towards the neighbouring building beyond the perimeter.

'Will your boyfriend still be there next year?' Katrin asked.

Frida's eyes hardened as she scanned the dozens of girls dotted around the gravel driveway, chatting in easy groups. 'Yeah. I can't wait to get away from these dickheads. They all think he's dropped me, but what they don't know is that we've still been messaging each other just about every day.'

'Is he good to you – is he kind?'

'Barney? Of course.'

'What I mean is, is he respectful – he must know you're not sixteen yet?' Katrin persisted.

'Oh, my God – Auntie Kat!'

'OK, OK,' Katrin laughed, conceding defeat. 'I get it: too much. At least let me ask, when will we get to meet him?'

Frida snatched up her bag with a good-humoured tut. 'Never, if I can help it! Well, maybe you, but I'd never let my psycho mum loose on him. He'd run a mile.'

A flood of feelings washed over Katrin: love and fear and hope and foreboding. 'What I said earlier, Frida,' she spoke into her hair in a final embrace, 'I meant it, OK? Whatever happens over the coming months or years, you will always – always – have me. You understand that? You've got my mobile number. Just call me if you need me, about anything at all.'

'Max and Ted – they're lucky boys,' Frida replied, and with that she exited the car, retrieved her weighty case from the boot, and carted it across the car park, skinny knees knocking as she went.

With a sudden sense of urgency, Katrin rolled down the window. 'Be careful!' she called after her.

Frida halted a moment, and turned, releasing her heavy case in order to wave back. 'Let me know if you find Thomas!' she replied with a thoughtful frown. And then she was off again.

Katrin stared after her niece, this recurring fear for her safety rising. She loved that girl so much. Was it talk of this boyfriend, or just the dangerous fact of Frida's beauty and youth that unsettled Katrin so? Perhaps it was her own hormones working against her, flooding her imagination and provoking maternal hypervigilance. Maybe it was because Katrin had the strongest sense that Frida wasn't telling her the whole story about this boy and the trouble at school last year. Or perhaps it was because she remembered being fifteen as though it was yesterday, and she knew better than most that the reckless choices we made in youth had a way of living on in us for the rest of our lives.

'*Barney*,' she murmured softly as she watched Frida disappear into the dark mouth of the school's imposing entrance. 'If you hurt a hair on her head, young man, I will destroy you.' Katrin restarted the engine and headed back to The Starlings.

20. Ginny

In the first week of May, every adult female resident of the Starlings community received an invitation to join Katrin and Ginny's new social club, the Starling Darlings, a group dedicated, the silver-leafed postcard read, to 'fun, friendship, conversation and culture'.

For Ginny, the first few months of the year had flown by peacefully, with Katrin staying true to her promise to remain on good terms with Bill, and Amélie thankfully keeping to herself right up until the arrival of a baby boy named Henri, born four weeks early on May Day, barely six pounds in weight and with a shock of black hair, just like his mother. And just like Hugo, as Katrin was quick to point out to anyone who asked after the poor scrap, as though her positive words might vanish all doubt from the world, as well as her own mind.

Frida had apparently settled back into life at St Saviour's and the twins, now five, were oblivious to their parents' concerns, and happy and mischievous as ever. Even Thomas's disappearance had failed to cast too permanent a shadow over life at The Starlings, and, since DS Samson had quickly discovered the missing red towel hooked up on a breakwater at the top of the beach, the police had more or less left them alone while they continued their investigation remotely. Of course, Katrin had been more affected than anyone by the sad conclusion that they must undoubtedly reach regarding Thomas's fate – especially given the note he'd left – but the distraction had meant that any questions he might have raised about Ginny had, for now, all but disappeared. Things really were starting to look up, Ginny thought, for all of them.

On the day of the inaugural social gathering in late April, Ginny drove Katrin into town, waving goodbye to Hugo and Bill as they set off for one of their boys' trips out on the water. It was just so good to see the family back to normal again, and this new project, the Starling Darlings, had been a beacon on the horizon throughout it all: something marvellous to look forward to. While the original idea had been Ginny's, she had insisted Katrin be the figurehead. And hadn't that secretly been Ginny's intention in the first place: to give Katrin something other than her marriage and business to focus on at this tricky time?

Ginny took charge of finding the right venue, ultimately deciding on the upper room of Tino's, a cosy private space away from the bustle of the restaurant, while Katrin had rallied to the challenge of arranging the opening agenda, promising Ginny they'd kick it off in style with a top-secret guest speaker she'd recently been corresponding with online. Was it a local author? Ginny wanted to know. Or an artist of some kind? A public figure? A celebrity chef? Never once bending to her constant fishing for hints, Katrin had remained tight-lipped, piquing Ginny's interest right up until the very day of the meeting.

At twelve-thirty, Katrin and Ginny formally greeted their fellow neighbourhood women – twenty-four of them in total – with champagne cocktails and canapés. The room was perfect, well-lit with leaded windows looking out on to the busy alleyway below, and low ceilings that lent an air of intimacy. Katrin was radiant; you'd hardly believe what the poor girl had been through with that blasted husband of hers – not to mention Amélie, who at least had the decency not to join them today. Katrin was a modern example of stiff upper lip if ever Ginny had seen one, and, as she took her place beside her, she felt proud.

'What a wonderful turn-out,' she remarked as Katrin gestured for everyone to take seats at the table, set out in a large arc, she noticed, not unlike the layout of the buildings still standing at Highcap House. At *The Starlings*, Ginny corrected herself silently, her stomach lurching at her casual slip of the tongue, albeit only within her own head; Highcap House had ceased to exist forty years earlier.

'Over half the women in the neighbourhood!' Katrin smiled buoyantly, bringing Ginny's thoughts back to the room, and with that she clapped her hands and brought the group to attention. 'Well, hello!' she said, raising her glass with one hand, resting the other on the gently protruding dome of her stomach. 'Welcome, one and all! Now, as I mentioned in my email, these meetings are meant to be fun, enriching and informal. Monthly subs will merely cover costs – so, lunches, guest speakers, etc – but today, this one is on me.'

'Bravo!' Marcie, the eldest of the group, interjected. Shakily, she tipped her glass in approval. 'I am very happy, Katrin,' she said, the remnants of her Polish accent still breaking through. 'I haven't been out and about like this in months! And oh,' she gasped. '*Champagne!*'

The women laughed and applauded Marcie's words, simmering down again as Katrin waved cheerily to regain their attention. 'So, the group is open exclusively to female residents of The Starlings, and, as the months go on, I'd like to invite any of

169

you to host a "specialist" meeting on topics you think might be of interest to the rest of us. Today, we're going to catch up a bit over lunch first, and then I'm going to introduce you to a mystery speaker, who is—' Katrin glanced across at Anne, who responded with an earnest waggle of her mobile phone '—who is on her way, as we speak! Before we eat, I'd like to ask you all to join me in giving a big thank you to Ginny for organising everything so beautifully – the food, the venue, and most importantly, the inspiration!'

As Ginny graciously accepted the applause, Tino's waiters appeared on the stairwell, and moved discreetly around the room to distribute platters of food, along with several bottles of red and white wine.

'*Anne* has arranged the guest speaker?' Ginny asked Katrin.

'I felt bad about the way I've been towards her lately – I mean, talk about shooting the messenger. So, I asked her if she'd like to lead the first meeting. I've never been terribly good at *actual* apologies,' she said sheepishly. 'And Anne was delighted.'

'Good,' Ginny responded. *Good to keep her on side*, was what she meant.

'What a lovely spread,' Andrea from next door commented, circling the contours of her own domed stomach.

It occurred to Ginny how rarely she ever saw Andrea without her husband Jim; until now, she'd only ever thought of them as Andrea-and-Jim. It was nice to see her here, among her fellow women, away from the domestic sphere. It was good for women, Ginny thought. Healthy. 'So many pregnancies at The Starlings at the moment!' Ginny said. 'You, Katrin – that nice young woman in the North Wing – and the other Mrs Gold.'

'Amélie,' Andrea said as though Ginny had forgotten her name. She hadn't forgotten; she just disliked uttering it, as though doing so would conjure her into the room.

'I've been meaning to ask,' Andrea said, lowering her voice. 'Any news on the gardener, Thomas? It's all gone a bit quiet and I wondered if the police had discovered anything more?'

Ginny shook her head quickly, anxious to shut the topic down. Katrin had suggested giving an update over lunch, but really, this wasn't the time or the place, was it? 'They haven't said as much, but I think the consensus is he took his own life. But I know Katrin's keen to keep today about the Darlings, so—'

'Oh, heavens, yes!' Andrea replied, intensely. 'Of course!'

Ginny patted her hand and cast an eye around the table to make sure everyone was alright, that the food had been evenly set out, and wine poured. As the waiting staff disappeared back down the creaky old stairs, a small, white-haired, olive-skinned woman arrived, loaded down with a backpack and a filing box of papers. While the rest of the group chattered loudly and helped themselves to lunch, Anne jumped up to greet the new arrival.

'Sorry I'm late,' the woman apologised as she slid into the empty seat Anne had saved. 'Traffic's a nightmare. I got stuck at the West Bay roundabout.'

Across the table Ginny – with, she hoped, her features somewhat obscured by the daylight streaming in behind her – felt her stomach drop. *Diana Bayo*. She'd know that face anywhere. Oh, God, she thought: if *she* had been so quick to recognise Diana more than forty years after they'd last met, was it possible that Diana might be able to place *her* in much the same way? Breath held, she watched as Anne encouraged the woman to fill her plate, chatting to her quietly in preparation for the after-lunch talk. So, this was Katrin's great secret? A visit from a former Highcap mother? A history lesson in shame and despair? Ginny's heart thumped faster, and despite the warmth of the room she suddenly felt desperately cold.

171

A few seats down, Joy Bassett waved brightly, wrenching Ginny's attention away.

'Ginny! Lovely lunch! I just love picky-bits, don't you? Aren't you having any yourself?'

Ginny tuned back into the room and, swallowing down her dread, rewarded Head Girl Joy with a gracious smile. 'Yes, of course, darling! Pass me some of those little stuffed pimentos, will you?'

Once the lunch plates had been cleared and the coffee and cakes brought out, Tino closed the door at the top of the stairs and the room was their own.

'Ladies! A bit of admin before I hand you over to our speakers,' Katrin said, calling the room to attention. 'Firstly, I'd like to welcome Jacky, Karen and Abi, our most recent female residents – whose presence means that every one of our Starling homes is now inhabited!'

There was a roar of applause around the table.

'Welcome, new neighbours! Now, I'd also like to remind you of our special date in two weeks' time, when we will be hosting our first anniversary garden party at The Starlings – something I hope will become an annual event. More details to follow, but needless to say, it'll be a day to remember!'

Another cheer went up, made more raucous by the quickly diminishing bottles of wine.

'Without further ado, I will hand you over for the afternoon's talk. As it's our first meeting, I wanted something close to home, and I'm delighted to say that Anne Ashbourne – our brilliant resident historian – has volunteered to launch us with a special talk exploring The Starlings' unique history. I warn you, it is a sad history, but I hope you'll agree with me that it's an empowering one too, and a reminder of just how far we women have progressed – and are progressing – in our battle for equality. Over to you, Anne!'

Wearing an unfortunate slash of pink lipstick, her face the colour of hot salmon, Anne gave a little two-handed wave, and opened with an apology. 'Sorry if I seem a bit nervous,' she said, breathily. 'I'm not a terribly good public speaker! *Sorry*—'

'Nonsense!' one of the women called out, and bashfully Anne gestured towards the far wall, where a large aerial photograph of The Starlings hung, taken just last year after the final building works had been completed.

'Right,' she began, indicating to areas on the photograph with an old-fashioned pointing stick. 'This is The Starlings as we know it today. Here's the clocktower, set in the centre of the original North Wing buildings, fanning out to the East and West Wings either side – here's the central green – Thomas's lodge house and greenhouse—' She halted briefly, her pointer suspended in mid-air. '*Poor Thomas,*' she murmured, almost imperceptibly, and, beside her, Diana Bayo's head tilted in interest.

Ginny's heart raced and she suddenly felt as though her lies were stacking up around her like tiny corpses, lie upon lie upon lie. Momentarily, she considered getting up and leaving – her panic causing her thoughts quickly to leap at notions of packing up, selling up, fleeing The Starlings altogether, because after all, this whole episode had been a big mistake, hadn't it? She hadn't meant for any of this to happen. It had only been that chance meeting with Bill and Hugo and the connection she had felt with Katrin – a complete stranger, for God's sake – that had propelled her into so rash a decision to overhaul her life. But as she sat there in Tino's, in close proximity to someone who might at any moment unmask her for the fraud she really was, she wondered whether any of the decisions she'd made were her own, or whether, instead, they had been driven by the sins of her past, destined to drag her down, to make her face up to the truth.

Mutely, Ginny concentrated on bringing her breathing into check, slowly in-out-in-out, grateful that no one seemed to have sensed the change in her, distracted as they were by Anne's presentation at the front of the room. Now, Anne was pinning up beside the aerial photograph an old ink-drawn plan, showing the original layout, from back in the early Highcap Workhouse days. It was extraordinary to see how little of the map had changed over the years, as the building passed through its various iterations. With the exception of an area of open space that had now been built on to create Katrin and Bill's house, the footprint of the land appeared almost unchanged.

'Most of you know that for the past twelve months or so,' Anne said, 'I've been working on a non-fiction book about the Mother and Baby Home years, investigating the stories behind the rumours, trying to build up a picture of what it was like to be a young mother forced to give up your baby in that way.' She paused as the group murmured with interest, her hands clenched in a wringing motion around the pointing stick. 'You may also know that I was one of the babies given up for adoption – and so was Katrin.'

This wasn't news to most here, but still, it was a reminder of just how close this dark history was to their cosy gated lives today.

'I found my birth mother a few years ago, and, in fact, that was what prompted me to further investigate the Highcap House Mother and Baby Home – one of the last of its kind to close in England.' Anne was reading from a handwritten script, clearly too nervous to deliver her talk without it. 'Sadly, all known records from the home were destroyed in a fire soon after its closure. In fact, I only found my mother through a chance match with a half-sibling on a DNA profiling website.'

Ginny could feel Katrin's rapt interest pouring off her in the adjoining seat. Ever since the recent shake-up of her family, she'd become more and more intent on unearthing 'her truth' as she called it, and to Ginny's disapproval she'd even got round to sending her DNA off to that ghastly genealogy website Anne was talking about. *Why are you so against it?* Katrin had asked her as she'd sealed up the envelope containing her spittle and dropped it into her bag. *You know how I feel about these things, darling. The past is the past,* Ginny had replied, *and sometimes digging around in it only turns up unpleasantness. Do you really want that?*

'And that's why word-of-mouth accounts are so important,' Anne continued. 'Which leads me on to our guest speaker, who has so generously travelled here all the way from Brighton.' She now indicated to the woman seated at the end of the table. 'May I introduce you all to Diana Lambley, former Highcap patient, and staunch campaigner for reparations.'

Katrin led the applause as Diana, a youthful sixty-something with a neat figure, joined Anne at the front of the room.

No longer Bayo, Ginny thought, as she pressed her back further into the seat, willing herself to disappear. She'll never pick me out, she told herself. It's been over forty years, for pity's sake.

'Thank you for having me,' Diana began. 'As Anne mentioned, I was a former patient at Highcap. And by patient I mean fifteen-year-old girl, pregnant after my first and only sexual encounter, and forced to leave my family and give birth alone at Highcap.'

The room was taut with shock at Diana's frank introduction.

'Were you the youngest?' Joy asked, breaking the silence.

'No,' Diana replied. 'There was a fourteen-year-old in the dorm with me. But I was the only brown-skinned girl there, and that caused me more problems than my age. A couple of the nastier nurses used to call me "the gypsy".'

Ginny cast her eyes down, trying to suppress the tide of emotions that roared within her. *No* differences had gone unnoticed in a place like that. Too spotty; too pretty; too skinny; too fat; too light-skinned; too dark; too impoverished . . . too 'posh'. Ginny recalled that particular taunt all too well. As Diana continued her story, Ginny glanced at Katrin beside her, noticing the unshed tears in her eyes, the need in her, and she felt a swell of guilt for deceiving her thus far, if only by omission.

'Katrin?' Diana said.

Seated directly next to Katrin, Ginny felt a fresh swell of panic run through her, her fear of detection intensified.

'I wonder if you can share what you know of your story? Of your adoption?'

Katrin pushed away her uneaten cake, the only sign of her discomfort. 'I was born in 1981, at Highcap House. In fact, it seems likely I was the last baby to be born there. Unlike many of the babies, I didn't go straight into adoption – I think the family I was matched with pulled out at the last minute – and with the institution in the throes of shutdown I ended up in the care system, moving from children's home to foster care right up until the day I turned sixteen.'

This was the part most in the room were unaware of, and their faces betrayed it. Katrin's sophisticated exterior, her refined accent and poise, Ginny had long ago concluded over late-night heart-to-hearts with her friend, were constructs, and convincing ones at that.

'What happened at sixteen?' Marcie asked.

Katrin hesitated, and Ginny suspected there was a lot more to her story than even the abridged version she knew. 'My social worker set me up with a local estate agent in Fulham, and I began a two-year apprenticeship – and, well, life kind of took off from there. In fact, that's where I met my husband, Bill.'

'Wow,' Joy murmured. 'I'd never have guessed, Katrin.'

'From hardship, strength.' Marcie nodded with warmth.

'But what about your birth mother?' the woman from No.12 asked. 'You never found her?'

'It took me years to follow the trail back here – to work out that I was a Highcap baby,' Katrin replied, folding her arms loosely. 'But when I got to Dorchester, to the records office, I found out that all the paperwork for Highcap was gone, in the fire Anne mentioned.'

'God, I thought that only happened in films!' Andrea exclaimed. 'Do you think the "fire" story was a cover-up?'

'I don't really know, except that adoptions from Highcap were what's known as "closed adoptions", which serves to prevent either party from ever knowing the identity of the other.' Katrin gestured towards their speaker. 'Diana might know a bit more about the cover-up theory. Did you ever find records for your baby, Diana?'

Diana pulled up a seat at the table and reached for her battered box of papers. 'My baby didn't make it,' she said, and the pain of it, even now, was still there in her downcast eyes, as she rifled through papers. 'So, there was no one to search for, in my case. But a few years ago, that girl I'd shared the dorm with at Highcap reached out to me on Facebook, and we ended up meeting for a coffee, and she told me more about her story. I thought my own experience was bad enough, but nothing prepared me for what I heard that day.'

Now, she took out a pile of photocopied news clippings and passed them around the table, so that every woman had a copy to look at. At the top was a column from a 1991 edition of the *Dorset Enquirer*, with the headline 'Highcap Governor Investigated'. For a couple of minutes, the women read together in silence, as Ginny's anxiety gained pace inside her chest.

For ten years the old Highcap House Mother and Baby
Home in Dorset has stood empty, slowly falling into disrepair
since the last residents and staff vacated the building in
1981. Little is known about the home's past as a church-
led maternity centre for unwed mothers, as all records
were destroyed in a fire of the same year. What is clear,
however, is that between 1971 and 1981 the home was
run on a private basis, by Dr Stanley Jarman, descendant
of philanthropist William Edward Jarman, who, in 1846, first
funded the building of Highcap House to accommodate
the poor of the parish.

Today, Dorset police have confirmed in a written statement
that Dr Stan Jarman is being investigated following multiple
historic claims of neglect, abuse and infanticide under his
care. The claims, which come from a 'significant number' of
independent witnesses, including ex-patients and their fami-
lies, are being 'vigorously examined', according to the police
statement. Jarman, now retired, has declined to comment.

'After they'd taken my friend's baby away, she stayed on for a
few months, to work off her debt as an orderly. That was how
the system worked, based on the Irish model of the fifties and
sixties. But during that time she became pregnant again – this
time, she claimed, with Jarman's child. She remained there
for another year – just long enough to see her second child
taken away.'

'The governor's child?' someone gasped, and Ginny found
herself shaking her head, along with the rest of them.

'She was fifteen at the time. And it's been suggested there were
many others,' Diana added. 'There is even a line of thought that
he was on some kind of a mission, to sire as many of his own
children as he possibly could. He was medically trained, and

it's said that in his student days he had a particular interest in genetics – in genetic hierarchy.'

'Jesus,' Belinda said, her eyes on Katrin. 'Unbelievable.'

'But what is your source?' another woman asked. 'It sounds far-fetched to me. Are you sure this isn't just one of those after-the-event trumped-up rumours?'

'Some said that about Hitler's crimes,' Marcie interrupted with a loud, accented voice, bringing break-out conversations back to attention. 'Just because something is terrible to hear – it doesn't mean it didn't happen.'

'*Are you OK?*' Ginny felt Katrin's hand on her leg, her lightly whispered concern. 'You've barely said a word.'

'What? Yes – yes! Sorry, just taking it all in. It's just so appalling,' Ginny replied as reassuringly as she could as she refocused on the lively discussion in the room. She felt nauseous.

'This article is from 1991? That's over thirty years ago,' Joy said, frowning. 'What happened to him in the end?'

'Oh, that reminds me,' Katrin said, suddenly reaching down for her bag. 'I have this photograph from 1971 – I assume that's Jarman in the front row?'

The black and white picture was passed down the table before Ginny could snatch a look. Diana cast a glance at it and scoffed, handing it along for the next woman to see.

'Yes, that's the old bastard. Nothing happened to him, of course. People in high places, etcetera, etcetera. Apparently, he was a generous Tory donor. The investigation fell apart, witnesses backed off, and Jarman lived out his days without punishment.'

'He lived up at White Rise,' another voice added. 'I think Gold Property have just bought it, haven't they, Katrin?'

Katrin nodded, her attention still on the article. 'This journalist mentions abuse and *infanticide*,' Katrin said. 'Did very many babies die?'

'Yes, certainly a much higher rate than you'd have expected in a normal maternity ward. And more, it's always been rumoured, than ever made official records. They used to say the bodies were buried in the basement of the old clocktower – but I think that was just an urban myth.' Diana reached for her water glass and drank deeply, as all around the table, expressions of shock were shared.

'You do read about these things,' Joy whispered to her neighbour. 'In Ireland, particularly.'

'Terrible,' Marcie said, firmly. 'Terrible.'

Diana set down her glass. 'My own baby died as a result of poor maternity care,' she said with a slight stiffening of her shoulders. 'I didn't know it was neglect at the time – how could I? I was fifteen. But later, when I had my first child with my husband, it all came flooding back to me – how I'd been treated so differently at Highcap. So brutally. One particular nurse was unbelievably cruel to us girls; she reminded us of the shame we were carrying every time we were in her company, and as misfortune would have it she was the nurse on duty when I went into labour.'

'What happened?'

'I was left on my own in the labour ward for half the night, in agony, crying for my mother. There was no pain relief offered, and each time the nurse stopped by to check on me she told me I wasn't ready, that I was making too much of a fuss, that I still had hours to go. *Did I think I was the first little slut to ever give birth – ?*' Diana broke off here, turning to look out through the leaded window to the street below. 'By the time I delivered her, alone, in the early hours of the morning, my baby girl was already dead.'

Silent tears ran down Ginny's face. She wanted to comfort that scared fifteen-year-old Diana. She wanted to tell her she understood, that she shared her pain. But of course, she didn't reach out. She couldn't.

The room was silent with shock; across the table that old photograph continued to pass from one woman's hands to the next, and Ginny wondered where on earth Katrin had found it, and what terrible secrets it might yet discharge.

Turning to see the tears on her friend's cheeks too, Ginny and Katrin embraced, as for a few moments the room mourned the loss of Diana's long-ago child.

Katrin was the first to speak up. 'Diana, it's so brave and generous of you to share your story. It's devastating, but important too, because I understand your and Anne's research has provoked some renewed interest in those old prosecution cases?'

'That's right,' Diana replied, glancing at Anne. 'With Anne's book release planned, we've contacted a number of news agencies, and we're going to put out a call to action – a request for any mothers or babies from the Jarman years to come forward and share their stories with us.'

'Aren't you worried about the reputation of The Starlings?' one woman asked. It was, in fact, the question on Ginny's mind.

'Absolutely not,' Katrin replied. 'The Starlings is a wonderful community, and we should feel proud to have created something special on the site of such hardship. I think helping these other women to find their voices is a tremendous gift we are able to give.'

There was unanimous applause, and, as though on autopilot, Ginny joined in.

Anne sat forward, more confident now. 'If enough women make themselves known, I think we'll have a case for the police – or the local authorities, perhaps – to reopen the investigation into Highcap House. And hopefully compensate some of those women for the trauma they've suffered at Jarman's hands.'

'But isn't he dead?' Andrea asked, cradling hands over her pregnant stomach in what now might be read as a protective stance. 'He's escaped punishment already, hasn't he?'

'Yes, he has,' Diana replied. 'But we want the world to know what he was responsible for. Stan Jarman was a monster. This is about so much more than just reparations or punishment – it's about the long-established tradition of *not believing women*. It seems there were always rumours about the governor abusing the women under his care, but no one was ever able to prove anything. When it came down to it, who was going to believe an unmarried mother over a celebrated doctor? That's what tortures many of these women, for the rest of their lives. Not only did they have to give up their babies, but they did so under a cloak of deceit.'

All the while, Anne sat beside Diana, her head nodding in earnest agreement, her eyes shining with life. 'The very least we can do is bring the truth to light,' Anne added. 'And that's why we're making this media appeal. Because we – unlike those before us – don't have to remain silent.'

Diana slid a few copies of a simply typed paragraph across the table.

HIGHCAP HOUSE MOTHER AND BABY HOME
Call to Action
Were you a young mother at Highcap House between 1970 and 1981? Or perhaps you're an adoptee who has discovered your roots there while researching family history? If so, we want to hear from you . . .

Ginny didn't need to read any further, in fact, she couldn't. She was too busy falling down a long-buried hole of memory, in which she could see him now, in her mind's eye, as clear as the day that she finally left that place. Tall, rangy and steely-eyed, with a darkness that poured off him like ink. 'You girls,' he'd murmured as she'd stood on the threshold to his office, cardigan wrapped tightly around her, waiting for her letter of recommendation to help her on her way in the outside world. 'Don't go the way of the rest of them, Virginia,' he'd said, his parting piece of advice. 'These days, all you girls seem to want is the pill and the poke.' He'd given a little chuckle and a sharp glance at his personal assistant Madeline, as though he hadn't already shared this piece of witty wisdom with a hundred girls before. 'Trouble is, when you lot don't take the pill, we're the poor blighters who have to clear up the poke.'

The poke.

Ginny turned to Katrin and whispered faintly, 'I'll see you in the car, darling. I'm feeling a little light-headed.' And she left them all to dig around in the past without her.

21. Katrin

When Katrin settled up with Tino after lunch, she discovered that Ginny had gone home in a taxi, leaving her Cadillac keys at reception for Katrin to drive herself home.

'She looked quite unwell,' Tino reported, looking anxious.

Keen to get back home to check on her friend, Katrin paid the bill and reassured Tino that his food was exquisite as always, before heading out to locate Ginny's car. As she adjusted the mirror, her mobile phone rang, and Bill's name flashed up on the screen. For a second she considered ignoring his call. It wasn't that things had been difficult between them since Christmas; in fact, humdrum would be a better description, even despite the arrival of Amélie's baby Henri. You'd think, when these life-changing events took place – like learning that your husband had cheated on you with his brother's wife, for example – that entire worlds would be turned upside down, that relationships would shatter beyond repair. But in fact, real life had a habit of simply carrying on.

Katrin's own child – a precious girl, she now knew – would be here before too long and, finances safely secured and a discreet divorce lawyer on standby, she'd have all the time in the world to work out her next move.

'Hi!' she said, picking up Bill's call, 'Are you two having a nice time out on the water?'

But Bill wasn't in the mood for small talk. In fact, he sounded furious. 'Katrin, have you any idea what Ginny has been up to with that bloody clocktower of ours?'

'Whoa, slow down a bit, Bill! What are you talking about?'

'The bird removal – the clearing of the asbestos!' The sound of wind buffered around Bill's handset, and she imagined him leaning up against the side of the boat, his silver hair flying wild.

'Ye-es. What about it? You know the various departments have been dragging their heels – I told you all this. Ginny's been chasing them.'

There was an angry pause at the end of the line, during which Katrin could hear Hugo telling his brother to calm down. 'Kat,' Bill said now, with a sigh. 'I've just come off the phone with Bob Ellis at the asbestos removal firm. I've dealt with him before; straight as they come. He tells me that he's never heard of Ginny LeFevre, and that the last correspondence he's had on the matter was way back in the summer, with you!'

'I don't understand—' Katrin began to say.

'She hasn't done a thing!' Bill shouted over the roar of the tidal wind. 'God only knows why, but Ginny has *not* been chasing up the bird certificate, Kat. I've just put in a call to environmental health myself, and they said we'll have to wait until the autumn now, as it's an offence to move the birds during nesting season.'

'God, I'm sorry,' Katrin said, but her mind was already racing ahead. Why would Ginny lie like that? Especially after volunteering to take on the project in the first place.

'You'll have to have a word with her,' he said. 'If you want to save her embarrassment, just tell her we've heard back from the council ourselves and we'll take it from here. Perhaps she's getting forgetful in her old age?'

'That's very generous of you, Bill,' Katrin replied, 'but I think Ginny could outdo the rest of us in the sharp-thinking stakes.'

'OK, well, I'll leave it with you,' he said, calmer now. 'Love you.'

It suddenly occurred to Katrin how Bill had never needed to call her trust into question, on any matter, and fleetingly she wondered how he'd react if he knew she'd been talking to lawyers and accountants behind his back. If he knew just how easily she could walk away.

'By the way, sweetheart,' he added. 'Don't wait up – we're stopping at the Anchor for supper, and I have a feeling it's going to be a late one.' A cheer went up from the fellas in the background.

She hung up, staring for a few moments at her own eyes reflected in the rear-view mirror.

'*Ginny*,' she murmured. 'What the hell is going on?'

On the close, Katrin eased Ginny's Cadillac over the speed bumps, fearful of damaging the undercarriage of the vintage vehicle if she took it too fast. As she dawdled past Thomas's crocus-flanked greenhouse, she spotted Anne, who had arrived back ahead of her to give Diana Lambley a tour of The Starlings.

'Katrin!' Anne scurried across to the roadside, leaving Diana to wait on the grass verge. 'What a wonderful meeting today!'

'It was, Anne,' Katrin replied. 'Thanks so much for organising the talk. You two were amazing!'

Anne's face broke into a wide smile. 'I meant to ask you – are you OK if my mother joins us for the anniversary party? She's coming to stay with me for a week.'

'Of course.' Katrin nodded, hoping they wouldn't have a repeat of the upsetting scene outside Thomas's house in December. She checked her watch in an obvious manner, keen to get away and locate Ginny.

'Um, is everything alright, Katrin?' Anne asked, her hand still holding on to the open window of the passenger door, somewhat proprietorially, Katrin thought in her impatience. 'It's only that when I saw you in the car at Tino's just now, you looked like you might be arguing with someone. On your mobile.'

'Arguing? No! It was Bill, just phoning in from the boat with Hugo.'

Anne gave an unconvinced little bob of her head, and with infuriating languor pushed her ugly glasses up her nose. 'Oh, *yes*. So, is everything good between you two now – I mean, since . . .?' And at this point she dropped her voice low, a suggestion that she and Katrin were in on some great secret. '*Did you ever find out who the other woman was?*'

Alarm swelled in Katrin's chest, suffocating, enraging. 'What are you doing, Anne,' she hissed in reply, 'bringing that up all these months later?! I'm pregnant, for Christ's sake!' she said, furiously gesturing to the swell of her belly beneath the steering wheel. 'Does this *look* like Bill and I aren't alright?'

Anne released her hand from the window frame, as though burnt, just as Diana joined them on the path, unwittingly bringing the exchange to a halt.

'*The starlings*,' Diana exclaimed, looking up towards the old building. 'They're still in the clocktower? Do they still flock at sunset?'

'They do!' Katrin replied, already releasing the handbrake, and trying to lose the anger from her voice. 'Anyway, I'd better return Ginny's car before she starts wondering where I've got to.'

She began to pull away again, but Diana stepped closer still, and stooped to the passenger window.

'Katrin – your friend Ginny – well, it's just I had the strongest sense I'd met her before. She's not a Highcap mother, is she?'

For a second, Diana's question silenced Katrin.

'No!' she laughed after a beat, and yet, her uneasiness was growing and she was suddenly unsure whether she knew anything about Ginny at all. 'Thanks again for today, Diana,' she called breezily as she pulled away, a little faster than she ought. 'Enjoy the tour!'

Nerves jangling, Katrin continued around the outer path, until she reached No.40, where she parked Ginny's car in the covered space at the rear of the property and made her way up the narrow garden to knock on the kitchen door.

For a minute or two she wondered whether Ginny had not yet arrived home, or if she'd taken a detour to the pharmacy to pick something up if she was feeling that bad – but, just as she was about to turn away, her friend's face appeared beyond the glass panel, and she unlocked the back door.

'Come in, darling,' Ginny said softly. Her face was drawn, her skin papery pale. 'Sorry to leave you in the lurch like that.'

Katrin followed her through the house, usually so neat, but today scattered with piles of paperwork and half-emptied boxes of books and belongings. At the foot of the stairs stood two large suitcases, a wool coat draped over one, an umbrella leaning against the other. Katrin took in the scene with shock, but, if Ginny noticed, she showed no sign. Instead, she led them into the living room, where they each took an armchair overlooking the central green and Katrin awaited Ginny's signal to talk. It was around teatime, and beyond the window, children played in the hiatus after school, while young parents and nannies chatted in small groups on the lawn.

'Where are Max and Teddy?' Ginny asked, her glance drifting to the space above the drinks cabinet where the clock read 5.45pm.

'Belinda said she'd pick them up for me,' Katrin replied, 'in case I didn't make it home in time from Tino's.' Was she imagining it, or did Ginny just roll her eyes? 'Ginny, is everything alright?' she asked. 'You don't seem – well, you don't seem yourself today.'

'*I* would've picked them up for you, if you'd asked. You didn't need to ask Belinda.'

'But I needed you at Tino's, for the Starling Darlings!' Katrin laughed, hoping Ginny would join her, but she didn't. She glanced around the room again, back into the hallway where those packed bags stood. 'Oh, Ginny, what is it? You're really starting to worry me now.'

At this, Ginny looked at her directly, with eyes so dull and depressed they didn't seem her own. She'd aged twenty years in an afternoon, all the spark and wit of her gone.

'Ginny, *please*,' Katrin wheedled desperately, 'you're scaring me.'

Now, Ginny broke down, weeping in her armchair, head dropped, shrinking in stature before Katrin's eyes. 'Darling,' she managed to say as Katrin rushed across the room to kneel at her side. 'I – I think it's time I moved on.'

'What?' Katrin snatched up her hand and clasped it between hers.

'Don't, Katrin,' Ginny said, meekly. 'I've loved it here, you know that – being with you and the boys, making new friends, the house, the gardens, it's all so lovely, but it's not enough, is it? I tried to make a new start, but, perhaps it's not for me – perhaps I'm not meant to.' She looked up now, her expression desolate. 'It was a mistake.'

'Is this something to do with that Diana woman?' Katrin blurted out, and Ginny tore her eyes away, fixing instead on the daffodils that flanked the lush green lawn outside. 'I just saw her with Anne on my way in,' Katrin pressed on. 'She said – she said she thought she recognised you . . .?'

'She's *here*?' Ginny whispered. 'She's at The Starlings?'

'Yes – she came back for a tour. Anne's showing her around.'

'Why must that woman keep digging up the past?' Ginny murmured, standing to move closer to the window.

Katrin joined her, feeling confusion and fear coursing through her in equal measure. 'You mean Anne? You know why – she's writing a book.'

'Yes, I know that! But to what end? It's *all* in the past. What's wrong with looking forward, Katrin? Would you want someone writing a book about *your* past? You've never actually shared the details of your own hardships with me, have you? But I know enough about shame to recognise it's something you'd rather forget. How would you feel if someone took your story, and wrote about it? Published it? Put it out there for all the world to see?'

Katrin swallowed hard, because of course, the idea of someone writing about the dark days of her own past was unthinkable. But this was different. The Highcap House story was history, wasn't it? It was a story that needed telling, whereas Katrin's story was, was . . .

Silently she had to concede, it wasn't actually all that different at all. Not when she really thought about it.

'Ginny,' she ventured. 'Your bags – it looks like you're going away . . .'

On the far side of the lawns, Anne and Diana passed by the sealed doors to the clocktower and began to cross the green, seemingly in their direction. Ginny leapt back from the glass. 'Don't let them in,' she murmured, heading for the drinks cabinet to pour herself a large brandy, now that the big hand of the clock had passed officially into cocktail hour.

Beyond the window, the sky was turning a deep shade of pink, and one by one, like fire motes, the starlings started to take flight through the broken bargeboards at the head of the clocktower.

'They're heading towards the south side, Ginny,' Katrin replied. 'Not here.'

By the time Ginny had returned to her seat a few moments later, so, it seemed, had her composure. She lifted the glass to her lips with a cool vacancy. 'I wish I could offer you a drink too,' she said, now turning her full attention on Katrin, 'but there we go. Will you sit, darling? I think I need to explain myself.'

Katrin nodded mutely, and pushed her armchair closer, and the two women sat side by side, as the colours of the living room slowly transmuted under the glow of a Highcap sunset.

'I've no idea how Diana recognised me today,' Ginny said, quite simply. 'After all these years. But yes, she's right – I was here, and I remember her too, quite clearly. I suppose some memories never leave you.'

Katrin shifted in her seat to better look at her friend, now lit up like a marble statue in the declining light. Why had Ginny never shared this with her, especially given Katrin's own links to Highcap House? Why the secrecy? Why keep lying about the child she must have given up, when it would surely be better to make peace with her past? And why come back here, to a place of such obvious pain? There were so many questions Katrin wanted to throw at Ginny right now, but she recognised the fragility in her and she knew she must tread carefully or risk driving her away for good.

'Was this why you wanted to visit Victor's stables?'

Ginny nodded. 'Poor Victor. He wanted to marry me, and I adored him – I've never loved anyone like that since. But my father wouldn't hear of it.'

Katrin took her hand. 'Go on.'

'I told you my father was a terrible man, Katrin. I wasn't exaggerating, you know. It was my school who worked it out, who broke it to my father – and when he found out about Victor – that I was involved with a stable boy, of all things – he flew into the most violent rage. He was mortified at the thought of his good name being sullied! He knew people, he told me – discreet people – who could "dispose of such problems", for a price. Oh, Katrin, I'd never been more scared in my life! We talked about running away together and starting afresh, away from Father, away from all the judgment – but in the end my stepmother persuaded him to bring me here.' She paused for breath. '*To hell.*'

Beyond the windows, the sunset grew deeper by the second.

'But why return here at all?' Katrin whispered into the growing shadows of the room.

'Because I'm a foolish old woman who doesn't know when it's time to leave! Katrin, if I hadn't dithered beneath the awning of the estate agents that day – if I hadn't bumped into Bill and Hugo and agreed to come with them here – I would simply have returned to my life in Kensington. But I don't know – there were greater powers at work that day, and truly, the moment you and I met, I felt helpless to do anything other than stay.'

For a moment, neither spoke. Katrin thought of what Diana had said at the lunch meeting, about rumours of dead babies buried in the basement of the clocktower, and then she thought of Bill's outburst on the phone, his suggestion that Ginny had been deliberately dragging her heels when it came to clearing the tower for development. She could see that Ginny was spent, that she'd had enough – that she wanted releasing from this confessional nightmare. But still, she had to ask the question.

'What happened to the baby, Ginny? Did it . . . did it live?'

For several seconds Ginny didn't reply, and, when she did, shame prevented her from meeting Katrin's eye. 'That's enough now,' she said, her features obscuring in the vanishing light. 'Please. Just leave it, or I really shall have to go. Promise me you'll never mention this again?'

'Ginny, I can't promise you that.'

'Katrin,' Ginny said, more firmly now, fixing her with haunted eyes. 'You have to swear to me you will *never* share this. I've kept it to myself for a lifetime – I've never let it break me yet, never let it define me. And I won't be made a victim of it now. I'd rather die! Swear it!' she begged, grasping Katrin's fingers with a violence that made her pull away.

'I swear it,' Katrin murmured, her hands now protectively cradling her own child as her heart hammered away. 'I swear it on one condition: that you'll stay.'

All at once Katrin recognised that the prospect of a life without Ginny was intolerable. If she could just keep her here until the party, perhaps then she might be able to change her mind? Ginny *couldn't* go! The powerful strength of feeling came as something of a surprise to Katrin, who had known this woman for not even a year. It was suddenly, patently clear that now she had Ginny in her life, she couldn't imagine a moment without her. Who would she confide in, if Ginny was gone? Who would she chat with, plot with, laugh with – cry with, even, if Ginny LeFevre really did walk out of those gates and never return. Perhaps if she had just a little more time to convince her just how much she was needed, with the new baby coming and everything that had happened with Bill, then maybe then she could persuade her to stay.

Ginny shook her head. 'Out of the question.'

'At the very least wait until after the party? *Please?* I'll get rid of Diana Lambley and make sure Anne is put straight – no one will be any the wiser, Gin! Just give it a couple of weeks. Do it for me? For the boys?' Katrin begged in a last-ditch attempt.

Ginny shot Katrin a look that told her she knew exactly what she was doing, a look that conceded defeat in the unfair face of emotional blackmail. 'Until the party, then,' she replied, flatly. 'But after that, I'm gone. I'm sorry, Katrin. I love you very much, but this is all too much. The past – *the past*. Katrin, darling, it just refuses to stay in the past—'

As the last of the daylight was blotted from the room, Katrin stood and switched on a side light. 'Let's get these bags of yours unpacked, hey, Ginny?'

Ginny rose, and the two women each picked up a suitcase and started up the stairs.

'The past is the past, darling,' Katrin said when they reached the top of the stairs, holding her friend in a steadfast gaze. 'Agreed?'

22. Frida

If it hadn't been for Auntie Kat pleading with her to come back for the anniversary party, Frida wouldn't have been in any rush to return home for the May half-term.

Of course Barney was away for the holidays too, but even so, she could really have done with the extra study classes St Saviour's put on in the run-up to GCSEs, and she had visions of trying to revise at home with a wailing infant now resident in the new nursery along the hall. Twice she had said no to Katrin, but then her aunt had said that she needed Frida's help in persuading Ginny to stay on at The Starlings, and that she couldn't do it alone. *Ginny's very fond of you*, the text read. *You'll be my secret weapon.* After re-reading her aunt's message several times over, Frida had set aside her reluctance and agreed to come home.

As arranged, Ginny collected her from school on Friday afternoon, as a favour to Katrin, who was 'unavoidably diverted'. Expecting to spend the journey in the passenger seat subtly drip-feeding Ginny lines about how much Katrin and the twins couldn't manage without her, Frida was somewhat blindsided to find her baby brother strapped into his carrier on the back seat of the Cadillac, earnestly regarding her with eyes like shiny boot buttons. Since his birth at the beginning of May, she'd seen him only once, in the crisp white setting of the private maternity hospital Hugo had forked out for, where she was introduced to the newborn Henri Pascal Gold, balanced like a fledgling on their mother's brittle arms. At the time, Frida had felt herself a bit-part in a film scene, one in which she tried and failed to conjure up any kind of authentic feeling at all. Why should she care? she'd thought at the time. She would barely get to know him by the time Amélie tired of him and parcelled him off to boarding school too. But now, through the salt-streaked glass of the rear passenger window, she marvelled at the smallness of the baby in his big padded seat, at the soft vulnerability of his tiny scrunched face.

'Is he OK in the back on his own?' she asked as Ginny lifted her bags into the boot, and it fleetingly struck Frida that perhaps she too was the target of one of Auntie Kat's peace missions.

With a fragrant waft of Givenchy, Ginny kissed her on the forehead, held open the door and told her she was sure Henri could do with some company. Despite Frida's well-established form for sickness while travelling in the back, she climbed in beside the baby seat, where she sat with Henri's miniature fingers resting in her palm for the entire journey, fighting nausea and blossoming affection in equal measure.

'He's going to need you, you know?' Ginny said as they drove through The Starlings and pulled up outside No.1. 'Henri. He's going to need you more than you can know. He's your brother.'

Her *brother*. Such an ordinary word, but one that was suddenly weighted with a significance she had, until now, not really understood. Frida's eyes met Ginny's in the rear-view mirror, and for what felt like the longest moment they studied each other with unspoken solidarity.

'And Katrin's going to need you, too,' Frida replied, unclipping her seatbelt with a resolute snap. 'I'm not meant to tell you, but I know you're thinking of leaving. Katrin won't say it, but she's devastated. She's asked me to help persuade you to stay. That's the only reason I came back from school, Ginny. She says you're the closest thing she has to family. She says she doesn't know how she'll cope without you. And her own baby will be here soon, and you're meant to be godmother. So you can't leave now, can you?' The words had come out in a spontaneous rush, and, while Frida knew Katrin would be horrified at her blunt delivery, if she didn't say it, who would?

In the mirror, Ginny's eyes seemed to darken, before disappearing as she turned her head in the direction of Starling House. For a few seconds, neither of them spoke. Across the green the new gardener was mowing pretty stripes over the lawns, and the buzz of the mower and the scent of roses in the air felt like summer come early.

With a sudden flurry of activity, Ginny lowered her sunglasses, unfastened her own seatbelt, and threw open her driver's side door. 'Right. Chop-chop!' she said. 'You'd better get your little brother inside, darling, before Hugo starts to think I've kidnapped the pair of you.'

As she watched Ginny set Henri's baby carrier down on the front step beside her bags, it seemed to Frida as though everything and nothing had changed, and a great exhaustion washed over her as she stepped inside the front door of her family home. Amélie was away at the gym in town, where, according to Hugo, she was intent on achieving her pre-baby weight before the party on Saturday. The fourth bedroom – previously Hugo's home office – was now Henri's depressingly chic nursery, carefully decorated in a palette of silver, cream and grey. And the rest of the house, despite the huge human alterations that had taken place over the past few weeks, showed little or no sign of baby life at all. Frida thought of those other women Amélie would no doubt pour scorn on, proudly driving their cars with bouncing 'Baby on Board' stickers; effortlessly switching designer clutch purses for bright nylon changing bags, taut complexions for sleep-deprived shadows.

'Where are all his toys?' Frida asked, rocking her little brother in her arms while Hugo heated a bottle in the microwave. It was strange to her just how competent she felt holding Henri like this, and she wondered if she'd feel the same if her mother were here in the room with them too.

Hugo nodded towards the storage bench beneath the kitchen window. Lifting the lid, Frida found dozens of brightly coloured toys, most of them still in their original packaging. She lifted one out, a fun crinkly caterpillar with a bell inside its head, and shook it towards her stepdad, like a question.

Indicating for Frida to sit with Henri, Hugo showed her how to encourage him to take his milk by gently tapping his lower lip with the teat of the bottle. 'We've been given so many lovely things, lollipop. People are kind, aren't they?' He smiled, but to Frida the expression looked forced, resigned even.

In Frida's arms, baby Henri suckled ferociously, stiffening with determination, the smooth orbs of his cheeks collapsing rhythmically as he drained the bottle, and all at once she had to bite down on her lip to stop herself from blubbing; to stop herself from making this about her. 'Why are all the presents still packed away?' she asked.

'Your mum doesn't want them cluttering up the house.' Hugo was met with a scowl and he winced. 'I mean, she's got a point,' he said, granting Amélie far more loyalty than she'd ever shown him, Frida thought. 'Henri can't even hold his head up yet. Amélie says he can have them when he's old enough to play.'

Frida replied with a roll of her eyes, and by the time Amélie returned late that afternoon every last garish gift had been unpacked and explored and strewn across the immaculate fawn living room, and baby Henri and big sister Frida had become firm friends.

'You look happy,' Amélie said impassively, eyeing them cautiously from the safety of the threshold.

Sitting cross-legged against the sofa, the sleeping baby propped on cushions in her lap, Frida gazed at her solemn Lycra-clad mother in the doorway. *If you only knew*, she thought, and she wondered why Amélie couldn't recognise in her own daughter the fear and conflict that pulsed through her body and spirit these days, every waking hour. She wondered again if it was something about her, something toxic. Something that made Amélie incapable of giving her the homecoming she so longed for.

'Did you miss me?' Frida asked, her tone more like confrontation than a genuine question.

Amélie replied with a curt nod of her head. '*Bien sûr, ma chérie.* I'm your mother.'

The following week passed quickly, as Frida yo-yo'd between No.1 and Starling House, taking advantage of the babysitting earnings on offer, while Auntie Kat tried to cram in extra hours of work before the new baby came in August and Amélie worked tirelessly on her figure down at the gym.

With her head firmly in her revision books, for the most part Frida had attempted to put Barney out of her mind, as he'd instructed. But this Saturday morning of the party, she'd woken early to find herself in an empty house, and once again anxiety began clawing at her insides. Slipped beneath her bedroom door was a scribbled note from Hugo: *Mum at the gym. I've got Henri – helping Bill to set up the party tables. Phone if you need me!*

Frida flopped back against her pillows and stared at the ceiling, thinking about phoning Barney regardless. She had messaged him late last night, feeling the distance that had now opened between them, given the heated manner in which they had parted. She hated it when they argued, but this time had been the worst ever. He'd said she was suffocating him; he'd said she was clingy. He'd said all the fun had gone out of their relationship. She'd just cried. But now she'd had time to think about it, and there were things she wanted to talk through with him, things she wanted to say in person. She loved him, she messaged, and she needed him, and she longed to hear his voice. *Please just phone me back?* she'd implored, already knowing he'd be annoyed that she'd messaged him at all. *I'm going out of my mind here. We can't just leave things like this.*

Through her open window came the sounds of happy raised voices, and of a jazz band warming up in the distant courtyard near Thomas's old cottage. Numbly, Frida watched from her bedroom view as Auntie Kat organised neighbours ferrying plates and glasses and trays of food across the sunlit green, for a party that would begin in less than an hour. Frida was meant to be down there helping like the rest of them. Putting on a bright face and being the confident girl they all wanted her to be, the girl her expensive boarding school prospectus had promised. But she wasn't that girl, was she? Right now, all she really yearned for was oblivion. Maybe she wasn't so different from her mother, after all?

On the green, Auntie Kat spotted her niece at the glass and she tapped her watch, beckoning her down. Frida raised a hand in return and stepped back from the window.

On a sudden whim, and having the house to herself, Frida headed to the drawer of Amélie's dressing room and rummaged around until she found what she was looking for. With some fear and deference, she set it down on the polished black windowsill and, turning to study her strangely disconnected reflection in her mother's mirrored wall, she wondered how she'd ever arrived at this place.

23. Ginny

The day had been an unparalleled success. Everyone said so.

Even now, as the sun descended on the horizon, and the older folk and the neighbours with younger children said their goodbyes, the party spirit was still in the air. Katrin was back at Starling House, briefly, along with Hugo, settling the twins and baby Henri there, ready for Frida to take over babysitting duties so that the grown-ups could stay on a little longer. As Ginny set down her chair in the fairy-lit courtyard, she spotted Frida beyond the throng of neighbours, sitting alone on the edge of the koi pond, gazing in the direction of Thomas's empty cottage, as though in a trance. Perhaps she'd been drinking, Ginny wondered momentarily, in which case she'd be no use to Katrin and the boys tonight.

She approached the girl. 'Darling? Are you alright?'

With something like alarm, Frida met Ginny with a gasp. 'You looked miles away. Is everything OK?'

Distractedly, Frida checked her phone. 'Oh. I'd better get going, hadn't I? Katrin's expecting me any minute.'

Ginny was struck by the girl's melancholy; so unlike her. She looked older than her years, her eyes darkly circled, her tone defeated. 'You know, I had a very good chat with Katrin earlier,' Ginny said, lowering her voice and perching on the stone ledge beside her. 'I told her I'd decided to stay after all.'

Frida looked up quickly, her expression momentarily light. 'You're staying?'

'I told her you'd managed to persuade me. I also told her it was a rotten trick, putting you up to it like that, the little minx.' She bumped shoulders with Frida and managed to extract a shy smile. 'Are you sure everything's alright with you, though, darling? It must be hard adjusting to having the baby in the house.'

Frida shrugged and got up to go. 'To be honest, he's the least of my worries.'

Ginny watched as the girl's gaze brushed over the dozen or so tipsy adults remaining in the dimming light, now dragging chairs and side tables into the more intimate courtyard setting, where the noise of their continued revelry might not disturb the rest of the neighbourhood. To one side, Michael Bassett was attempting to connect his phone to a Bluetooth speaker balanced on the edge of a geranium planter, while an uncommonly drunk Joy laughed at her husband from the distance of her deckchair, heckling him for his outdated taste in music. Bill, by now already ruddy-faced with too much sun and drink, was loudly popping a fresh bottle of champagne, while Belinda and Poppy Parsons handed out yet more of their signature vol-au-vents, and Dylan from No.21 threw a ball for No.12's sausage dog while Graham filled up the pretzel bowls and sang along to the Commodores. Sitting discreetly on the sidelines were Anne and her mother, whom Ginny had successfully managed to avoid all afternoon, and who, judging by their body language, wouldn't stick around for much more of the evening.

Looking back at Frida, Ginny realised that the girl's attention was now fixed on the fluid lines of her mother, Amélie, draped as she was over an ornamental bench, shoulders bare and deeply tanned, plunging black jumpsuit clinging to her frame, as one arm theatrically summoned Bill to top up her champagne, *tout de suite*. There was a loose cannon if ever she saw one. She would have to keep an eye on Amélie tonight, Ginny thought; something about her signalled trouble.

'I'd better go,' Frida repeated, looking away in what Ginny could only interpret as disgust. 'Katrin and Hugo are waiting for me to take over.'

Ginny reached out and touched her wrist lightly. 'I didn't only agree to stay because of Katrin, you know, darling? There are other people here whom I've grown very attached to . . .'

The girl's eyes filled with unexpected tears and she leant in to grab Ginny in a brief and fervent hug, before jogging off in the direction of Starling House, without a backward glance. For a while, Ginny remained there, apart from the crowd, reflecting on all she had found here, in this last-chance home of hers, and watching the light change as the first starlings of the evening began to take flight.

'Ginny, you gorgeous creature!' Bill cried out, breaking her from her thoughts, bottle and glass thrust aloft as he spotted her sitting alone at the pond. 'Come on, gal! The *real* party's only just starting!'

With a wry smile, Ginny accepted his heavy embrace, just as the opening bars of Nick Drake's 'Pink Moon' rose from the speakers and Hugo and Katrin arrived back from Starling House to rejoin the party.

'What a day,' Katrin said, now slipping her arm through Ginny's with a happy sigh, her gaze captured by the rare spectacle of a spring starling cloud now swirling darkly in the sky overhead. She ran her hand over the beautiful dome of her pregnant belly. 'What a perfect day.'

PART TWO

Present day

24. DS Ali Samson

From where DS Ali Samson is standing, the detective inspector doesn't look pleased to be called out on his weekend off. Shoulders hunched, he stomps in her direction over the dew-damp grass, lit up in the glare of squad car headlights.

Ali steels herself for his disapproval, something she's grown accustomed to since her return to work last month on 'light duties'. What is it about these senior officers, she wonders, that drives them to be so punishing in the face of another's struggle, when compassion would be the more obvious response? Would his attitude be the same towards Johnson or Garner, if *they* were back from sick leave? Of course not.

'Sergeant,' Trelawney grunts on arrival, hands deep in the pockets of an overcoat too heavy for a mild night in late May. 'Debrief?'

They're standing on the path adjacent to the clocktower, the entrance of which has been cordoned off with yellow incident tape. Beyond the tape the floodlit figures of paramedics create a loose screen around the victim as they go about their work, urgently assessing the woman's condition and preparing to move her. Outside, around the paths and across the lawns, uniformed officers briskly patrol the residential area, as neighbours are name-checked and directed back to their homes.

'Who phoned it in?' Trelawney asks.

Ali lifts the tape and ducks under, while her superior hangs back on the other side, casting his gaze about the expansive lawns and mansion blocks. The sea breeze is picking up, flapping at his coat-tails and lifting his thinning hair to reveal a high forehead he works hard to conceal.

'The initial caller didn't give a name, guv,' Ali replies. 'We're trying to trace the number now. The handler said the line was poor, hard even to ascertain whether it was male or female. Approximately twenty minutes later, right before we turned up, the girl found the victim – Katrin Gold – and raised the alarm here.'

'The girl?'

Ali indicates towards the family group huddled outside No.1. 'Frida Pascal. Fifteen years old – she's the victim's niece. According to neighbours, her scream pretty much alerted the whole estate. I've had some dealings with the family before. Nothing serious, but I know Katrin Gold and her niece are very close.'

'And the victim's status?' he asks, glancing past Ali towards the floodlit activity within.

'PC Bloom was first on the scene, and, like the husband, he struggled to find a pulse. But the paramedics were only a few minutes behind and they were able to confirm that she was unconscious but still breathing. I'll go over and update the family in a second – the husband was escorted off the scene before the paramedics arrived, and I'm afraid he may still be under the misapprehension that she didn't make it.'

From their distance, DI Trelawney studies the family group, the girl with her face pressed into her father's shoulder, the older woman beside them, stoic, upright. 'So, you think the fall scene looks suspicious?'

'Uh-huh – the clocktower roof is an asbestos hazard, so it's been locked up for years. The floor is thick with dust and debris, meaning every movement leaves a trail – and there are footprints everywhere. We can account for the first two sets to the right of the victim, as belonging to Ginny LeFevre, her friend and Bill Gold, her husband, who both attempted to bring her round and find a pulse immediately after she was found. They didn't move her, though – they were afraid to, in case they did more damage. But then there are other footprints, to the left, unlike the victim's, heading up and down the steps and across the stone floor from the entrance here. It looks as though someone has tried to obliterate them, and it seems the handrail has been wiped haphazardly too. Combine all this with the unidentified call, and we're certainly building up a picture of something more complicated than a simple accident.'

Trelawney scratches his chin. 'You spoke with the husband?'

She nods. 'He's a mess – blames himself for not going to look for her sooner. The family liaison officer took him back to his house. They've got two little boys, so—'

'And any reason to think the niece might be involved?'

'Frida? No. As I say, they're close. She was alone when she discovered her aunt, and she says she didn't enter the area – just called for help. We've taken her shoes, to eliminate her footprints, and PC Bloom has fingerprinted her, again for elimination.'

Trelawney gestures towards the family. 'Who are the others?'

'The woman is Ginny LeFevre – the friend I mentioned – and the man is Hugo Gold, Frida's stepdad, and brother to the victim's husband.'

'And they were all present at this party, you say?'

'It was a first anniversary bash – a year since The Starlings opened as a residential estate. Apparently the whole community was here throughout the day – but by the time this happened they were down to – let's see . . .' Ali counted down her list of names. 'They were down to less than a dozen people still up and drinking in the courtyard, with most of the others having returned to their homes.'

Now the DI lifts the tape and steps in beside Ali, taking care not to cross the forensic markers set wide of the woman at the bottom of the marble staircase, where paramedics are preparing to move her. She is dressed in cerise silk, and her hair inadvertently fans out in such a way as to almost appear as though she is still falling. A pair of small stacked heels lie kicked off in the dust near her feet. The DI takes a couple of steps closer, before stopping in his tracks.

'Jesus, Samson,' he hisses, shooting her a fierce glare. 'You didn't tell me she was pregnant.'

Ali feels her blood rising, her anger these days ever close to the surface. She doesn't answer, instead fixes her attention on the form of Katrin Gold, forty years old, managing director of Gold Property, wife and mother of two, six months pregnant; unresponsive. It doesn't matter whether she's pregnant or not, Ali tells herself. She's a victim, and they're the police, and she deserves the best attention they can give her.

'I would never have let you attend if I'd known,' Trelawney starts to say, but she cuts him off with a warning glance he can't ignore. 'For Christ's sake, Ali,' he says now, appealing to her with the use of her first name, 'you've only been back four weeks.'

They stand aside as the ambulance crew swoop in and expertly lift Katrin Gold on to a stretcher, hurrying her away to the emergency vehicle waiting outside. White-suited forensics officers move in on the scene, setting down more evidence numbers and taking photographs of the fall site from various angles.

Ali shakes her head. 'And in those four weeks, guv, I've been going stir-crazy. You know I like to get my hands dirty – if I get even one more traffic violation to investigate this week, I think I'll lose my mind.'

'Yes, but this – this isn't the case for you, sergeant.' DI Trelawney's demeanour is hard, but Ali suspects the intent comes from a good, if archaic, place. 'You can complete all the preliminaries tonight, as you're here,' he conceded, 'but then I'll get one of the fellas to take over in the morning, OK?'

Ali grabs Trelawney's sleeve and steers him towards the entrance again, away from their fellow officers. She points across the green to the large modern building lit up on every floor. On the very top level a figure can be seen watching the events, two small children at his side, an officer a little distance apart. 'See that house there?' she says. 'That's Katrin Gold's house, and the person at the window is her husband, Bill.'

The DI sighs impatiently.

'Over there,' she says, pointing to No.1. 'Frida, the niece, and her stepdad Hugo live there along with Frida's baby brother Henri and their mother, Amélie Pascal, who is currently refusing to give a statement, despite having been at the party all evening. Suddenly taken unwell, apparently. And this person here, in the blue dress,' she says, pointing across the lawns towards a woman standing beside a shawl-draped teenage girl, 'is Belinda Parsons, who was very quick to ask me whether we thought it was the husband who pushed her.'

Trelawney's brows knit in interest.

'Over there,' she says, indicating towards the very end terrace on the East Wing, 'is the home of Ginny LeFevre, whom I previously met in my dealings with The Starlings earlier this year, concerning the disappearance of their groundskeeper, Thomas King.'

'OK, sergeant,' DI Trelawney says, folding his arms. 'What's your point?'

'I *know* these people – at least, I know them better than you or any of the rest of the team do – and I reckon I've got a better shot at getting answers from them. They trust me. You're always banging on about gaining the trust of our community, aren't you? What was it you told me on my first day at Highcap? *Get the public onside, and you're halfway there.*'

The inspector stuffs his hands deep into his pockets and glances about the grounds again, his baby hair billowing above his head like mist. She's got him. He looks back, at the now empty space at the foot of the clocktower stairs, and exhales through pursed lips.

'You're stubborn, Samson,' he says, 'I'll give you that,' and he hesitates a moment, clearly deliberating over his next words. 'OK. You take the case – but be warned, if I get even a sniff that you're not up to the job, you're off it, alright, and I'll put Johnson on in your place. Your mental health is important,' he adds, looking uncomfortable.

'My mental health is absolutely fine,' Ali replies coolly.

He stares at her for a few seconds, and she can tell he's regretting his concession already. 'I still think it's too soon, and if this case gets the better of you, sergeant, it'll be my backside on the line.'

But DS Ali Samson has heard enough. The warrior in her wants to tell him he's a dinosaur – to threaten to report him for discrimination, for sexism, for misogyny, even – but of course the police force doesn't work like that, and she won't say a word. She'll suck it up, because the case is hers, and that's all that matters. She'll prove to him that a woman, a grieving one at that, is entirely capable of separating the personal from the professional – and of getting a result.

'I'll send you an update later, guv,' she says with a respectful nod, and she strides off towards the ambulance to get the latest on Katrin Gold.

25. Frida

Standing on the path outside No.1, Frida watches the distant ambulance crew entering the unfamiliar space beneath the clock-tower, their hi-vis uniforms offensively bright in the glare of floodlights now erected there. An unstoppable sob escapes her, and she breaks down again, allowing her stepdad to pull her close, where she presses her face into the warmth of his jumper.

Since the officer took her prints and statement at the kitchen table, the air outside has grown cool and damp, the buzz of police radio a stark contrast to the warmth of laughter and music that less than an hour ago had floated high in the air above The Starlings, back in the *before*. Behind her closed eyes, she can still see the fallen body of her aunt, laid out on the stone-cold floor, the mound of her unborn baby the picture of vulnerability beneath the crumpled cerise of her ruined silk frock. Now, Ginny prises Frida from her stepfather's arms, cushioning her face against the fragrant cashmere of her neck scarf, and murmuring soothing words as she holds her there.

'Don't look, darling,' she tells her, 'don't look,' and fleetingly Frida wonders who is comforting whom.

Beside them, Hugo shrinks away, made useless by Ginny's intervention, and Frida senses him disappearing through the doorway of No.1, where she imagines, somewhere, Amélie is hiding, ignoring the cries of her baby boy and turning a blind eye to the traumas of the night. Nothing seems real. Frida can't stop thinking about her last words to Auntie Kat, the wrongness of them, the selfish ingratitude of them; the violence of them. *You're not my mother!* she'd hissed, and, even in the moment she'd said them, the irony of those words was not lost on her. Because all she had dreamt of, these past few months, was to have a mother like Katrin – a mother who cared enough to fight for her and with her, to protect her, to tell her she was getting it all wrong – to catch her when she fell.

It really is her fault, isn't it? All of this. A good person wouldn't have lost their temper like that, they would have simply returned to the party together, to eat cake and light table fireworks and dance to Ella Fitzgerald and forget about their troubles, for a short while at least. But Frida isn't a good person, and she never will be, because everything she does is infected by the bad choices she makes, and she just keeps making them, over and over. She's toxic. That's why Meg and Rose dropped her; it's why Barney has blocked her messages; it's why her own mother is nowhere to be seen when she's really needed; it's why Auntie Kat has been taken away.

'What will we do without her?' She looks up into Ginny's desolate face, as the panic of reality hits her. 'Ginny? If Katrin hadn't come looking for me—' But Ginny isn't listening. Her focus has turned back towards Starling House, across lawns suddenly absent of neighbours, broad and empty.

In the lamplight, Frida follows Ginny's gaze to the bleak figure of Uncle Bill, walking towards them from Starling House, a sleeping twin over each shoulder, an awkward-looking police officer trailing in his wake. Bill's gaze is distant, his expression confused, and as he halts beside them Frida's breath halts in her chest. She wants to make this all stop; to put back the clocks – to have not fought with Auntie Kat this evening, to have walked on past the snug room instead of pausing, to have never met Barney, never gone to that school – to never have been returned to her mother all those years ago in Paris when she was too small to cause any harm—

Uncle Bill's focus, Frida suddenly comprehends, is firmly fixed on the paramedics outside the clocktower, who are now loading Katrin's body into the back of the ambulance. *Her body*. Time seems to stop for a moment, as Frida takes in the horrific implications of that scene, and of Uncle Bill's bereft expression. But then, her attention shifts as she spots the police officer, the one who let her off with a caution, now jogging across the grass from the clocktower, towards Uncle Bill.

'Mr Gold?' DS Ali calls over, waving her arm in a wide arc. 'Mr Gold! She's breathing!' she says, coming level with the gathered family outside No.1. 'Your wife. *Katrin*. She's in the ambulance now, unconscious, but breathing.'

A member of the crew jumps into the driver's seat and starts up the engine.

'*She's breathing?*' Bill murmurs. 'You mean she's not dead?' His face appears to fall in on itself.

To Frida, it is as though a collective breath is held for one-beat, two-beats, three-beats, four – until the sirens scream out into the night air, and her broken-up world slams back together into a new shape.

In what feels like slow motion, she pulls away from Ginny and turns to Uncle Bill, scooping up the boys as he lowers them, half-sleeping, into her arms. Without stopping to ask any further questions of the officer, Bill breaks into a run, only skidding to a halt as he reaches the emergency vehicle containing his wife.

Hugo reappears in the doorway, and together they stand and watch – Ginny and Hugo, Frida and the twins – mute with shock and confusion as Bill disappears into the back of the ambulance and, yellow lights spinning, sails off into the night with his broken wife.

Frida drops to her knees and hugs the tiny boys to her, the damp of the grass cold against her bare legs. But even in her relief and gratitude the bad part of her rises up, and she hates herself all over again. Because her overriding thought, once she's allowed herself to believe this good news to be true, is this: what will Auntie Kat tell them, if she wakes up?

26. DS Ali Samson

It's not yet seven when DS Samson arrives at the station to prepare the interview room, a stress headache forming at the back of her skull after little sleep and a tense drive in through the thick valley fog.

The moment she steps through the door, she is irritated to see DI Trelawney already in his office. At first she pretends not to have spotted him, and slides behind her monitor, powering it up, hoping to get a few minutes alone before he interrupts. But, only seconds after she's logged in, his door flies open with a thump, and he's stomping across the office, the customary scowl etched firmly on his face.

'It's Sunday,' he says, stopping wide-footed at her desk, handing her an official-looking envelope she already knows is from the police liaison officer in charge of her case.

Without a word, she pushes it to the bottom of her bag and looks up to meet Trelawney's gaze.

He folds his arms. So, they're playing that game, are they? He won't mention it until she does.

'You're not on today's rota.'

'Uh-huh,' she replies, looking away now and fixing her eyes on the screen.

'What are you doing here, Samson? Forensics won't have anything for you until next week – and the interviews can wait too.'

'I've set them up for today,' Ali replies, clicking away at her emails. 'I thought we should get the family in for formal statements while it's all fresh in their minds.'

'You took statements last night, didn't you?'

'Yes, but witnesses often recall new details with the passing of time – or realise they got something wrong in the initial shock. I thought it would be prudent—'

'What about your own family?' Trelawney asks, and the unexpectedly personal nature of his question quite throws her. 'Well, it's the weekend, isn't it?' he adds, when she doesn't respond. 'Haven't you got anything planned?'

'Haven't you?' she retorts, heart racing. Does he know Margo has moved out? Is that what he's digging for? It's none of his damned business what she does on her weekends.

Trelawney flushes a deep mahogany and takes a step sideways. 'Point taken,' he mutters. 'If you'd rather be here working, then I suppose—'

'I would,' she says simply.

'Then you'd better tell me what the plans are for today.'

'What – you want to sit in? I was going to ask Johnson, as he's due in this morning anyway.'

'Why not? I'm quite interested what the husband's got to say, if I'm honest. Something didn't sit quite right about him last night. I mean, he was clearly shocked when I told him she was still breathing.'

Ali spins her chair round to face him. 'I know what you mean. I followed them down to the hospital after we'd finished up at

The Starlings, and he was strange – well, inconsistent, at least. At first he seemed completely shattered by what had happened – head in his hands, questioning why he hadn't been there – but then, the next minute, all smiles and charm with the doctors and nurses, as though she was in there with nothing more than a fracture. Maybe it was just the shock but it seemed off to me.'

'Any update from the hospital?'

'No change. They're monitoring the baby, and so far all seems well.'

Trelawney nods thoughtfully. 'How many months pregnant is she?'

'Six,' she replies flatly. If Katrin Gold has to deliver early, it's a hit-and-miss stage in pregnancy, Ali knows only too well. She holds Trelawney's gaze for an uncomfortable second too long, until he looks away and she can let out the breath that's all backed up inside her chest. 'But as for Katrin, they're not sure yet. She was unconscious for almost an hour before they got her to hospital, and since then she's been in an induced coma. They're worried about a bleed on the brain.'

'Will she make it?'

'The doctor wouldn't commit – but for the purposes of inter-view we need to stress the likelihood of her recovering, so if the husband's hiding anything he'll see the sense in getting it off his chest now.'

'Agreed. What time is he in?'

Ali checks her watch. 'He's been at the hospital all night – the neighbour Ginny stayed over with the kids, so he wants to check in on them before he comes down. I told him to get himself showered and freshened up and we'd see him here at eight. Interview Room One.'

'Righto. I'll see you then.' Trelawney returns to his office and shuts the door. A second later he opens it again. 'Samson – you said one of the neighbours last night asked if you thought the husband had pushed her. What do we know about the state of their marriage?'

'Not much yet, guv. Ginny LeFevre is in later, and she's close to the family, so I'm hoping she might give us a bit more insight.'

'OK. We'll take it nice and gently with the husband to start with – after all, he's probably still in shock. You can kick off with the basics – get him to go over his version of events again, and ask after the family – and if the time is right I'll come in with the heavier questions.'

Good cop, bad cop. Trelawney really is old-school, Ali thinks as she types 'Bill Gold' into her search bar and trawls through the various local news articles and unrelated hits that pop up. An image search brings up multiple photographs of Bill at fund-raisers and social gatherings over recent years, many of them with Katrin on his arm, but also a good few taken alongside any number of women who could be connected with him in some other way. Ali has a feeling things aren't going to be completely straightforward with Bill Gold.

She zooms in on a photograph that catches her eye, in which Bill and Katrin Gold stand with their beautiful twin boys at the sealed wooden door of the clocktower, shoulder to shoulder with brother Hugo and wife Amélie, all four dressed stylishly, champagne flutes in hand. Amélie's eyes are obscured by large dark sunglasses, while Katrin wears hers atop her head, causing her to squint very slightly against the bright light of a spring morning. Either side of the women, the two men wear expensive linen suits, their easy postures matching, each smiling brightly, the younger one dark-haired, the other a silver fox. Beneath the picture is the caption *Starlings Fly High This Spring*, together with a short article, dated almost exactly a year earlier, announcing the launch of the new Highcap development. There's something unsettling about the photograph, and it's not until Ali is on her way down to the front desk to meet Bill Gold that she realises what it is.

They're perfect. The Gold family, to the outside world, appears glitteringly blessed, and entirely, flawlessly perfect.

Bill declines DS Samson's offer of tea or coffee, explaining that he's swilling with the stuff after a night spent at Katrin's hospital bedside, attended by kindly nurses on the ward. Ali suspects most visitors don't get such privileged attention; Bill's charm, even in his traumatised state, is unmissable. Apparently they'd even let him use the ward shower to save him having to detour home on his way in, and she wonders how it feels to sail through life as someone like Bill Gold, easy passage a given, never to be questioned.

'How are you feeling this morning?' she asks, placing a plastic beaker of water on the table in front of him.

At first he doesn't answer her question, and instead focuses on the curve of his hand around the white ridges of the cup, opening and closing his fingers as though testing whether the object is really there at all. 'I honestly don't know,' he replies. 'It's a cliché, but it all just feels like a bad dream. Even this, here – I suspect I'm going to wake up any minute.' He breaks into one of his disarming smiles, all teeth, eyes gleaming with despair. 'I expect you hear that all the time, don't you? You'll be used to dealing with relatives in shock.'

Ali returns a polite smile and pulls out the seat opposite, turning to a clean page in her notebook, and hoping the DI won't keep them waiting now he's decided to gatecrash the interview. Bill Gold seems unembarrassed by the wait, and for the next few minutes he sits quietly looking into his water, his sorrowful gaze never shifting. Overhead, the strip light tremors slightly, and instinctively Ali angles her chair away; the last thing she needs now is one of her blinding migraines. The guv would see it as a victory, proof that she's still not strong enough to take on anything so weighty as a case of this kind, anything so sensitive as this.

'Morning, Mr Gold,' DI Trelawney says, striding in confidently and stepping into a firm handshake across the desk. With a loud clatter, he pulls out his chair and sits side-on to the table, his posture relaxed, one leg crossed over the other, his arms lightly folded. As though it's an afterthought, he leans across Ali and flicks on the recording device. 'I'm sure DS Samson here has put your mind at ease, but I just want to reassure you that this meeting is purely informal. Now, please can you confirm for the tape that you're William Gold, husband to Katrin Gold, and you're here voluntarily to go over your statement about the order of events last night – and that you don't object to us recording our conversation?'

'Er, no,' Bill Gold replies with a startled blink, clearly stirred in some way by Trelawney's 'reassuring' introduction. 'I mean yes, I agree with all that – that's fine.'

'Also in the room with Mr Gold is me – DI Dave Trelawney – and DS Ali Samson. Over to you then, DS Samson.' He sits back in his seat with a hand gesture that borders on dismissive.

Ali makes a mental note of Bill's change in demeanour at the arrival of Trelawney. Gone are the flashing smiles, the emotional appeals for empathy. He's clearly a man more intimidated by another man; that insight might come in useful later.

'So, Bill, if I may?' she begins. 'I want you to take us through the order that things happened last night – right from the point at which you last saw your wife, through to Frida raising the alarm.'

Bill blinks in reply, casting a glance in Trelawney's direction, and Ali reframes the question.

'Let's start with when and where did you last see Katrin?'

To her surprise, Bill reaches into his breast pocket and pulls out a crumpled handwritten sheet of paper, smoothing it on to the tabletop before him.

'I had the whole night to think about it,' he says. 'I just kept going over and over it, trying to work out if there was anything more I could tell you. Anything useful. But I have to say, nothing new occurred to me.'

'OK, do you want to take us through it again, then?' Trelawney asks, nodding towards the sheet.

'Right,' Bill says. He rakes fingers through his hair, rubs the back of his neck. 'The first thing to say is we'd all been drinking. Except Katrin, of course – she never touches a drop when she's pregnant. I mean, we weren't plastered – there were still the kids to think about at home – but they were being looked after, so – but we'd been drinking fairly steadily, in between food and so on, since midday.' He pauses for a breath, looking from one officer to the other for some response. 'So if I get some details wrong, it's just—'

'We understand,' Ali says with a smile. 'We're not here to judge you, Bill. It was a party, yes? Of course you'd been drinking – it was a celebration.'

'No law against that, is there?' Trelawney adds.

'Yes, OK,' Bill replies, relaxing a little.

'Who was looking after your children?' Ali asks.

'Oh. Frida, my niece – well, not really my niece but she calls me Uncle Bill – my brother's stepdaughter. She was babysitting the twins at Starling House, along with their cousin Henri – her brother. Hugo's new baby. Sorry, I'm not being clear, am I? It's a bit confusing—'

'You're fine,' Trelawney interrupts. 'Frida was babysitting all three of the little ones at your house, yes? Yet she was the one who found Katrin? I take it she hadn't left them unattended?'

Bill shakes his head. 'No, of course not. That was when I'd gone back home to check on them. When I got there, I told her to go and get some cake while I took over for a bit. She's close to Katrin, and I didn't want her to miss out on the party. She'd got some table fireworks she wanted to light.'

'OK, all clear,' Trelawney says, with a gesture that says everything is just fine. 'Let's just go back to the courtyard now, before you left to take over from Frida.'

Bill runs both hands through his hair again, his face a momentary blank. 'Yes. Yes, OK. By about half-seven, those of us remaining all moved round to the courtyard at the back of the North Wing. It's the large cobbled area you see directly to your right as you come through the entrance gates – opposite the lodge.'

'Where you had your Christmas tree last year,' Ali says with a smile.

'Exactly.'

'Who was there at this point?' Trelawney asks.

Bill refers to his list. 'Me, Katrin, my brother Hugo, his wife Amélie. Ginny. Belinda Parsons, her daughter Poppy. Graham and Dylan from the maisonettes. Anne Ashbourne and her mother for a bit, but they didn't stay long. Joy and Michael Bassett. And a few others were there for a short while, but that was the main group who stayed on – those are the ones I remember.'

'And how was the atmosphere?' Ali asks, her voice still light.

'It was good. Really good. The whole day had gone wonderfully – it was a big deal to us, you know? This project has been incredibly personal, especially to Katrin – I don't know if you know, but she was a Highcap baby? Possibly the last born there.'

'Is that right? Fascinating.'

'Katrin, Hugo and I are all equal partners in the business, but she's been the driving force behind it all. She poured all her compensation money into The Starlings, every penny, even when Hugo and I wondered if we'd ever see any of it back. Because it was a wreck when we found it – well, you probably remember it as the derelict hospital? Five years, it took to renovate, so, you know . . .' He trails off, a crease forming between his eyes as though he is trying to remember where he was going with this.

'Compensation money?' Trelawney asks the question on Ali's lips. Money is always a good motive to follow.

Bill looks up from his cup, suddenly anxious. 'Oh, I shouldn't – Katrin is really funny about it; she doesn't like people to know. She . . .' He hesitates, his caution appearing sincere, and then he sighs, perhaps realising there's no point in holding back. 'She grew up in care, you know, in and out of foster homes the whole of her early life.' He pauses momentarily, as though deciding whether or not to go on. 'When she was a teenager, she was moved to a children's home, and she and some of the other kids there were, um—' he struggles to find the right words '—taken advantage of.'

'By the people running the place?'

He shakes his head. 'It was one of these appalling grooming rings you read about in the press. These girls had no one, and apparently the problem was reported again and again to Social Services, but nobody stepped in. They were barely teenagers, most of them. Turns out it had been going on there for years.'

'Jesus,' Ali murmurs, shocked to hear the truth that Katrin Gold's life had really been less than blessed.

'The local authority was finally investigated, and that's why she got all that compensation money. So, when she found out – just weeks after it had cleared into her bank account – that she'd been one of those babies born in Highcap, and that the building was up for sale – she thought it was a sign, kind of a full circle, if you like. She persuaded me to uproot from Battersea, to move here – to invest in the place, to start a new property business, a family. The Starlings was a big deal to Katrin. Family was *all* she ever wanted.' His face crumples.

'You know you're talking about her in the past tense, Mr Gold?' Trelawney says, softly, leaning in. 'The doctors tell me she has a very good chance of making it through. A *very* good chance.'

At this, Bill Gold gets a grip of himself. He takes a strong breath and nods. 'Yes. I hope they're right.'

And then he runs through the timings again, the same as before: at half-seven they were all in the courtyard; at 7.50pm he left to check on the twins at Starling House; by the time he returned around 8.20pm, Katrin had already left, apparently in search of him. At 8.55pm, Frida's scream rang out across the square, and Katrin was found.

Bill Gold slumps back in his seat, and rubs both hands across his face, apparently spent. 'And that's it,' he says, raising his palms in what could only be described as bemusement.

Ali glances at her superior, and from his closing posture it seems obvious to her that he's not going to ask anything more pressing. But Bill Gold is holding back, she's certain; he's only giving them the version of events that suits him – the version that paints him as traumatised husband and devoted father. It seems strange to her how easily he gave up information that he knows his wife would rather keep quiet. A diversion tactic, perhaps? A smokescreen from the past to prevent difficult questions about the present? Frustration eats away at her as the clock on the wall ticks loudly in the silent moments that follow.

'Thank you,' Trelawney says at last, and Ali lays down her pen with studied care. 'I think that'll do us for today. But just one last question, Mr Gold: do you recall anyone else leaving the courtyard in that time period before Katrin was found?'

A brief flicker of something like irritation crosses Bill Gold's face. 'Er, no, not that I know of,' he says, biting down on his lip, making a show of giving it serious thought. 'No, definitely not. Not unless they were very quick. Everyone I mentioned was still there when I got back to the courtyard. Everyone except Katrin, that is.'

'OK,' Trelawney says, pushing back his chair. 'Thank you, Mr Gold. We'll keep you posted on everything, and of course, you know where we are if you need us – or if you recall anything else.'

Bill Gold starts to rise from his seat, but Ali Samson's frustration gets the better of her. 'Mr Gold,' she asks, remaining seated so that he is left hovering uncomfortably. 'May I ask: do you love your wife?'

He straightens up now, turning to DI Trelawney, an appeal, perhaps, but Trelawney says nothing, his face remaining impassive.

'Yes,' Bill Gold replies, his eyes now brimming with tears. 'Yes, I do,' he says, in a sonorous tone Ali thinks would not sound out of place on a West End stage. 'I love my wife very, very much.'

Ali rises now, and gestures towards the door. 'I'll walk you out,' she says, with a flat smile designed to make him feel not quite at ease.

And it seems to work, because it's then that he remembers something new. 'Oh, yes – actually, someone *did* leave the party while Katrin was gone. Ginny LeFevre. After I got back, she went off to fetch us all a nightcap, and she was going to see if she could track down Katrin while she was at it. She was gone for a while, now I think of it. Maybe she saw something?'

27. Ginny

Just give it a couple of weeks. Do it for me? For the boys?

The words play over and over in Ginny's mind as she lies awake in bed, nudged too soon into consciousness by the sun rising brightly over the sea, pouring daylight in through the uncovered windows of Bill and Katrin's spare room. She had been so exhausted by the time she'd got the twins back to sleep last night, and a distraught Frida settled in the snug, that she hadn't even paused to draw the curtains before she had dropped into bed, still fully clothed. She'd fallen deep, quickly, but, even as she slept, her mind had roved endlessly, busy with dreams and distant memories and half-remembered conversations.

Just give it a couple of weeks. Those had been Katrin's words, that day of the terrible lunch at Tino's, when Diana Bayo had arrived, reawakening the nightmares of the past. Why must these women pick away so? What kind of masochism compelled them to keep opening their own wounds, to prod and poke and feel the pain all over again? That day, she really had been ready to go; she'd made up her mind – she'd begun packing her bags, for heaven's sake. But no, along came Katrin again, her Achilles' heel, the one person who could persuade her into staying, so pathetically grateful was she to feel part of her family.

If only she'd gone with her instincts; if only she'd simply left, there and then. If she had, perhaps the chain of events would have been broken and Katrin wouldn't be lying in a hospital bed, close to death, and those darling children downstairs wouldn't be waking to a house absent of their mother.

I'll go tonight, she concludes. *Once Bill is back home with the boys, I'll pack a bag and tell him I'm off for a fortnight to visit an old friend, and then I just won't come back. They'll soon forget me, and me them*, she thinks, though of the latter she's not entirely sure. She had, not so long ago, allowed herself to believe these beautiful people would remain in her life forever.

Ginny eases her legs from the bed, feeling the deep ache of her age running through every limb. She tunes in to the sounds of the house, making out the light voices of Maxie and Ted on the floor below, rousing their big cousin from sleep, no doubt. With a cursory tidy-up in the mirror, Ginny centres herself and heads out into the corridor on stockinged feet.

'Frida? Is that you, darling?'

The twins appear on the landing below her, each with a croissant in hand, squealing in their excitement to find Ginny upstairs in their house at so early an hour. 'Gin-gin!' Max cries, clapping his little hands together, sending pastry flakes flying, and it is all Ginny can do to keep from folding in on herself and sobbing as the events of the night before come flooding to the front of her mind again.

Frida catches up with the pair on the stairwell, her face mascara-streaked, her hair a crazy mess, and even in her own upset her face registers the pain in Ginny's. 'Come on, boys,' she says, herding them back down the steps like naughty puppies, 'we'll put the kettle on for Auntie Ginny, shall we? Make her a cup of tea?'

'Coffee, please, darling,' Ginny replies gratefully, and she follows them down to the kitchen, and allows Frida to wait on her while she takes a stool at the breakfast bar and tries to make sense of this new world she finds herself in. It feels so wrong to be here without Katrin or Bill present; and it is unthinkable that Katrin might never return.

'Have you spoken to your stepdad yet this morning?' she asks Frida. 'Does anyone have news yet – from the hospital?'

Frida is pouring hot water into a mug, a triangle of toast poking from one side of her mouth while she stirs. She drops the toast on to her plate with a bob of her head. It is a wonder to Ginny, the resilience of youth; last night Frida had been near-hysterical, and Ginny had begun to wonder if the girl had witnessed the fall, or been present for some part of it.

'Hugo texted me earlier,' Frida replies. 'Uncle Bill was at the hospital all night. They let him stay. But he said Auntie Kat's still asleep.'

'*Asleep?*' Ginny repeats in horror as Frida places a mug of insipid-looking coffee on the counter beside her. *Asleep* is no term to use for a grown woman at death's door; *asleep* is the kind of word etched on the gravestones of infants, like *gone too soon* or *finally at peace*.

'Oh, no,' Frida quickly replies, reading Ginny's dread. She slides on to the bar stool beside her. 'Hugo said it was a good thing – what did he say? The kind of coma the doctors put you in, just so you can recover?'

'An induced coma,' Ginny murmurs as a new image assaults her mind, of Katrin, tubed-up, machines whirring.

'He said they're keeping a really close eye on things. Apparently Mum's refusing to speak to the police – they tried last night and again today but she's pretending to be ill. Anyway, she seemed absolutely fine to me last night. Which is a bit sus, don't you think?'

Ginny takes this in, her thoughts galloping ahead. Amélie *is* an obvious suspect, if indeed the police conclude foul play. And she's got one very big motive they don't even know about. 'Yes, it is.'

'I wouldn't be surprised—' Frida starts, but Ginny raises a hand to stop her from saying something she'll regret.

'*And the baby?*' she asks, in a whisper that the twins shouldn't hear, wrapped up as they are in the DIY breakfast Frida has laid out for them on the kitchen table. Already Ted's fair hair is streaked with chocolate spread.

'Katrin's baby? Hugo says, so far, so good.'

'Oh, thank God.' *The baby is going to be fine.* Ginny brings a hand to her mouth, only now releasing the pent-up terror she's been wrestling with all night, a fear not only for Katrin, for herself even, but for that precious unborn child. She swipes a tear from her cheek, waving a dismissive hand at Frida's concern. 'No, no, I'm fine. I'm absolutely fine, darling – but what about you?' She reaches out to the girl. 'How are you feeling this morning? Such a terrible shock, Frida – you should never have had to find her like that – for you to think she was, she was—'

Now Frida, up until this point so together, so strong, collapses into spontaneous tears. 'I thought she was dead,' she sobs into Ginny's shoulder. 'I thought she was dead. *I thought she was dead,*' over and over, as though saying it will secure the fact that she's not, that, with hope, she's going to be alright.

'There, there,' Ginny soothes, despising the girl's mother all over again. Last night, after the police had gone, Ginny and the twins had walked Frida home to No.1, only for Hugo to tell them that Amélie was in a bit of a state, and ask could Frida stay with them

232

at Starling House? *Amélie* was in a bit of a state? *Amélie?* It was only the girl's silence on the matter that showed Ginny just how crushed she had felt, to be sent away from the family home all over again, and after witnessing something as traumatic as that. Some people didn't deserve children. The woman was a disgrace.

'I don't want you to worry about a thing, darling,' Ginny says, drawing away now to look at Frida directly. 'You can stay with me and the boys for as long as you like, OK? While things are up in the air with Katrin and Bill. We'll make a funny little family between us, but a family we'll make, agreed?'

She kisses Frida in the centre of her forehead, and they allow themselves to smile and let the tears run for a few private moments together. This is one of those heart-over-head moments Katrin so often talks of, Ginny recognises. Her head is screaming at her to leave this place, to get out while her secrets are intact. But her heart, it would seem, is stronger, after all. Because how could she leave now? How can she, with a clear conscience, just walk away from this unparented girl, from Katrin and this family, at a time like this?

'Thank you, Ginny,' Frida says, wiping her face on a tea towel as the doorbell rings out and they break apart.

Ginny watches her sprint into the front hall, all limbs, and her heart sinks. *You wouldn't thank me if you knew the truth about me,* she thinks. *If you knew the truth, darling girl, you wouldn't want a thing to do with me.*

Anne Ashbourne bustles into the kitchen, radiating the infectious kind of stress that women like Anne run on. Even in her own anxious state, Ginny is immediately irritated by the woman.

'Oh, Ginny! Have I called too early? I'm sorry – *sorry.* I barely slept, did you? I waited as long as I could, and I know it's only just gone eight, but there are police everywhere and I thought you might all be up early too, what with Katrin and everything. I just, I just needed to see someone – it's just so, *so* upsetting.' She stops for a breath, her face a desperate portrait of grief, and glances apologetically at Frida. 'Do we know yet – will she be OK?'

Anne hovers expectantly, round-shouldered, hands briskly rubbing her own upper arms like a Dickensian character, Ginny thinks; like the Ghost of The Starlings Past. Anyone would think it was *her* best friend who'd fallen down those steps last night, the way she's wincing and sighing. How dare she come round here looking for information so soon, when none of those closest to Katrin know how this is going to play out?

'Bill's still at the hospital,' Ginny replies curtly, putting the island unit between her and Anne, and busying herself at the counter. 'We'll know more when he gets home.'

Beyond the glass doors to the garden, Frida is now kicking a ball around with Max and Ted, who are still dressed in their matching onesies which drag at their ankles, damp with dew. Ginny gazes after them, her nerves racing with guilt and fear, and she wonders how on earth Bill will tell them if the worst really does happen. If Katrin doesn't make it.

'I thought you were taking your mother back to the nursing home this morning,' Ginny says.

'Oh. Oh, yes, well, I decided it was best to take her back last night in the end. After we left—' she blinks at Ginny uncertainly '—after the party, Mum just wouldn't settle, kept getting out of bed and making a fuss. She doesn't mean to, it's the dementia – sometimes she forgets whether it's night or day.' There was no doubt that the woman's condition was getting worse; she hadn't recognised Ginny at all throughout the party, and for the most part she'd sat quietly with Anne, vacantly pushing a sandwich around her plate. 'She knocked her water glass off the bedstand three times in a row, just to get my attention.'

Ginny nods, trying not to show her annoyance at the way in which Anne describes every tiny event in her life in the minutest of irrelevant detail. She looks up after a moment's silence and realises the woman is trying to gather courage to speak of something.

'What on earth was she doing up there?' she asks finally. 'In the clocktower of all places?'

Ginny shakes her head. 'It's an absolute mystery to me – and it seems no one saw her at all after she left the courtyard.'

'But that's the thing, Ginny – I *did* see Katrin last night.'

Ginny looks up with a start.

'My bedroom window looks straight across the lawns, you know?' Anne continues. 'Towards, well, here – Starling House.' She seems to be waiting for Ginny to give her a sign of encouragement.

'Go on,' Ginny says, impatiently placing her folded tea towel on the counter.

'It's just, she looked quite frantic – rushing across the green on her own, and then, well – she stood for a while looking towards Starling House, and . . .'

'And what, Anne?'

'Well, that's it, really. It was just strange. I went outside to check on her a few minutes later, but she'd gone. I assumed she'd gone home as all the lights were on over here, but – well, I just wanted to tell someone. I feel terrible about it all.'

'What have you got to feel terrible about?' Ginny asks.

'Oh, I don't know, I can't help feeling I might have stopped her going up into the clocktower if I'd gone out sooner, if I'd talked to her. Because she was obviously in a bit of a state. But Mum was getting herself worked up, saying she could see the governor outside her window—'

'The – the *governor*?' Ginny stammers.

'I know, it's so upsetting, isn't it? I think perhaps I oughtn't to bring her back here any more – I think it triggers too much of the past, even now.'

Blood rising, Ginny snatches up the towel and returns it to its hook, before striding ahead of Anne towards the entrance hall. 'There's nothing you could have done, Anne. OK? If the police ask, just tell them the truth, that you saw her heading home, alone. Yes?'

'Should I mention the, you know—' Anne lowers her voice. 'The *affair*?'

Ginny casts a warning glance over her shoulder and reaches for the door, lowering her voice. 'Do as you see fit, Anne.'

'And you know our ITV appearance is scheduled for Wednesday?' Anne says, stalling her departure. 'The television appeal for Highcap mothers?'

Ginny stares at her, wide-eyed.

'Diana Lambley was on the phone this morning, wanting to confirm arrangements, and I had to tell her the terrible news. Of course, Katrin won't be able to join us now, but Diana wants to go ahead.'

'And do you think Katrin would want you to go ahead without her?' Ginny asks, coolly.

Anne's eyes fill with tears. 'Yes, I think she would,' she replies, giving Ginny exactly the opposite answer to the one she had hoped for.

Ginny opens the front door for Anne, and she is startled to find a uniformed police officer on the doorstep, arm raised, poised to knock. Anne gives a little gasp and pushes her spectacles up the bridge of her nose. Beyond the officer, across the lawns, two other unknown figures move about while the yellow tape of the crime scene flutters in the coastal breeze.

'Now, Anne, I don't want you to worry about Katrin,' Ginny says with purpose, before she's even acknowledged the serious-faced man on the doorstep. 'I'll let you know as soon as we hear anything.' And with that she gives Anne a little rub on the shoulder and waves her away.

'Good morning,' the officer says as Ginny turns to him with a welcoming smile that isn't returned. He looks at his notebook. 'Are you Mrs LeFever?'

'LeFEVre,' she replies. 'And it's Ms.'

'*Msss*,' he says deliberately, unimpressed. 'The DS wanted me to stop by and tell you that Mr Gold will be at the station until eleven or twelve, to go over his statement.'

Ginny nods blankly, aware of Frida's presence close behind her in the hall. 'Are we talking about Bill or Hugo?'

'Er, William,' the officer replies, checking his notes. 'The victim's husband. You're looking after the children, I think?' He gestures towards the house with his pen. 'Well, DS Samson said I should stop by and let you know. And also to say, can you come in and go over your statement later this afternoon too, about five?'

'Me?' Ginny smiles, masking her nerves. 'I'm sure I've got nothing to add to what Bill's already told them. Did the DS say why?'

Now the officer smiles, but there's no warmth in it. 'Purely routine. We're interviewing everyone who was around Katrin last night, anyone who was away from the party when the accident happened.'

'But I wasn't—' she begins to say, but the officer cuts her off.

'Five o'clock, then?' He tilts his head to see past her now, one eyebrow cocked, and Frida steps out of the shadows. 'I don't suppose you're Frida Pascal, by any chance?'

She nods.

'Excellent, two birds with one stone!' His demeanour has brightened up no end with the appearance of the pretty young thing in her shorty pyjamas. *She's sixteen*, Ginny wants to hiss in the officer's face. *She's a child.* 'I've just spoken to your stepdad,' he continues. 'And he's agreed to take you down to the station to go over your statement at twelve, OK?' He waits for an answer, his eyes restlessly roaming up and down the length of her.

'OK,' Frida says, flatly, crossing her arms over her chest and stepping back inside, out of view.

As the officer turns to walk away, Ginny notices another man in overalls up a ladder at the near end of the East Wing.

'Is he anything to do with you?' she calls out, pointing in the workman's direction.

The officer slides his notebook into his pocket. 'CCTV engineer. We're checking all the footage from last night. You've got reasonable coverage here, by the look of things. With any luck, *Ms* LeFevre, we'll get to the bottom of this in no time at all.'

Ginny retreats inside the house and leans heavily against the closed door, her heart hammering. She can't just let this all play out, can she? She needs to act, not just for her own sake, but for the sake of the others too.

A couple of hours later, Ginny walks Frida over to No.1 with the boys in tow, where a sleep-deprived Hugo greets them at the door.

He looks relieved to see them, and after hugging Frida he scoops up his two nephews, one on each arm, and leans in to kiss Ginny on either cheek. The boys giggle and make squishy kissing noises, and Hugo, smiling at last, sends Frida off to get them a treat from the freezer.

He leads the way into the living room. 'Bill should be back soon,' he says, with a shake of his head. 'God, Ginny, what a – excuse my French – fucking nightmare this all is. I can't stop thinking about Katrin. I can't get the image of her lying there out of my mind.' He gestures for her to sit on the sofa opposite.

'I know, darling,' Ginny says, brushing lint from her trousers, grateful that Hugo is too distressed to notice her shabby appearance. She hasn't even fixed her face this morning. 'The boys have been asking after their mother since they woke up at six. I've told them she's at work, but they're not buying it – there was a bit of a meltdown when I didn't prepare their Weetabix the right way, and Max is refusing to eat anything else. I just hope Katrin wakes up soon so we can at least take them in to visit her and explain it all properly.' She pauses a moment, taking in Hugo's shock. 'Hugo, they want to interview me this afternoon,' she says, trying to keep the nerves from her voice, 'because apparently I left the party for a minute or two,'

'Did you?' Hugo asks with a frown. 'I don't remember, Gin. I mean, we were all a bit blotto by then, weren't we?'

'All but Katrin,' Ginny replies, sadly. She casts her eyes around the room. 'Where's Amélie? And baby Henri?'

Hugo rolls his neck out. 'Upstairs,' he says after a pause, and there's a weariness in his reply. 'You know, the police want to interview her too, but she's refusing to come down, or to let anyone up to see her. She's asked me to get a doctor to come out, but she doesn't seem to understand that you've got to be near death to get a home visit these days.' He grimaces at his choice of words.

'What's wrong with her?' Ginny asks.

'Bladder infection, she *says*.'

'Is she aware of what Frida went through last night?' Ginny can't keep the incredulity from her voice. 'She actually thought her aunt was dead, that she'd discovered her *body* – right up until they took Katrin away in the ambulance. She was beside herself when I put her to bed, absolutely heartbroken. Has Amélie asked after her at all?'

Hugo looks down at his hands and doesn't reply.

'Right, I'm going up to see her,' Ginny declares suddenly, snatching up her bag and standing. Hugo seems to consider objecting, but lets it go, and before she has a chance to change her mind, Ginny is halfway up the stairs and on her way to Amélie's bedroom.

After trying a few wrong doors, Ginny enters what must be Amélie's dressing room, a walnut-lined double room, wall-to-wall with wardrobes and mirrors and slide-out drawers housing more shoes and accessories than a fully stocked Knightsbridge boutique. There's something unsettling about the excess of the room, which is a reminder of Ginny's stepmother, a woman she probably only met a handful of times, but one who left a deep and lasting impression on the young Virginia.

Ginny casts her eyes about the room and is drawn to Amélie's make-up drawer, left open to display the chaos within. Old tissues lie balled up beside gleaming Lancôme lipsticks and Nars shadow compacts, in a drawer that must contain thousands of pounds' worth of products. Without hesitation, Ginny reaches into her bag and stuffs a small item to the back of the drawer, covering it over with cosmetics. As she goes to push the drawer shut, she spots the little stack of paper wraps tucked into the nearside corner, and she lifts one out, laying it on the dresser top to gently unfold the corners and reveal the white powder within.

Calmly, she refolds the tiny paper envelope, arranges a couple more beside the vanity mirror, and returns downstairs without even stopping to look in on Frida's mother. In the lounge, Hugo is still sitting on the sofa alone, the sound of the children's voices safely distant.

'Is Amélie breastfeeding?' Ginny asks, in a low voice.

Hugo's brow wrinkles. 'Yes . . .?'

She leans in and drops the cocaine wrap on the glass coffee table before him. 'Well, she really ought not to, darling,' she says gently. 'I wasn't snooping,' she lies, 'but there's more of it up there, in plain view on her dressing table, where anyone could find it.'

Mutely, Hugo picks up the wrap and heads directly for the downstairs bathroom where he flushes it away, with not a single word said on the matter. His manner is neither angry nor upset. It's simply defeated.

Following him into the hallway, Ginny calls out to Max and Ted. 'Boys! Time to go! Uncle Hugo and Frida need to go out now!' She opens the front door as the twins bomb through the house and out on to the front path, wielding small sticks as weapons. Ginny hugs Frida and Hugo in turn. 'Just tell them everything as you remember it, and you'll be fine,' she says to Frida.

Hugo drapes an arm over his stepdaughter's shoulder and watches as Ginny and the boys head along the path towards Starling House. 'Thank you,' he mouths silently over Frida's head, when Ginny turns to wave.

And, with that one small gesture of gratitude, Ginny is reassured that her actions are entirely reasonable. No one in this family would miss Amélie.

28. DS Ali Samson

After Bill Gold has left the station, PC Bloom checks in from The Starlings, confirming he's caught up with Ginny LeFevre at Starling House, and that she'll be attending the station at five, as requested.

Ali is curious as to why the woman omitted to tell them she'd also been away from the courtyard during the period Katrin was missing. These cases are always made so much more complicated when alcohol is involved, where lies can be so easily passed off as drunken amnesia, or inaccurate accounts mistaken as deceit.

Sitting at her desk, Ali gazes across the office, running over last night's scene in her mind's eye, recalling each detail like a series of snapshots. There's Katrin Gold's lifeless-looking body at the foot of the clocktower steps, lit up beneath hastily erected floodlights, unmistakably pregnant, robed in shimmering silk. Across the central green, the neighbourhood gathers in shock as the last of the evening's starlings come to roost in the attic space overhead. Beyond the lawns, there's Katrin's husband Bill, in outline, watching from the window of his own glass tower, while the rest of the family huddle outside No.1, emergency lights illuminating their haunted features, as the sea breeze picks up and the officers seal off the crime scene. Yellow tape flaps noisily. An elderly woman watches sorrowfully from a ground-floor window, her palm pressed to the glass. Hugo, Frida, Ginny LeFevre. Belinda Parsons and her daughter Poppy, a shawl about her shoulders. And then, as residents are slowly persuaded back indoors, the lawns are lit up by the spinning lights of the ambulance, as the driver readies to tear through the night, sirens screaming, in the hope of saving Katrin Gold.

In all of these snapshots, there is no sign of the sister-in-law, Amélie Pascal, who is still avoiding police questions, according to Bloom. Unwell, awaiting a doctor, her husband claims. Of course, they have no reason to suspect Amélie Pascal in any way, but it seems odd, to check out so completely in the face of a family emergency of this kind.

Ali will ask Hugo Gold herself shortly, when he gets here with his stepdaughter, and you never know, she may uncover any number of other incidental snippets of information while she's at it. Hugo's account was one of the few straightforward ones from the evening, as several people quickly confirmed that he'd remained in the courtyard for the entire duration of the time Katrin was absent, but that doesn't mean he doesn't hold something of significance not yet mentioned, no matter how small.

With its shrill ring, the phone on the desk startles Ali, and in her haste to answer she sends a cup of water flying.

'*Shit*,' she curses as she picks up the receiver. 'DS Samson?'

It's the front desk. 'Frida Pascal and Hugo Gold to see you, sarge.'

'On my way down,' she replies briskly. Upending a box of tissues, Ali Samson blots up the mess and heads to meet her next interviewee: Frida Pascal, aged sixteen, niece of the victim and primary witness.

Hugo Gold, in the clear light of day, appears to be a good decade younger than his brother, and in Ali's opinion a whole lot less arrogant. For starters, he seems to be far more anxious about everyone else, asking the questions you'd hope a worried relative might. Bill, in contrast had given Ali the impression of a man wallowing in his own shock, perhaps more concerned to present well to onlookers than to move the investigation forward. The DI hadn't been keen on him either, and, for all Trelawney's shortcomings, Ali respects his judgment.

In the interview room, one of the team has already laid out a couple of cans of drink and a few snacks, and rearranged the chairs into a more informal setting, with the table moved to one side.

'I wasn't sure if you'd be hungry, Frida,' Ali says as Hugo and his stepdaughter take their seats, and Trelawney joins them. 'Feel free to help yourself. Mr Gold – are you happy for me to call you Hugo?'

DI Trelawney sits heavily in his chair and leans on to his knees to go through the preliminary 'nothing to worry about' intro. Frida and her stepdad sit close together, her hand in his, and already she looks like a trapped animal, fearing the worst, desperate to leave.

'Before we start, I must ask, Hugo,' Ali says, 'how's your wife doing? I hear she's unwell. You've got a young baby, haven't you?'

Hugo shifts uncomfortably, while beside him Frida lowers her gaze. What's that in her expression? Embarrassment? Shame?

'She's got an infection,' he replies. 'It's pretty exhausting having a new baby in the house.'

Ali nods, letting a pause hang between them for a second or two. 'We were hoping to speak with her today, as she was one of the last at the party – one of the last to see Katrin before the accident.'

'Do you think it was an accident, then?' Frida asks, now alert.

'We're not sure,' Trelawney replies. 'Hence all these tedious interviews.' He smiles at the nervous girl, with a roll of his eyes, and Ali Samson likes him a little more. 'We'll know once we've spoken to everyone who was there.'

Frida extracts her hand from Hugo's to gnaw at the corner of her thumbnail. She glances at him, almost furtively, before asking, 'Is Amélie really that ill?'

Amélie, Ali notes. Not Mum.

Hugo is evidently thrown by the question, because he breaks into a wide smile, and Ali can immediately see the striking resemblance between him and his brother. 'Well, she hasn't left her bed since last night, so I'd say yes.'

'She seemed fine the last time I saw her.'

Ali sits forward and reaches for the M&Ms, opening the packet and popping one in her mouth, offering them around before setting it down on the empty chair beside Frida. 'When did you last see your mum?'

At this question, Frida sits more upright, her eyes scanning the floor between them as though searching for the right answer, the best answer. 'Last night, when she checked on Henri. When I was babysitting.'

'Henri's your baby brother? You were looking after him and the twins, at your Auntie Katrin's house?'

Frida nods.

'They're lucky to have you on hand, for babysitting duties,' Ali says, smiling at Hugo. 'I hope your stepdad's paying the going rate.'

Hugo laughs; Frida makes wide eyes. 'As *if*.' She helps herself to an M&M.

'So, what time would that have been, Frida? When your mum popped back to Starling House to check on Henri?'

Frida looks startled again, and Ali worries she's pushed her too soon. She's clearly still skittish after the events of last night.

'Was it before or after your Uncle Bill came back to check on the twins?'

Frida opens her mouth to reply; closes it again, her eyes moving restlessly across the lino floor. 'Before,' she replies, decisively. 'But I wasn't really keeping track of the time.'

'That's fair enough,' Trelawney says. 'It had been a long day, hadn't it? I understand the party started at midday – you must've been tired by then.'

She bites her lip. 'Henri took ages to settle, but I know he was asleep by the time Mum came back to check.'

Trelawney smiles encouragingly. 'Maybe your mum texted you to say she was on her way over?' It was a good line of questioning; young people marked the passing of time by their technology these days, like early humans used the sun.

Frida shook her head.

'Or anyone else – if you sent or received any other messages, it could give you a time stamp, if you can remember whether it was before or after your mum's visit.'

'I didn't get any. I wasn't really on my phone that much last night. I didn't get any messages.'

'None?' Hugo asks, nudging her lightly. 'Really? You're always messaging someone on that bloody phone.'

'Well, I wasn't last night,' she replies, avoiding his gaze.

There's something she's not saying.

'OK, let's try it another way. How about we work backwards from the moment you found your Auntie Kat? Maybe we can build up a timeline that way? That's all we're trying to do here, Frida – build up a set of timelines to see if everyone's recollection matches. That way, any gaps or differences will show up, and might give us an idea of what happened to cause Katrin's fall. We're not here to trick anyone. OK?'

Frida glances again at her stepdad. 'OK.'

'Right,' Ali starts. 'At 8.55pm, you sounded the alarm – that's when you found Katrin. Where had you been directly beforehand?'

'Um. The beach.'

'OK – with a friend?'

'On my own.'

'How long were you there for?'

'Maybe half an hour? Mum told me to have a break while she stayed with the boys for a bit, and I didn't want to be too long, so I just went down to the beach. I do that sometimes, just for, you know, a bit of time on my own.'

'So, you went to the beach, alone, before Uncle Bill arrived?'

'Er, no.' She blinks hard, once, twice. 'I mean *Uncle Bill* told me to have a break. That's it. Mum went back to the party, then Uncle Bill came, then I went off for a break.'

Ali lets the discrepancy hang in the room for a second or two.

'Tell you what, let's use the time your Uncle Bill gave us, shall we?' Ali checks back through her notes. 'Your Uncle Bill reckons he left the party at 7.50pm to check on the kids – let's call it 7.55pm by the time he gets to you. And you recall his arrival being after your mum had come and gone from checking on Henri.'

Frida nods.

'Now, after you'd left, did you go back to Starling House at all in the time before you found your aunt?'

'No.'

'Hmm, that's odd.' Ali muses. 'Bill's timeline says he got back to the courtyard at 8.20pm. If you didn't go back in between,

Frida, that would mean the kids were on their own for the next half-hour or so. Wouldn't it?'

'That can't be right,' Hugo interjects, but DI Trelawney raises a warning hand, and he sits back in his seat.

Frida looks panic-stricken. 'Oh,' she murmurs, pulling at her bottom lip. 'Oh, maybe Amélie – Mum – came back again.'

'I thought you said you were there, at Starling House, when you last saw your mum?'

'Yes. Yes. *Sorry*. Mum came back again so I could to the party for a bit.'

'Another break?' Trelawney asks. 'Let me get this straight. First your mum came back to check on your baby brother. Then your mum left, after which Uncle Bill arrived to check on his boys, and you went to the beach. Once he left, your mum arrived back again, and at that point you went off to join the party?'

Frida nods slowly. 'Yup, that's it. But I never made it to the party.'

'Did anyone see you leaving Starling House?'

'No,' she replies quickly. 'I don't think so. I used the back door.'

Hugo is silently frowning in his seat, clearly desperate to ask a few questions of his own.

'I had some table fireworks I wanted to light for Auntie Kat,' Frida replies. 'And Mum said she was probably going to turn in for the night soon anyway.'

'Did she?' Hugo asks. 'I don't remember that.'

'But you do remember her going to see to Henri?' Trelawney asks, and Hugo nods, slowly, thoughtfully.

'I do. Yes. But I seem to recall she was planning to fetch more champagne while she was at it . . .' He trails off, shaking his head. 'I think you need to ask her yourself.'

'I think we do,' Trelawney replies with a meaningful nod.

Ali doesn't want to lose Frida's focus. 'Now, Frida, on those two occasions when you were out on the beach, and around the courtyard on your way back to the party, did you see anything unusual, or anyone behaving suspiciously?'

She shakes her head. 'There were still a few people around, but not many. It just seemed normal. Oh, except for the clocktower. I saw lights behind the clockface, and I thought maybe Auntie Kat had lit it up especially for the party.'

'Lights? What time was this?' Ali asks, sitting forward in her seat. 'The first time you left the house, or the second?'

'The first. I noticed it when I was coming from the beach, from a distance, you know? It was dim, but you could definitely see a glow behind the clockface, which isn't normal.'

'And the doors below?'

'I wasn't near enough to notice. But later, when I found Auntie Kat, they were open – like how you saw it, with Auntie Kat l-lying there.' Now, Frida stutters, covering her face with her hands, and her shoulders shake uncontrollably.

Hugo draws her to him as Ali passes over a box of tissues. She glances at Trelawney, a silent request that they wrap it up.

'You've done brilliantly, Frida. I mean it – well done. Now one final question, and then we'll let you go.'

Wiping her face and breathing out through trembling lips, Frida sits up again. She's not putting this on, it's clear. She's torn apart by what's happened to her aunt.

'Do you know anyone – anyone at all – who might want to hurt your Auntie Kat?'

For a second, Frida's mouth falls open. She turns to look at her stepdad, who is studying his own hands.

'Let's put it another way, Frida,' Trelawney says, 'does Katrin have any enemies?'

'Enemies?' Hugo repeats, incredulous.

'The question is for Frida, Mr Gold.'

Frida glances at her stepdad apologetically, before turning back to DS Ali with resolve. 'Only my mum,' she says.

'Frida!' Hugo gasps, turning in his seat to meet her gaze face-on.

'What?' she retorts angrily, wiping her nose on the bunched-up ball of damp tissue. 'It's true, Hugo, and you know it. Mum absolutely *loathes* Auntie Kat.'

29. Frida

After the interview, Hugo is anxious to get straight home to Henri, and it strikes Frida for the first time that maybe he doesn't completely trust Amélie to look after her baby brother.

'But the hospital is on the way,' Frida pleads as they cross the police car park towards the car. 'We could just go in and see Auntie Kat really quickly, and still be home in half an hour?'

But Hugo won't hear of it, and Frida wonders if it's her words that have got him spooked; her suggestion that Amélie is capable of harming others. But the truth is, Mum's been out of control for months, and it's about time Hugo faced up to it. She just feels sick with guilt that she was the one who had to say it out loud.

They reach the car and face each other beneath a darkening sky.

'Listen, why don't you go with Ginny later?' Hugo suggests. 'She said she was planning to stop at the hospital on her way to give her statement this afternoon. I've already said I'd mind the boys to let Bill catch up on his sleep.'

'Don't *you* want to see Auntie Kat?' Frida asks, slapping the roof of his precious Audi in a last attempt to get him to change his mind. 'I thought you "love her like a sister"?' she adds sarcastically, mimicking words she's heard him use in recent weeks, in response to another of Amélie's jealous rants.

He sighs heavily and takes his seat behind the wheel, turning to regard her sadly. 'She's in a coma, sweetheart. She won't even know we're there. And, well, I'm not sure I can handle that, if I'm honest, Freeds. I'm sorry, sweetheart. You understand, don't you?' He pauses for a moment before starting the engine. 'And, lollipop, don't worry about what you said in there – about your mum being Katrin's enemy. I'm not mad at you, and I won't be repeating it to your mum.'

Frida folded her arms over her chest and forced a smile, and gazed from the window for the rest of the journey home.

Back at home, No.1 is in silence, and Frida notes the speed with which Hugo scales the stairs, two steps at a time, calling Amélie's name in a phoney light voice. The chaos of the kitchen counter shows signs that she's been out of her bedroom with Henri. Until now, Frida would never have imagined the monumental impact the arrival of a baby could have on a household. It seems that the smaller the human being, the more time and space and attention they take up. Evidence of Henri is everywhere. The island unit is covered in discarded baby items and markers of Amélie's presence: bottles and teats and rings and caps; a tin of formula powder with the lid left off; a big splash of spilled water beside a still steaming kettle; a dummy in the fruit bowl (or a 'pacifier' as Amélie says, which makes it sound only slightly less icky). A silk sleep mask hooked on the back of a bar stool; an empty bottle of prescription tablets, again, lid off; a half-drunk mug of black coffee and an iPad left open on the Jo Malone home fragrance page. It's as though Amélie has sprinted away the second Hugo put the key in the front door; everything appears abandoned, and it is both normal and tragic to Frida to come home to a house like this, to feel so little a part of a family.

As her eyes rest on that open bottle of pills, an uninvited thought pops into her mind, confirming what she already knows about herself: that she is a bad, bad person. *Why doesn't Amélie just get on with it, and spare them all?* She imagines Hugo standing at the side of the four-poster bed upstairs, checking Amélie's pulse and finding none. Henri is there too, in his cot, peacefully sleeping, oblivious. Hugo doesn't know what to do, and so Frida is the one who calls the ambulance, but when it arrives it is too late, and together they must make the best of life without her, without Amélie—

Frida is suddenly ferociously hungry. On inspection, other than a couple of bottles of champagne and a large tray of unrecognisable cheeses the fridge is empty, and, when she thinks about it, she can't remember the last time it was full. She heads back towards the front door and stands at the foot of the stairs, tuning in to the raised voices overhead, and the fragile wail of baby Henri, caught between the warring adults. *That poor baby*, Frida thinks. *What will become of poor baby Henri?*

She picks up her bag and opens the front door. 'I'll be over at Starling House,' she calls up, but neither of the adults upstairs hears or replies.

At four, Ginny and Frida drop the twins with Hugo, along with a stack of DVDs and the best part of a platter of homemade lasagne cooked this afternoon, after Frida had arrived, looking for food. Hugo stands in the doorway, a baby over one arm, a twin boy either side of him, his pose at once shattered and grateful.

'How's Bill?' he calls after Frida as she steps into Ginny's car.

Frida shrugs. 'I dunno. Still asleep, I guess. He's been in bed since he got back from the police station this morning. Maybe you should visit him while we're out?'

'Good idea,' Hugo replies, but Frida's not convinced he will. What is it with these grown men, that they can't even show each other support at a time like this? If Bill needed help lifting a table or changing a tyre, Hugo would be round in a shot. But an emotional problem, well, that's an ask too far, it seems. 'Maybe I'll walk the boys back round to him later, if your mum doesn't need me.'

As the car pulls away, the leaden skies seem to split open and the rain begins to fall hard against the windscreen. Fear vibrates beneath Frida's skin, and she looks back to wave at Hugo, now staring bleakly after them through the rain.

Pulling out on to the main road, Ginny turns the car stereo up high to compensate for the drumming downpour, and Frida checks her various message threads and finds nothing new since her texts with Katrin the night before. No one is thinking of Frida, her phone confirms; no one, nowhere. If I died tomorrow, who would miss me? she wonders. Would anyone cry if I had been the one they'd found at the bottom of the clocktower steps? Her mind draws up the vision of Katrin's motionless body, her pregnant shape a reminder of the fragility within, and, shuddering, Frida crosses her arms tightly over her own ribs as though doing so might save Katrin, save that unborn child. Beyond the windscreen, the rain lashes down and Frida does her best to hold back the tide of fear and horror that threatens to wash her away.

At the hospital, Ginny parks up and they dash through the rain, heading for the critical ward, where they're told that it's strictly family-only visits for Katrin Gold.

'I'm her niece,' Frida says quickly, cocking a thumb in Ginny's direction. 'And this is my granny,' she says, sensing Ginny wince at the old biddy word. 'Katrin's mum.'

'In that case, this way,' the desk nurse replies brightly, leading them down the hall. 'We had your son-in-law in earlier.' She smiles at Ginny. 'Bill. What a lovely man! Had us all quite charmed!' She halts now, outside a private room, and her face grows more serious. 'Now, you'll already know Katrin has been placed in an induced coma for the time being, so she won't be able to communicate in any way – but do feel free to chat to her as you would normally – there's some school of thought that it aids recovery. At any rate, it can't do any harm.' She opens the door and leaves them with one last sympathetic smile.

Inside, the two women stand side by side, shocked into silence. Katrin is lying on her back, neck held in a thick brace, skin sallow against the white of her bedsheets, with tubes poking out all over and machines bleeping like something out of a movie. *This isn't real, is it?* thinks Frida. *This isn't Auntie Kat lying there, looking like a wax imitation of herself – looking like a corpse.* Her arms appear thin and veinless against her sides, her usually glossy hair now flat and dull against her forehead. Most alarming of all is the prominence of her stomach, so obvious beneath hospital sheets pulled taut over her motionless body.

Ginny must be feeling it too, because Frida is suddenly aware of fingers linking with hers, and for a minute or two they linger in the doorway together, neither speaking a word. *This is all my fault*, Frida's mind kicks in again, taking her back to the events of that night. *My fault; my fault; my fault.*

As her thoughts return to the room and the reality of the present, nausea rises up in her, and she makes a bolt for the door. Hanging her head over the freshly bleached bowl of the ward toilet, she wonders, what if Auntie Kat doesn't wake up at all? What then?

30. DS Ali Samson

DS Ali Samson sets a mug of tea down on the table for her last interviewee of the day, along with a mug of strong coffee, three sugars, for DI Trelawney.

'Thanks for coming in to see us so promptly, Ginny. We won't keep you too long.'

Ginny LeFevre appears poised and warmly confident. She has the naturally platinum hair many older women pay a fortune for, and the skin of a woman at least a decade younger than her age. With her pillarbox-red lips and jauntily tied neck scarf, she reminds Ali of a fifties film star, all sharp cheekbones and equally sharp wit.

'Anything I can do at all,' she replies, crossing one leg over the other and smoothing out the expensive fabric of her trousers. Her eye contact is steady, sincere. 'I'm still in shock, if I'm honest – but of course it's nothing to what Bill's going through, or poor Katrin. Or those little boys.' At this, Ginny's manicured veneer wrinkles a little, and the affection she has for the Golds is apparent. 'They're the closest thing I have to family,' she adds.

Trelawney enters the room and pulls up his seat with an inelegant scrape. 'Sorry about the delay. Carry on, DS Samson,' he says brusquely, pressing the record button and sitting back to listen in.

'Now, in your original statement, you said you hadn't left the courtyard during the time Katrin was absent. But one of your neighbours told us you were actually gone for at least twenty or thirty minutes.'

Ginny sets her cup down with a rueful smile. 'They're completely right, of course. I did leave during that time – to fetch brandy nightcaps for those of us remaining – but at that point we didn't know Katrin was missing, or "absent", as you say. I'm sorry about the inaccuracy – entirely unintentional and completely stupid of me. I wasn't thinking straight last night at all.'

Warm self-assuredness pours off Ginny, and she's not even conscious of it – and it's that, Ali suspects, which makes her so magnetic.

'And what do you recall about the period before Katrin went off? Where was she going, do you know?'

'It's hard to be entirely clear with the order of events, sergeant, because it had been such a lovely relaxed day, and of course no one was taking note of comings and goings. I mean, there was a fair bit of drink consumed, and pretty much everyone left the area at some point.' She pauses in recollection, her fingers lingering at her throat. 'I can't give you times because I wasn't clock-watching, but what I do remember is that Amélie left the courtyard first, to check on little Henri – he's only three weeks old – and I think that prompted Katrin to suggest checking on the boys too. But Bill insisted he do it as he needed "a gentleman's detour" as he called it.' She gives a little smile at Trelawney's frown. 'He needed a pee, inspector. Anyhow, he headed off maybe five minutes after Amélie. Oh, yes, that's right – Amélie had mentioned fetching more champagne and Bill made some joke about chivvying her along while he was at it.'

257

Interesting, Ali thinks, making a note. In his statement this morning, Bill Gold had omitted to mention that he and his sister-in-law had been away from the party simultaneously. No wonder Frida had got confused about which of them had told her to take a break.

'So, Bill and Amélie were away at Starling House at the same time?' DI Trelawney asks, clearly on the same track.

She nods. 'I believe so, briefly.'

'And what was Katrin doing at this point? Did she seem happy, concerned, indifferent . . .?'

'Actually, I remember very clearly that Katrin was chatting with Poppy – Belinda Parsons' teenage daughter – and I don't know what it was about, but I must say I did notice Katrin was looking distracted.'

'Distracted? Can you explain?'

'Maybe "preoccupied" is a better description. She was checking her phone a fair bit, and her demeanour with Poppy was rather earnest, as though she was pressing her about something or other. I know it's none of my business, but I did hear a volley of alerts from Katrin's phone right before she left to check on the boys. She has these dreadful ringtones, one for texts, another for emails – all of them grating!'

'And which type was she getting that evening, would you know?' Ali asks.

'A mixture, I'd say. I only remember because it was getting on my nerves, and I called over to her to turn the damned thing off!'

'Did she?'

'Turn it off? I doubt it; she can't bear to miss a message. But anyway, right after that she decided to go and check on the kids, and I was left wondering what had got her looking so anxious.'

'You didn't think to go after her?'

'No, it was only a fleeting thought. Although I did try to tell her to leave it – to stay put. I mean, how many adults does it take to check on three children and a babysitter?' Ginny laughs lightly now, looking slightly worried. 'That's not fair of me. Of course, it's completely natural for parents to want to check in on their children. And Katrin and Bill are devoted parents.'

'Of course,' Ali agrees. 'And who did that leave in the court-yard with you?'

'OK, let's see. There was Belinda and Poppy, Graham and Dylan, the Bassetts – Joy and Michael – and of course Hugo. Anne had already taken her mother home before all this toing and froing, which was at 7.30pm because I remember her mentioning the time as they left. I think that was everyone.'

Ali is struck by Ginny's recall, far sharper than anyone else's. 'You said Bill returned to the courtyard, but not Amélie?'

'Yes. He returned perhaps half an hour after he'd left, and he was wondering where Katrin was as he hadn't seen her back at home, or passed her on the way. Very soon after, I offered to fetch those brandy nightcaps, and I said I'd have a quick look for her on my way.'

'Where did you look?' Trelawney asks.

'Well,' she says, picking up her tea mug and taking a sip, 'I started at Starling House. Amélie came to the door and told me Katrin wasn't there. She couldn't get rid of me quickly enough, to be frank. But then she's always fairly rude.'

As DI Trelawney made a note, Ali followed Ginny LeFevre's eyes taking it all in.

'And then I headed over to my own place – it's only a stone's throw – to fetch the brandy, and I tried calling her mobile while I was there. She didn't answer, so I put my phone away, fetched the bottle and a tray of glasses, visited the cloakroom to powder my nose, and returned to the party. I can't have been gone more than twenty minutes. I was back in the courtyard, handing out drinks by, well, it must have been a quarter to nine.'

'You weren't worried about Katrin by this point?'

'Not at all, why would I be? The Starlings is renowned for being one of the safest places to live. I just thought we must have missed each other and that she'd turn up any moment. But I didn't really get a chance to worry, did I? Because only minutes later, we were all up on our feet and running to see what poor Frida was screaming about.'

Ali lays down her pen. 'Your account is so helpful, Ginny,' she says. 'Really good. One thing we do now know is that an anonymous call came into Emergency Services at exactly 8.34pm – a full twenty-one minutes before Frida found Katrin. That means the doors to the clocktower were already open by the time you returned to the courtyard, and Katrin would have already been lying there – surely you would have noticed such a scene as you passed?'

'Goodness,' Ginny murmurs. 'Goodness, yes – if only I *had* walked that way. But you see, there's a perimeter path around the edge of the estate – you'll have seen it when you've driven in. I very often come and go via my back door rather than the front, and that's what I did that night on my way back to the courtyard.'

'Even though it's the longer way round?' Trelawney probes. 'Across the green is certainly shorter.'

'I don't suppose I was really thinking about the shortest route so much as the simplest. My kitchen is at the rear, and I was laden down with my drinks tray – so it would have just made sense for me to leave through the back.'

'I understand you and Katrin are very close friends,' Ali says. 'Is there anyone you can think of who she might have fallen out with last night?'

Ginny flexes one hand, and she studies her neat fingernails, one eyebrow slowly arching. 'Well, there is . . .' She looks up now, between the two officers and pulls a tight smile, a tiny shake of her head. 'No, no, I don't think – no.'

'You looked like you were about to suggest someone there, Ginny?' Ali presses.

'It's silly, really.' Pause. 'OK – but don't quote me on this, because it's completely ridiculous. But I was thinking of Katrin's sister-in-law, Amélie. She's a terribly jealous woman, and she's been up and down ever since she announced her pregnancy, and I know she and Katrin are far from friends. But that doesn't mean . . .' She blinks hard. 'Look, I really don't think she'd do anything, but of course her addiction *does* make her rather unpredictable.'

DI Trelawney inclines his head. 'Addiction?'

'Oh, yes, inspector. From what I hear, she's been in and out of The Priory a few times. Cocaine, I think. And depression. Gosh, I hope I haven't spoken out of turn – I'd hate to cause anyone unnecessary trouble – or to ruin my relationship with Hugo and the rest of the family, for that matter.' Her hand returns shakily to her throat.

'I promise we'll be discreet in our investigations, Ginny,' says Ali. 'But that is useful to know.'

'I'd just like to go back to that anonymous call, if we may,' Trelawney interrupts. 'One of our officers spoke with the call-handler this morning.'

Ginny LeFevre nods gravely.

'He said that the line was poor, and that, while he initially took the caller to be female, on reflection it could just as easily have been male.'

'Male?' Ginny repeats, aghast. 'You're not suggesting Bill—'

'No, I wasn't suggesting that,' DI Trelawney replies, exchanging a glance with Ali, 'but it's interesting that you are.'

'I'm doing no such thing!' she protests. 'Katrin and Bill are one of the happiest couples I know. Katrin would be mortified if she heard you suggest Bill was involved. In fact, she'd laugh. I mean – no – no, it's impossible. He's devoted to her.'

'*Oh-kay,*' Trelawney says with a that-told-me tone. 'So, no marital problems that you're aware of?'

'Not at all.' Her words are firm, but Ali notices that Ginny seems unable to make eye contact as she delivers them.

Trelawney rubs his jawline, looking unconvinced. 'No affairs, that you've heard of, then? It's just that one of the neighbours made a comment that got us wondering.'

This time, Ginny doesn't reply, not even to ask what that comment might have been.

'Of course, you and Bill Gold were the first on the scene, once Frida raised the alarm,' Ali says, moving the interview on before they lose her. 'You didn't happen to notice Katrin's mobile phone in the area?'

'No, why? Is it important?'

'Didn't we mention that?' Ali says, looking up from her notebook. 'This anonymous phone call to emergency services – well, we traced the caller's ID, only to find that it came from Katrin's own mobile phone – which at this point has still not been found.'

'No! You mean – it wasn't an accident? I can't . . .' Ginny shakes her head, as though the whole scenario is incomprehensible. 'Are you saying,' she murmurs as her eyes scan the wall opposite, 'that the person who made that phone call is responsible for Katrin's fall?'

'It's possible.' DS Samson nods, and with that thought she calls the interview to an end.

Trelawney offers to walk Ginny LeFevre out, and Ali agrees gratefully, glad that this long, intense day is finally at an end.

But, just as Ginny is leaving the stuffy interview room, she halts in the doorway and turns back with a bright smile.

'Oh, darling, I meant to ask you,' she says, one hand resting on the door frame, handbag hooked over her arm, looking every bit like a 1950s catalogue model. 'What did you have?'

'What did I have?' Ali replies, flashing eyes at DI Trelawney.

'Yes! Boy or girl?'

For a long, horrible moment, from her low position at the interview table, Ali can only stare back up at the woman. 'Oh,' she finally says, her hands suddenly icy cold. 'I didn't.'

And at that the DI clears his throat and escorts Ms LeFevre away. In the distance, Ali can make out what she assumes to be the hushed words of Trelawney's explanation, followed by an outpouring of apology from the woman. *Oh, my, that poor girl,* she says. *My goodness, will you apologise for me, inspector? I'm so sorry.*

By the time Trelawney returns, Ali is back at her own desk, where she has returned her expression to one of neutral professionalism. 'I'll check in with that other neighbour in the morning,' she says. 'Ref the rumours of an affair.'

'And we need that bloody sister-in-law's statement, pronto,' Trelawney replies, 'even if it means you have to camp out on her doorstep to get it. We've heard from both Ginny LeFevre and Amélie Gold's own daughter that she had issues with Katrin – and this addiction story adds a whole new dimension in my book.'

'Agreed,' Ali says, making notes. 'And I'll get on to the technical department first thing Tuesday, to see if they've had any luck tracing the location of Katrin's phone. They said it would take no more than forty-eight hours.'

Trelawney locks eyes with her now, and she knows he is thinking about asking if she's OK. 'What did you make of Ginny

LeFevre?' he asks her instead, and she is grateful that he is at least sensitive enough to recognise that, for now at least, the topic is off-limits.

'I think she was charming and articulate. She's obviously a popular resident, and very close to – very loyal to – the Gold family. But I also think she seemed fairly keen to cast the finger of suspicion around her fellow neighbours, however obliquely,' Ali adds.

'Agreed,' Trelawney concurs, giving the desk a short rap with his knuckles as he heads back to his office. 'Until we can confidently discount her, Ginny LeFevre is a suspect.'

31. Ginny

Up on the top floor of Starling House, Ginny looks out across the green, watching her neighbours go about their business, almost as though the weekend's events had never occurred at all.

It's Tuesday, and, other than those with children young enough to be home for the half-term holidays, life has returned to the everyday. For Ginny and the Gold family, a temporary kind of normal has descended, as today Bill rose at seven and showered, while, sensitive to his unspoken need for quiet, Ginny pressed a hearty breakfast on him, and kept the boys entertained in the TV room. Last night, Bill had explained to them that Mummy was in hospital for a few days, for a rest, and that she'd be back soon. Resilient as they are, the boys took the news in their stride, apart from a few tears from Ted at bedtime when he realised Mummy wouldn't be tucking him in. This whole awful business has unsettled Bill more profoundly than one might have imagined it would, and, despite his recent poor behaviour, his devotion to Katrin is clear, and Ginny's opinion of him is recovering.

Once Bill had set off for the hospital, she had dressed Max and Ted in much the same way as Katrin would any other day of the working week and delivered them to their kindergarten for what she hoped would be a day of relative normality.

Now, she is alone with her thoughts, and as she stands here high above The Starlings she replays pieces of her police interview from Sunday evening, worrying over the details she'd shared. The detectives had seemed especially interested in the ins and outs of Bill and Katrin's relationship, and Ginny wonders which of the neighbours it was who tipped them off about the fractures within the marriage. If Ginny was a betting woman, she'd put her money on Anne Ashbourne. Mind you, any number of the other residents could have heard about Bill's extramarital affairs on the neighbourhood grapevine by now. She supposed it could have been busybody Joy, or perhaps Belinda Parsons, who always seems to know what everyone else is up to on the close. Or one of the men, jealous of another man's conquests – Hugo even? Ginny sighs sadly at the mess of it all.

Overhead, the gulls are circling noisily, as they do when the fishing boats come in further along the shore, and the sky is a stippled canvas of blue and white, the kind that promises heat later in the day. Please, Ginny prays, please let Katrin be alright. Whatever the repercussions. She thinks again of Thomas and her role in his disappearance, and she thinks of her own fears of being found out as someone other than the person she now presents to the world. How has she become so deceitful a human being, so easily? Last night, when Bill was in the shower, a text had popped up on his phone, from his pal in the environmental health office, informing him that the bird removal man would be in touch with him about the starlings next week – and without a thought Ginny had swiped it into the delete bin and carried on chopping onions, glad of the excuse to let her tears fall. She'd give it all up – the lies, the secrets – if only they could have Katrin returned to them in one piece.

At the end of the West Wing, the door to No.1 opens and Hugo appears on the path, baby Henri in his arms, a muslin cloth draped over his shoulder. Right behind him is Frida, who is carrying the baby rucksack and what appears to be a bottle of milk in one hand. Even from this distance Hugo looks frazzled, while Frida appears far older than her sixteen years as, grave-faced, she pulls the door shut and heads towards Starling House, towards Ginny. Still no sign of Amélie, Ginny notes, taking in the closed upper curtains of No.1 before heading down the stairs to greet Hugo and Frida at the front door.

'Hello, darling,' she says as Frida embraces her. 'This is an early visit.'

Hugo plants a kiss on her cheek and passes her the baby. 'Sorry to barge in on you,' he says, grasping the muslin cloth and blotting furiously at a milk stain on the cuff of his expensive linen shirt.

'It's Amélie,' Frida says, leading the way through to the kitchen, as though it were her own home. 'She's done a runner.'

Hugo flops on to a chair at the kitchen table, and exhales heavily.

'What do you mean "a runner"?' Ginny asks, securing baby Henri under one arm as she pours Hugo a coffee and sets the formula milk to warm.

Frida casts a glance at her stepdad, who nods for her to continue. 'Hugo got a call from Social Services, and basically someone reported Mum for using drugs and now they want to come round and do a home visit. They take this kind of thing very seriously,' she reports knowledgeably. 'He had it on speakerphone,' she adds by way of explanation.

Ginny sets Hugo's coffee down. 'I hope you don't think that "someone" was me, darling?'

Hugo shakes his head emphatically. 'God, no, Gin. It could've been anyone – from what Frida tells me, Amélie's been getting pretty sloppy at covering up.'

'There's always white dust on the tiles up in her bathroom,' Frida says, slotting a piece of bread into the toaster.

Hugo draws a hand over his face. 'Of course Amélie also heard the whole conversation. And when they said they wanted to come over late morning – *today* – she went into panic mode. I tried to stop her from leaving, but short of restraining her, what could I do?'

'She left *without Henri*?' Ginny pulls out the seat opposite and settles there with the baby. With no fuss, she teases the teat of the milk bottle into his mouth.

'Without much of anything at all,' Hugo sighs, exhausted. 'She ranted a while, accusing everyone and his cat for reporting her – she even accused Frida, for Christ's sake – then she threw a few things in a holdall and took my car. And she's switched her phone off, so there's no way of contacting her.'

'What can I do to help?' Ginny asks, reaching out to lay a gentle hand on Hugo's wrist.

Frida eases herself up onto a bar stool with her buttered toast. 'See? I told you Ginny would help. She's a guardian angel. That's what Katrin calls her. Her Guardian Angel.'

Ginny rises from the table to clear away the sink top, desperately fighting back the tears. 'Katrin always was prone to a bit of exaggeration,' she says lightly, wishing she could swallow back her use of the past tense. 'But really, Hugo, I'll do anything I can.'

At No.1, the house is as spotless as ever, the cleaner having been in only yesterday.

'I can't see that you need much help making it look good for the Social Services people,' Ginny says, casting around the place. 'Although, I suppose if I didn't know better I'd think this was the home of a couple with no kids.'

'Exactly!' Frida exclaims. Something has altered in the girl, Ginny thinks; it's not precisely relief she's displaying, but there is a lightness of sorts – a clarity. 'That's what I said! It's not a good impression. Has Amélie hidden all those toys again?'

Frida crosses the living room and opens a wooden trunk, and proceeds to arrange various plastic play things over the sofas and carpet, presumably to give the appearance that they'd all been engaged in a morning of educational play. Chucking a few scatter cushions across the room, she hesitates a moment, assessing the scene, before taking off her own shoes and kicking them randomly into the hall.

'That's better, isn't it? More lived-in? Hey, we should put a roast dinner in the oven or bake some bread – like they do on those house selling programmes.'

'This isn't some TV show,' Hugo says, laying a sleeping Henri down in his Moses basket. 'If these people don't like what they see, Frida, they could take Henri away, you know?'

Frida looks momentarily chastened and then, seconds later, incensed. 'Fucking Amélie!' she growls, and she kicks hard at the corner of the sofa, leaving a dirty great boot print on the white velvet.

'Nice one, Freeds,' Hugo says, 'Social Services will love that,' and it is a relief to Ginny when they all laugh.

When the doorbell goes, Hugo's alarm is instant. He checks his watch and tucks his shirt down like a schoolboy about to meet the head teacher.

'This can't be them. It's only just gone ten – they said eleven. They said eleven o'clock.'

It is Ginny who answers the door, ready to give Social Services the impression that she's a kind of surrogate grandmother to Henri, and to report that Hugo is a wonderful dad and that they're not sure where Amélie is at the moment, but she's bound to be back soon . . . But in fact, it is DS Ali Samson she finds standing on the doorstep. With her is another plain-clothed woman, along with the person she was introduced to on Sunday as the family liaison officer.

'Oh, Ginny, hello,' DS Samson says, with a little frown. 'I was hoping I might see Amélie Gold. Is she in?'

'I'm afraid not, sergeant, and actually it's not a terribly good—'

'What about Hugo? Is he at home?'

Hugo steps forward to take over. 'Sorry,' he mumbles, 'we're all at sixes and sevens today. We're expecting the health visitor any minute, and Amélie has popped out again, and we're trying to get the place straight.'

'I wonder if we can come in?' the DS asks, ignoring his attempt to deflect her.

Hugo steps aside and ushers them through to the kitchen, where DS Samson launches into a direct line of questioning.

'It's now been nearly three days since Katrin's fall, and we still haven't managed to speak with your wife, Mr Gold. It's imperative that we do, as she is one of the few people we can't account for during the time of what we now suspect was an assault at the very least.'

There is a sense that everyone in the room has stopped breathing.

'I take it Amélie has recovered from her illness?' she asks, never taking her eyes from Hugo, who is doing a very poor job of not looking shifty. 'Do you happen to know where she is, Hugo?'

Ginny's eyes flicker up towards the ceiling, and the younger officer notices.

'Sarge,' she says. 'I think she might be upstairs.'

'She's definitely not,' Hugo says, but his smile comes off as disingenuous, and Samson steps out into the hall to glance towards the upper landing.

With all the disturbances around him, baby Henri begins to grizzle and Hugo is quick to go to him, picking him up and rocking him against his shoulder.

'Do you mind if I take a look?' the detective asks. 'If only to satisfy my curiosity?'

'Be my guest,' Hugo says without resistance, and Ginny offers to escort DS Samson while Hugo attempts to arrest little Henri's cries.

On the landing, Ginny steers the sergeant along the hallway, where she begins a room-to-room search for Amélie, peering under beds and inside wardrobes as she goes. Ginny leaves her to continue, stopping in at the dressing room, where she pulls open Amélie's make-up drawer and rearranges the contents a little before returning to the hallway as DS Samson emerges from the master bedroom.

As Samson enters the dressing room, Ginny gives a little laugh and says, 'Oh, you won't find her in there – there's nowhere to hide!'

But by this point DS Samson's eyes have already fallen on the bright red object on the top of Amélie's expensive pile of make-up, and she's blocking Ginny's entrance and leaning out into the corridor to call down to the floor below.

'DC Shepherd, can you join me up here, please? And Mr Gold, I need you to join us too.'

By the time the social worker arrives twenty minutes later, the police are filing through the front door, clutching three clear evidence bags, one containing small wraps of cocaine, another holding the shoes Amélie wore on the night of the party, and the last one containing a cherry-red phone, which Hugo has confirmed looks exactly like Katrin's.

As the DS passes the social worker in the hall, she looks back at Hugo, who stands grey-faced at the foot of the stairs, with little Henri in his arms and Frida and Ginny either side of him. Ginny notices the way in which DS Ali's eyes linger on the soft curve of the tiny baby's form. We're all of us presenting something other than our real truth, Ginny is reminded. That young woman, standing there strong and in control, is more grieving mother than she is police officer; that part of her will never hang up its uniform.

'Go easy on him,' DS Ali says to the social worker as she passes. 'This is a difficult time for the family, but from what I can see, Mr Gold is doing a good job with the baby.'

Without looking back, DS Ali Samson steps out on to the path and closes the door.

32. DS Ali Samson

Ali is spooning yoghurt into her muesli when a message comes through from Trelawney on Wednesday morning.

Switch on ITV – women from the starlings being interviewed now.

Hurriedly Ali takes her bowl into the tiny living room, where she flicks on the TV, and tries to turn a blind eye to the layer of dust that's settled on the surfaces in the past few weeks. She's barely used this room since Margo moved out, a room she thinks of as belonging to an earlier, better time. They had been in this very room, watching *Cinema Paradiso*, when Ali had announced the long-awaited news that she was pregnant. And it was also here when five months later she had experienced those first alarming cramps forewarning her that she was not.

She pushes the intrusive feelings of guilt away and turns up the volume, as the television presenter introduces the section.

. . . investigation into historic abuse claims at the former Mother and Baby Home, Highcap House, which last closed its doors in 1981. The institution, which is the subject of

a forthcoming book, is said to have placed an undisclosed number of babies into the adoption system in southwest England, and is alleged to have covered up the deaths of countless others. I'm pleased to have with me today former Highcap mother and investigator Diana Lambley, along with the author of the book, Anne Ashbourne, who was born there in 1979.

Ali listens intently to the women's descriptions of unlawful imprisonment, deceit, rape, even infanticide, under the rule of the feared Governor Stan Jarman way back in the sixties and seventies – even just into the eighties. She thinks of the women at The Starlings today, and she is slowly seized by an inexplicable sense that their experiences are yoked to this past in some unreachable way. There's Katrin, herself a Highcap orphan, six months pregnant, currently laid out on a hospital bed, in her own state of dreadful imprisonment; there's Frida, hardly older than this Diana woman was when she gave birth to her child there under the most dreadful of circumstances; and then there's the mysterious Amélie, so far voiceless, a new mother, on the run, perhaps out of guilt, perhaps out of fear? And Ginny; what is it about Ginny, mother to no one, yet in her own peculiar way matriarchal, the most motherly of them all?

Host: And what is it you want to say to Highcap mothers and babies out there, Diana – people who may have kept this secret for many, many years?

Diana: We would urge them to make contact using the number on the screen or via the ITV website. We are a growing community of Highcap women, who seek to bring comfort to one another through our shared experiences, but also to put together, through our oral accounts, a true history of what happened there – and potentially join forces to seek reparations.

Host: Anne, a final word?

Anne: Don't let fear or shame hold you back. When I found my mother a year ago, through the use of DNA, she was forced to tell her story, to face the truth about what happened to her. But, rather than the shame she had anticipated, she says she felt liberated – uncaged – for the first time in forty years. This is what we want for all those Highcap mothers, and for every one of the children they brought into the world. We want our truth to be told; we want our voices to be heard.

Ali turns off the TV, brushes her teeth, snatches up her keys, and heads to the station for an 8am briefing. That TV interview seems only to have added another layer of static to the noise inside her mind. The threads of this Katrin Gold case seem to be floating loose, like seaweed underwater, threatening to tangle in the currents, to break free, and right now she's finding it impossible to know which thread to grab on to.

On her way in, she buys a tray of doughnuts at the petrol station, which on arrival she slides on to the photocopier outside the boss's office, before giving him the nod and signalling for the team to gather.

'Morning all!' Trelawney bellows, hands in pockets. 'You're all aware that this stair fall case at The Starlings has developed somewhat since Saturday night. For any of you new to the case, we're talking about the suspicious fall of Katrin Gold: forty years old, married mother of two, and partner in Gold Properties – the development company behind The Starlings development. And in light of forensic evidence, and the fact that it was phoned in anonymously, we have to consider the strong possibility that Katrin Gold's fall was the result of an altercation. Mrs Gold is six months pregnant, and at this point remains in an induced coma while the doctors monitor her progress. She's not yet out of the woods, and we're keeping everything crossed that this does not become a manslaughter – or murder – investigation.' He glances about the room, checking for full attention. 'Now, DS Samson tells me there was no sign of forced entry to the clocktower, yet it's understood that the building is always locked. All three sets of keys have been accounted for – one set is held by the Gold family, another by neighbour Ginny LeFevre, and a third set is kept in the lodge cottage, which has been uninhabited for several months – so it's possible someone could have used that set without anyone noticing.'

'We didn't get any useful prints off them, guv,' Benny Garner pipes up with a regretful shrug.

'Shame,' Trelawney replies. 'OK. In better news, thanks to the dusty condition of the building, Forensics have been able to confirm that there was more than one set of footprints on the scene at the time of her fall. Mrs Gold's partial fingerprints were found on a piece of broken railing from the top landing of the clocktower, which certainly puts her up there, but doesn't tell us how she, or the railing, came to fall so catastrophically to the bottom. If it was an innocent fall, why did our anonymous caller flee the scene? And if it was intentional, what possible motive could there have been? In fact there are several sets of footprints – was there more than one assailant, or did someone else help Katrin's attacker to cover up their tracks? Well, that's what you're all here for.'

He nods at Ali to take over.

'So far, our best suspect is Amélie Gold, the victim's sister-in-law – married to Katrin's husband's brother, Hugo. It was her sixteen-year-old daughter who first found Katrin and raised the alarm. Since the fall, Amélie has refused to give us her statement, and her husband has now admitted that yesterday she left the family home, leaving her teenage daughter and three-week-old baby behind, and hasn't been heard from since. Clearly this is highly suspicious behaviour. On a brief voluntary search of her home yesterday, we quickly discovered what we believe to be Katrin Gold's phone in an open drawer in Amélie's dressing table, together with a small quantity of cocaine. While there, Hugo Gold gave us permission to take away the shoes his wife was wearing on the night of the party, in order to compare with the footprints left on the steps inside the clocktower. I've asked Hugo to keep track of any unusual movement on their joint bank and credit accounts, and he called me this morning to say his online statement showed up new transactions for a Wessex Hotel and a train ticket, suggesting Amélie checked out somewhere this morning – and that she's on the move.' Ali looks around the small team. 'Benny, any news on that CCTV?'

'It's a funny system, sarge, one that was already in place before the building was renovated – really outdated, so it's not as simple as downloading it from the Cloud. This one works on a tape system, operated from the lodge cottage, but the guy that lived there went AWOL about five months ago, which means the tapes haven't been maintained. It's not looking very promising.'

'OK, keep at it, Benny. And keep in mind, everyone: while Amélie Gold is our most promising suspect, she's not been cautioned or officially named. Yes, she had Katrin's phone in her possession, but until we get the print work done on it – DC

Cooper, can I get you to arrange that? – we can't rule out the possibility that somebody else planted or hid it in her room. We still have questions over Amélie's daughter, Frida Pascal – she's very close to her aunt, but she gave a flaky account of the evening. She's putting her inaccuracy down to being so upset, but I'm not entirely convinced she's telling us everything.'

PC Bloom raises a pen. 'Sarge, we've got another neighbour, Belinda Parsons, coming in tomorrow morning – her daughter goes to school with Frida. She caught us before we left The Starlings yesterday, said she might have some useful info.'

'Excellent,' says Ali. 'Fill me in on the time later, and I'll make sure I'm back for it. Now, husband Bill also had opportunity that night, but while he's a bit arrogant—'

'More than a bit,' Trelawney interjects, reaching for a doughnut and enjoying the team's ripple of amusement.

Ali rolls her eyes. 'While he's *distinctly* arrogant, he seems genuinely upset by the situation with his wife and their unborn child. That said, we'll be taking a very close look at him as a potential suspect. Finally, neighbour and friend Ginny LeFevre was also away from the party shortly before Katrin was discovered in the clocktower, so we'd really like sight of that CCTV footage to timestamp her movements.

'Now, as far as Katrin's phone is concerned, we've been trying to contact Bill Gold to confirm that it's definitely hers, and to see if we can access her messages. Apparently he's been keeping vigil at his wife's bedside most days, but the mobile signal at the hospital is pretty shoddy. According to Ginny there was a lot of activity on Katrin's phone – text messages pinging, etc – shortly before she disappeared, so we'd very much like to know who they were from, and if they were relevant. If I can't get through to Bill this morning, I'll drive down to the hospital and get him to ID the phone in person.'

'Good job, DS Samson,' Trelawney says, when Ali indicates she's done. 'OK, all hands on deck, everyone. We've got a pregnant woman in a coma at Highcap Hospital. Let's try to get this solved before she wakes up, yes?'

At lunchtime, Ginny LeFevre answers the home phone at Starling House and confirms that Bill Gold is still at the hospital, where he's likely to remain until five or six. Still getting no reply on Bill's mobile, Ali Samson drives the high coastal road to the hospital and heads for the intensive care ward, where she asks to be shown to Katrin's room.

Sunlight streams in through the open blinds of the private room, slashing broken lines across the dome of Katrin's pregnant stomach. Standing at the foot of the single bed, Ali finds she is suddenly trembling, grateful that the nurse had simply deposited her there and walked away. She wasn't prepared for this – the raw truth of this woman's vulnerability. The truth that she might lose her baby, if some unseen damage is at work beneath her skin, beneath her skull; if her body fails to restore itself. It's the frailty that is so crushing. Ali sees herself, reduced to all fours in the bathroom of the home she once shared with Margo, blood pooling between her knees, shock rendering her speechless, helpless to make it stop. She sees Margo's disappointment, at Ali's refusal to acknowledge that her recklessness was in part to blame; and she sees Margo's drive to save their love ebb and diminish, until she too seeps out of Ali's life forever. Determined as she is to put it all behind her, it sometimes feels to Ali as though neither of them – neither Margo nor the baby – had ever really existed at all.

'Hello, there!'

Ali turns, startled by a strange voice, and finds a doctor in the room beside her. She swallows a gasp and quickly shifts back into professional mode.

'And you are?' he asks in a friendly manner.

'Detective Sergeant Ali Samson,' she replies, 'I'm the investigating officer – looking into Katrin's fall.'

The doctor draws down the corners of his mouth. 'I'd assumed it was an accident – that's how the husband described it, when she was first brought in.'

'Well, it's looking a little more complicated.' She gives the doctor a straight-mouthed smile. 'How is the patient doing?'

'Actually, she's doing really well – as is the baby. She's been very, very lucky – the brain scans this morning show no bleeds at all. We're monitoring her constantly, and, without over-promising, it's quite possible she'll get out of this with nothing more than a fractured collarbone. Of course, I wouldn't say that to the husband yet – false hopes and all that.'

'Actually, I was hoping to find Bill Gold here. I think he arrived about seven this morning, so maybe he's popped out to fetch some lunch?'

The doctor hugs his clipboard to his chest. 'Mr Gold? No, he hasn't been here for a couple of days now. I thought he must be away or something, because he barely left her side for the first forty-eight hours.'

Ali doesn't wait for any further comment. She thanks the doctor and heads straight out to her car, already dialling Bill's mobile number. As far as Ginny LeFevre told her earlier, she has been minding Bill's kids for the past few days while he devotedly tends to his wife. So, if he's not been at the hospital, where the hell has he been?

On the third ring, he answers.

'DS Samson! Hello? Have you got news?'

Momentarily, Ali is floored by his upbeat manner. 'Erm, yes, in fact, I have. We think we've recovered Katrin's phone, but I wanted you to formally ID it and see if you could help us to unlock it. There may be messages that cast some light on her last movements. Can I visit you at home – I'm nearby now?'

There's a pause, the rustling of a hand around the receiver. 'You know, I'm not there right now – I'm at the hospital. I really don't want to leave Katrin if I don't have to. Maybe you could call in at The Starlings this evening?'

'Listen, don't worry for now,' she replies, cautiously, her mind racing to formulate a plan. She doesn't want to spook him, but she doesn't want to let him go without some progress. 'But in the meantime, Katrin's phone – can you describe it to me?'

'Yep,' he says, without hesitation. 'It's a cherry-red iPhone SE with a matching red protective case.'

'Great. Any identifying marks or scratches?'

'Um, let's see. Oh, yes! If you remove the case, there should be a photobooth pic of the family – I remember her putting it in there when she first set up the phone.'

'That's excellent, Bill, thank you.' Ali notes the lack of obstruction, his desire to be helpful on this matter, at least. 'Do you happen to know her passcode?'

'Really sorry, but I don't. I'm not sure how you're going to get in without it.'

'If we're able to, Bill, are you happy to grant us access to Katrin's messages, in her absence?'

'Absolutely,' he replies. 'By the way, where did you find it?'

Ali hesitates before answering, weighing up the benefits of Bill Gold knowing the truth against the disadvantages. 'We found it at your brother's house.'

'Hugo's?' Bill replies. '*Really?*'

'It was in your sister-in-law's belongings,' Ali adds. 'In fact, Bill, we haven't been able to speak with Amélie at all since Katrin's fall. I don't suppose you've any idea where she is right now, do you?'

281

The moment's silence before he replies is enough to pique Ali's suspicion. That and the ease with which he lies. 'Not at all. I take it you've asked Hugo? Listen – I'd better shoot. Don't like to be away from Katrin's room for too long. Keep me posted, yes?'

He hangs up, and Ali stares from the seat of her car, at the sunlight bouncing off the glass windows of the hospital building where Bill Gold definitely is not.

When she arrives at the station the next morning, Belinda Parsons is already waiting in reception, and DS Ali Samson takes her straight through to the interview room, along with PC Bloom.

'You have some information for us, Belinda?' Ali asks without ceremony.

'I think so,' Belinda says in a faltering tone. 'I – I'm really good friends with Katrin, and I feel so bad talking behind her back. But, you know, now that there's talk of this not being an accident . . . Still, I'd hate to break her confidence.'

Ali doesn't have time for this. 'Sometimes we prove ourselves to be better friends by breaking confidences,' she says, mimicking a line she recalls a superior officer using in an interview years ago. 'Your friend is gravely ill, and it's just possible that some small thing you tell us could help in finding her assailant.'

Belinda nods nervously. 'OK, well, it's two things really. The first one is, my friend's husband is a financial advisor, and, when she mentioned the accident to him, he told her that Katrin Gold had been to see him at the start of the year, wanting to move funds around. He said she moved a load of cash out of joint accounts and into accounts in her name only.'

Ali nods for her to continue.

'And apparently Bill and Katrin have very high-paying life insurance policies, so – it just got me thinking: what if Bill found out about her siphoning off money, and got angry or something . . .'

She seems to be waiting for Ali to fill in the blanks for her, which she doesn't. 'Anyway, listen, I shouldn't even be telling you this and I don't want my friend's husband to get in trouble.'

'Understood,' Ali replies, laying her pen down. 'And the second thing?'

'*Right*. I'm going to break yet another confidence, I'm afraid.' Belinda takes an unsteady breath. 'I was speaking to my neighbour Anne Ashbourne yesterday morning. She was in a real tizz, wondering if she should get in touch with you. It seems that last year, Bill was having an affair – or a fling, at the very least. She said Katrin definitely knew, because Anne had been the one to break it to her.' She chews the inside of her mouth distractedly. 'Apparently Ginny LeFevre had called on Anne the very next day, asking her to keep it to herself as Bill and Katrin were trying to work things out.'

'Ginny knew about the affair?' Ali asks, recalling Ginny LeFevre's insistence that Bill and Katrin Gold were the most happily married couple on the planet.

Belinda nods. 'Ginny was there with Katrin when Anne phoned to tell her. Evidently Katrin just wanted to forget all about it – let it blow over, which is so sad, isn't it? I would've thought Katrin of all people would have been strong enough to kick the cheating so-and-so out!'

Ali gives no response, sensing Belinda Parsons doesn't need much encouragement.

'But the thing is, I've got my own theory about who the affair was with. Because Anne's friend – the one who spotted Bill in the hotel – she said she thought the other woman was French.'

'French?' Ali repeats.

'That's what she said. And from the description she gave, I'm certain it had to be Amélie – Katrin's sister-in-law! She and Bill were both away from home at the time, so it all added up.'

'And do you think the affair is ongoing?'

'I don't know, but the evening of the party, Bill and Amélie went off within a few minutes of each other, and it must have been at least half an hour before Bill came back alone. I certainly thought they were up to no good, and I think Katrin did too, because it was soon after that that she decided to go and check on the boys, even though she really didn't need to. She looked troubled, I thought.'

'This is really useful, Belinda,' Ali says, eager to follow the lead up.

'It's a motive, isn't it?' Belinda says grimly. 'I mean, Amélie always made it clear she hated Katrin, and then the affair, and then – this. Not to mention the question the whole thing might pose over baby Henri's paternity.' She blinks wildly, and it takes all of Ali's self-control not to stop her face from registering her astonishment at this latest revelation. 'I just thought, what if Katrin had gone off and confronted Amélie that night, unable to stay quiet about it any longer? What if they'd had an argument?'

'We'll look into it, Belinda, thank you. Before you go, one of your neighbours mentioned that your daughter Poppy was talking with Katrin before she left the courtyard that night. I don't suppose you know what they were talking about?'

Belinda's face is a blank. 'Probably something and nothing. Poppy's a very sociable girl, and Katrin's lovely at ensuring everyone feels included. I expect it was small talk, nothing more. Poppy's at her dad's for a few days now, but I can text and ask her if you like?'

DC Garner knocks on the door and hands DS Samson the evidence bag containing Katrin's phone. 'I've taken prints, and it's fully charged,' the constable says. 'We found the photograph in the back, so it's definitely hers. Just wanted to check whether you'd got hold of the passcode yet, before I attempt to unlock it.'

'That's Katrin's,' Belinda says.

Ali nods. 'I don't suppose you know her passcode, do you?' She's half joking, but Belinda surprises her by nodding furiously.

'I think I do! Last time I was with her, I ticked her off for having one so easy to access. Unless she's changed it, it's 4321.'

Once Belinda has left the station, Ali fills Trelawney in before returning to her desk to attempt the suggested passcode. It takes her by surprise when, just like that, Katrin Gold's mobile phone lights up, and she's in.

Scrolling past all the unread emails that have arrived since Katrin last used the phone, Ali finds a series of messages from Ancestry.com that landed at 8pm on Saturday night, notifying Katrin that she has 'new close matches'. Ali had herself signed up to Ancestry a couple of years back when researching her family tree, and she now recalls the regularity with which the company flung out emails to entice you back on to the site. Other than these, there are no other emails from that two-hour time period she is interested in. It's likely it was these emails that were the cause of the pinging alerts Ginny described hearing from Katrin's phone that night, before she left the courtyard.

Judging by the lack of apps on her home screen, it would appear that Katrin Gold is not a regular user of social media. And so the only other place to check is her SMS text folder, and it is here that Ali makes the discovery that Frida Pascal was far from truthful about her communication with her aunt on the evening of the party.

'Sarge, I think you should see this.' It's Benny, hovering at the side of her desk and holding out an iPad showing a freeze-frame of the exterior to Katrin Gold's house, from Saturday night. 'So – turns out they've got *two* security systems at The Starlings.

One is the pre-renovation system I already mentioned, operated via a tape system in the lodge cottage. We've been in and checked, and there's definitely nothing to see, 'cause the tapes haven't been maintained since the groundsman vanished a few months back. But then we find out there's this second system, with footage stored in the Cloud, which Hugo Gold described as a bolt-on, to cover a couple of black spots. It doesn't show us the clocktower, but it does give us Starling House and the entrance gates.'

Ali beckons Trelawney from his office, and they gather around the screen and press play. Together, they watch intently as Benny speeds through the various comings and goings at Starling House between 7.48pm when Amélie first returned to check on the baby, and 8:34pm, when the anonymous call was made from Katrin's mobile. During that time, Bill arrives five minutes after Amélie, and stays for a full half-hour. Frida doesn't appear, and they can only presume she left through the back entrance as she'd claimed.

'So, if Frida *has* left by this point, we can assume Amélie and Bill were together in the house alone for almost half an hour,' Ali muses. 'Which could support the rumour Belinda Parsons provided this afternoon – that they were engaged in an affair. In fact, it might explain who Bill has been with while he was pretending to be at the hospital these past couple of days.'

Trelawney raises an eyebrow. 'But doesn't this mean Amélie Gold is off the hook? There's no sign of her leaving the house from the point she arrives at 7.48pm,' he says.

'Not necessarily. Ginny LeFevre mentioned how she habitually uses her back door – Frida too – and it got me thinking: there's no reason why any one of this lot couldn't have nipped out the back, done the deed and returned without any camera picking it up at all.'

'And what about the girl? She lied about Bill and Amélie being there together, and, according to this recording, her movements are unaccounted for for the best part of an hour.'

'That's not all she's lied about, boss,' Ali says, reaching for Katrin's phone. She locates the thread of messages between Katrin and Frida that night, and hands it to the DI.

Trelawney scratches his head, causing his hair to stand up in wispy peaks. 'So, we've got Amélie Gold – potential love rival, who is to all intents and purposes on the run; we've got Bill Gold, who's screwing around behind his wife's back and pretending to visit her in hospital when he's really God knows where; and we've got Frida Pascal, who's lying about just about everything on the night in question.' He looks between Benny and Ali. 'Is it just me who's confused?'

'No, boss, you're not alone. What is clear, though, is that we urgently need to track down Amélie Gold – and we definitely need to speak with Frida Pascal again.'

33. DS Ali Samson

Hugo Gold is heading up the path as DS Samson arrives on his doorstep on Friday afternoon.

'Sergeant,' he says with a frown, reaching past her with his house key. 'Were we expecting you?'

'Sorry about the unannounced visit,' she replies. 'Have I caught you at a bad time?'

He smiles ruefully. 'Sorry, no – you're absolutely fine. I've just been up at this new development of ours. White Rise, just along the coast here. We had reports of trespassers overnight, so I've been up there with the security guys, shoring up the windows and doors until the builders can get started. Anyway – do you want to come in?'

Ali follows Hugo inside, accepting his offer of a hot drink, just as Frida appears in the doorway to the kitchen. She's wearing cut-off jeans and flip-flops, cradling baby Henri in one arm and holding a milk bottle to his mouth with the other. His eyes are locked on his big sister's, determinedly anchored to that young face as he suckles away, and there's something deeply unsettling about the image to Ali, somehow taking her back to that

TV interview with the Highcap women, and their descriptions of so many teenage girls, giving up their babies, like it or not.

'Hi, Frida,' she says, gently. 'Seems like you're a dab hand with your little brother. He can't take his eyes off you.'

'I don't know what we'd do without her,' Hugo says, fetching down the cups.

Frida smiles, a shy, genuine smile, and Ali notices just how darkly circled her eyes are, in stark contrast to her youthful complexion. Why is she lying to them? she wonders. What has this girl got to hide?

'I thought we could have another informal chat, if that's OK?' Ali makes a show of addressing the question to both of them, taking a seat at their kitchen table as Hugo prepares drinks and Frida perches on the seat opposite with Henri. 'By the way, how did the meeting with your health visitor go?' she asks.

'Full disclosure,' Hugo sighs after a few seconds' thought. 'That woman was actually a social worker.'

Ali nods benignly, anxious not to make him feel judged on the subject of his new baby boy.

'You'll have guessed from the items you found here yesterday that Amélie has had, erm, a bit of a past.' He glances at Frida, who is chewing at her lip, glassy-eyed. 'A bit of a problem with—'

'Drugs,' Frida interjects impatiently. She rearranges Henri over her lap, absently stroking the hair away from his soft forehead, fixing her eyes on Ali across the table. 'Mum's an addict. I don't know why he has to pretend like it's a big secret – I don't know why he can't just say it like it is.' But then her manner softens as she looks back at her stepdad, and she sounds more like an adult talking to a child. 'Because, you know, Hugo, if you were honest with me, I might actually be able to help. I'm not a kid any more.'

Hugo looks up from his tea-making and nods, without grievance. 'I know, lollipop,' he says. 'But it's not fair to saddle you with the worry of it. You shouldn't have to be worrying about things like this at your age.'

Frida chews at the inside of her cheek, clearly holding back on her real thoughts.

'Anyway,' Hugo continues, addressing Ali, 'Social Services usually follow up with new parents who've had a history with substance abuse, and so when they got a call reporting her for using again – well, hence the visit. Good news is, they're happy with Henri being under my care, but I'll have to let them know when or if Amélie returns.'

'We still don't know who reported her,' Frida says. 'My money's on Cathy, the cleaner. Mum's so rude to her, and she's bound to have noticed stuff when she's here.'

Hugo brings the mugs to the table and sits with a heavy sigh. 'I've told you, Freeds, it wasn't Cathy. Let's just stop speculating, yeah?'

'Anyway, that's good news about Henri, Hugo. All you need now is Amélie back,' Ali says lightly, taking in the non-committal nods of agreement from both Hugo and his stepdaughter. Are they sorry Amélie has left, or relieved? Ali is finding it almost impossible to read the emotions at work here.

She helps herself to a posh brown sugar lump and stirs it into her tea.

'And have you seen much of Bill?'

'He's at the hospital every day,' Hugo replies with a shake of his head. 'I've barely seen him. I've been trying to pick up some of his work, emails and so on, but I just wish there were more I could do. I can't imagine what he's going through.'

'You get on very well, don't you?' Ali asks, her mind on the information Belinda Parsons brought them only yesterday. She takes out her notebook. 'It must be hard on him, all this. I just popped in and saw Ginny at Starling House – she's still there, looking after the boys. In fact, she said he didn't even come home last night.'

Hugo frowns. 'Really? I've been visiting Kat in the evenings, because Bill said they're really strict about visitor numbers, so our paths don't tend to cross. I didn't know you could stay over at the hospital.'

'Neither did I,' Ali replies, searching Hugo's face and finding no sign that he's any clearer than she is about Bill's where-abouts. What she does know is that DC Garner tailed Bill Gold yesterday morning, and, instead of driving to the hospital as he'd have everyone believe, he headed out of town, getting as far as Poundbury before Benny lost him at the roundabout. 'Now, let's get to these questions of mine.'

Casually, Ali places Katrin Gold's red phone on the table.

'It's definitely Katrin's?' Hugo asks, his face lighting up briefly, before clouding again. 'I don't understand why Amélie would have it in her room. Does it tell you anything useful?'

'It does.' She glances at Frida, reading the girl's body language, the way in which she shifts the now sleeping baby, for distrac-tion. 'Frida,' she says, softly, 'we've seen all of the texts between you and your Auntie Kat that night. And they throw up certain questions I'd like to go over with you.'

Frida looks up, tears already springing to her eyes, and she draws Henri closer, as though his small innocence might afford her protection. She nods, swiping away a tear and setting her jaw against the formation of more.

Ali picks up Katrin's phone and opens the text folder. 'So, we can see here that Katrin first texted you at 8.01pm that evening, saying: *Tell your mum you need a break – I want to talk to you about Barney.*'

Frida nods; Hugo scowls. 'Who's Barney?' he asks.

Ali reads the full set of texts aloud:

Frida, 8.01: Why?

Katrin, 8.02: I've been talking to Poppy. I'm worried x

Frida, 8.04: What's she been saying? Don't worry about it Auntie Kat – she's just chatting shit. I'm not even seeing him any more x

Katrin, 8.04: Frida, I'm your auntie, it's my job to worry. Meet me by the greenhouse in 5 mins and you can put me straight x

Frida, 8.04: I can't, I'm looking after the boys

Katrin, 8.05: I happen to know Bill and Amélie are there right now! Just meet me!

Katrin, 8.05: I really am worried, Frida. Please? And then I'll leave you alone, promise x

Katrin, 8.05: ps LOVE YOU!

Frida, 8.05: OK

Frida, 8.05: Love you too

Frida, 8.05: xxx

Katrin, 8.05: OK I'm leaving now – see you in a minute xxx

For a few moments, no one speaks, and Ali watches the confusion working its way across Hugo's face, as shame and regret play out on Frida's.

'You told me you hadn't seen Auntie Kat all evening,' Hugo says.

'I *didn't* see her.' She can't meet his eye.

'OK,' Ali says, steering the conversation away from Hugo. 'In your official statement, Frida, you said you were at the beach at that time.'

'I was.'

'But these texts suggest you were meeting your Auntie Kat at the greenhouse – and you can't have done both. Several witnesses agree that Katrin left the courtyard at around 8.05pm. And your Uncle Bill says he arrived back at Starling House by 7.53pm – which we've now confirmed via CCTV.'

She pauses to let this information land. Frida's eyes flicker in Ali's direction, and it's clear she's unnerved.

'Of course, the CCTV also shows us your mother's exact arrival at the house just five minutes earlier. Now, you told us that it was Bill who sent you off for a break, after your mother left – although there's no sign of her leaving on the recording, incidentally. I think we can all agree that it would be impossible for you to get to the beach and back in the short time before your planned meeting with Katrin.'

Frida growls in frustration. '*I didn't meet Katrin!* Why won't you believe me? I told her I would, but I didn't go! I went to the beach instead, so she couldn't find me and grill me. I didn't want to talk to her about all that, all that – *stuff.*' At her raised voice, baby Henri wakes with a start, his face crumpling, and Frida hands him to Hugo and crosses the kitchen to run herself a glass of water.

'Do you mean all that *Barney* stuff?' Ali asks patiently, noting Hugo's ongoing confusion.

Frida keeps her back to them, and drinks from her glass.

'OK, Frida. Let's just get to the bottom of this, shall we? I have the strongest sense that you're doing that thing that we police officers encounter so often, which is when witnesses attempt to confuse us by changing their story over and over, leaving a trail of knots for us to entangle – in the hope that eventually, we'll give up.'

Frida returns to the table, and meets the detective's gaze.

'Frida, just for the record, *I* will never give up. Not until I get the truth.'

'*Uh,*' the girl murmurs as she drops her head on to folded arms in defeat. 'I lied,' she says, barely audible. Slowly she lifts her head. She looks beaten. '*I lied*. Yes, I was there, at Starling House, when Bill arrived just a bit after Mum. He came in and went straight upstairs, saying he was checking on the boys. Then Mum told me to go off for a break, she insisted, and – well, I did go, 'cause I know when I'm not wanted. I went out through the back to shortcut down to the beach, but then I remembered my coat was on the chair outside the snug. So I went back up to get it, and that's when I heard them, in there – Mum and Bill. Together.'

Hugo is listening intently, his colour gradually draining from his face.

'What do you mean "together", Frida?' Ali asks gently.

'I mean, I could hear what they were saying, and, and sounds – kissing.' Uneasily, she turns her eyes on Hugo. 'I'm sorry, Hugo! I didn't want you to find out. I didn't want you to know, because, if this has been going on for – I dunno . . .' She trails off briefly, casting around for the right words. 'I just couldn't bear it if – if . . .' And now her gaze lands on baby Henri, and Hugo is shaking his head, a shockwave motion of denial.

He really had no idea, Ali is sure. 'Frida, did you hear anything of what they were saying?'

Reluctantly, she nods. 'Amélie said she wished they could just run away from The Starlings. She wished they could leave it all behind. And Bill didn't really say anything, you know – he didn't really sound like he was in the mood for talking. But . . .'

'But?' Ali nudges.

'But then, Amélie said, wouldn't it be good if they could just get rid of Katrin and she could move into Starling House, which was a much more suitable home for a classy *femme* like her, and then he laughed and said she was terrible – and, urgh, I couldn't stand to listen to them for a second longer, and that's when I left.'

'And Katrin's text to you?'

'It arrived that same minute, as I got out the back door, and, I don't know, after what I'd just heard, it threw me into a spin. I had to get away, and I answered saying I'd meet her, just to get her off my back. And then I went down to the beach on my own, like I said. I wasn't even thinking straight. By that point, all I wanted to do was curl up on the beach, and – and die.'

Beside her, Hugo cradles his baby while a single tear rolls down the contours of his face, soaking into the linen of his shirt. He reaches out and places a hand on her shoulder, and nods for her to carry on.

'She phoned me about five minutes later – when I didn't turn up,' Frida murmurs, 'and she just kept going on at me. We had an argument. She wanted to know where I was – I wouldn't tell her, and eventually I lost my rag and said . . .' She trails off.

'You said what?' Hugo asks.

'I told her, *You're not my mum!* And then I hung up, and those were the last words I ever said to her.' Frida drops her head, and she looks small and so young, diminished by her confession.

'Frida?' Ali ventures, cautious to tread carefully now that the girl is speaking the truth. 'Your Auntie Kat's going to be alright, you know? You'll get a chance to make it up to her.'

Frida looks up, hope in her eyes, and Ali takes her advantage.

'May I look at your phone too, Frida, to see the text conversation for myself – to make sure it tallies with the one I have on Katrin's?'

Robotically, the teenager unlocks her own phone and passes it to Ali. 'I'm sorry,' she tells her stepdad, reaching out a hand to rest it gently on his.

'You've got nothing to be sorry for, lollipop.'

'I have. I'm sorry I knew about it and didn't tell you. I wasn't taking her side. You know that, right? I just didn't want her to hurt you any more.'

The tenderness of that touch threatens to weaken Ali, and she breathes deeply, and focuses on the messages on Frida's phone. After confirming the Frida-Katrin exchange is consistent, she attempts to close the text folder, but inadvertently opens the message thread above it – a thread between Frida and this boy called Barney. Before she can stop herself, Ali is reading their last exchange:

Frida: I'm not making it up, I swear! I nicked a test kit from my mum's room earlier and I got two blue lines. It's positive. Please answer me B! I don't know what to do!

Barney: I've got pills I can give you. Monday, 12.30 in the refectory. Not a word.

Frida: Are you sure they'll work?

Barney: 100% – Miseferon – look it up. Delete this thread.

Frida: Will you stay with me when I take them? I'm scared.

Barney: Remember to delete this thread. OK?

And that's where the conversation ends. Six days ago, on the night of the fall, less than an hour before the texts from Katrin.

Ali clicks on Barney's profile picture to see a handsome young man in a rugby shirt, fresh-faced with floppy blond hair falling over one eye. He certainly looks a couple of years older than Frida; old enough to know better. If Ali is right about the uses of the drug mentioned, this poor girl must be desperate. So, this was what was on Frida's mind in the moments before she discovered her mother was sleeping with her uncle. This was why she wanted to see nobody and speak to no one and curl up on that dark lonely beach and die. With sinking dread, Ali reads Frida's last words again. *I'm scared.* If she didn't fear for this poor girl before, she does now.

'You board at St Saviour's, don't you?' Ali asks Frida, casually switching off the phone and sliding it back across the table. 'When are you due back?'

'Monday.'

'Damn, I'll have to get a hire car sorted before then. Unless you want to stay home for a few days longer?' Hugo asks.

But Frida shakes her head vigorously. 'It has to be then 'cause of exams. I've got an exam the next day. It has to be Monday.'

Hugo nods sadly. 'Of course. Sorry. Yes, of course, you have exams.'

'What time do you have to be there on Monday, Frida?' Ali asks.

'Lunchtime.'

Impetuously, Ali speaks, a plan formulating before she even has a chance to think about it. 'Listen, we're going to need you to give us a formal statement, to capture everything we discussed today, Frida. So, how about you two come down to the station first thing Monday morning, and then I'll drive you back to St Saviour's myself? Give Hugo a bit of time alone with Henri? It won't put me out – the regional police branch is en route, so I can drop in some overdue paperwork on my way back. What do you say?'

'Thank you,' Hugo says, softly murmuring the words into the warmth of his baby's head.

Ali stands to leave.

'Keep an eye on him over the next day or two, Frida?' she tells the girl on the way out. 'Look after each other, yes?'

Quite unexpectedly, Frida throws her arms around the sergeant, and she cannot think of anything else to do but pat the girl's back, uncertain what is correct protocol in these instances. The girl is tall, but she feels fragile in Ali's arms, so very much a girl and not a woman.

'I think I'd like to be a police officer,' Frida says, letting go, stepping back with that small shy smile of hers.

'Really?'

'Yeah,' she replies, thoughtfully. 'It's heroic.'

Ali offers her a gentle farewell fist bump and heads to her car. With a growing sense of dread, she pulls up on the roadside just beyond the security gates, and Googles the drug Barney had mentioned, her heart sinking as her suspicions are confirmed. *Miseferon is a medication typically used to bring about an abortion during early pregnancy . . .*

She's sixteen, for Christ's sake; she's just a kid. How can she be going through this alone? Glancing back at the wrought-iron gates, Ali's eyes are drawn to the gleaming brass plaque attached to the pillar there. *Welcome to The Starlings, Dorset's Safest Community.*

With rage building in the pit of her stomach, DS Ali Samson releases the handbrake and pulls out on to the main road.

34. DS Ali Samson

'Go home, sergeant!' DI Trelawney barks at Ali, when she arrives at the quiet station a little after ten on Sunday morning. She had, after all, assured him yesterday that she'd be taking the day off.

She argues with him, of course; after all, he's there on his day off too. And no one is telling him *he* is overdoing it. Or, more to the point, no one is suggesting he isn't up to the job. It's no wonder she looks like hell, she wants to yell back at him, because she's barely slept for two days, fretting over the messages she saw on Frida's phone, not to mention trying to untangle the Katrin Gold case. She wants to make sure she's got her facts straight before she sounds any alarms; she's certain Hugo Gold could do without the added heartache, if it turns out Ali is wrong. Of course, the right thing to do would be to run it past Trelawney, if it weren't for the fact that he seems more triggered by anything related to pregnancy than she is. His kid-glove approach is slowly driving her demented.

'You need to learn to pick your battles, sergeant,' he says when he returns from fetching a coffee and finds her still at her desk. 'This is one you're not going to win.'

'You know, thousands of women miscarry every year, boss,' she growls now, slamming her laptop shut.

Trelawney perches on the desk beside hers, eyeing her over his coffee cup.

'And, eventually, they get up and get over it and carry on as before!' This, she realises is the first time she's used the word. *Miscarry. Miscarriage. Miscarried.* And instead of feeling debilitated by speaking the subject out loud, she feels empowered. She's caught Trelawney out, she knows. How could he possibly argue with her logic, pragmatic and unemotional as it is?

'I'm sure that's true,' he replies, not unkindly. 'But most of them don't miscarry after being assaulted by a prisoner in custody.'

Ali tries to hold his gaze, but she fails as tears of fury spring to her eyes and she turns away. 'It looks as if the niece is in the clear,' she mutters, aggressively stuffing papers into her bag. 'I was hoping to spend a bit of time looking into Ginny LeFevre's background today.'

The boss shakes his head. 'I've checked your time sheets, Ali, and you haven't had a shift off for twelve days straight. You're still getting over the – *the assault* – and you look like crap, if I'm honest. Listen, it's a week since that letter arrived for you, with the date for Holmwood's hearing. Is that what's on your mind? I think maybe it would do you good to see him in the dock, Ali; I think it might help you to draw a line under things. What do you think? You're not on your own in this.'

Ali can't even meet his eye, and for a few moments they remain in silence, the spectre of her assailant having somehow crept into the room. What does the boss know about what's good for her? It's not as though he's ever experienced anything like this. How dare he presume—

'Did you even have breakfast this morning?' Trelawney asks, his voice uncharacteristically tender.

At this, Ali stands and shrugs, for some reason unable to articulate a straightforward answer. What the hell is wrong with her?

Trelawney puts a hand on her elbow, and it is instantly evident that the physical intimacy of it feels wrong to them both. She stiffens; he retracts his hand.

'Look, all roads seem to point towards the sister-in-law, especially given this new info about the affair, and until we find her I think you can afford to park the case for a few hours, OK?' He walks her to the door. 'Go home, Samson, and we'll see you back here tomorrow morning. And have a think about that court date, yes? I'm happy to go along with you.'

For half an hour or so, Ali drives around the town, crying angrily at the wheel, cursing her boss, her losses, her sad empty life.

She thinks of Trelawney's offer, to accompany her to Neil Holmwood's hearing next week, for the harm he inflicted on her on that bright spring morning back in April; but what of her unborn child, too young to be considered viable as a victim in its own right? Too tiny to bring a charge of child destruction down on Holmwood's worthless life. Is Trelawney right? Would it help her to heal, facing her attacker across the courtroom?

If Margo were here, she'd know what to do. She'd be the one getting her through this. There was so much Ali regretted about that period, not least the way she treated Margo, coldly rejecting the care she so unconditionally gave. It had seemed at the time that Ali was incapable of accepting any real kindness in the face of her loss. But Margo had also experienced loss, hadn't she? She had been the other expectant parent in this story, and Ali had done nothing to acknowledge the fact. The crushing loneliness Ali felt weighing down on her was no one's fault but her own.

She turns into the car park of the supermarket and stops the engine, checking her reflection in the rear-view mirror. Her skin, normally a Mediterranean brown, is sallow, the whites of her eyes almost translucent. What did other people do, she wonders, when their partner had left them? She has no family nearby, and her only real friends here are those she made through Margo, or through her job. And there's no way she'd confide in her colleagues; God, can you imagine? It's bad enough that she's a woman, but it'd be worse still if she showed weakness so intrinsically linked to the condition of her sex. The only way out of this pit she finds herself in is to forget she was ever pregnant, and to move on. To 'pull herself together', as her mother helpfully suggested on her last visit home.

She rifles through her bag to locate a crumpled prescription the doctor wrote out for high-strength iron tablets weeks ago. Checking her sallow reflection one last time, she leaves the car and strides towards the supermarket entrance with its green pharmacy cross, making a mental shopping list as she goes: iron tablets, steak, spinach, mushrooms, milk, wholemeal bread, eggs, multivitamins, red wine. Food to raise her red blood cells – food to put the colour back in her cheeks.

She won't have Trelawney taking her off the job just because she looks like shit.

On her way towards home on the outskirts of town, Ali parks up at the seafront just a mile along from The Starlings, and walks down to the beach, where she devours a sausage roll and large latte picked up from the supermarket café.

From here, she has a clear view along the coastline, and can just make out the perimeter fence to Katrin and Bill Gold's property at the south side of the estate. Further along the coastal path, the amber shade of the majestic cliffs grows deeper, all the way out to Golden Cap and beyond, where the occasional house is dotted here or there, enjoying unspoilt sea views. One of them will be White Rise, she presumes, the renovation project Hugo Gold has been working on. It's such a beautiful landscape, at once gently rolling and gloriously wild. For the past three years, since they moved to Highcap, Ali and Margo had talked about hiking the South West Coast Path. Of course, with Margo's city job and Ali's police work, they never found the time, and now, well, now—

On a whim, Ali photographs the wide blue landscape on her phone and sends it to Margo's number, with a simple message, an olive branch, perhaps: *Hope you're ok x*

The sun is high and warm in the cloudless sky, and Ali heads up to the coastal footpath, slipping off her light jacket and striding with purpose in the direction of The Starlings. Out at sea, a few fishing boats bob about in the breeze, while the odd yacht passes along the horizon, heading off, perhaps, for a lazy weekend, picnicking on the water. She thinks of Bill and Hugo Gold, keen sailors, apparently. Will they ever get over what's happened? Not just with Katrin, but the affair? The betrayal? It's not something Ali could forgive, she knows from experience, and she thinks how different people are: their drives, their breaking points.

It's low tide, and as she nears The Starlings Ali drops back down on to the beach and walks close to the water's edge, where a cluster of sanderlings gathers and rises in genial formation. From this distance, the commanding outline of the old workhouse rises high above the safely fenced borders, its clocktower peering down on the day-to-day lives of its residents. To Ali's trained eye, an obscured cut-through gate is just visible in the nearest corner of Katrin's hedge, and it reminds her of the visit there back in the New Year, while she was looking into the disappearance of their groundskeeper, Thomas King. Afterwards, Ginny LeFevre had given Ali a brief tour of the estate, and they'd walked through Katrin's garden, retracing the route Thomas would have taken to the beach for his daily swim, ultimately leading them to his discarded red towel and walking boots. *Katrin was among the last babies born here,* Ginny had told her then with some pride. *It's what brought her back to Highcap – the search for her family.*

Ali takes out her phone and taps a message to her deputy, asking him to look into Ginny LeFevre. *Check if that's her maiden name. Previous address, marriage status, criminal history etc.* Something about Ginny LeFevre isn't quite stacking up for Ali, though she's at a loss to put her finger on exactly what it is. There's a subtle restlessness in her that Ali can identify with, and she wonders if Ginny's poised confidence is all it appears to be.

Resting against the breakwater where Thomas's belongings were found, Ali closes her eyes and turns her face to the sun, letting the whispering drag of the tide wash over her mind. Trelawney thinks this case is so simple: that Katrin was the victim of her husband's covetous lover, a crime of passion. Jealousy: the oldest motive in the book. But Ali's instinct tells her it's so much more complex than that. What is it about this place, The Starlings, that has its grip on these women, or at least binds them together in some way? She has a sudden flashback from the night of Katrin's fall: of the woman she now knows to be Anne Ashbourne at the ground floor window of her maisonette, overlooking the green. Beside her is an older woman, her mother, who gazes out, vacant-eyed, one palm resting on the glass. *It's motherhood*, Ali realises; that's the connection. It's to do with motherhood and childbirth and babies and confinement. Katrin; Amélie; Frida; Ginny; Anne. Despite never actually meeting Amélie nor seeing the others' interactions for more than a few minutes at a time, she thinks of them as women bonded in some unspeakable way. But the Mother and Baby Home closed four decades ago; long before Frida was born, before Amélie arrived here from France, before Ginny made Highcap her home. Apart from Anne, the only other person with a connection to those days is Katrin.

Taking her phone from her pocket, she dials Anne Ashbourne's number.

'Hello, Anne? This is DS Samson. Sorry to call you at the weekend.'

'Oh,' Anne replies, nervily. 'Hello.'

'Just a quick question. I saw you on the TV, talking about the Mother and Baby Home and your own DNA discovery, and I thought you might be able to help me with something. We recovered Katrin's phone, and one of the things I noticed was that she'd had a series of emails from Ancestry.com right before she left the courtyard on the night of the party. I hear she was interested in tracing her family – I just wondered if she'd mentioned anything about it to you?'

'Really?' Anne's voice brightens. 'Do you know what the emails said? Katrin sent off her DNA a few weeks back.'

'Right. There were three emails in a row and they all had the subject line: "You have close family matches".'

'Wow. Goodness. Had she opened them?'

'No. It looks like her DNA has been matched to others on the database, so I'd imagine she'd have been keen to open the emails if she had seen them.'

'Oh, yes, she was really looking forward to finding out if she had any real family out there,' Anne says breathily. 'You know, "close" could mean anything from great-grandparent to parent to half-sibling.' There is a pause on the line, while Anne takes in the information. 'Gosh, this really is amazing. You know, since the TV appeal, we've been inundated with calls from Highcap mothers and babies reunited through DNA – and now it looks like Katrin will be one of them.'

'It does look that way, doesn't it?' Ali wonders at the courage involved in making contact with new family like this, in the way Anne must have done with her own mother. 'By the way, Anne, how's your mum doing?'

'My mother? Um, she's fine. You know, a bit confused these days but, yes, fine.'

Ali had only asked out of courtesy, but again she seems to have unsettled Anne, whose nerves appear to live under the surface of her very thin skin. She only ever seems fully at ease when discussing her professional areas of knowledge or interest.

'Good. Well, thanks for that – and have a nice weekend.'

She hangs up and gazes towards Starling House, the wind snatching a tendril of hair from her on-duty up-do. Releasing the pin from the back of her head, she lets her long black hair fly, to whip freely on the coastal breeze. The altercation with Trelawney this morning seems to have opened something up in Ali and she feels as though she's on the brink of some great discovery, some revelation that will expose truths far wider reaching than just the answer to Katrin Gold's clocktower fall—

Her phone, still in her hand, rings out.

'How far are you from the hospital?' It's Trelawney, who seems in the space of a couple of hours to have changed his tune about her need to work at the weekend.

'Five minutes, boss.'

'Good. Get yourself down there straight away. Katrin Gold is awake.'

35. Katrin

When they brought Katrin back into consciousness, the awakening had been nightmarish, like swimming up through ink, weighted down.

At first, she had thought this was all part of the dream: that the brightly lit room and buzz of machines, the doctors and nurses in scrubs, were all figments of her imagination, not real at all.

'Katrin? Katrin, this is Dr Bantam. Can you hear me? Take your time. You've had a fall, and you've been in a coma . . .'

For a moment she had lain very still, her mind crawling drowsily over this strange new information. But then her boys had come to mind – her beautiful boys – and Bill, and Ginny, and, and—

Suddenly recalling the existence of her unborn child, Katrin had flown into a wild panic, gasping for air as she scrabbled to sit up, all the while holding defensive hands against the swell of her stomach.

'The baby is fine,' Dr Bantam swiftly assured her, taking a cautious step back to give her space. 'The baby's doing really, *really* well, Katrin.'

She had sunk back against her pillow then, the groggy hang-over-like sensation suddenly tamping her flame. The baby is fine. *The baby is fine.*

Now, three hours later, she is sitting up in bed in her private room, drinking a strong cup of sweet tea and eating toast and marmalade, perhaps the best toast and marmalade she's ever tasted. A nurse checks in on her.

'You look a bit perkier!' she says, planting hands on hips.

'Is Bill here yet?' Katrin asks, flinching at the pain in her collarbone. She's desperate to get out of this neck collar, which stifles her movements even more than her pregnancy. 'I want to see my boys. Have you heard from him?'

'Your husband? Sorry, we think he's got his phone switched off. But we'll keep trying, love.' The nurse checks Katrin's temperature again and leaves her with the strict instruction to keep drinking water and to leave the neck support alone.

For a few minutes Katrin stares at the clock on the wall, zoning in on snatched memories of the party night, many of them jumbled or unclear. She recalls how they'd all moved to the courtyard, carrying drinks and dragging chairs and fetching fleecy blankets to ward off the late May evening air. There'd been fairy-lights, music, champagne for those drinking. And there was a fight with Frida, she remembers with a sick lurch, so uncharacteristic of their warm relation-ship, and those words, aimed to wound – *you're not my mum* – ringing in Katrin's ears. She fixates on the memory of first Amélie leaving the courtyard, then Bill, and what felt like their long period of absence, together, so brazen, so cruel. Amélie, already looking enviably chic just a few weeks post-birth; Bill, with that hunger in his eye, but not for his pregnant heifer of a wife. She'd gone after them, hadn't she, on the pretence of checking on the twins? Or was it Frida she was in search of?

Or Ginny? Either way, Hugo had called after her, *Don't go*, offering up a lazy smile, docile on champagne. *Leave them*. But despite the warmth in his plea and the smile playing at the edge of his mouth and her wanting to stay, so very much, she'd forged onwards, into the darkness, like a kicked dog in search of its master. But no, she's getting things muddled; Bill's Amélie phase had ended months ago, and that rogue vision of Hugo took place somewhere other than the courtyard, in a London bar perhaps, years earlier, on an evening when they'd both stayed on too long.

Katrin curses her tangled mess of memories. She focuses again on that night, on leaving the courtyard, and for a while all is dark, until her recollection lands on the damp earth smell of the greenhouse – and Ginny's laughter – and the face of the clocktower faintly glowing, like an invitation. And overhead, the sky turns from pink to red, and everything feels wrong. *I can't find Frida*, she's saying, one step in, her shoes leaving prints in the decades-old dust.

But then – then there is only the sound of Frida's screams of terror, going on and on and on—

'Kat!' Hugo is standing in the doorway, cradling an enormous bunch of yellow roses, Katrin's favourite, along with a highly inappropriate bottle of champagne. He swoops in, dumping the gifts on the guest chair and enveloping her in a careful embrace. 'Oh, my beautiful pal,' he exhales into her hair. 'I thought we'd lost you for a minute there.' When he lets go, Katrin can see his pain clearly, and the love there.

'Where are Max and Ted?' she asks, wiping her face dry. 'I want to see them. Are they with Bill?'

'The boys are fine – Ginny has them. They're absolutely fine.' He stares at her strangely, as though trying to assess the damage. 'Do you remember what happened, Kat? At the party?'

'I – I remember the party, but I don't remember falling.' She blinks at her brother-in-law, hoping he'll fill in the blanks for her, but instead he just shakes his head sadly. 'So? Where's Bill, then?'

'We – I haven't seen him for a couple of days, Kat,' he stammers. 'Ginny's been staying at Starling House with the boys, so they're OK. But Bill – well, he's been telling us he's here, visiting you, but the staff here say they haven't seen him since Monday. I phoned him first thing, to tell him you were awake, because the hospital hadn't been able to get through to him, and he said he was going to drive straight here. But when I dropped Henri with Ginny she said he'd packed a bag the minute he'd hung up from me, saying he had to go away for a few days. On business.'

Hugo's face says it all: he knows it's bullshit.

Katrin's thoughts jumble around in her head, lurching about in search of some sense. 'How long have I been here?' she whispers. She knows the consultant has already told her, but that was hours ago, and she hadn't been in a state to retain the detail.

'The party was a week ago – a week yesterday,' Hugo replies. 'Katrin, we thought you were – well, it doesn't matter what we thought, because here you are now, so—'

'And you really don't know where Bill has gone?' she demands.

Hugo shakes his head, and there is something hidden, something reluctant in his expression that makes Katrin ask her next question.

'And Amélie?'

His eyes now anchor on hers. 'Gone too.' He looks down, a gathering of courage. 'Did you know about them?' he asks.

Katrin feels the shame of her knowledge, and, when she nods, all his hurt pours into her, to merge with her own.

There is a knock on the open door, and Katrin is relieved of the interruption from Hugo's grief. The woman in the doorway is familiar to Katrin, but it's not until she speaks that she realises where they've met before.

'Katrin, I'm DS Ali Samson. I hope this is a good time?'

'Yes, I remember you.' She was the one who let Frida off that shoplifting charge with a caution. 'You dealt with Thomas's disappearance at the start of the year, didn't you?' She blinks at the woman, bemused. 'Oh, have you found him?'

DS Samson casts a glance in Hugo's direction. 'How much have you told her?' she asks, and he simply shakes his head.

The detective pulls up a chair. 'Katrin, the doctors tell me you're in great shape, all things considered. Just a small fracture?' She indicates towards the neck brace. 'Now, you'll know that you suffered a fall – did they tell you that you were found at the bottom of the clocktower? At The Starlings.'

Katrin nods slowly. Yes, Dr Bantam had mentioned it, but she'd not had a chance to process his words until now. 'The clocktower,' she repeats. 'But – that door's kept locked. Why on earth would I have been in the clocktower?'

DS Samson crosses her hands over her notebook. 'That's what we're trying to find out. I'm really sorry to have to tell you this, but we're treating your fall as suspicious.'

Katrin finds she can't even answer; is this woman trying to tell her she was pushed?

'Forensic evidence suggests you weren't alone, that there may have been at least one other set of footprints on the stairs apart from yours – and, as none of your friends or neighbours have come forward to admit they were there with you, almost everyone is under suspicion. In fact, Hugo here is one of the only people at the party with a cast-iron alibi.'

'Barely left my seat all evening, apparently,' he says.

'We're currently trying to find your sister-in-law, who's been missing since Tuesday—'

311

'And Frida? Is Frida OK?' Katrin asks with urgency, suddenly certain she should be worried for her. 'Can I see her?'

'She's fine, Kat,' Hugo says with a reassuring nod. 'Honestly. She's been helping Ginny out with the boys. Those two have been lifesavers, I can't tell you.'

DS Samson leans in, clearly anxious to gather everything she can before Katrin tires. 'So, as I said, Katrin, Amélie's missing, and, from what Ginny tells us, it would seem Bill has also disappeared now.'

She hesitates for long enough to make Katrin uncomfortable.

'They were having an affair,' Katrin confirms, offering Hugo her hand. 'That's what you want to know, isn't it?'

Samson nods.

'I thought it was over. I'd known about it for a while – but Hugo . . .?'

'Yup, this has been a hell of a week,' he scoffs. 'I didn't have a clue.'

'Assuming Bill is with Amélie, have you any idea where they might be headed?' the detective asks.

Katrin is numb. She shakes her head, feeling useless.

'We discovered a Find My Phone app on your phone,' Ali says, 'but it's password-protected.'

'My phone?' Katrin replies. 'Yes – if he has his mobile with him, I can track him. Can you get me my phone?' she says with some urgency, glancing at the bedside cabinet beside her. 'Actually, that's a point – where *is* my phone?'

Samson reaches into her bag to bring out Katrin's fully charged phone. 'We had to check it over, Katrin, and access some of your text messages, as it became an important piece of evidence.'

She frowns.

'It went missing after the fall,' DS Samson explains. 'And then we realised that the emergency call we received that night had actually been made from your phone.'

'So, where did you find it?' Katrin asks.

The officer glances at Hugo.

'In Amélie's dressing room,' he says. 'That's why they want to talk to her. Kat, it's not looking very good for her at all.'

'Or Bill, at that,' Katrin adds, and the detective nods frankly.

Mind racing, Katrin turns to the phone screen and opens the app. It only takes seconds and she has him located, somewhere in southwest London, his signal steady. She hands it to DS Samson, who for a fleeting second looks as though she's won the lottery.

'OK. Katrin, we're going to have to hang on to this for now,' she says, waving the mobile between them, already on her feet. 'Wait here – I'm just going to hand this to my deputy outside, so we can get straight on it.'

She disappears into the corridor, leaving Hugo and Katrin staring at each other as though frozen.

'Do you think she could have done it?' Katrin whispers, allowing her mind to travel further, as she adds, 'That *they* could have done it?'

Hugo appears not angry or bitter, she realises, but troubled. It occurs to Katrin that he is in many ways Bill's opposite: the dark and still waters to Bill's silver fox charm, his quiet, thoughtful laughter a tonic against Bill's bellowing bluster. If only she'd met Hugo first, a previously unacknowledged thought floats up, shocking in its clarity. What life might they have had then? How different the world would look today.

'Oh, Kat,' he replies, his dark eyes gleaming with sadness, 'I don't know what I think any more. Honestly, I don't.'

Their conversation is cut short as DS Samson returns to the room, briskly shutting the door behind her and again reaching into her bag to bring out an iPad.

'We've got a couple of officers on it now – our city colleagues should be able to catch up with your husband before the end of the day. *And* Amélie, with any luck.' She studies Katrin a moment, assessing her, perhaps. 'This must be a lot to take in, Katrin. At the risk of bombarding you, I'm going to play you a recording, if that's OK? It's this anonymous call we received from your phone. The quality was very poor, but I've just had this back – our tech team have managed to clean it up a bit. I want you to take a listen, and tell me if you recognise the caller.' She hands her iPad to Katrin, and a light, raspy voice plays out.

Hello? Hello? Yes? Ambulance, please? Yes – no. No, listen! There's a woman – she's fallen. At Highcap House. No, no, I mean The Starlings! On the main Highcap Road. She's hurt! Hurry, please! The caller hangs up.

'Do you recognise the voice?' DS Samson asks, a hopeful crease scored between her dark eyebrows.

'Of course,' Katrin replies, and in her mind's eye she is standing at the top of the clocktower steps, looking down on the solitary figure framed in the backlit doorway below, feet planted firmly in sturdy old walking boots. She looks at Hugo and sees confused recognition in his face too. 'It's Thomas. Thomas King – our groundsman.'

36. Ginny

On Monday morning, Hugo and Frida set off for the police station, to write up a revised statement before Frida heads off to school again.

As Hugo hands over baby Henri at the door of Starling House, Ginny cannot take her eyes off the girl. She has that aura, the one Ginny not so long ago described to Katrin as being able to see with a kind of sixth sense, and the sudden awareness of it causes her to stiffen up as Frida hugs her goodbye and disappears behind the door of the waiting taxi.

For a moment Ginny remains in the open doorway of Starling House, a baby over her shoulder, two little boys bombing around in the hallway to her rear, and the morning sunlight streaking across the green expanse of lawns before her. When she'd imagined her new life in The Starlings on that May Open Day, just over a year ago, could she ever have imagined how events would play out? Gazing towards the red-brick mansion blocks and the central clocktower, she recalls another time, other babies, other girls, other fears, and it feels to her as though she is losing herself, a little more with each passing day.

For the rest of the morning, Ginny occupies herself delivering Max and Ted to nursery, before returning to Katrin's home with baby Henri for feeding and nap time. It is a marvel to Ginny, the resilience of youth, and it is clear to her that Amélie's baby doesn't miss his errant mother one bit, contented little chap that he is. As she cleans the kitchen and bakes cupcakes in anticipation of the boys returning home, her mind continuously strays to that unsettling feeling she had about Frida this morning, and over and over she bats it away, rejecting it as the foolish imaginings of an overwrought old woman.

Bill has been out of contact now for a full twenty-four hours, his last call to Ginny being soon after he'd set off yesterday morning, when he'd phoned simply to say, sorry, he'd be gone a while, before breaking down and adding that he'd made a terrible mistake. And with Bill's call, any thoughts of her own escape evaporated in the sure knowledge that Katrin really did now need her more than ever. Of course, yesterday's news that Katrin has regained consciousness is joyous, but, while Ginny is desperate to go to her dear friend, she fears what Katrin will see in her when they come face to face; she fears what she will remember.

When she opens the front door to shake out the doormat, Ginny is dismayed to see Anne Ashbourne rushing over the dewy grass of the green, waving a large envelope in the air. She's agitated, exhilarated even, and Ginny's first instinct is to step back inside the house and bolt the door.

'Ginny! Ginny, hang on! You must see this!' Anne calls out, puffing and shiny-faced as she comes to a halt at the doorstep, bending over to rest on her knees a moment.

With no choice other than to invite the woman in, Ginny directs Anne towards the kitchen, where she immediately commandeers the table, spreading out several sheets of A4 paper

316

along with the 1971 Mother and Baby Home photograph she'd borrowed from Katrin.

'Can't this wait, Anne?' Ginny demands, wincing at the sight of that dreadful picture. 'I've got a lot on my plate right now.'

'No, you'll want to hear this. It's huge news!' She pushes her thumb-smeared specs up her nose and taps her pen on the palm of her hand, smiling broadly. 'We've been completely inundated with responses from the TV appeal! I've been poring over emails all weekend. Let me show you. You won't believe it!'

Ginny would believe it, she thought, given the unsettling email alert she herself had received late last night.

Anne holds up a sheet of paper covered in tables and pie charts and percentages that make Ginny's eyes swim. 'Now, this is a printout I was given permission to access by a member of the Ancestry DNA community who contacted me shortly after the TV appeal. What we're looking at here are the DNA matches for Sonia Glaser, a forty-six-year-old woman who grew up with her adoptive family in Cornwall. In the first section—' Anne points to a list entitled *Close Family* '—you'll see her birth mother, here, and then, over here, one half-sibling who grew up with that mother.'

Ginny's pulse is pounding so loudly in her ears, she feels quite faint.

'Sonia was recently reunited with him, which is how she learned she was a Highcap baby. Now, if we follow Sonia's list, the DNA tells her she has five more half-sibling matches—'

Without warning, Ginny snatches the sheet of paper from Anne's hands, and together with the rest of the documents she slides it briskly back inside the unmarked envelope, out of sight.

'Ginny! Whatever's the matter?' Anne gasps, taking a step back.

Ginny slaps the envelope down on the breakfast bar and pushes it away. 'How insensitive can you be, Anne Ashbourne?'

'*Insensitive?*'

'Poor Katrin is lying in a hospital bed right now, quite possibly in danger of losing her own child, and you're here in her house, jumping up and down like an excitable puppy, harping on about other people's families – other people's babies!'

'Oh, good grief, I didn't think . . .' Anne stuttered, her face grown quite pale. 'I just thought it would be a nice thing for her to see when she got home – I thought she'd be interested.'

'Interested in what?'

The two women both start at the sudden appearance of Katrin in the doorway, alone, pale-faced, dirty-haired, in a neck brace and sling, wearing a pair of white hospital Crocs and, appallingly, her torn silk dress from the night of the party. At Ginny's shocked expression, she laughs, glancing down at her outfit with a rueful smile. 'Don't judge me. I didn't have anything else to wear.'

Ginny rushes to her, taking up her good hand, cautious of her injuries. 'Darling! What on earth—'

'I couldn't take another second in that place,' Katrin replies. 'They didn't want me to leave, but I discharged myself. My brain scan was clear last night, so I'm fine – just tired.' She casts about the room, looking for her boys. 'And I didn't have my phone, so I couldn't call anyone or check my messages – but there's something else. Ginny – I've remembered what Frida and I were arguing about that night. What Poppy Parsons told me—'

Unceremoniously, Ginny steers a startled Anne out through the front door. 'I'll call you later,' she says, just to be rid of the woman, and she pushes the door shut behind her.

With dread, Ginny returns to Katrin. 'I know about Frida, darling,' she replies, softly. 'I realised it too, only this morning, as I watched her leave. It's this Barney – this boy at school, isn't it?'

Katrin nods. 'She's pregnant. And this "Barney" is no boy.'

37. DS Ali Samson

The drive to St Saviour's takes an hour and twenty minutes, and for most of the journey Ali and Frida chat easily, the girl having relaxed in her company since getting the truth about her mother and uncle out in the open at last.

Yet still there is the secret knowledge she possesses about Frida's condition, about this boy she's about to meet in the school refectory, with his black-market abortion pills and demands for his girlfriend to delete any damning evidence. Ali had lied to Trelawney this morning, messaging him to say she was heading back to The Starlings to follow up on a couple of interviews, but she doesn't feel bad about the deception; this girl's safety has leapfrogged the urgency of finding Katrin's attacker. Katrin Gold is safely recovering in hospital, whereas, right now, everything points to the clear and present danger for Frida Pascal.

'Did you get to see your Auntie Kat before you left?' Ali asks, knowing the answer, but wondering at the reasons behind it. These two were meant to be so close.

Frida shakes her head and turns to look out of the passenger window, attempting to shut the topic down. 'Didn't have time.'

'That's a shame. I know she was keen to see you.'

Frida starts scrolling through her phone, and Ali lets it go, granting the girl silence for the rest of the journey.

After the best part of an hour, they turn on to the long driveway towards the mansion buildings of St Saviour's and Frida puts her phone away, stiffening and checking her reflection in the visor mirror.

'Looking forward to seeing your friends?' Ali asks.

'What friends?' Frida scoffs. 'They all dumped me months back. After – after I got suspended.'

'I'm sorry to hear that, Frida. Have you got a boyfriend, perhaps – or a girlfriend, for that matter?' she says with a warm smile.

Frida shrugs. 'Kind of.'

It's now midday, and after pulling up in the parking area Ali helps Frida with her bags, says goodbye to her at the front steps and wishes her good luck with her exams. But as Frida disappears inside the building, instead of heading back to her car, Ali stops another student and asks directions to the refectory.

'Is that the canteen you share with the sixth form college?' she checks, and the girl nods before picking up her own bags and tramping across the gravel towards a waiting cluster of friends.

Ali slips off her jacket just as her phone rings. 'Garner, what've you got for me?' she asks, simultaneously pulling on a more casual hoodie and checking her watch.

'Ginny LeFevre, sarge? I managed to trace her to the purchase of her last address in London back in the late eighties, but earlier than that, she disappears. No birth or marriage certificates. No passport or employment records.'

'And you checked under her full name, "Virginia", too?'

'Yup, there's nothing, sarge. Ginny LeFevre appears to be a ghost.'

'Ha, fancy that.' Ali is struck by her lack of surprise. 'Good stuff, Benny,' she says. 'I'll follow up with you at the station in the morning.'

By the time she has tucked her hair inside a baseball cap and changed into sneakers, Ali reaches the refectory at 12.20, where she buys a vending-machine coffee and takes a seat near the main entrance. As she tries to blend in beneath the noisy din of teenagers and teachers at lunch, she scrolls through her messages, spotting a new email sent by the boss this morning, asking her if she's made up her mind about Holmwood's hearing tomorrow. *Happy to come along for morale support*, he signs off, without fanfare. Spelling never was his strong point, she thinks, feeling a rare flash of affection for the old bastard. He thinks it will be 'good for her' to see her attacker face justice, but the truth is, the idea of seeing the man who robbed her of what may well have been her one and only chance at motherhood terrifies her more than anything she's ever faced before. What if he changes his mind about pleading guilty? What is she's forced to give evidence? She's not scared that she'll go to pieces; she's afraid she'll lose her control. She's fantasised about it often enough to know she's capable of it.

Without another thought on the matter, Ali deletes Trelawney's message and concentrates on the matter at hand. *Frida*.

No sooner has she put her phone down on the table, than it silently vibrates, flashing Ginny LeFevre's number with blinking insistence. Ali rejects the call, annoyance setting in when the woman attempts to get through again seconds later, and then again four or five times in the next few minutes. Flipping her phone over, Ali scans the refectory, lingering on a group of non-uniformed sixth-formers, wondering if one of these harmless-looking boys is Barney, or whether he's even here at all.

At 12.30 sharp, Frida appears at the edge of the refectory and hovers near the entrance, studiously scanning the large hall. Ali watches intently, waiting for this Barney to appear, expecting to see the fresh-faced young man she'd glimpsed on Frida's phone last week. But instead, to her dismay, she sees a young man dressed in a grey suit rise from the teachers' table to stride confidently across and out of the hall, closely followed by Frida, whose eyes never leave him.

Abandoning her coffee, Ali follows at a distance, along the busy corridors and out towards the residential wing, where Frida now leads the way, up the staircase, one flight, two flights, three – and on to a dormitory landing. The young man is still following, a few feet behind her, and, as Frida reaches her own room and pulls out a key, Ali drops her head and continues past as though on a mission elsewhere. As soon as she senses it's clear to do so, she looks back to see the grey-suited man step swiftly inside Frida's room behind her.

Heart pounding, Ali races back to the door, setting her phone to video record, where she stands motionless, phone close to the frame, listening in.

'You take this one now, and then this one the same time tomorrow,' he says.

There is a pause, a horrible lull when Ali wonders whether her presence has been detected. 'You're sure it's safe?' Frida asks, in almost a whisper.

'I told you, my brother's a doctor. Honestly, you've got nothing to worry about.'

Another pause. 'That's easy for you to say. You've never had to take one.'

Barney doesn't answer.

'Will I bleed a lot?' Frida asks then, in a child's voice.

Again, there is no response, and it is at this point that Ali turns the handle and throws back the door, chest out, head high, while her phone captures the whole scene on video: a girl in school uniform palm outstretched, a man, *a teacher*, handing her a foil wrap of tablets.

'Who the hell—?' he asks, clearly thinking this baseball-capped woman is a student. 'Don't you know how to knock?'

'I'm Detective Sergeant Samson,' she replies coolly, showing him her ID. 'And what's your name, sir?'

'Oh,' he says, his tone switching instantly to one of affability. Now she recognises him, that smiling young rugby player with the floppy blond hair; clearly the profile pic she saw on Frida's phone had been taken a good few years earlier. 'I'm Mr Barnaby. I teach here.'

Ali turns to Frida, whose expression is a brutal blend of regret and relief. 'Barney?' Ali asks, and Frida simply nods, dropping to perch on the edge of her single bed, her narrow shoulders slumped, her bare knees pressed together in shame.

'What's your first name, Mr Barnaby?'

'Ed,' he replies with a frown.

'Ed Barnaby,' DS Ali Samson says, loud and clear, 'I'm arresting you on suspicion of child abuse and attempting to elicit abortion through unlawful means.'

38. Katrin

The call from DS Ali Samson had been brief: Barnaby is in custody; Frida is safe; the detective is bringing her home. All they can do now is call Hugo back from the office and wait anxiously for Frida's safe return.

'Katrin, you're going to need to treat her with kid gloves,' the detective had instructed. 'Right now, she's appalled that we've arrested him. She also denies that she is pregnant, or even that she and Barnaby are involved at all. I just wanted to forewarn you, as this kind of denial is very common in abuse cases.' Katrin had wept silently as the detective spoke; denial was something she knew only too well about. Thanking the detective, she had hung up and headed downstairs to update Ginny.

By late afternoon, Ginny has fetched the twins, and alongside Katrin, baby Henri and a visibly shaken Hugo they assemble in the living room at Starling House, attempting to conjure up some semblance of normality before Frida gets home. The boys, ebullient in their delight at Mummy's return, have worn themselves out after an hour or two of excitable running around, and they're now flopped out on the beanbags watching TV.

When Frida finally arrives, despite not having seen her aunt since the night of the fall, it is clear she can barely look at Katrin.

'Can I go straight upstairs, please?' she asks Hugo, ignoring the pleas of her little cousins to play. 'I just want to go to bed. I just want to sleep.'

'Of course,' Katrin answers for him, careful to respect Frida's need for some space. 'You know where your room is, sweetheart. You just make yourself at home.' It has been agreed that she will stay at Starling House for a night or two, along with Ginny, who can keep an eye on both Katrin and Frida while continuing to care for the boys.

'She's in a state of shock,' DS Samson tells them, once the teenager is out of earshot. She gestures towards the sofa, and the three of them sit side by side, facing her across the coffee table. 'This Ed Barnaby is a teacher at the sixth form college next door to St Saviour's, but this past year he's also been teaching a few hours in the girls' school, to cover staff shortages. Twenty-nine years old. Clearly he has no business being in the single room of a then-fifteen-year-old pupil – and no business handing out abortion pills either.'

An unwanted memory rises in Katrin's mind, of herself and Bill on their very first date in Soho, she, at seventeen, so young and inexperienced, he the man of the world, talking her through the wine list, enjoying his role as teacher. How much she'd loved him, she thinks now; but how much she'd missed out on, tucked beneath his wing. She feels sick with betrayal at the recollection, as though the rest of the world had somehow colluded in embracing their imbalanced union as acceptable.

Hugo's hand trembles as he runs it across his face. 'How could we have missed this? Is this the same teacher she had all that bother over last year? Amélie was so hard on her about it. She told her she should grow up and get over it.' He meets Katrin's gaze, his jaw slack. 'I – I didn't do enough, did I, Kat? I'm meant to be her stepfather. Nobody believed her, not even me.'

Katrin rests her good hand on Hugo's shoulder and gives him a little shake. 'How could you have known, Hugo? At least you were kind to her, which is more than can be said for Amélie. You can't blame yourself.'

Hugo glances overhead and lowers his voice. 'You know it was me who reported Amelie to Social Services? I thought I was doing the right thing at the time – I was at breaking point, and I thought it was the only way she'd get help. But now – for Frida – well, now I think I've probably only made everything worse.'

Beside him, Ginny takes Hugo's hand in hers, regarding him sympathetically, and for a few seconds no one speaks.

'Someone had to do it, Hugo. You've got nothing to feel guilty about,' Katrin says with finality, before turning back to the detective. 'Ali, what happens now?'

'Let her just rest tonight,' DS Samson says, 'and see how she is tomorrow. From what Frida's texts tell us, she was about three weeks late at the time of the party, so if she is pregnant it's very early days. Barnaby will be held in custody overnight, and in the meantime I'll be liaising with Social Services and working with the CPS to take advice on moving the case forward.'

'Is there any news on Bill and Amélie?' Ginny asks the next question on Katrin's mind.

The twins pad barefoot across the room and clamber on to the sofa, snuggling either side of their mother, like ducklings. Katrin pulls them close and plants a kiss on the top of each head.

'Yes. Amélie's shoes came back from forensics – they're not a match for the footprints in the clocktower. We think Bill must be turning his phone on and off, because the Find My Phone signal keeps dropping off your mobile, Katrin. But Roehampton seems to pop up frequently. Any ideas about that?' DS Ali asks, glancing between Katrin and Hugo.

Suddenly, Hugo sits upright. 'The Priory. It's where Amélie goes for rehab. Bill must be visiting her there.'

DS Ali Samson grabs her bag. 'I'll keep you updated,' she says and, without looking back, she races through the hall and slams the front door behind her.

For long moments, nobody speaks, as Katrin draws up the memory of waking, terrified, in her lonely hospital room, without Bill. In the moment when she most needed him by her side, he hadn't been there. He'd let her down.

'I'm divorcing him,' she says finally. 'I never want him in this house again.'

At suppertime, Hugo cooks, grateful for the distraction, but Frida still refuses to leave her room, insisting that she'd rather eat there alone. With the little ones in bed, Katrin, Ginny and Hugo dine on their laps in the living room, with the television turned low to blot out the uncomfortable silence that has descended since DS Samson phoned to confirm they have now taken Bill into custody for questioning tomorrow. Meanwhile, the detective had said, with some relief, Amélie is being interviewed in her private room at The Priory, and her prints taken to compare against those left on Katrin's mobile phone. The police should have some news to share with them soon, she'd promised, some answers, perhaps.

After everything that has happened, the developments are something of an anticlimax, because Katrin knows all about Bill and Amélie's crimes, and they don't involve pushing her down the marble stairs of the clocktower at the anniversary party. Their crime is far more pedestrian, a simple case of infidelity. As the three sit together, lights turned low, Katrin studies Ginny across the room, a friend who is normally so in tune with her, but now so absent. And Hugo – well, Hugo seems to be sinking further inside himself by the minute. So, at just before midnight, when a call comes in reporting another security alert up at White Rise, it is almost a relief to see Hugo jump up in response, a breaking of the inertia they find themselves locked in.

'We'll keep Henri tonight,' Ginny says, getting up as he pulls on his coat to leave. 'I'll check on him – I'm heading up to bed anyway.'

Instinctively, Katrin follows Hugo into the entrance hall and hugs him goodbye, telling him to be careful and handing him a spare set of keys before closing the door behind him. She returns to the kitchen and sits at the table, watching Ginny as she stacks their dirty plates in the dishwasher and wipes down the worktops. Beyond the dark panes to the garden, the solar lanterns twinkle across the lawn, and Katrin is once again struck by a sense of unreality, of disbelief. Neither woman says a word, and, when Ginny has at last finished clearing up, she runs herself a glass of water and turns to Katrin with a weary smile.

'Goodnight, darling,' she says. 'I'm going up.'

But Katrin only shakes her head. 'Sit down, please,' she says with an expression that can only communicate one thing to this woman who stands before her, whoever she might be. 'I remember everything, Ginny. From the night of the party. I remember it all.'

39. Katrin | Eight days earlier

Katrin made her excuses and left the courtyard, her heart hammering with urgency.

Quite out of nowhere, Poppy Parsons had confided in Katrin that there were rumours circulating at school about Frida and Mr Barnaby, the music teacher. 'They're saying he visits her bedroom at night,' Poppy had said, her eyes aglitter with the glee of divulging gossip. The girl's mother had allowed her a glass of champagne, and it had loosened her tongue. 'Meg and Rose say she's been throwing up a lot lately, but I said loads of girls at our school do that. I mean, it doesn't have to mean you're pregnant, does it?'

Cutting through the twilight paths of The Starlings, Katrin tapped frantic words into her phone, as echoes of her own past loomed large from the shadows. This wasn't the kind of thing you left unspoken; she had to talk to her niece about it right away, before it ate into the heart of her. Whether she was pregnant or purging, Frida was evidently carrying her torment alone, and that was wrong, so very wrong.

Katrin arrived at the greenhouse as arranged, where she waited for ten minutes or more, dialling and redialling Frida's number, and cursing under her breath. But when finally her niece answered, Katrin's anxiety spilled over and she demanded to know the truth in so bullish a way that she felt Frida withdraw in a breath.

'Frida, please!' Katrin insisted. 'Just come and talk to me, sweetheart? If you really are spending time with that man – spending *nights* with that man, Frida – he's breaking the law. You do know that?'

But instead of answers Katrin was rendered powerless by Frida's response. 'Just leave me alone, Auntie Kat,' she sobbed, as the wind howled around her handset. 'You're not my mum!'

Those words. *You're not my mum.* A faraway memory surfaced, of Katrin yelling that very phrase herself, decades earlier, aiming them at some kindly foster mother intent on saving her, on stopping her from climbing into that Mercedes and away into the darkness beyond. She recalls her palms flying out and connecting with the shoulders of that good woman, rejecting her help, dogged as she was in her pursuit of self-obliteration. Still Katrin felt the guilt of the memory, the shame at how easily she – a child – had been coerced into believing that that adult world was something she wanted to be a part of—

Alone in the gloom of the greenhouse, Katrin dialled Frida again, sobbing herself now, begging her niece to please come, to please talk to her! But something in Frida had hardened and she had become unreachable, even to Katrin.

'Worry about your own problems, Auntie Kat,' she hissed, her voice subdued against the drag and pull of the night tide. 'Worry about my mum and Uncle Bill playing Happy Families at Starling House right now, why don't you?'

Leaving the greenhouse behind her, Katrin began making her way home, crossing the lawns towards Starling House, with its unoccupied top floor illuminated from within like a cinema

330

screen against the darkening shoreline beyond. Was it true, what Frida had said? Were they really there, together, their affair alive and flourishing?

When she was halfway across the green, a wave of false contractions tightened like a band beneath Katrin's pregnant belly, and she found herself stooped, leaning into her knees as she caught her breath. Her pulse was throbbing, and, though the evening was growing cool, perspiration beaded at her brow like a fever. She prayed that none of her neighbours were watching from their windows, flanked as the lawns were by all three wings of the old building; she couldn't bear to think there might be witnesses to her downfall. But when she righted herself there were no neighbours to be seen, only a new image now visible, a monstrous tableau of mother, father and beloved infant, frozen in their common focus: studying her. With slow deliberation, the woman – Amélie – peeled away to reposition the lens of the adjacent telescope, inclining herself to zoom in on the scene below. Her gaze weighed in on Katrin like a body blow and, overwhelmed by the shock of fresh betrayal, all Katrin could do was turn away.

'Darling?' Ginny murmured, setting her drinks tray down on the cobbles outside the clocktower. 'What on earth—'

'It's Bill . . .' Katrin stuttered, turning to look back towards her home in the distance. 'Oh, God, he'll be coming after me – I don't want to listen to any more of his excuses,' she confided through laboured breaths. 'Can we go back to yours, Gin?'

'Come in here a sec,' Ginny replied, already rifling through a bunch of keys before slotting one into the entrance door beside them. 'I just spotted a light behind the clockface on my way back – I think Bill must have left a lamp on after the bird inspectors yesterday. Come on, darling, in you come. Tell me what's going on.'

331

Easing the great door open a few inches, the two women slipped inside, and sure enough, high above the landing at the top of the dusty marble staircase, a lit construction lamp hung on a cable from an exposed beam.

'And I can't find Frida either,' Katrin started to say as cautiously she followed Ginny up the steps, taking in the morbid gloom of the space, and the elusive shifting sounds of a legion of birds roosting in the rafters overhead. In the damp half-light, the clocktower felt as though the very fabric of the place contained all the grief and torment of the past two centuries gone by, all of it held right here, like a silent heartbeat pulsing, palpably, at core of The Starlings.

A solitary bird broke from the darkness, chittering through the open space above, causing the lantern to swing and cast long dust-moted shadows up and down the flaking plaster walls. Katrin reached for the railing, but Ginny was quick to stop her, an arm shooting out to grasp her wrist.

'No, the barrier's not safe to lean on,' she said, steering her clear. 'In fact, you shouldn't be up here at all, in your condition. The woodwork's rotten all over. Now—' she fixed Katrin with concern '—what were you saying about Frida? I thought it was Bill you were upset with.'

Katrin ran her hands over her face, careless of the make-up she'd applied so carefully just hours earlier. 'Oh, Ginny, I don't know where to begin.'

Faintly, beyond the narrow opening in the door below them, they heard Bill's voice, calling her name across the courtyard. 'Katrin?' he called out, all singsong, so as not to raise an alarm. So as to keep up appearances. 'Katrin? Sweetheart?' His voice passed and grew fainter.

'He was up there with her, in our bedroom – with Amélie and her baby. *Their* baby. I saw them!' She swivelled to meet

Ginny's eyes, shining champagne-bright in the lamp glow. 'It felt like I was looking at – at – it felt as though I'd just vanished, been erased somehow. As if I'd never existed at all.' A sob rose in her chest, and Ginny opened her arms to draw her close. 'He promised me it was all over, Gin. I'd even managed to convince myself that Henri was nothing to do with him, that Amélie and Hugo were reconciled – that we should just forget about it all, and look to the future—'

Gently, Ginny pulled back to look at her. She exhaled heavily, her features losing all softness. 'I could kill him,' she murmured. 'That stupid, stupid man! What are you going to do, darling?'

All these years, and one way or another she'd always let him off the hook; Bill, the golden boy. Why? Even now, he continued to have his cake and eat it – greedily, carelessly, spraying crumbs all around for his little wife to clear up. But this time felt so much worse, gorging as he was on his own family's doorstep, right here for all to see.

'I can't do it any more, Ginny. I just can't.'

'What can I do to help, darling?' Ginny asked, her devotion like that of a mother desperate to take away her child's pain. She clasped Katrin's forearms and gave her a gentle shake. 'Tell me what you need, Katrin – what can I do to make this all better? You're not on your own, you know. *I'm* here now.'

Something in Ginny's self-possessed tone triggered a shift in Katrin's mindset, and she found herself adopting the same steely certainty as she answered her friend. 'I want him to pay this time, Ginny,' she whispered. 'I want them both to pay.'

On the floor below, a heavy creak alerted them to the presence of another. Snatching for the cable overhead, Ginny angled the light towards the newcomer, and, expecting to see Bill, Katrin was astonished at the sight against the backlit glow of sunset of not her husband, but Thomas King. Thomas, not drowned, and not dead – not dead at all. Above them, the roosting birds broke into a sudden clamour of deafening noise, before bursting out through the broken rafters for their nightly display in the red sky above The Starlings.

'I don't believe it,' Ginny growled at the sight of Thomas, a low, hostile tremor in her voice.

'Virginia?' Thomas replied, craning his neck stiffly, one hand shielding his eyes against the glare. He looked older and thinner, unkempt, a patchy white beard now adorning his chin. 'Is that you?'

'Yes!' Katrin replied on Ginny's behalf, the wonder of his reappearance briefly releasing her from the drama of her own life. 'And me, Thomas – Katrin! Are you alright? Where have you been all this time?'

Thomas dropped his hand to his side and his face was bathed in white lamplight. 'Why don't you ask Virginia?' he said.

'What?' Katrin turned to Ginny, whose jaw was set rigid.

'Katrin, there are things you should know about Virginia,' Thomas continued. 'She's not who you think she is. She's been here before. She's lied to you about everyth—'

'Wait, I'm coming down,' Katrin called, raising a hand.

The next three seconds unfolded like a silent dance: both women stepped forward, one in friendship, the other to censor. Preparing to descend, Katrin pinched up the hem of her silk dress, just as Ginny released the lamp flex, causing the bulb to sway madly, the strobe of it passing over the figure of Thomas below, his shadow shrinking and stretching like a warning scene in some long-forgotten film noir. Flinching against the light, Katrin reached for the crumbling rail as her foot slid out on the dusty marble step, and, shock-faced, Ginny grabbed at the empty space between them, too late to save her, too late to stop the future rolling, too late to stop the truth from spilling out. Into the darkness, Katrin fell.

40. Ginny

'I don't understand why you lied, Ginny.' Katrin's expression is challenging, confused. 'I don't understand why you said you weren't there.'

Ginny rises from the kitchen table and, under the glow of the hob lamp, begins to make cocoa, the old-fashioned way. The way Cook used to make it on birthing days, a rare treat for the girls after they'd returned to their dorms, exhausted, childless, bereft. She recalls how the girls all quietly rallied around these hollow mothers, with kindness and murmurs and strokes of the hair. *Ginny gives the best hugs*, she recalls one dorm mate saying. *Ginny will know what to do.* It all seems like a thousand years ago now. A different world; a different version of herself, and one she is now resigned to own. There is nothing to protect herself from any more. All she can do is tell Katrin the truth and accept the consequences, even if that means relinquishing all the warmth of belonging she has basked in over the past year.

'The fall,' she says, placing two mugs on the table between them. 'You do realise it was an accident, don't you? You know you just slipped.'

Katrin gapes at her. '*And you didn't think to tell anyone?*'

'I thought—' Ginny starts, but Katrin isn't finished.

'All this time the police have been wasting their energy searching for Amélie and Bill – tracing his phone, checking her transactions. Trawling through CCTV and fingerprinting the entire bloody community, for God's sake, Ginny! And don't even get me started on what you've put poor Frida through – Hugo says she's convinced it's all her fault, that I threw myself down the stairs because of something she said. What the hell were you thinking?'

Shame washes over Ginny. She cups her fingers around her mug, drawing it closer, mooring herself to the heat she finds there. 'I thought it was what you wanted,' she replies, looking up into Katrin's fierce gaze.

'What *I wanted*?' Katrin repeats, her shoulders dropping a little, a crease forming between her brows.

'That night, you – you were so desperate, Katrin. *You'd had enough*, darling, and the last thing you said to me was that you wanted them to pay.'

'Not like this!' Katrin gasps. 'Divorcing him, taking him to the cleaners – humiliating the pair of them even, yes! But framing them for murder? No one in their right mind—'

'I *wasn't* in my right mind, Katrin! Don't you see? It all happened so quickly! The fall – the sight of you and your precious unborn child tumbling down those marble steps – the rage I felt towards Bill and Amélie for everything they'd put you through! I rushed down after you, and when we found you were still breathing I got Thomas to call the ambulance, while I tried to bring you back round.'

'Oh, Ginny, why didn't you just stay put, and tell the police what had really happened?'

'I panicked, Katrin! I'd had more than a few glasses of champagne by then, and I wasn't thinking straight. And then, of course, there was Thomas, back from the dead like bloody Lazarus—'

'But what was he doing there, Ginny? I mean, even the police had given up on him. I honestly thought the poor man had drowned.'

'I thought so too.' Ginny exhales through trembling lips. 'It was pure chance that he should turn up that evening – he said he was on his way to gather a few of his belongings from the lodge, expecting the close to be quiet at that time of night. He'd come up from the beach side, you see, so he'd spotted the light from the clocktower – and you know how protective he is about the starlings. That's when he found us.'

She pauses, waiting for Katrin's response, but her friend only stubbornly sips from her mug. Ginny throws her hands up, defeated.

'Well, you know what happened next. After Thomas phoned the ambulance, I told him to get out of there, or else I'd tell the police that I'd seen him push you.'

'But why—?' Katrin tries to interject, but, now that she's started, Ginny has to get it out, has to *just say it*.

'It would be my word against his, I said, and who did he think they'd believe? Me, a close family friend, or him, an old employee who had left unexpectedly, harbouring a grudge?' Across the table, Katrin is unreadable. 'He must have believed I'd do it, because without another word he handed me your phone and fled.' Ginny lowers her gaze again. 'That's when I had the idea to blame it on Bill and Amélie. It had been so easy to scare Thomas off with the threat, and I thought, why not them? I was so angry, Katrin, and in many ways it *was* their fault! You would never have been up there with me if you hadn't been upset like that, if you hadn't come face to face with their treachery, yet again. And just like that, I convinced myself that the idea was simply perfect, because, let's face it, who had a better motive than them, the cheating husband and sister-in-law? It would have dealt with everything, Katrin, just like you'd wanted – what better way to make them pay?'

For a few long seconds Katrin stares at her, her thoughts appearing very far away, giving Ginny no clues with which to guess at her inner workings. What is she thinking? Is this it? Is this where their brief time together finally ends?

Katrin's eyes come back into focus, meeting squarely with Ginny's.

'What did Thomas mean, Ginny? When he said you weren't who you said you were? What secrets are so terrible that you would threaten an old man like that – that you'd rather see him homeless than face the truth he seemed so anxious to share?'

Ginny opens her mouth to speak, but her lips struggle to form the words, to wrestle her confession into the room. 'He's not all he seems either,' she says finally. 'He's more connected to this place than you could ever understand.'

Gently, Katrin places her hands over Ginny's. 'Then help me to understand? I'm still here, aren't I? I haven't run from the room so far – I haven't kicked you out. Just tell me everything. *Please*. Did Thomas do you harm when you were a patient here?'

After decades of denial, the moment Ginny had feared so gravely has finally arrived. *No more running*, she tells herself. *No more lies*.

'Before I tell you all this, Katrin, I want you to know that I only lied to you out of fear. Out of shame. And you know, it has taken me a lifetime to realise how that shame has held me back – how it prevented me from trusting and loving in the way normal people do. Before I came here, I had nothing – at least, nothing of true value. But then I met you, on that unexpected May day last year, and it was as though you'd been here waiting for me all along – here, where it all started. I *knew* you, instantly.'

338

'You knew me . . .?'

'Of course, I didn't *really* know you, darling – I'm talking in riddles. Forgive me. My point is, I adored you, all of you, at once, and I had never felt any such feeling of that kind years before. And so, I came here to be part of this new world you had built. But as my feelings for you and your beautiful family grew, so did my fear. I became more and more terrified that my past would emerge, and that I'd lose the one good thing in my life – you. Shame is a powerful poison, Katrin.'

'But surely you now realise there's no shame in what happened to you, Ginny? You were a young unmarried mother, a teenager – a victim of circumstance. A victim of a terrible, corrupt system!'

'No!' Ginny snatches her hands away, to bring one palm crashing down against the tabletop. 'I was no victim, Katrin. Don't you understand? Haven't you worked it out yet? I wasn't a victim. I *was* the system!' Breathing raggedly, she slumps back in her chair, covering her eyes with her hands. 'I was one of the nurses, darling. I looked after those poor girls – hundreds of them over the years – and that's what Thomas had on me. That's what I was trying to keep from you.'

'But you *told me* you were a mother here,' Katrin gasps, reaching across again, forcing Ginny to drop the barrier of her hands.

'I – I just let you believe what you wanted to, darling. I just didn't correct you.'

'And Victor? And your father? Were those stories all lies too?'

'Victor was real, and it's true he wanted to marry me, just as I said. And my father, oh, yes, he really was as terrible as I made out. Worse, in fact. When he said he knew people who could make problems disappear, he wasn't talking about a baby, Katrin – he was talking about Victor. So, without consultation he withdrew me from school and brought me back to Highcap, where I'd be safely out of temptation's way. I was to have a career in nursing, he announced, to "keep me out of trouble". My stepmother's idea. My apprenticeship began the very next day, at the Mother and Baby Home. I was sixteen.'

'No baby, then? *No baby.* You know, Ginny, I had even started to imagine it was possible you might be my—' And now it is Katrin's turn to look shamefaced. 'Stupid of me.'

'If I had been one of those poor girls, Katrin, and I found out you were my daughter—' a sob rises in her chest '—I'd be the happiest woman alive. The proudest.'

'But you weren't one of those girls, were you?' Katrin retorts. 'You were their nurse! You were their jailor!'

Ginny puts her mug down and meets Katrin's challenge, all pride gone. Now is not the time to minimise her role in this; now is the time to lay everything bare. 'Katrin, I wasn't just a nurse, darling. When you and I met for the first time last year, it was my father's death that had brought me back here. I was signing off papers for his estate. For White Rise.'

Katrin opens her mouth to speak, but it seems she cannot find the words.

'Stan Jarman,' Ginny confirms, instinctively lowering her voice as she finally utters the dark truth. 'The governor – he was my father.'

Ginny reaches for the envelope Anne brought over just hours earlier and places the documents on the table between them.

'You'll remember this photograph?' Ginny says, sliding the 1971 image across. She indicates a young woman, no more than a teenager, to the right-hand side of Governor Jarman.

'That's *you*?' Katrin gasps.

Ginny touches the edge of the picture with a wary fingertip. 'I remember the day that photo was taken, outside the clocktower. The building hasn't changed a bit, has it?'

'Ginny, did I tell you Bill had a full inspection carried out a few weeks back? After he took the clocktower project back from you. I had this theory that you were dragging your heels on getting the starlings moved because you were worried what we might uncover in there– after we'd heard Diana Lambley's rumours of infants buried in the basement . . .'

There is no answer Ginny can give to this, because Katrin is right: this is precisely what she had feared, exactly the disclosure she had, in some irrational way, hoped to defer. Because it was bad enough to know of the wrongs her father had committed in plain sight, but something else altogether to learn he had knowingly erased the evidence of so many infants who never even got to take their first breath.

'Ginny,' Katrin says, 'there is no concealed basement in the clocktower.' She waits for Ginny's response, but none comes. 'No buried secrets. No buried babies. Just starlings and bird shit and woodworm and dust.'

Ginny feels the sting of tears behind her eyes, and a fresh shame: that of cowardice. With the slightest bob of her head, she draws Katrin's attention back to the photograph. 'And you'll have spotted young Thomas here in the picture? Does he remind you of anyone?'

Katrin peers at it uncertainly.

'I would never have guessed it myself, until Anne mentioned that her mother had got herself in a state on the night of your fall. She was convinced she'd seen the governor from her bedroom window after they'd retired to bed, at just around the same time Thomas turned up and found us in the clocktower. Have a good look at Jarman,' she says, pushing the photograph back towards Katrin. 'I don't know how I'd never noticed the resemblance before, but if you took away my father's heavy moustache and spectacles . . .'

Katrin studies the picture again, suddenly aghast. '*Thomas*. Thomas is the *image* of him. Does he know?'

Guiltily, Ginny shakes her head. 'I didn't know, so why should he? All I can tell you is that his mother had worked up at my father's house for years, long before I was even born. She was his housekeeper; devoted to him, apparently. She was a nice woman, I seem to recall. And my stepmother loathed her.'

Katrin sits back in her chair. 'Do you think there are others? When Diana visited, she seemed to think there were many more, fathered by Jarman here, in the Mother and Baby Home.'

With a heavy sigh, Ginny turns over the Ancestry document Anne had tried to talk her through earlier. 'This DNA profile belongs to an ex-Highcap baby who came forward after Anne and Diana's television appeal last week. The woman was adopted, but after sending off her DNA she discovered not one, but six half-siblings she knew nothing about – one of which shared the same mother. That's how this Sonia found out she was born here: when they were reunited.'

Katrin nods slowly. 'And those other five half-siblings?'

'I assume they share DNA on the male side – meaning they all have different mothers.'

Katrin looks up with a slow frown. 'Jarman?'

Ginny's hand hovers at her throat. She nods, and then pushes the document closer to Katrin, indicating towards Sonia Glaser's six half-sibling profile names, stacked one on top of the other, like transactions on a bank statement.

'Soon after you'd sent your DNA off, I did the same. Because once Diana had planted that seed in my mind I needed to know if it was true – if my father had really been capable of such an atrocity. And then, last night, I received an email with a half-sibling summary just like this one.' She taps the very last profile name on Sonia's list: *VJ1955*. 'This is me.'

'VJ?' Katrin murmurs. 'Virginia Jarman.' For long moments, her eyes don't leave the list as she runs her finger slowly over each name, breath held. When Katrin finally looks up, Ginny sees her face is now tear-streaked, her lips parted in wonder, or perhaps disbelief. It is now Katrin's turn to tap a profile name, the one directly above her friend's: *Darling1981*. 'Ginny,' she whispers, '*this* is me.'

In awed silence, the two women remain, until their mugs grow cold and the first fingers of light appear over the garden, streaming in from the ocean beyond.

41. DS Ali Samson

Early on Tuesday morning, DS Ali Samson makes her way over
to Starling House to see how the family are faring, and to give
them an update on yesterday's interviews with Bill and Amélie.

As she approaches, the morning light paints a smooth, hazy
line across the horizon, a sign of better times ahead, perhaps,
Ali allows herself to hope. She parks on the perimeter path
and walks the short distance across the tranquil lawns of The
Starlings, shielding her eyes to gaze up towards the distant
sound of a light aircraft, sailing through the dappled Dorset
skies. It's an idyllic scene, and one completely at odds with
her own inner turmoil.

In the back of her mind is the hearing in Bournemouth Crown
Court, later this morning, of the case of thirty-two-year-old Neil
Holmwood, the man who stamped the unborn life out of her back
in April, but who, despite his admission, will only face charges for
the damage inflicted on Ali's body. Because she wasn't pregnant
enough for the baby to count. Because that's the law.

Margo phoned her last night, in response to the message
she'd sent, and they'd talked easily for a while, and it had felt

good. As they said goodbye, Margo had told Ali that she would be attending court in the morning; that she hoped Ali might be there too. But today Ali has woken exhausted, her ragged nerves worsened after a new message arrived from Trelawney, asking how she's feeling, and if she'd like a lift to the courthouse. Deep down she knows the boss is right, that it probably *would* do her good to see Holmwood in the dock, but, despite the additional bolster of Margo's support, Ali's not sure she has the strength for it – or the courage. And anyway, she's got other, more pressing business to attend to right now.

Since she delivered Frida Pascal home yesterday evening, Ali hasn't been able to stop thinking about the girl, and so she made it her priority to follow up with her Bournemouth colleagues, who had damning insights to share regarding Ed Barnaby. Now armed with this information, Ali hopes she might be able to persuade Frida to make a statement against him; she hopes that together they might be able to put that predator behind bars for the maximum sentence available.

Standing on the step of Starling House, she sets her face to neutral and leans into the front doorbell.

It's Ginny who comes to the door, with the twins close at heel, excitedly asking if it's Daddy come home.

'Not yet, darlings!' Ginny tells them, meeting Ali's eye as she winces at the heartbreak of their ignorance.

In the kitchen, Katrin is fully dressed, looking fresher than she had the last time Ali saw her, and sitting up at the table with Amélie's baby in her arms, feeding him from a bottle. The boys return to their game on the rug, constructing tiny brick towns and road systems around the empty baby basket.

'Oh, good, I was hoping you'd all be up,' Ali smiles, accepting a cup of coffee from Ginny. 'I just wanted to check in on you – and see how Frida is feeling.'

Katrin and Ginny exchange a sorry glance. 'Ginny took her up some breakfast an hour ago,' Katrin says, 'but she was still asleep. She hadn't even touched her supper from last night. I'm worried about her – she really does need to see a doctor sooner rather than later.'

Ali gazes beyond the parted glass doors to the garden, where gull cries fill the air, soaring in and out from the shoreline, feeding their young.

'I don't need to see a doctor.'

The three women turn at the sound of Frida's voice, and find her standing in the doorway, barefoot in soft lilac pyjamas, her hair a mess of curls. Her brown skin is pale, and her eyes are wet with tears.

'You don't?' Katrin asks, shifting baby Henri to her shoulder as she attempts to stand, her large pregnant belly hindering her pace. For a few taut seconds the adults can only stare at Frida, a multitude of possibilities washing between them, each one terrifying in its own way. She's keeping it? She isn't sure?

The girl drops her gaze, and with a little shake of her head, says, 'It's gone. I woke up with cramps in the night and when I got up to go to the loo, I – well, I'm pretty sure it's gone.'

'Oh, darling, why didn't you wake one of us?' Ginny asks with a small gasp.

Frida shrugs weakly, looking close to fainting. 'I took some ibuprofen a few hours ago, but it still hurts quite a lot—' Her palm hovers over the flat of her abdomen and she appears suddenly so very small.

Without thought, Ali crosses the room and draws the girl into an embrace. 'It's OK,' she tells her, aware of Katrin now passing the baby to Ginny to settle in his Moses basket beside the twins. 'Everything's going to be just fine. *You're* going to be just fine.' She steps aside to allow Katrin to take over.

Leading her niece to a seat, Katrin wraps a throw around her shoulders and pours her a sweet tea, and together the women gather at the table in the warm morning light. Frida shivers beneath her blanket, neither girl nor woman, with Ginny and Katrin close on either side. Her mother is, as ever, absent, but who needs a mother in name only, when you have women like these in your corner? Regarding them from her position across the table, Ali is suddenly struck by the privilege of sisterhood; what strength, in every one of them, she thinks. In every one of us.

'Frida,' she says, cautiously. 'You know, you'll still need to see the doctor. They'll want to make sure everything is OK.' She waits for a reply, but Frida remains silent. 'I know you were only three or four weeks late, but still, it's good to get checked out. And you're still in some pain, I think? I – I had a miscarriage last year, and the doctors were very kind to me.' These words, Ali finds, come out with unexpected ease.

Now Frida looks up with something like trust in her weary eyes. 'Will he go to prison? Barney?'

'If we can prove he's done something wrong, then, yes, he will,' Ali replies.

Katrin clasps Frida's hand. 'Are you afraid no one will believe you, sweetheart? After last time?'

Frida hides her face behind her mug and nods.

This is Ali's moment. 'Frida, my police colleagues in Bournemouth have been working with St Saviour's since I brought you home, and I can tell you that already they've uncovered four other allegations made against Ed Barnaby – before yours – allegations that the school managed to make disappear. They knew about these complaints well before they suspended you for, in their words, "lying" about him.' She waits a moment, letting this information settle. 'Agree to make a statement against Barnaby, and I can promise that you will

347

be heard, Frida. If you and these other girls are brave enough to speak up, you *will* be believed.'

'*We* all believe, you, darling,' Ginny says firmly. 'And you've got DS Ali on your side now, too.'

Something in the girl's appearance toughens – no, strengthens – and her eyes lock on Ali's. 'Yes. I want to do it. He told me he loved me, you know? I believed him.' She looks away, blinking back tears, before returning with resolve. 'And then, as soon as I told him about the, the . . .' She chokes back a sob, and it hits Ali that despite her youth Frida had begun to think of this as not just an unwanted pregnancy, but as a child. And why wouldn't she? That might have been the reality, after all. 'About the *baby*,' Frida says at last. 'As soon as he knew about that, he just threw me away.'

'Then let's stop him doing that to someone else, shall we?' Ali says, and Frida allows herself a small downturned smile, the grateful smile of someone released from a solitary burden.

A clatter at the front door announces the arrival of Hugo, calling out through the hallway to signal his return. As he steps into the kitchen it becomes clear that there is someone else with him, in the hall to his rear.

'Oh, look,' Hugo says, appearing tired but somehow enlivened, despite the trials of the past few days. 'Four of my favourite people. Oh, seven, if you include that motley crew down there,' he adds, pointing to the twins building a train track on the rug around baby Henri's basket. The boys giggle and wave him away.

'Heya,' Frida says softly, casting her stepdad a careful glance.

'Hey, lollipop,' he smiles.

Katrin jerks her chin towards the hall. 'Who's with you?'

'Ah,' Hugo replies with an air of mystery, 'you'll never guess who I found up at White Rise last night. Looks like we've solved the puzzle of our elusive trespasser.'

348

Hugo stands aside, and Thomas King steps into the room, now bearded and scruffier than the man in the photograph that Katrin had shared with Ali back in January, but Thomas King without a doubt.

'Thomas!' Katrin cries out.

Ginny rises from the table with something like fear in her expression, and Ali observes the way in which Thomas avoids her gaze.

'We've just come from a slap-up breakfast in town,' Hugo says, clearly delighted at Katrin's response. 'Thought the old trouper looked like he could do with a bit of feeding up!'

Ali stands, ready to escort the older man directly to the station, to take his full statement and to account for his voice being identified as the anonymous caller reporting Katrin's fall. 'Have you been at White Rise this whole time?' she asks.

But before Thomas can reply, Katrin is on her feet too, her good hand raised, effectively silencing his words.

'DS Samson, I need to fill you in on some developments,' she says, flashing warning eyes at Thomas. 'Last night, I remembered everything about my fall, so you can call off the investigation.'

'Hang on . . .' Ali starts to say. With all that has happened with Frida this morning, she's not yet shared her own update. She hasn't had a chance to tell Katrin about the interview with her husband last night – how his absence, he claimed, was down to his fear that Amélie really was responsible for Katrin's fall, and his concerns that he, as a result of their affair, was in some way culpable too. She hasn't yet passed on the message that he's booked into a hotel nearby, in the vain hope that Katrin might speak with him at some point soon, might forgive him. And she hasn't been able to ask Ginny why it was that Amélie's prints were entirely absent from Katrin's mobile phone, while hers were inexplicably present. 'Can I just—'

'That night of the party, I was up there, in the clocktower, on my own,' Katrin says, firmly cutting her off. 'The bird inspectors had been the day before, and on my way past I happened to notice that Bill had left a light on in the clocktower. I was worried it was a fire hazard to leave it lit up like that, what with the state of the old place. So, I thought I'd just pop up and unplug the lamp.'

'Without keys?' Ali asks.

'I can only think Bill must have forgotten to lock up the day before,' Katrin replied, without missing a beat. 'Anyway, it was stupid of me to go up on my own, I realise now, because the steps were so thick with dust that no sooner did I reach the top than I lost my footing. I was still conscious when I landed, and thank God, Thomas just happened to be passing at that very moment.'

'Thomas happened to be passing at that exact moment, after being missing for *six months*?' Ali asks, pulling her chin in.

'Pure chance,' Ginny murmurs, with a shake of her head.

'Yes. Pure chance,' Katrin echoes, and they exchange a look that makes Ali feel as though she's standing on the outside of a joke. 'I asked him to phone an ambulance, which he did – and for which I'm eternally grateful to now be able to thank you, Thomas.' She ends her monologue with a curt nod in Thomas's direction, and when Ali sees the stunned response on the man's face it is all that is needed to confirm to her that the entire story is untrue.

A brief glance at Hugo tells Ali that, like her, he hasn't a clue what's going on either.

'Mr King?' Ali says. 'Is that how you recall the events of that night?'

Thomas turns his gaze in Ginny's direction and gives a solemn nod. 'Absolutely,' he replies. Just that one word, and nothing more.

Hugo motions Thomas into the kitchen, to take a seat at the breakfast bar, where Hugo proceeds to prepare a fresh pot of coffee.

'And your phone, Katrin?' Ali asks. 'How do you explain it turning up in Amélie's drawer like that?'

Katrin shakes her head again, giving a good impression of bemusement. 'No idea. Maybe someone picked it up by mistake. Everyone else had been drinking that night, you know?'

'So you all keep telling me,' Ali says, frowning.

'I remember *every* second of it now,' Katrin states resolutely, 'and I'd like that to be the end of it.'

From the doorway of the kitchen, Ali takes in this strange broken family unit, with Katrin Gold at the centre, one arm in a sling resting on her expectant belly, her neck in a brace, cheekbone still darkly bruised. Beside her Ginny stands steadfast, Katrin's champion, her friend, stubborn devotion in her eyes. They've closed ranks. Ali knows there's no changing these women's minds. She turns to Frida, in whose expression she sees the quiet calm of release – both from her own nightmare and her aunt's – and Ali concludes that while she may never know the truth of what happened that night, in the end no one has been irretrievably harmed. Ali thinks of the work she has to do now, to help bring Ed Barnaby to justice, and she picks her battle.

'Frida, I'll be in touch in a few days, then?' she says, pulling on her jacket. 'Once you've seen the doctor and been given the all-clear. We'll get the ball rolling then, yes? Get this thing sorted once and for all.'

'OK,' Frida replies, and in her tone Ali detects the courage she knows will see the girl through. 'Can I walk you to the door?'

Ali says her goodbyes and follows Frida into the hallway, where the girl surprises her with an unexpected show of affection.

'Thank you,' she whispers, releasing Ali from a tight hug.

351

'No, thank *you*, Frida, for being so strong. It takes courage to stand up to men like Barnaby; and to stand up to the system that lets him get away with it. I'm proud of you.'

As she steps out into the bright light of The Starlings, Frida calls after her. 'Where are you going now?' she asks. A simple question; small talk, really.

Detective Sergeant Ali Samson hesitates a moment and checks her watch. If she hurries, she can just about make it in time. She'll call Margo now, tell her she's on her way.

'Bournemouth,' she replies. 'I've got a hearing to attend.'

ACKNOWLEDGMENTS

Homecoming was written through the various stages of the 2020–22 pandemic, at a time when all our horizons closed in and the future felt uncertain. Under lockdown, in a house unusually crowded with unsettled young adults, I wrote a full first draft, only to despairingly tear it up and start again. *Completely* start again. In the second version, written as restrictions began to lift, my original characters and Dorset locations remained, but the novel itself had evolved to reveal the real story hidden beneath the first, something like a fossil nestling at the heart of a smooth pebble. Particular thanks go to my agent Kate Shaw and my editor Sam Eades, for their patience, warmth and enduring belief in my storytelling, and to Linda McQueen, whose forensic eye and shared humour make the copy-editing part of the writing process a joy. Between them, their wisdom, skill and encouragement are woven through this book in no small measure. Thank you, wonderful women.

Huge gratitude also to the Society of Authors and the Royal Literary Fund, two organisations which exist in the service, support and celebration of writers. I am proud to have received grants from both over the past two years – grants which encouraged and assisted me to keep writing through the rocky times.

Fellow writers can find out more about help available by visiting their websites (below).

www2.societyofauthors.org
www.rlf.org.uk

CREDITS

Isabel Ashdown and Orion Fiction would like to thank everyone at Orion who worked on the publication of *Homecoming* in the UK.

Editorial
Sam Eades
Lucy Brem

Copy editor
Linda McQueen

Proofreader
Linda Joyce

Audio
Paul Stark
Jake Alderson

Contracts
Anne Goddard
Dan Herron
Ellie Bowker

Design
Charlotte Abrams-Simpson
Joanna Ridley
Nick May

Editorial Management
Charlie Panayiotou
Jane Hughes
Bartley Shaw
Tamara Morriss

Finance
Jasdip Nandra
Nick Gibson
Sue Baker

Comms
Alainna Hadjigeorgiou

Production
Ruth Sharvell

Rights
Rebecca Folland
Barney Duly
Ayesha Kinley

Sales
Jen Wilson
Esther Waters

Victoria Laws
Toluwalope Ayo-Ajala
Rachael Hum
Anna Egelstaff
Frances Doyle
Georgina Cutler

Operations
Jo Jacobs
Sharon Willis

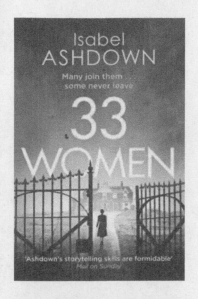

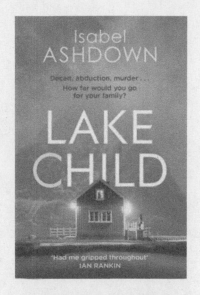

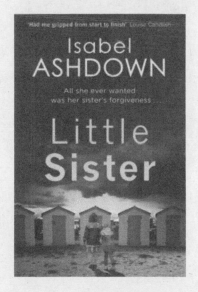

AVAILABLE TO BUY NOW